THE GRYPHON KING

"A twisty feast of politics and fantastical beasts—
I cannot wait to read more of Omer's work."

Shannon Chakraborty, *New York Times* bestselling
author of *The Adventures of Amina al-Sirafi*

"Omer has created an engulfing fantasy world, as vicious as
it is human, not shying away from the brutality of conquest
or the deeply complex characters who fight for it. The
monsters are horrific. The slow-burn yearning is borderline
inhumane. I stan an angry woman reaping vengeance with
a scythe from the back of a nightmare fanged pegasus."

S. A. MacLean, *Sunday Times* bestselling
author of *The Phoenix Keeper*

"A sweeping, magnificent epic of elaborate worldbuilding
and intricate court politics. Omer skillfully explores the
complexities of conquest and the flawed characters at
its helm. One of the best fantasies I've read in years!"

Hadeer Elsbai, author of *The Daughters of Izdihar*

THE GRYPHON KING

SARA OMER

TITAN BOOKS

The Gryphon King
Print edition ISBN: 9781835412831
E-book edition ISBN: 9781835412855

Published by Titan Books
A division of Titan Publishing Group Ltd
144 Southwark Street, London SE1 0UP
www.titanbooks.com

First edition: July 2025
10 9 8 7 6 5 4 3 2 1

Map artwork by Allen Omer.

A CIP catalogue record for this title is available from the British Library.

EU RP (for authorities only)
eucomply OÜ, Pärnu mnt. 139b-14, 11317 Tallinn, Estonia
hello@eucompliancepartner.com, +3375690241

Typeset in Palatino LT Std.

Printed and bound by CPI Group (UK) Ltd, Croydon, CR0 4YY.

For everyone who wishes they could pet the man-eating monsters in their favorite fantasy books.

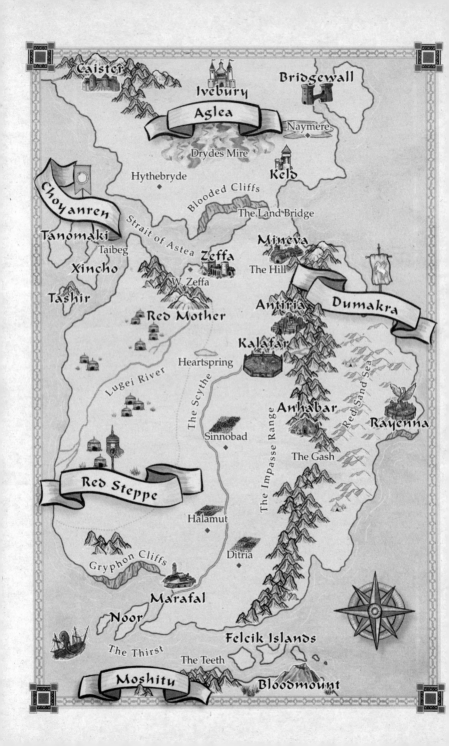

CHARACTERS

DUMAKRA

HARPY KNIGHTS

NOHRA ZULTAMA, princess, wielder of the sickle-staff *Bleeding Edge*

SAFIYA ZULTAMA (Saf), princess, Nohra's half-sister, wielder of the sword *Queen of Beasts*

CALIDAH (Cali), Clemiria's daughter, Nohra's cousin, wielder of the crossbow *Covenant*

AALYA ZULTAMA, princess, Nohra's half-sister, wielder of the shield *Segreant*

MERCY, Nohra's pegasus

PRUDENCE, Safiya's pegasus

ROYAL FAMILY

RAMZI ZULTAMA, zultam, ruler of Dumakra

HIMMA, queen mother

THORA, Aglean-born Dumakran queen, Nohra's mother

RAMI ZULTAMA, crown prince, Nohra's brother

MERV ATTAR, Ramzi Zultama's first wife, Dumakran queen, mother of Aalya and Nassar

NASSAR ZULTAMA, prince, Nohra's half-brother

CLEMIRIA ZULTAMA, Nohra's aunt, queen of Rayenna, former Harpy Knight, former wielder of *Queen of Beasts*

FARRAH ZULTAMA, Nohra's aunt, former Harpy Knight, former wielder of *Bleeding Edge*

HANA ZULTAMA, princess, Nohra's half-sister, Syreen's twin

SYREEN ZULTAMA, princess, Nohra's half-sister, Hana's twin

ZIRA, concubine from the islands north of Moshitu

SURI, former concubine from Moshitu, Safiya's mother

MURAAD ZULTAMA, cousin of Ramzi

ABAYAE, Nassar's monkey

QUEEN PURRI, Aalya's cat

SERVANTS

DARYA DAHEER, Nohra's talmaid, a cook

FAHAAD, stablemaster, Zultam Ramzi's servant-ward from Moshitu

LAILA, Safiya's talmaid

ADEEM ADEN, court physician, medicine maven

RAMMAN MYTRI, head servant

CAPTAIN MADY, captain of the palace guard

ORIK, former stablemaster

KAATIMA, kitchen maid

Others

ERVAN LOFRI, Minister of Commerce,
Merv Attar's cousin

JAWAAD LOFRI, Ervan Lofri's son

KASIRA LOFRI, Prince Nassar's betrothed,
Ervan Lofri's daughter

YARDAAN NAJI, grand vizier

MAHVEEN NAJI, Yardaan Naji's daughter

MAJEED JABOUR, Minister of Faith

FAKIER, a general

VIZIER SARTARID, formerly controlled the town of
Mineva

WAEL BAHDI, captain of the Kalafar city guard

ZAREB, one of the guards at the
Forked Tower

DIACO SHAAM, son of the Minister of Agriculture

TAMYR ALI, emissary in the village of Halamut

Historical Figures

NUMA ZULTAMA, former zultam

OMAAR THE
PEACEMAKER, former zultam

ROKSANYA ZULTAMA, Nohra's great-great-grandmother,
former queen

SHASSAM NAJI, former Master of Architonics

OBEYD, strategist

RED STEPPE

BATAAR RHAH, rules all the Utasoo tribes

QAIRA, Bataar's wife, Shaza's older sister

TARKEN, a general, Bataar's bloodsworn brother

SHAZA, a general, Qaira's younger sister

ERDENE, Bataar's eagle

BOROO, Bataar's healer/shaman

OKTAI, Bataar's footman, Tarken's cousin

MARAN, Qaira's handmaid

CHUGAI, Tarken's little brother

GANNI, Bataar and Qaira's daughter

BATO, Bataar and Qaira's son

TOBUKAAH RHAH, fought against Bataar in the war for the Red Steppe

MUKHALII RHAH, fought against Bataar in the war for the red steppe, kidnapped women and children

CHOYANREN

RUO SACHA, empress in Tashir, leader of Choyanren

YEEON, councilwoman in Tashir

AGLEA

MERIC WARD BARRISTER, lord of Bridgewall

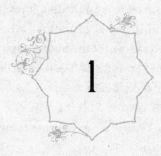

1

AUTUMN, 355

Over a decade after the Sunless Months, food remained scarce, especially among the nomadic tribes west of Dumakra.

— *A Dark Era*

The eagle screeched as she wheeled through the sky high above camp, her tethers waving like the hair on a war banner. Whoever had cut her leash was probably watching and laughing. Bataar weighed a piece of uncooked meat in his hand, disgusted at himself when his stomach growled. Coaxing her down using the chunk of liver felt wasteful, but it couldn't be helped.

"Going hunting? There's good game at the foot of the mountain," an old man called out, gesturing toward the snow-capped red peaks in the distance. With a broad smile, he warned, "Watch out for the gryphons, though."

Bataar stiffened. The man's drinking companions broke into riotous laughter.

"Hah, his face! Like you shoved an arrow up his ass."

Fermented milk sloshed from a cup, splashing Bataar's

boots. He stepped back, grimacing. He was only fourteen, but he'd been hunting since he could ride a horse. His pride was already mangled and dirty—it could take a hit, and so could he. These men were shadows of the hunters and fighters they'd been before wars and vermilrot outbreaks had left them scarred and gaunt. The rot took better men—it had killed Bataar's father two summers before. Still, he wasn't going to start a brawl with a gaggle of drunks over some teasing. He already lost more fights than he won.

These wrinkled sots had never seen a gryphon, and neither would Bataar. Each year, the gryphons moved closer, but never near the mountains. Attacks on the steppe were so rare that the stories had begun to sound like fables to fill children's heads when their bellies were empty.

Soon, winter would freeze the river. The herds would shrink, forcing everyone to ration, just like last year, and the years before. Hunger was the real monster, and Bataar knew how deep its fangs pierced.

He tossed the meat, and Erdene dove down. When she'd scarfed back the chunk of liver, he snatched up her leather jesses where they trailed in the dirt.

"You better still be hungry," he whispered. He needed her ravenous.

Turning away from the mocking laughter, Bataar slung his bow over his shoulder and set off across camp to gather his friends. Tarken crouched near one of the cookfires, binding fletching to the shafts of arrows with cord.

Bataar nudged him. "You ready?"

Shaggy hair fell in Tarken's face as he squinted up. "Why do you look like your eagle crapped in your porridge?"

Bataar's ears burned. "Just get your brother."

Tarken held his hands up. "Alright, alright."

As his friend disappeared beyond the threshold of his tent, someone snickered. "Getting a little hunting party together? It'll be gerbil stew for dinner, then." Bandages covered the boy's head, hiding where an eagle had almost gouged out his eye.

His lackeys cackled. They were still milking the scratches from their hunting accident. Lately, these losers had done nothing but hang around camp, picking on the girls, stuffing their faces, and sneering at anyone they thought was below them, which was almost everyone, especially Bataar.

Respect was earned on the red steppe, and Bataar seemed wholly unremarkable, with his black hair, plain face, and no accomplishments to boast of. He wasn't the cleverest or tallest or most vicious, but these useless idiots were wrong to underestimate him.

The boy's good eye narrowed. "What are you looking at, whelp?"

"I was just thinking it's unfair for someone to be both horse-faced and stupid," Bataar said, then bolted before the other boy's thick tongue could form a response.

Tarken burst out of his tent, running to keep up. "What'd you do?"

His little brother Chugai clung to his side, too big to carry like that anymore, his eyes screwed shut and small hands clenched into fists around Tarken's tunic.

"What makes you think I started it?" A rock flew past Bataar's cheek. A second struck him in the back, and he almost fell. On his arm, Erdene screeched and thrashed her wings, buffeting his face.

"Cut it out, bird meat!" a girl shouted, emerging from her home across the circle of round tents and throwing a stone back at the older boys. A pained groan answered her hit. Shaza was tall and strong for a girl. Smirking and satisfied, she turned on

3

Bataar and Tarken. "If you dog-brained idiots are going to start a fight, at least finish it. I can't always save you."

"Like we needed you!" Tarken snapped.

Bataar winced. "We were coming to tell you I found a good hunting spot."

She looked at them doubtfully. "I'll believe that when I see it."

"You coming or not?" Tarken balanced his brother in one arm, rubbing a spot on the back of his own head where he must have been hit by a rock.

Shaza shrugged, impassive as ever. "Tell you what: let me bring my sister and I'll come."

Bataar scowled, picturing her older sister Qaira's annoying big ears and stupid blushing face. Finally, because he couldn't think of a good enough excuse, he said, "Fine, bring her."

❧

Bataar flung up his arm, casting his eagle into the air. Erdene flew swifter than a storm, shooting across the field. The hare leapt above the tall grass, narrowly evading her talons. Bataar whistled for Erdene to circle back. She arced around, diving to sink sickle claws into its neck and dragging its thrashing body hard across the red dirt.

This side of the river, eagles were the most dangerous predators, alongside the falconers who hunted with them. The hare's kicking legs went limp. Something iridescent spilled out of its slack face, disappearing like smoke on the wind.

Not everyone could see spirits.

Bataar had been born with his umbilical cord constricting his neck, his skin tinged blue. As soon as his soul had come into this world, it had almost left it. If anyone knew he could see souls, they'd make him become a shaman, reading rune stones and interpreting smoke signs for the great rhahs. But the spirits didn't whisper wisdom to him. Instead, every death he witnessed was a reminder that he'd robbed Preeminence of a life it was owed. The universe hunted him, and Bataar knew never to look a beast in the eyes unless you were ready for a fight.

He had a plan. He'd keep his sight a secret and get stronger. When he was tougher than everyone in their camp, he would challenge a steppe king, be named a rhah, and rule not only their tribe, but all the Utasoo. And after that, he'd become a king of the world. Then he would finally be worthy of what he'd stolen.

He tried not to grin like an idiot as he imagined riding into battle one day with Erdene on his arm. He'd have a long mustache, a sable cape, and hundreds of thousands of men sworn to his cause.

For now, he just shooed Erdene off the hare before she could rip open its belly, tempting her with a piece of organ meat from his bag. He tied the dangling creature to his saddle and climbed back on his horse. Erdene choked down the heart meat and squawked, gliding up to perch on Bataar's forearm. Her bloodied talons dug like needles into his vambrace.

"What do I have to do before the men let me hunt with them?" Shaza asked. Her black rope of a braid swished as her mare came abreast of them.

"Are we not good enough for you?" Tarken said around a mouthful of orange berries. He and his little brother shared a horse ahead of Bataar, its legs deep in the ruby-tinted grass.

Shaza let her icy silence be an answer.

"That's insulting," Tarken grumbled.

Tarken's little brother bounced in the saddle, holding a child-sized bow. Chugai was only six, but Bataar had been even younger when he first rode with his father, watching the eagles take down wolves in the snow.

Shaza's rabbity sister Qaira brought up the rear, wearing ribbons in her braided hair. She caught Bataar looking back and glanced away, flushing. He bristled. Everyone admitted Bataar was a passable shot, better than most of the boys, but he wasn't as good as Qaira. Still, Shaza's sister was older than him, yet she bawled when sheep were slaughtered. Bataar didn't even flinch as he watched souls rip free from bodies, shimmering in the air and evaporating into the sky.

A timid rabbit like her couldn't even see what was really worth being scared of.

As the noon sun began to dip, they dismounted by a stream to let the horses drink. Surveying their kills, Shaza scoffed. "They'll laugh us out of camp."

"Food is nothing to laugh at," Bataar told her. Blood matted the raked-through pelts of the hares. Erdene ruffled her feathers as she preened, surveying her mangled quarries proudly.

Tarken glanced over his shoulder. "Hey, where's Qaira?"

Shaza fixed him with a look. "She's picking berries. We passed the bushes ages ago. How'd you two not even realize she left?"

"She's so quiet, how could we?" Bataar muttered. "Why'd she bother bringing a bow anyway if she's going to close her eyes whenever there's something to kill?"

"She just doesn't have the stomach for it."

"Well, at least she's not useless," Bataar admitted, starting to smile. "Someone's gotta mend our clothes and cook for us."

Tarken laughed. Chugai laughed because his big brother was laughing.

Shaza rolled her eyes. "You two are idiots. You'll ruin the kid."

The four drifted apart, refilling water skins and cleaning their knives. Bataar sheathed his, watching Tarken and his little brother kick stones along the river's burbling edge.

Winter was a biting song on the wind. High above, a perfect blue stretched over the horizon. People said the Preeminent Spirit looked like the calm sky, but that wasn't true. Bataar could see Preeminence's face leering down at him from above, and They were terrifying.

Ahead, the snow-capped Red Mother stretched into the sky. Except for the wind and his hunting party's voices, the hills were quiet. A sulfurous smell hung in the air, fouler than any fire. Gooseflesh prickled on Bataar's neck. Instinctively, he drew his short bow off his shoulder.

"Look at that shiny one, Chugai." Tarken's voice became smaller the farther he walked, blabbering about rocks.

Erdene cried in Bataar's ear, insistent, digging her talons deep. A twig snapped, and the horses whinnied, shuffling nervously. Bataar turned, expecting to spot the black eyes of an antelope.

Instead, his gaze fell on a gryphon.

Golden irises locked with his, and Bataar stood paralyzed. A clear membrane slid over the gryphon's eyes. It looked like a huge lion, except for its beak and feathered back legs ending in taloned feet. Its tufted tail lashed the air.

Bataar's chest tightened, his body trembling and heart pounding. The gryphon rose from its crouch. Standing as tall as Bataar's sternum, it spread its wings. They could all have made a line, arms outstretched, and they wouldn't have reached as far as the tips of its longest feathers. It was darker than sable, than tar, like a hole torn in the night sky. Its footfalls were soft as it slunk forward, hardly disturbing the grass with its bulk.

Beside him, Shaza gasped. The gryphon was lean and gaunt, its ribs pressing through its rippling pelt, eyes flashing as its head moved sharply, watching them, then the horses. Not wanting to turn away, Bataar inclined his head at Shaza. The

7

two of them moved in tandem, nocking arrows and pulling bowstrings taut. Maybe they could distract the gryphon, giving Tarken time to get his little brother away. The ponies whickered, breaking the quiet.

Up ahead, Chugai asked, "Find something?"

His older brother thumped him on the back of the head. Tarken whispered, "*Shut it*. They're hunting, you'll scare their quarry away—*oh*, Spirit." Tarken's eyes went wide, and he dropped the berries he'd been eating. They spilled across the dirt, garish orange on red.

Erdene screamed and tore into the air, circling above the field as the ponies fled, veering off across the stream.

The gryphon moved quickly. It reared on its hindlegs, flapping its wings, and leapt. Suddenly hulking over Chugai, it craned its neck down, beak inches from his head, breath stirring his brown hair. It put one paw on Chugai's head, the other on his shoulder. Bataar and Shaza loosed their arrows—they glanced off the gryphon's shoulder. Tarken's bow was on his horse, so he threw his bag. It missed, splashing into the water.

Chugai only had time to squeak, like a mouse. *Snap snap snap*, a sound like so many sticks breaking, a little boy crumbling. The gryphon's beak opened and shut around the broken body. It threw its head back, swallowing him whole.

Bataar watched bonelessly as Chugai's soul swirled out through the gryphon's nostrils.

He told himself *don't look*. But he had to watch, to bear witness to that moment when the gaping mouth of Preeminence at the precipice of the sky drank in Chugai's soul.

"*No!*" Shaza shouted, firing more arrows. "Tarken, move!"

The gryphon didn't flinch as barbed heads sank into its flesh. It circled, eyes gleaming, and batted Shaza away with a crunch. She fell on her back, the front of her tunic torn. Scarlet bloomed across the fabric. Her ragged gasps told Bataar she was still alive, for now.

Tarken collapsed to his knees as the gryphon neared. Bataar tried nocking another arrow, but his fingers were clumsy. His ribs constricted, tight around the hollowness in his chest. Bile burned in his throat, and his eyes stung as his quiver spilled into the bank.

The gryphon's paw thumped against Tarken's face. He wobbled, whimpering, a thick red line welling across his nose.

The gryphon tilted its head curiously.

Bataar thought of the oath he'd whispered to Tarken, when they camped together last year; no longer just friends, but bloodsworn brothers. Memories of skating on the Lugei river in the winter came to him. He remembered laughing so hard his sides ached when Tarken fell and slid into a snowdrift.

Numbing powerlessness overcame Bataar, loosening his grip, making it hard to stand on shuddering legs.

"*Tarken!*" he yelled. *Run, fight, do anything*.

Everything was happening too quickly, a smear of motion and choking terror. He didn't want to cry, but the world was already blurring.

An arrow shot into the dirt beside the gryphon's talons. Bataar couldn't tell where it had come from. The gryphon spun away, leaving Tarken gasping, the front of his breeches darkening. The wind carried Qaira's smell, honeyish, like edelweiss flowers.

Bataar reached uselessly for his spilled quiver.

The ribbons in her horse's mane flashed a rainbow of color as she gripped its bridle. "*Shhh, shhhh,*" Qaira whispered. She dropped the reins and raised her bow.

Bataar had once watched her split one arrow with a second, bursting them through the back of a target the older boys had put up, but he'd never seen her kill anything. Her hands didn't tremble as she loosed an arrow toward the gryphon's face. It deflected off its beak. The gryphon screeched, loud as a peal of thunder.

They were all going to die like Chugai.

Bataar didn't want to meet Preeminence's gaze, to watch its horns and teeth and black eyes as his soul joined it in the sky, but he'd face death, if it meant the rest of them lived. The blade of his knife was short and straight, tapering to a hatchet-point. He unsheathed it and stumbled forward, uncoordinated with panic. With both trembling hands, Bataar sank the blade into the gryphon's flank, sliding it between dense quills.

"Take your sister and Tarken! Get out of here!" he screamed to Qaira as the gryphon's beak thrusted toward him.

Bataar pulled the knife out and fell onto his back. He scrambled through the dirt, kicking the gryphon's chest. His pulse pounded as claws raked across his face and burned down, over the top of his chest, into his shoulder. More of Qaira's arrows sank into its body. Shadows oozed from the wounds. Bataar put his dirty fingers in his mouth and whistled. Erdene swooped down, her talons slicing through black feathers. Smoke seeped out and dissipated in the air. Bataar blinked in confusion, vision fading on his right side as something warm and wet flooded his eye.

There was something hypnotic about its eyes; they made Bataar want to freeze up and pee himself, like a mouse cornered by one of the camp cats. But he wasn't prey. Stabbing again, his blade pried some of the huge feathers loose. His vision was obscured by blood, tendrils of smoke, and plumage floating in his face.

He blinked, and as it cleared, the gryphon's bare purple skin came into view. The claws on one paw slashed at him. Bataar ducked away, squeezing himself down toward its midsection.

He jammed his blade into the gryphon's stomach. Hot droplets hit his face. *It bled.* It could be killed.

Qaira yelled his name. Her gentle voice had never sounded so hoarse.

The gryphon curled its underbelly back. A fervor overcame Bataar. His hands moved on their own, faster than his mind could think. The knife sank in and out of the muscles on its throat as its beak snapped toward his face. Blood ran over his hands, coating his arms down to the elbows. His fingers turned raw, palms splitting and chafing against the knife's hilt. He recognized Erdene's brown feathers on the arrows Qaira fired now, from his spilled quiver. With a scream, Bataar plunged his blade into one of the gryphon's yellow eyes.

Its soul seeped out of its body, pulling close and snarling in Bataar's face. The gryphon's spirit was shimmering nothingness, but it caressed his skin like fevered breath before it was swallowed up. Its hunger smelled sour, the same desperation and fear that roiled through Bataar. He kept stabbing even after the gryphon's weight collapsed on top of him. He didn't stop until Qaira pried the knife from his fingers and groaned, struggling to roll the gryphon's body off his. She didn't vomit at all the blood. She didn't cry or shake. He stood dizzily, throwing her hands off when she reached for the scratch across his face. He wiped the blood out of his eye, his vision turning red again in seconds.

"I'm fine." His voice scratched, clawing its way out of his throat.

Near Tarken's stunned body was one of Chugai's shoes. Bataar limped forward. Inside was a little foot. Bataar had only had a few bites of dried meat to eat in the last several hours, but it bubbled in his stomach as his eyes fell on the white bone protruding from bloody flesh.

"Let me help," Qaira said softly.

They worked together. Qaira wrapped wounds using clean strips torn from their clothes. Shaza moaned, eyes unfocused as Bataar hefted her onto his shoulder and laid her across her sister's horse.

"We need to get her to Boroo quickly," Bataar said. She'd already lost a lot of blood. The shaman wouldn't be able to do anything if Shaza died before they could get her to camp.

Qaira whispered gentle things to Tarken as she helped him stand. "He was embraced by the Preeminent Spirit. I felt it," she said, voice full of kindness.

Her words were well-meant, but Bataar had *seen* it, the moment Chugai's soul disappeared. The universe had swallowed him with blank eyes. Bataar tried to keep from quivering. He couldn't tell Tarken, not now, or ever.

Tarken's voice cracked. "My brother. His body, I can't leave it."

"I'll come back for him," Bataar swore.

He gave Tarken the wrapped shoe to hold. Tarken slotted his other fingers through Shaza's limp ones and walked. Qaira rode, steadying her sister against her. Bataar tried to staunch his own bleeding, so the red seeping through his tunic wouldn't drip and create a trail. Every step made his head spin, but he waved away Qaira's offer to ride with a stiff upper lip. They moved slowly, in silence punctuated by groans and stifled sobs.

Twilight was smoldering, coloring the sky in melting pinks when relief twinged in Bataar's chest. Shaza's shoulders still rose and fell in shallow breaths, and their camp grew in the distance.

Ignoring the gasps and concerned expressions as they entered the circle of tents, he took Shaza off the horse and laid her down near the cookfires. Qaira ran to get the shaman.

Bataar stood in a daze as Boroo worked. He let his mother fuss over him, dabbing his face with a damp cloth. Across camp, a woman cried, clinging to Tarken—his mother. Chugai's shoe dangled in her hand and fell. She looked down, her ragged sobs turning to a keening wail.

"Thank Preeminence," Bataar's mother whispered, gripping him with desperate fingers, squeezing his uninjured shoulder like she was reassuring herself he was really there.

☙❧

When night fell, Bataar led the men to the gryphon's carcass. His wounds burned as they skinned the pelt by the light of a torch, revealing purple flesh underneath. *Chugai is inside there*, he thought, as the men dressed the kill.

Back at the camp, they burned Tarken's little brother on a funeral pyre. His body reeked like something rotten as tongues of flame lapped up at blackness.

"You did well," Shaza's father said, clasping Bataar's shoulder, careful around the bandages. The hardened poultice itched.

Shame settled, iron in Bataar's gut. He hadn't brought them all home. The horses were gone with the hares, and the gryphon that had murdered Chugai was no feast, its ribs bulging through its skin. So little meat clung to its hollow bones, as if most of the fat and muscle had burnt up in the tendrils of smoke that had curled off its wounds. Every bite was dry and charred, a mouthful of ash.

Boroo, a shaman old enough to be a grandmother's grandmother, stood near the fire, chanting into the blaze. Families shuffled close to Tarken's mother, offering flat condolences. Her gaze looked beyond the feathery pelt hanging on a rack near the fire, searching for something far away, past their world and gone forever. Tarken stood frozen at her side, as still as he'd been when the gryphon attacked. Bataar turned away from them, looking out at the emptiness, the stoic mountains and distant stars.

The face in the sky never slept. Some creature was always dying, sustaining the Preeminent Spirit on a banquet of souls. He pretended not to see, and tried to convince himself it wasn't beautiful.

Soft steps rustled dry grass. Qaira stopped beside him, close enough their fingers could brush if he flexed his. Her sudden gasp made him instantly alert.

"What is it?" Bataar's hand shot to his knife in its sheath.

He scanned the darkness, following her line of sight in the sky. Shapes came into focus just as the screeches reached camp. Bataar took a breath and held it as the shaman's chanting quieted. Tarken's mother shook. Some other women whispered prayers.

Qaira stood firm, but if the wind blew, she might have fallen like a leaf. Bataar clenched his jaw, waiting. A few heartbeats later, the swarm of gryphons passed over and disappeared. When their shrieking faded, Bataar finally let himself take another shaky breath.

"Strange," Boroo muttered, as expressions on the faces around the pyre relaxed.

Bataar flexed his fingers, brushing Qaira's. Every living thing had a soul, had a place in the divine web of things, but no other animal Bataar had seen moved like shadows come to life. His hand twitched.

He turned away, leaving Qaira stranded at the edge of the darkness. He wouldn't turn around to check if that face suspended in the canopy of night watched her with a familiar hunger.

All around, people were looking at Bataar, *really looking*. He'd fought a gryphon and survived. More than that, he'd killed it. He studied his palms, wondering what people saw when they looked at him now. Steadying his breathing, he tried to still his fingers. How many times would he have to scrub his skin before all the traces of the day disappeared?

❦

That night Bataar woke up covered in sweat, staring around the unlit tent in a haze. The iron stove looked like a crouched body with a long neck, and the furs on the walls seemed alive. The fire had died. Nausea rolled over him, but his stomach growled at the smell of burned fat. Pain had ripped him out of dreamless sleep, as sharp as the claws that had maimed his face.

He was on fire. *He was dying*. Bataar couldn't call out as the fever burned through his body.

In the moonlight coming through the crack in the door, he found his mother's shape. He took a few ragged breaths. The poultice itched, especially his chin, and the front of his tunic was plastered to the wound on his chest, but he couldn't scratch it. He just stared up at the roof, waiting to face Preeminence.

The shadows never took shape. Morning came. The next day, his fever broke.

❦

His scabs scarred, enduring in twisted knots across his face, neck, and chest. As the years passed, people began to say Bataar's dark hair looked inky, like gryphon feathers. They said that he had a severe, serious face, that his scar meant he was gryphon-marked.

Gone was the boy desperate to prove himself. Now, when his enemies saw him, they were afraid.

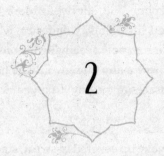

2

SPRING, 357

Sixteen-year-old Ramzi led the forces that conquered
Keld in 336. The Dumakrans occupied the holy city for
five bloody years.

— *The Southerner's Child King*

A gust of wind blew through the entrance to the sanctium.
Nohra stopped scrubbing at the handwashing fountain and
looked up, catching a glimpse of blurred feathers and massive
wings as her aunts landed their pegasuses on the steps outside.
Bellowing whinnies turned into keening falcon shrieks,
cracking through the cool morning air. The pegasuses' yellow
eyes rolled, and their sharp teeth bit down hard on the metal in
their mouths, steel-shod hooves lashing stone. Nohra's aunts
tied them off and tightened their blinder hoods. Finally, the
feathers on the pegasuses' fetlocks and necks settled.

Her aunts brushed past, not bothering with the crowd
gathered outside or a glance her way. Their family's insignia
glittered on their feather-steel breastplates. The royal crest, a
rearing pegasus, signaled them as her father's Harpy Knights,

but everyone in the capital would recognize their faces even if they were wearing rags.

"Lend me a wing, little bird," her mother said. Turning from her aunts' retreating backs, Nohra walked deeper into the sanctium and took her mother's arm.

Nohra should have outgrown pet names by now. She was tall enough to meet her mother's eyes without straining her neck up and hopping like one of the sparrows in the palace courtyards. But hardly a moment passed when Nohra wasn't flying, so little bird she was.

Seeing the other pegasuses made her miss Mercy. Her colt was as black as a raven's wings, as wild as wind. The trainers up in the mountain were breaking him now, making him obedient and rideable like the ones in the stables she'd learned on.

A hip and elbow jammed against Nohra's back.

"Have you had a good look at his latest acquisition?" Merv asked the concubines. She glanced disinterestedly down at Nohra, pretending to be surprised to find her at the end of her sharp elbow.

Merv Attar, the zultam's first wife, was Dumakran-born and older than Nohra's father. She was gossiping about the new girl, young enough to be the zultam's daughter, with red hair and freckled skin.

"She's Aglean," another concubine whispered to Merv, looking pointedly at Nohra's mother. Merv Attar arched a perfect eyebrow, her lips twisting. If they hadn't been in the prayer hall already, Nohra would have threatened to wipe the sneer off the queen's face.

Merv had good reason to be a jealous bitch. It was no coincidence that the blue tile covering the walls matched Nohra's mother's eyes. This was Thora's Sanctium, erected in her name. It reflected her beauty back in gilt-edged arches and pillars.

Thora had come from South Aglea to Dumakra when she was scarcely older than Nohra, claimed in a skirmish as a gift for the zultam, or sold by her parents. She never spoke of it. Her Dumakran was still accented fifteen years later, and her beauty hadn't waned. Her skin was milky and easily burned by the hot sun, and her hair fell in pretty waves like spun gold. Nohra knew she was only a tarnished approximation of her mother.

"Chin up," Thora said, tapping the space between Nohra's shoulder blades. She didn't seem to hear Merv's mocking laughter, or maybe she just didn't care.

Merv and Thora, the two imperial queens, always traveled with concubines, princesses, servants, and eunuch guards. But their retinue only followed as far as the prayer hall in the inner sanctum before taking their places in the outer ring. After fussing with Nohra's tiara, her mother drifted away to the middle of the room.

A chill slithered through the sanctium, and the floor in the innermost circle was cold on Nohra's bare feet as she hurried to her spot with her half-sisters. Hanging incense burners sparkled at the cleric's dais. Nohra breathed in the smell of burning olive leaves, familiar and warm. As she knelt, the natal-day rings encircling her fingers tapped the smooth tile. At fourteen, she'd long since run out of fingers for new rings; now four fingers had two bands each.

Safiya appeared like she always did, a sun suddenly blinking to life in the room. "I'll race you to the training yard after the ceremony," she whispered conspiratorially, knocking Nohra's shoulder with her own. "It'll be a good warmup. Captain Mady says he'll teach us grappling. They say he fought some of the best Utasoo wrestlers at the Blood Rhah's wedding and won."

Nohra snorted. "Who says?"

Saf beamed. She always thought everything was funny.

Her tiara glittered under the light of the swaying lamps, resting on her dense black curls. Nohra's own was itchy in her brown hair.

Like Nohra, Safiya had been born a concubine's daughter, but her mother hadn't become a queen. Saf was the firstborn princess, their father's oldest child and his favorite, probably. She liked playing with swords and gaping at pretty concubines, and everyone loved her. For more than a year now she'd been studying history, alchemy, medicine, mathematics, and fine arts at the Conservium, and was infuriatingly good at everything.

Nohra had always been jealous of Safiya, but she was impossible to hate, except maybe when they fought. It was annoying that Saf hardly broke a sweat on the training ground. In the last few years, Nohra had grown taller and heavier than her half-sister, which made her slower, even if she had the longer reach.

"Don't tell me you'd rather have dinner with Grandmother?" Safiya raised an eyebrow. "Like a polite little lady?"

She wouldn't. "I'll come fight." The bruises would heal, the scabs would scar, and adrenaline always tasted sweet. Of course, her maid Darya would gasp in the baths, where the clouds of steam couldn't hide the purpling battle marks, but Nohra didn't need her approval.

Safiya smiled. "Then we'll have dinner with the men in the guard house."

"I know you don't care," Nohra grumbled, "but I won't eat what they're having." The soldiers garrisoned at the palace were foreign-born and impious.

"Oh yes, 'I profane my mouth on feathered flesh'. Don't worry. We'll send someone to fetch you something else from the main kitchens."

From the smell of cooked chicken alone, Nohra would picture pegasuses, gryphons, and the Goddess's winged daughters, nausea stirring her gut.

At least her manners wouldn't be criticized between each bite. Nohra would as likely meet her end in Grandmother Himma's stuffy quarters, to the tune of music and etiquette lessons, as she would on the training ground.

"You know we *could* sneak out early, before Father notices," Safiya said, nodding toward the doorway. Around them, their half-sisters, girls with pudgy cheeks and tiaras askew, knelt with their faces screwed up in concentration.

Nohra shook her head. "You might try to learn something from the Godsbreath."

Safiya looked like she wanted to pinch Nohra's face. "It's adorable you believe in all this."

"*Saf!*"

"Really, you're such a good girl." Safiya laid a hand on her heart. "May the Goddess have mercy on my unworthy soul."

"She won't."

Nohra relished the calm of the inner sanctium. She found strength in her faith, more than she found in her father's armory or in getting her ribs sprained by her sisters in the training yard. If she prayed hard enough, she would wear divine armor no weapon could puncture, and peace would be her guiding light.

Unlike Safiya, she didn't fight because she enjoyed it. Nohra fought for Father, for her country, and for *Her*—Paga, the incarnation of peace.

Their father knelt on the stairs to the cleric's dais, surrounded by his sisters in their gilded armor, his four Harpy Knights. He was separated from full view of the crowd by an ornamental grille, but all of Kalafar clamored for a rare glimpse of him. Through geometric cutouts in the metal screen, all that was visible were fragments of his white turban and the dark brown hair at the base of his neck, his shoulders that to Nohra had once seemed wide enough to block out the entire sky.

He didn't turn, but he must have felt her watching. He beckoned. "Safiya, Nohra, to me."

Curious eyes bore holes in Nohra's back. It was special to be signaled out by the man everyone knew was Goddess-blessed. Even if he was their father.

For a second it was like they were little girls again, going with him to watch falconers fly the royal birds and have supper in his private quarters, back when they were his daughters instead of his guards in training.

"*Princesses*," Clemiria greeted, her voice clipped.

Their aunt surveyed them with narrowed eyes. Only last week, Nohra's father had crowned Clemiria queen of the Sister City across the desert. Soon she would leave to take up her throne, and her lion-headed sword *Queen of Beasts* would need a new wielder. Safiya was the obvious choice. She was nearly seventeen and as skilled with a blade as any of the Rutiaba Palace guardsmen.

It was *Bleeding Edge*, the sickle-staff, that Nohra wanted. Her eyes fixated on its red crescent blade, strapped to Aunt Farrah's back. Nohra would have to train hard to beat out her sisters and have a chance to stand next to Saf at Father's side. Any daughter who could ride and fight could become his soldier, but only four could become his Harpy Knights.

Safiya's smile was saccharine as she inclined her head with false politeness. Nohra tried not to scowl or trip over anyone's hands.

Now flanking their father, they crouched again. Nohra's knees were beginning to ache, and the cold tile raised goosebumps on her arms. The zultam didn't say anything, didn't smile or acknowledge them. But joy blossomed, thick in her throat, as if the moon had chosen to shine only on her.

Ahead, the hems of the priestesses' robes puddled on the floor of the platform. Paga's priestesses wore veils trimmed with coins. The other women wore hoods and half-masks: these were Nuna, the chaos incarnation's silent daughters. They wouldn't sing Her praises until the Long Reconciliation began, and the Goddess was of one mind and body again. Immaculate and whole.

A hush fell over the murmuring crowd as the cleric cleared his throat. He wore unadorned gray robes, nothing like the women's costumes. His face was unlined, beard steely and cropped short. The arms of the young boy holding the Godsbreath wobbled under the weight of the illuminated tome.

"Before man, the Goddess carved bodies from the bones of the first demonking," the cleric said, picking up from his marked page.

A god's soul was too large for just one body, so when the Goddess took a mortal shape, She tore Herself in two: peace and chaos, life and death, Paga and Nuna. Nohra remembered looking up at the frescoes of the incarnations' blank faces as a child. Even before she knew their names and the stories of the godswar, she'd already thought they were perfect, the queens of her dreams and nightmares.

"During the first godswar, the Goddess's Harpy daughters fell, and the last demonking was chained in servitude, harnessed as an agent of havoc."

Like in lessons, it was difficult to focus. Especially because Nohra already knew these stories, had memorized the words. She tried not to be distracted by the whispers from the back of the sanctium, the fly buzzing around the red water from the

Heartspring, or the light refracting off the ornaments on her father's turban. One of her aunts cleared her throat.

"A final time of turmoil will usher in a long and peaceful era, the Long Reconciliation." The cleric's words rolled over each other in a soothing cadence, like a tired song.

Nohra could go to the private sanctium at the palace after she trained with Saf. It didn't have a magnificent skylight, but its domed roof was decorated with images of bat-winged Nuna in her cloak of shadows and stars, and Paga, resplendent with Her white hair, red skin, and scythe. And there were fewer distractions there.

One of the priestesses held cupped hands overflowing with red water close to Nohra's face. The half-veil covering her nose and mouth meant she was one of Nuna's. Sweat sheened the priestess's forehead, though Nohra was still shivering. The woman watched the room, gaze flickering between the doors to the inner sanctium, the zultam, and his Harpy Knights. Her eyes were light, a honey brown Nohra hadn't seen in the capital. Some people in the north had features like that, where Dumakra brushed South Aglea.

Nohra's heart hammered as she took an irony gulp of the water from the priestess's hands. When her lip awkwardly brushed the woman's fingertips, the soft touch fanned flames under her skin. A swarm of bugs fluttered against the walls of her stomach. Every nerve in her body thrummed, just like when Fahaad—a servant she was *only* friends with—had stolen a kiss from her behind the stables. The priestess met her eyes, holding her gaze; for a moment, Nohra could have died of embarrassment.

Then the priestess's pupils burst in sudden panic. She rushed forward, the tip of a blade poking out from her sleeve. Nohra's aunts hadn't even looked up, and the cleric hadn't paused his reading, but Nohra stood, pushing in front of her father.

"What are you doing?" he said as Nohra crashed into the priestess.

"Down with Dumakra's heretic emperor!" The woman's hissing voice was muffled by fabric.

Shouts exploded around the room. Concubines and viziers' wives screeched, servants screamed and children wailed. Nohra grabbed the assassin's wrists, pinning one arm behind her back. The other one wriggled free. A hot ache bloomed in Nohra's stomach as the knife slashed across her dress, splitting through silk. A strangled sound, half-gasp, half-groan, escaped her lips. She gritted her teeth, trying to keep the pain contained, her blood pattering as it dripped onto the marble.

The rings on Nohra's knuckles caught the priestess in the jaw. The woman reeled, her eyes unfocused as Nohra wrestled her down onto the floor. The cleric, mouth agape, stepped away from them as they rolled on the ground. The knife fell from loosened fingers, hitting every step on the dais and skittering into the crowd.

The Harpy Knights formed ranks around the zultam. One of Nohra's other aunts raised her crossbow, *Covenant*, aiming at the assassin. "Move, girl," Clemiria ordered.

Safiya lunged forward, hands outstretched to pull Nohra back to safety. The screams coming from around the room were dizzying. Nohra went lightheaded as she touched her stomach, hoping to stanch the bleeding. With a grunt, the attacker kneed Nohra in the abdomen and broke free. Something glistened under the wrist in the assassin's other sleeve—not a knife, some kind of apparatus, with a dart jutting out. Nohra winced, stumbling to her feet. Her palm came away from her stomach painted crimson.

Paga was here, in this sanctium, in the sun spilling through the skylight, in the olive leaf incense, in Nohra. Peace was fragile and fissuring and sprinkled with Nohra's blood.

Aunt Clemiria wrestled *Covenant* from her sister and fired a bolt from the crossbow just as the assassin raised her arm, aiming her wrist at the zultam. Nohra wrenched the woman back. The dart arced off course. It shot too high, flying toward the sky window instead of Nohra's father.

The woman's head cracked against the marble step, light draining in an instant from her honey eyes. The crossbow bolt hit Nohra in her shoulder. Her body jolted. The noise of the crowd faded to a distant drumbeat, an ache pulsing where her arm joined her torso. Nohra didn't see Paga's featureless face in the throng; her eyes landed on her friends, Fahaad and Darya, at the room's fringes with the other servants, their expressions contorted with concern. Her mother was pushing through the crowd, but Nohra was already in Safiya's arms, letting her sister help her limp toward the outer sanctium.

The decorative divider that separated the zultam from the world wobbled and fell with a cymbal clang, and suddenly sound flared back, ear-bleedingly loud.

"This is bad," Nohra whimpered. "I fought in the sanctium. People go to hells for that." The house of the Goddess had been soiled by blood and death, but still beams of golden sunlight shone down.

The hard line of Saf's mouth softened. "You're not going to hells."

Nohra took a trembling breath, stumbling. "Am I going to die?" She wanted the truth, but she knew her sister wasn't above telling a lie in the sanctium.

Safiya attempted to smile, lips twitching. "Of course not. You'll be in fighting shape in no time."

Nohra tried to respond, but her words came out gurgled. She could tell Saf's smile was hollow because her dark eyes were shiny with unshed tears. Nohra groaned. Everything hurt.

"*Nuna*," Safiya swore. "It's—you're fine. It isn't—you're going to be okay. Paga's holy ass, you're so stupid, Nohra."

Saf had learned medicine at the Conservium. She'd even shadowed the royal physicians. If she was crying, Nohra was doomed.

She prepared for her vision to flood black. Instead, she found herself sinking into white bed linens and the smell of lemony soap.

☙⸙❧

The cleric's bed was surprisingly soft. He smiled patiently as Nohra apologized over and over for bloodying the bedclothes. The court physicians had dulled the pain in her shoulder and stomach with numbing salves and plied her with a red tincture that made her feel deliriously at ease.

"You should've stabilized the shaft of the bolt and cleared out the inner sanctum instead of moving her," the physician scolded Safiya, who had insisted on watching as the broadhead was removed from Nohra's shoulder. When Nohra woke toward the end of the surgery, through the fog of the opium, she remembered seeing her sister gawking like she was watching a toad being dissected.

"Yes, maven," said Safiya, sinking a little at the doctor's chiding.

"We'll prepare a room in the palace infirmary, Your Majesty," the doctor told Nohra's mother.

Thora's voice was still shaky. "Thank you, Adeem."

Adeem Aden was a young man, but his beard had started graying when Safiya and Nohra began training to be Harpy

Knights. He continued, "If it isn't a stab wound, it's a broken wrist from a fall, glass in her knee, a dog bite. Better than a broken neck"—he paused, scrunching his nose—"I suppose."

"Everyone's worried. I should tell them you're alright," Safiya said, ducking out of the cleric's room, clearly glad to be out of there. All the fun had ended when they'd finished sewing Nohra up.

Nohra looked to the physician. "I can go riding, can't I?"

He frowned. "No."

"Flying?"

He looked unimpressed. "No, and if one of your sisters tries to sneak you out, she'll find herself in a bed beside you."

Nohra slumped. On bedrest, she couldn't practice with Saf in the training yard, fly pegasuses at the stables, or even hobble to the palace sanctium to pray. She'd have to work twice as hard to become a Harpy Knight now, before one of her sisters stole *Bleeding Edge*. Nohra didn't care about Clemiria's lion-headed sword, but she'd dreamed of the sickle-staff for as long as she could remember. Its feather-steel flashed red like the Goddess's scythe, jeweled with rubies dark as welling blood.

She pouted. "Then what's the point of living?"

The doctor blinked unsympathetically. "Learning. Your tutors can visit, so your education will continue. Let this be a long-needed lesson in recklessness."

"But—" If she hadn't intervened, someone could have died. If not her aunt or her father, *the zultam*, then someone else among the innocents and courtiers gathered to pray. Everyone should be celebrating her! This was basically her first act as a Harpy Knight. There'd been a whole week of feasts when her stupid half-brother got circumcised.

"The assassin's dart was tipped with a neuromuscular blocking agent," the physician said. "If it had struck its target, paralysis would have afflicted the lungs, resulting in respiratory failure." It was as close as he was likely to get to outright praising her. "You should have alerted your father's guards when you noticed, not charged at an assassin bare-handed."

When Adeem Aden had finished admonishing her and departed, Nohra surveyed her ugly stitches. Her aunt's crossbow bolt had cut through to the other side, but a part of the broadhead had lodged itself in the meat of her shoulder. The jagged wound on her stomach was hidden under a plaster dressing and layers of bandages. Gingery turmeric wafted up from the muslin wraps. '*What a lucky girl,*' the doctors had said as they poked at her. She was probably the unluckiest girl in Kalafar.

Tearing her gaze away from the wounds, Nohra sighed. Sighing hurt even worse than talking. Her mother perched at the foot of the bed, eyes red-rimmed, tear tracks staining her cheeks. In the light of late afternoon, even her mother's alabaster skin was bronze-touched. Nohra's blood was matted in her hair and smeared across patterned brocade, spoiling the fine fabric of the robed dress and white skirts.

"I thought I'd lost you," Thora said. A sob caught in her throat.

The cleric had given Nohra his necklace as something to hold before the anesthetic tincture had gone into effect. She'd clutched it so tightly it had left an impression of flowy script on her palm. Now she ran her fingers over the words engraved on the flower-shaped pendant. *Peace sows complacency, Chaos begets order.* In her poppy-addled head, Nohra couldn't seem to understand what the words really meant. Something about how there was good and bad in everything?

By a small window, the cleric tilted his head, his gaze aimed at Thora's flat belly. "A son?"

She balked. "How could you know?"

"Paga put the question in my head." When he smiled, his straight teeth and easy grin made Nohra flush. Even with strands of silver threading through his hair, the cleric was handsome.

But what had he said? *A son?* A brother? Nohra's surprise was a blade of ice cutting through the fog. She studied her mother's profile, that small smile, like Thora had already known she was having a baby.

Most of the women in the harem were only permitted to bear the king one child, like Safiya's mother, who had retired to an estate outside Kalafar. And Dumakran court wasn't kind to boys. Nohra had grown hardened to her half-brothers crying, stuffed away in private wings of the Rutiaba Palace until they were weaned and sent off, exiled to live as wards in distant parts of the country, or even farther. But Nohra's mother was Father's favorite. If she had a son, he would be raised as the next zultam. He'd become the crown prince, Nohra was sure of it.

Thora took Nohra's hand and squeezed her fingers.

"I'll ask Paga for an easy pregnancy," the cleric said, "and a quick labor."

∽◦∽

For the next seven months, Nohra held onto those words the way she'd clung to the cleric's necklace. But it turned out even the incarnation of peace and mercy could be cruel.

Nohra was almost fifteen when her little brother was born. That same day, her mother died. The medicine mavens frowned sympathetically when they gave Nohra a box to take to the palace in the mountains, to put in the tomb with all the other dead queens' hearts.

3

WINTER, 367

Gods of granite do not crumble when men die and
empires fall.
— The Supreme School of Thought in Xincho

The siege would end before the night did. Bataar stood behind
the palisades, watching the battering rams and projectiles meet
the wall with earth-shaking sound. Smoke hung over the last
stronghold of Choyanren. The city wall surrounding Tashir had
once glistened. Now, the stone was streaked with gore, dented
from projectiles thrown by Bataar's catapults. White flakes of
ash rained down, collecting on the backs of their horses. Hot
sand and boiling water hissed as enemy guards on the walk
defended against Bataar's siege towers. The night exploded in
light as a cannon fired on one of the siege machines. A torch fell,
and fire spread. Burning wood popped and cracked, splitting
apart like logs in a stove.

Bataar nearly fell from the saddle when one of the battering
rams finally breached the city wall, sending up a cloud of dust
and debris. At the horses' hooves, Tarken's dogs salivated and

snarled. The cavalrymen swirled in formation, waiting for the opportunity to storm in as Shaza and her archers picked off guards on the wall.

"Watch the longbowmen in the crenels!" she shouted. "If you lot die, I'll pack your ashes into gunpowder."

High above, sabers clashed. The sound of metal rang through the night like talons raking steel. A flash of gunpowder illuminated the dirt-smeared faces of soldiers as a cannon ball pounded out of an iron bore, wedging into the wall. Two more shot out, the sound like a heartbeat.

"Whoa, whoa," Bataar soothed, wrestling with the reins on his gelding. High above, Erdene screeched as she wheeled through the smoke. Her feathers had darkened over the past twelve years, her body a golden-brown gash in the starless sky. Bataar whistled for her just as a firework exploded in the air above Tashir.

"What's that signal mean?" Shaza yelled. Her fingers dripped with red as they pulled away from a slice across her cheek.

Tarken grimaced as his dogs howled at the explosion. "Bataar?"

In the sky above the city, a spray of gold shimmered in the air, like a flower blooming among white stars. The second explosion was red. At the third pop, an ocean spray of blue erupted across the smoke-clouded sky, and the Choyanreni on the walls laid down their arms.

Hollowness settled in Bataar's gut as snow began falling.

Someone shouted, "The emperor is dead!"

‿◦‿

Come dawn, the cinders and snow were nearly indistinguishable. Bataar's nose wrinkled at the reek of sickness mingling with smoke. The smell of gunpowder had haunted his nightmares since the start of the campaign last winter, and the odor of rot was as unwelcome as it was familiar.

"They're waiting for you in your war tent," a messenger said, "Your Eminence."

Bataar tore his eyes away from the wisps of souls rising into the sky to reunite with the Preeminent Spirit. His fingers twitched, an eyelid fluttering. Qaira would smooth his brow, concern twisting her smile into a frown. He didn't like to see her worry, but the reminders of the cost of this war piled higher every day. More souls swirled into darkening skies, and a taller pile of charred corpses built up around the edge of the wall, bodies thrown out by the city guards.

Tashir's people had paid a heavy price for their emperor's defiance. The smell of burning corpses hung over the encampment. Each new body tossed out of the city gates disturbed the growing pile of ash, crunching charred skin and sending up dust clouds. The first weeks of the siege, Bataar had helped drag twisted, broken bodies to the funerary pyres, most of them belonging to the elderly and poor who'd starved after Bataar's ships sealed the port. The last few weeks, the dead thrown outside the wall had all shown obvious signs of vermilrot, eyelids crusted with gelatinous blood, mouths filled with red. Bataar knew the symptoms well. Years ago, the disease had torn through their camp and claimed his father.

All three of the Federated Kingdoms' major cities had fallen. First he'd beaten the dragonlords, wealthy distributors of Dumakran opium who ruled Tanomaki. Xincho, a fortified haven of scholars, had surrendered next. Now Bataar would have Tashir, this port city perched above gem-filled cliffs.

The Federated Kingdoms had rejected Bataar's initial offer of peaceful surrender, just as they'd spat on his initial proposal for a union between their nations, refusing to swear fealty to a steppe king. *The Choyanreni royal line has been selected by the granite gods for a thousand years, and the oracles will determine succession for the next thousand years*, the letter had said.

So the kingdoms had burned.

He'd wanted to take the Federated Kingdoms first for Choyanren's gunpowder. He also needed Tashir's fleet of lugsail ships, with their towering battened sails the color of cloud jade. The vessels could outmaneuver even nimble Aglean ships. Their cannons would give them an advantage against Dumakra's navy, and would be especially useful if Bataar had to sail to Dumakra's far eastern city of Rayenna and seal its port.

In anticipation of their arrival, the Tashiri emperor had razed the forests surrounding the city, giant birch trees burnt to nubs. Bataar's soldiers had traveled hours away to carve out the closest pine forest, clearing a portion to construct the palisade. With sweat on their brows, they'd dug ditches and constructed siege engines. Behind the palisades, hundreds of tents dotted the horizon, conical roofs sagging under piles of snow.

Bataar whistled for Erdene. The eagle answered with three short screeches, and he caught her on his vambrace. By the time he passed the medicine tents, he had stilled his spasming fingers, prepared to present a strong face.

Honorifics spilled from the doctors' mouths in hushed tones. They bowed their heads as if cowering when their eyes fell on him. The physicians captured in Xincho were skilled in traditional medicine. The scent of their tinctures spilled out of the tents, filling this corner of the encampment with the musky aroma of bitter herbs, almost as strong as the necrosis.

The smell shed the years away. Suddenly Bataar was a boy again, watching the rot take his sallow-faced father. He shook his head, clearing it of thoughts that made his breath come too quick, clouding the cold air. Now, they had the knowledge and resources to fight the rot, to fight anyone.

Outside the triage tents, men, women, and boys lay still and quiet on cots. Gauze covered burn wounds from boiling water. Bloody stumps were capped in poultices where incendiary weapons had blown limbs from bodies. Doctors were moving a soldier into the quarantine tent. The patient quietly groaned, infected with the early stages of vermilrot. Soon, their fever would break as coagulated blood oozed from their eyes, ruby tears as viscous as molasses. From there, the rot marched untiring through its victims until it was nearly impossible to tell if a shallowly breathing body was alive or dead.

One boy screamed as a physician tightened a tourniquet. "S-spirit! I see Preeminence," he shouted. "The teeth!"

A voice pacified, "*Shhh, shhhh*. It's alright."

Past the threshold of Bataar's war tent, his council was assembled. Heat off the stove warmed the space between walls. The spacious canvas-and-felt room was sectioned off with exotic pelts, lacquered furniture, and plush Dumakran rugs, all fealty presents from the steppe kings. Erdene chirped as she flitted off Bataar to her perch.

"*My rhah.*"

Bataar stiffened as his wife brushed into the tent behind him. Cloth was tied around the bottom half of her face, obscuring her mouth and nose like the Dumakran silent priestesses.

For a moment he was distracted, intoxicated by the flowery smell of Qaira. She was entirely soft edges since giving birth to their son. Bataar grasped for her but she flowed out of reach, a teasing light sparkling in her hazel eyes.

"You shouldn't touch me. I was in the rot tent."

Near the seated advisors, one of her handmaids rocked a swaddled baby. Both Bataar's and Qaira's gazes were drawn to little Bato, his thick coppery hair and ruddy cheeks. His fingers were tangled in the beads of his sitter's headdress. She clenched her jaw as she eased his small fist open. In this tent in the middle of the war encampment, surrounded by so much death, Bataar smiled.

Tarken smirked. "I was worried I'd be ashes and he'd be leading a battalion before we left these damned islands."

Qaira laughed. "Our Bato doesn't like war. He cried whenever anything hit the wall."

"Ganni's going to be the fighter," Shaza said, brushing Tarken's hand off her knee. Her grin was wolfish, beaming with pride.

"My daughter is gentle, like her mother," Bataar said. It was only half true; when the seven-year-old was around Shaza, she was her aunt's dutiful shadow. "I left her with her grandparents to keep her out of your claws." Bataar was glad his daughter would have memories of skating on the Lugei river and chasing her friends through a sea of red grass. A happy childhood built in the shadow of mothering mountains, as it should be. Qaira's parents might ease Ganni out of her shell.

Shaza shrugged. "Remember they raised me, too."

If Shaza was the dark sliver of a waxing moon, and just as cold, then her older sister was a meadow soaking up the sun. Qaira wasn't so different from how she'd been as a girl with her wide eyes and big ears. But she'd traded undyed wool for silks; now she dressed like a queen, and carried herself like one. She politely thanked one of her handmaids, who was scrubbing her arms in the steaming water at the washbasin.

Bataar tore off his gloves as he approached his generals and scribes. They squatted near the map spanning between the floor cushions, its edges weighted down with everything from metal goblets to a knife half out of an ornate sheath, to an eagle

Tarken had carved from a hunk of bone, and rocks smeared with ash. Mismatched game pieces covered the map.

"We need to start thinking about Kalafar," Shaza said. "Their zultam is weak, his wealth waning. The poorer cities on the fringes are restless. Soon, gryphons will circle the farm towns like vultures."

She had her sights east toward Dumakra, an insular nation that bordered the red steppe and which had refused the Utasoo tribes' pleas for aid in the horrible years after the Sunless Months. No one in that tent had much love for the country that had spit in their faces. Bataar probably least of all.

Zultam Ramzi was Dumakra's puppet king. His xenophobic ministers had weakened the red steppe with embargos, leading to the raids that had killed Bataar's mother and almost took Qaira away from him. At the border, Dumakrans settled on Utasoo tribal land, infringing on old treaties. Bataar was compelled to seek retribution, by duty, and by a divine force even greater than the united will of his people.

"So hasty," Tarken chided. "Does the esteemed general know how many pegasus fliers we should be looking out for? Give me numbers, and I can start training my men to keep one eye on the skies and the other facing forward."

Shaza scowled. "We need those pegasuses for ourselves." She had already moved her marker, a tigress piece plucked from the popular token-capture game Eagles & Lions. If the continent were a gameboard, currently they possessed half the lower level; when they captured Dumakra, the entire playfield would be theirs, ready for a clean sweep of the Aglean kingdoms to the north, the Moshitu tribes south of the Thirst, and whatever was in the far east, undocumented on any maps. The pegasus knights were a threat now, but soon, they'd be another weapon in Bataar's arsenal.

"You act as if everything's done here," Bataar said.

Shaza turned pensive, absently swatting Tarken when he tugged her long braid. "Isn't it? The emperor is dead. The council is surrendering, and Tashir is yours. All of Choyanren."

A few of the older men nodded in agreement. The gray-bearded generals with creased faces had once led armies of thousands for the most powerful rhahs. After Bataar's stomp of the warlords, they now commanded even larger companies for him. The old rhahs were back on the red steppe, sending tribute like vassals.

"After Choyanren," Shaza said, "the zultam, his viziers, and the lords in the north are going to take notice, quickly. We'll send demands and make a plan for when your terms are rejected. We need to strike first."

Even if their zultam was weak, Dumakra commanded the air, and its capital Kalafar was bordered by feather-steel reinforced walls. Bataar's empire was a beast that would gorge on their Conservium's knowledge and grow larger. He wanted the zultam's pegasuses and iron mines, his ports and fertile farmland. Dumakra's land bridge would make moving troops into Aglea easier, and their impossibly light steel would equip his troops to sweep the armies of the northern lords.

"We'll send terms demanding the zultam pledge Dumakra and her soldiers to your empire, consenting to open borders and free trade with the west in exchange for protection and an era of peace," Shaza said. "Everything could be formalized with a marriage pact, exchanging of wards... and representatives of your choosing being made ministers and viziers to revise inequitable law in Kalafar and the surrounding cities."

Tarken twirled the end of his dark beard, which was comically out of place on his boyishly handsome face. "Well, while you lot plan for battles on a front thousands of miles east, I'll

37

celebrate the war we just won. Don't worry, I'll drink enough for all of us."

Unimpressed, Shaza knocked over Tarken's leopard piece, making it look as if his battalion had fallen.

Now clean of any blood, Qaira made her way to the advisors and sank down, reaching for the bread on plates in the center of the circle. Her body was warm curled against Bataar's side.

Tarken groaned. "Fine, Dumakra. If their walls don't fall, we can still break Kalafar." He straightened his token. "We starve my war dogs, then lower them over the rampart and release them into the capital. We keep a few dozen vermilrot corpses, hurl them into the city; they explode, spreading rot—"

The older advisors' smiles turned to expressions of awe and unease as Tarken outlined his methods.

"You shouldn't worry your pretty head with thinking." Shaza sounded unfazed, used to his horseshit. "You're more useful when you aren't coming up with plans. *Time* won the siege in Choyanren, not your dogs."

"Time was our enemy too," Bataar muttered. He stroked Qaira's knuckles. The next nearest town was full of granite and bone, the Silent City where the Choyanreni entombed their dead in stone crypts. This last cold snap could have forced a retreat, and then they would have had nothing but gravel and the leathery dead to gnaw on.

Shaza cocked her head. "Tarken is right about one thing. Vermilrot is more deadly than any siege equipment."

Bataar shook his head. "We want them to surrender, not start an epidemic."

Destructive wars drained resources. Fires had been burning inside the walls of Tashir for weeks. The lugsail ships they needed could have been put to the torch any day.

Qaira took Bato from his sitter, rocking him in her arms. "What has Preeminence said?" she asked hopefully.

Her words weren't directed at Bataar, but she interlocked their fingers, squeezing in a silent question. She knew he saw souls, but he'd spared her from the reality of the Preeminent Spirit she loved. Bataar wasn't a child anymore, feeling unworthy of his stolen life, but he still felt primal fear under Their gaze. He fed the Preeminent Spirit like a man throwing meat into a wolf's den. His shaman had declared he was the arm of Preeminence, but Bataar was terrified that his insatiable god would claim more than just his bloodied hands; it would take him, body and soul. For now, forever, it was better to be a blind servant than a seeing vessel.

Boroo, his grandmotherly shaman, pulled away from a corner of the room as if her thin body had been an extension of the bentwood rafters. Her wrinkled face was painted with black streaks of dried lamb's blood from the night before. "In the east, you'll lose the first battle but win the war," she said, studying Bataar with her rheumy eyes. "It ends almost as soon as it starts."

Passing years didn't touch Boroo, who had probably been born with liver-spotted skin. She was a gifted seer, conversing freely with spirits in her trances around pyres, and her rune-stones had accurately predicted the outcomes of every battle he fought. Her abilities were nothing like Bataar's. He saw Preeminence in the sky; she heard Their whispers in the flames.

"If you say so, it will," Bataar said, voicelessly dismissing Qaira's probing touch.

Shaza took his declaration as a sign to unfurl a new map, this one of the palace in the Dumakran capital. She began repositioning markers.

The baby gurgled, his lips wet with milk. Bato had Qaira's

hair and ears, but his eyes were Bataar's. The boy reached out, small fist curling around the saber in its scabbard at Bataar's belt. Bato had been born in Choyanren after the sack of Xincho, into a conquest of saltpeter and sulfur. Would he take wobbling steps and babble his first words in another military camp?

A footman appeared on the threshold. "The empress's envoy approaches."

◦◦◦◦◦◦

Bataar stood at attention at the front of his retinue as the gates screeched open. Beyond Tashir's walls, silver finials decorated pagoda roofs. The sky carried a hint of fetid sweetness, at odds with the taste of iron and melting ice on the air.

"A clear sky means Preeminence smiles on your victory," Tarken commented.

Bataar said nothing as he straightened his cloak. The black sable lining was soft and warm about his neck. At his hip, the hilt of his saber sparkled. His blade hadn't seen blood since they clashed with the Choyanreni army on the farmland outside of Tanomaki. He'd wanted a surrender, not a bloodbath, and he'd received one.

Beyond the generals standing stiffly, soldiers made lines, solemn in their tension. Shaza's cheek was dressed with gauze, covering the cut she'd received from a longbowman on the wall. "*That archer's mine*," she'd hissed after the smoke cleared. Bataar wasn't sure if she wanted to kill or recruit them. She'd been collecting the best bowmen since their campaign against the steppe lords, years ago.

Boroo lingered at Qaira's side, watching Bataar with an inscrutable expression he didn't wish to study too closely. The knuckles on her hand clutching Qaira's arm were white, and her fingers shook with exertion.

Bataar shared a meaningful glance with his wife. "You look every part the queen," he whispered.

"I'd hope so. This is very heavy."

The hammered silver headdress brought out golden undertones in her thick auburn braids. Her damask dress was a crimson so dark it looked blood-dyed. The ornaments haloing her head chimed as she lowered her face to their son, her half-lidded eyes never breaking contact with Bataar's. The expression she wore ignited heat that coiled in his stomach.

He shuffled in the snow. After the guardsmen on the wall laid down their arms, Bataar had dictated a message to one of the captured scholars. The scribe wrote succinctly, without the flourishes he'd seen in the tomes of Xincho's famous library. The message had been delivered using one of the birds liberated from a dragonlord's coop, and the reply came quickly.

"Finally," Shaza muttered, uncrossing her arms.

Guards in plate armor conveyed a litter through the gates. The tall men lowered the carrying poles, and a historian walking behind quickly drew back the curtains. The crowd grew hushed as the woman inside was let down by the hand of a guard. Her slippers crunched into the snow.

"Presenting the personal envoy of Her Majesty Ruo Sacha," the historian announced in a reedy voice.

Bataar nodded to his footman. The boy, one of Tarken's cousins, stepped forward and cleared his throat, speaking in clumsy Choyanreni: "Announcing His Eminence, the Rhah of the Red Steppe, Son of the Red Mother, the Scourge of Xincho, and future prince of Tanomaki, the re—resplendent Bataar Rhah."

His soldiers shouted his name, pounding their chests and hitting the hilts of their weapons against the ground.

"'*Resplendent Rhah*,'" the envoy said, as if she were spitting the honorific through gritted teeth and asking a question all at once.

At the nod of her head, her retinue knelt in the slushy snow. Even the historian didn't hesitate to dirty his honorable white robes and coat.

The empress's representative wore brightly colored brocade. Her cheeks and lips were stained red, and jade pendants hung from a pronged headdress in her hair. Condensation swirling under the milky green surface gave the stone its name: cloud jade. Painted porcelain bells and sachets of incense were tied to the sash stretching around the hips of her jacketed dress. Bataar breathed in the citrusy-smelling orchid perfume that hung in a cloud around her.

He was instantly suspicious. The woman before him was an absurdly well-decorated delegate.

"Word reached Tashir that during your conquest, your men destroyed the Supreme School of Thought," she said, facing the translators, her voice fierce even as she kept her expression blank. "That they used the leather covers of priceless books to make sandals for your dirty feet. The empress has heard rumors that you made the Taibeg river run red with the blood of their greatest thinkers and skilled physicians."

"Xincho's doctors are at work in my encampment, stalling vermilrot," Bataar said without hesitation. It would be better to ease her anger. There had been blood, so much death the hungriest gods would be sated, but he hadn't slaughtered doctors. "Your country's academics are already sharing their knowledge with my historians and clerks, constructing an accurate description of the conquering of the Federated Kingdoms and their absorption into the Utasoo nation."

She pursed her lips. "Your pronunciation is... better than

I anticipated," she conceded, facing Bataar now instead of the translators.

The Choyanreni historians and high scribes had already proven useful as language instructors. One day, Bataar might employ them as private tutors for his own children, if the Conservium-educated scholars in Dumakra didn't impress him more.

"But I can tell you mean to trick me with soft words," she continued. "I won't let you construct a false history. They say in Tanomaki—"

"What you might have heard about Tanomaki is true," he admitted.

The dragonlords had fought filthily. Their insults had been unforgivable. A few of those men had been drawn and quartered. Others had been stripped naked and tossed into their own drug dens. Tarken fed one to his dogs. Bataar could only watch that for a few seconds before he'd averted his eyes, but others had gawked as the man was turned to a lump of meat. So much for dragons breathing fire. In Choyanren, the only dragons left were mere men, wearing a frightening name like a shield, and they had died whimpering.

"Tashir is not Tanomaki," she said. "The Cloud Jade Empress expresses—"

For a moment, Bataar had forgotten he was talking to an "envoy." He wouldn't let this farce continue.

"The empress wrote that she was sending a representative. I didn't anticipate parleying with her directly. Would Your Majesty be more comfortable in a tent, near a fire? Something befitting your station." He met her eyes. Hers still betrayed nothing. "You're younger than I anticipated," he said. "*You* were the emperor's wife?"

The royal family in Tashir was a mystery, even to the

historians at the Supreme School of Thought. The emperor had been frail and white-bearded, hidden behind paper screens, but not much else was known about him.

The disguised empress squared her shoulders. "I'm his daughter, Ruo Sacha, and I could say that you're young, for an illustrious warlord."

She was right. Mukhalii Rhah's raid that had stolen his mother, Qaira, and more women and children from their camp had taught Bataar when he was still young how war was waged. He had been sixteen, then, leading a conquest for their return—and for revenge. His childhood had been taken from him by bloody swords and talons. Victory was only ever bittersweet.

"I'm new to war, but not naïve." The empress's breath steamed in the frosted air. "I have a sharp mind."

He almost smiled. "You were right to surrender. The wall was falling. Inexperience doesn't mean you lack good judgment. Tell me. How'd the emperor die?"

Ruo's expression was stony. "He succumbed to vermilrot. If it's true you have the physicians from Xincho, I beg of you... I've repurposed the council hall, but we can't stop the spread of infection." Her jaw worked, not quite disguising the flash of terror that suddenly pulled at her brow and twisted her red lips. So her stone facade could crack. "I'll swear fealty."

That wouldn't be enough. Bataar would *demand* fealty. It was claimed, won, owed, earned, not given. He strained to keep his expression blank. "The empress of the cloud jade city begs before me," he said in both their languages, loud enough to carry through the crowd. Soldiers snickered, some laughed. Others shivered. Most looked grim. "What does Her Eminence present in exchange for peace?"

Annoyance flickered in Ruo's dark eyes. "All I have is our

fleet, and myself. If my scribes draft a peace pact pledging mutual support in emergencies, sealed with marriage vows, would you accept? You'd be king consort in Tashir. It's an honor."

Bataar had planned on taking another wife to solidify the union with the Federated Kingdoms. One of the dragonlords' princesses would have sufficed. The opium merchants ruled Tanomaki and wielded power in the Federated Kingdoms. He would have let Qaira pick her favorite of the sulky girls with their powdered skin. But the empress?

This *was* a better offer.

Bataar turned to Qaira, eyebrows raised in question. At her small, assenting nod he looked back toward Ruo.

"Then your city has my protection."

It wouldn't all end so neatly, but the war was unwinding, melting like snow. And sediment—unrest and revolt—would need to be skimmed off as white ice became clear water. But today there would be feasting and sex, music and wrestling and archery tournaments, *victory* blurred by alcohol and delirious laughter.

Bataar didn't want warm and comfortable. He was already burning for more. There was so much of that map still unclaimed. A god that would never be satisfied, but he couldn't blame Preeminence alone. Perhaps he did want bloodshed, revenge for a thousand injustices.

Maybe he was a monster.

4

SUMMER, 368

*Never were there more dutiful children
than Paga's Harpy daughters.*
— Dumakran holy writ

Nohra was elbow-deep in a pegasus's birthing canal, her grip slipping on the legs folded inside the sac. Cool, pre-dawn dampness hung in the air, mingling with the heady scent of tanned leather and the fust of wet straw. At sunrise, grooms would feed the pegasuses, and the royal stables would reek of iron, the ornate columns spattered with meaty flecks of viscera.

The laboring mare thrashed the wing not tucked under her body. A keen yellow eye zeroed in on Nohra's face, and suddenly Faith was canting her head sharply, teeth snapping. If the mare weren't lying spineless on the ground, she might have bitten Nohra's nose off.

"Easy, you monster." Over her shoulder Nohra called, "Some help? The wings are stuck." *See their worth*, Nohra prayed. *Don't smother a flame yet unkindled.*

The young stablehands cowered, hesitating behind the safety of the paddock gate.

Uneven footsteps stomped down from the stablemaster's loft. "Out of the way," Fahaad said, weaving between the boys. The top of his tunic was open, revealing a triangle of smooth umber skin. He ran fingers over his hair, cropped too short to ever appear disheveled. His other hand held an amber bottle sealed with wax.

"For health." He pulled out the cork with his teeth and poured the zultam's good liquor over his hands. "For courage." He wrapped his lips around the stem. His throat bobbed as he swallowed. "For luck."

He knelt, extending the bottle to Nohra. Blending scents of licorice and plum tickled her nose. The swig burned down her throat, sending needles of warmth stabbing to her fingers and toes.

Goddess, it was so good she could whimper.

"For *Darya*." Fahaad drew out their friend's name as he stood, holding the lip of the bottle to her. Darya shrunk back, pressed flat against the wall. She had been green-faced since the foaling started, but now roses bloomed on her cheeks. "Watch this for us, will you, love?" Fahaad winked. "And not a drop for these useless gits."

A lifetime ago, back when Fahaad was a scrawny stablehand, Nohra and Darya would often sneak out here at night. Nohra remembered waking up in the stalls with straw in her hair, her head against Fahaad's shoulder. They used to fall asleep to Darya's lullaby voice reciting the names of constellations.

Dar's brown hair was sleep-mussed, her shawl askew and black eyes bleary. She was all mousy softness and ample curves, so non-threatening that even her penetrating eyes only intimidated a few clumsy girls in the palace kitchens who were terrified of her gentle scolding. "You don't need my help, right?"

"No, you're safe, Dar," Fahaad told her.

There were already too many hands in the pegasus. Nohra dragged an arm out. She attempted to wipe the perspiration off her forehead with her shoulder. Darya fluttered forward with a handkerchief.

"You don't have to mother hen," Nohra reproached her.

"Paga's ass, it's light," Fahaad said. His hip prodded Nohra's as they repositioned the foal, bending the tiny wings and legs. It slid out into the peat and hay while its mother panted heavy, labored breaths.

"Knife." Nohra flexed her fingers expectantly. Her hand closed around a blade, its embossed hilt inset with diamonds. She recognized the shape of the constellation by touch—she'd drawn the design out for the royal smith for Darya's natal-day present. The Demonking's chain: perhaps a gauche gift from a princess to her servant, but Dar was her friend first, her talmaid second, and the stars in that cluster were Darya's favorite.

Nohra sliced through the umbilical cord and peeled back the amniotic sac. After a few tense minutes, the pegasus foal swayed upright on spindly legs. The rubbery fingers on its hooves would harden quickly, and its naked wings would fill in with feathers as it grew. Nohra held her breath. She'd already begged Paga for its life. Asking for more would be selfish.

Its body shook, and it collapsed into the straw. Nohra sagged with it. Another long labor ending in a newborn pegasus made of glass.

"Brittle," Fahaad explained to Darya and the new stable-hands. "A congenital effect, makes them birdlike and infertile."

She murmured, "So the poor thing has hollow bones."

The mare stirred, her breaths steadying, nose rooting

toward the afterbirth she'd just delivered intact. She ate, the placenta painting her white muzzle scarlet.

"This is Faith's second brittle foal. We should send for new breeding stock from Antiria. Start fresh. Need a hand?"

Nohra brushed Fahaad off and climbed up. She squeezed through the audience that had gathered, moving toward the fountain in the center of the opulent stables to scrub discharge off her arms. The stablehands could coax the foal to stand properly and nurse, separating it from its mother if she rejected it.

Darya and Fahaad followed, sweeping off Nohra's bad mood.

"Before I forget, from the apothecarist," Darya mumbled. "And something for the taste."

Fahaad's voice rasped as he took the proffered vial. "Thanks. I'm filthy, would you mind?"

Nohra stole a glance at them. Back stiff, like she was prepared for him to nip her fingers, Darya stood on her tiptoes to pop a sweet pastry between his lips. Fahaad smirked like he was using all his self-control to restrain from sucking its honey sweetness off her fingers.

Darya made an unconvincing show of wiping off her hand and looking repulsed. "What about the infertility tonic?"

He grinned. "I like what you make better, Daheer."

Even the pegasuses were probably rolling their eyes. Nohra put distance between them.

"You should say something to her about… you know," Fahaad whispered, lowering his voice and leaning close to Darya.

"No. You should."

"I know my place here. Yours is by her."

Nohra pretended not to hear them. *Goddess*, she wanted

to go flying. Day was dawning, tinting the sky in orange and pink hues. She wanted to soar high above the city, until all the browns, reds, and oxidized blues in Kalafar smeared. To look down on the glistening building that housed the Maraq Cistern, the crests of the turquoise domes on top of Thora's Sanctium, and the sprawling grounds of the Rutiaba Palace. She wanted to savor the crests of the domes on the sanctium as if they were little round candies, drinking it all in. To watch Kalafar's early-morning lights flare to life, and the capital glisten, a sea of fallen stars.

Her chest clenched. Before long, she'd only see that view in her memories.

"Thirsty?" Fahaad asked, coming up beside her and wiping his hands dry on his shirt.

Nohra finally grinned. "Always."

Crystal clinked as Fahaad poured water from a covered carafe into cups. "Daheer?" he prompted, and Darya reluctantly poured. In contact with water, the oils in the alcohol turned creamy white, which was why they called the drink Gryphon's Milk.

"Sure you don't want some?" Fahaad asked, taking a slow sip.

Darya set down the bottle and took his cup. She flinched, coughing when the brandy hit her mouth. "It's too early to drink," she choked out.

"We should have started earlier."

Nohra leaned back against Mercy's stall door, resting her head against the iron bars. "This is from my father's cellars," she observed, studying the paper card secured to the neck of the bottle.

"A gift, from a vizier pleased that I taught his wife to ride so well."

Nohra smiled in earnest. "*Oh?*"

He pulled a face. "Not everything's a euphemism, you child." He took the blue vial out of his pocket and tipped the infertility tonic into his cup.

"And what happens if you forget to drink that one morning?"

Fahaad winced as he swallowed. "Fevers, chills." He looked annoyed. "Maybe Mytri would notice the withdrawal symptoms and kick me out. I'd have to find a boat back to Moshitu without any money."

That might be wishful thinking. The truth was, Fahaad was too valuable as a political prisoner. He might be punished and sent away from the palace, but his presence in Dumakra guaranteed uneasy cooperation with the southern tribal lords.

"At least they don't use the old way of making eunuchs." Nohra nudged Darya's thigh with the toe of her boot. She squirmed away, refusing Nohra's baiting. "The tonic's effects are reversible, if you ever find a nice vizier's wife and want to settle down."

Fahaad stared daggers at her. Nohra jerked at a tug on her scalp. The black gelding inside the stall had put his lips around her hair and pulled.

"He probably thinks it's straw. Dar, brush that rat's nest better for our princess, and maybe the pegasuses won't get confused."

"Hey!" Nohra tugged her braid free. "I'll have you know the Minister of Roads said my hair looked lovely yesterday." She'd almost spat on him when he said it.

"Recently widowed, isn't he?" Fahaad snorted, knocking back the glass he'd poured for Nohra. "Oh, I almost forgot you're already spoken for."

Nohra's smile fell. Darya looked down, at her own hands, the recently swept floor, anywhere but at Nohra.

It had always been the three of them carving time out of the almost-morning for each other. But they weren't children anymore. Change came, like waves breaking around her body, and Nohra would have to keep wading forward, even if it was without them. The Godsbreath said it was a trap to become complacent. Her duty was to Dumakra.

"Tomorrow, same time?" Fahaad asked.

Darya would be back, leaving little blue vials outside the gate with a tenderness that contradicted their contents.

"Before dawn?" Nohra ribbed. "Goddess, I hope not. I have other responsibilities than playing medicine maven for horses." As if she wouldn't return as soon as she could, wheedling the foal to suckle from a bottle. She'd prick her own finger and let it latch on her blood. She'd done it countless times. And Nohra would need to savor every moment she could steal with her friends, to remember when she left.

❧

Steam rose from the washbasin as Nohra stripped off her riding clothes. The windows were thrown open in all the rooms in the harem's wing, the coolness of morning replaced by the heat of a Dumakran summer. Outside, bees buzzed at the rose bushes and giggling serving girls passed under covered walkways, balancing stacks of linens on their way to the washroom. Water dripped from Darya's wrung-out cloth.

Most servants only worked at the palace for a handful of years before finding gainful employment or a marriage match. But Darya's grandmother had been a favorite of Nohra's family and had raised Dar at the palace. Since Nohra's swearing-in almost ten years ago, her friend's official title was talmaid, dedicated lady-in-waiting and squire to a Harpy Knight.

After Nohra wriggled into her undergarments, Darya

pulled the straps tight on her vambraces and helped her into the rest of her gold-plated armor. She braided Nohra's hair in intricate interlocking plaits, not a strand out of place.

Nohra's quarters in the palace were mostly empty. The only real decoration was a tapestry her stepmother had chosen. Since Darya had already stripped the clothes off the bed, the only signs the room had an occupant were all the weapons and the stack of books on a table.

"You know, I never actually see you reading," Darya said, following her line of sight. "I'm beginning to think you just borrow those to look smart."

"I read, when I have the time."

Titles like Obeyd's *Wartime Strategies* and *The Second Conquest of Noor* jumped out, the pages yellowed and brittle. Beyond that, the rooms could have been secondary storage for the armory. Sharpened blades and whetstones littered every surface. By the end of the year, Nohra would have left the palace, and Kalafar, and her room would look just as lived-in as it did now.

"You know, I could speak to my father," Nohra said. "Arrange a marriage match. I think Fahaad would agree to it. He's always been soft for you."

Fahaad had been brought to Dumakra from Moshitu when he was only a boy. He'd been their prisoner for long enough. After more than a decade, it was time he assumed a more important role than stablemaster. As Father's ward, he should be an ambassador to Moshitu to strengthen their tenuous relations with the southern tribal lords. Taking a Dumakran wife, one from the zultam's palace, would project a strong image of unity. And Dar would be good for Fahaad. Never mind that he wouldn't know something good for him if it put a hoof through his head. He'd always been carefully aloof. Maybe that was her family's fault.

Darya peered around Nohra's head. Her reflection in the mirror grimaced. "You don't want me with you in Aglea?"

Nohra pinched Darya's side, and she jerked back, bumping the table with her hip. The murky water in the basin sloshed but didn't overflow. They both laughed.

Nohra's teasing smile fell quickly. "You don't have to follow me."

Darya's eyes were earnest, dark like midnight, as endlessly deep as the sky. "Then don't leave."

"*I have to.*" Her tone was sharper than she'd intended. Darya flinched.

Nohra should go to the private sanctium. The words that didn't come easily with Darya would flow out of her mouth into the Goddess's ears. Once she'd sat with it, prayed on it, it would all become small. She'd recognize how immature it was to be resentful of her father when he had Dumakra's best interest at heart. Nohra had been born knowing the weight of duty, whether she was to be her father's sword or his bargaining chip. Half-Aglean herself, she'd be well matched with the northern lord's son. In the foreign court, she would be a powerful diplomatic asset.

She might even enjoy Aglea. Feel some connection to her mother there, *become* a mother there.

Goddess.

Crossing the room, Nohra pulled her red sickle-staff from its pedestal and slung it into the scabbard strapped across her back. *Bleeding Edge* was finally hers after years of wanting, but for how much longer? She chanced a look back at Darya. A lump caught in her throat. Darya would stay at the Rutiaba Palace in Kalafar when she left, or go to the Sister City, to her grandmother in Rayenna; Nohra would order it.

Instinctively, Nohra touched the cleric's pendant. The

necklace she'd been given over a decade ago stayed yoked around her neck like the Demonking's chain. She rubbed her thumb over the inlaid letters. *Peace sows complacency, Chaos begets order.* She understood that better now.

"Nohra, I—"

She turned and left Darya before she could finish speaking. Outside her rooms, the covered causeways were tightly packed with servants. In the distance, hounds howled and a peacock screeched. Nohra failed to stifle a yawn.

"Couldn't sleep?" Safiya asked, falling into step beside her.

"Looks like I wasn't the only one."

Her sister's black hair was disheveled, her eyes red. "At least I enjoyed my night," Safiya said conspiratorially. "Why didn't you?"

"I had my arm up a pegasus's birthing canal."

"I can think of six things right now I'd rather put my fingers in than a horse's twat. Next time call the Conservium. Make a maven soil their hoods and hands." Safiya's grin turned teasing. "I was in far better company."

"Zira?"

Zira was a concubine from the islands north of Moshitu. One of their father's recent favorites—and Safiya's. It was an open secret. Everyone knew—except, hopefully, Father.

"I'm surprised you actually keep up with my—what does Grandmother Himma call them?—'*dalliances*'." Safiya sighed. "I'll be lonely tonight, though. Grandmother wants Zira to join Father in his room. Play queen mother for me, would you, and send someone to *my* rooms?"

Nohra grunted. "Like you need my help."

Queen of Beasts, Saf's wickedly curving sword, swung from the scabbard at her hip. The swirling patterns in the steel glistened as the sun hit them. Like always, dressed in their armor

55

with their weapons bared, Nohra and Safiya attracted the eyes of curious maids, concubines, and little girls.

"Hells, it's too early to be responsible," Safiya muttered. "Rami, what in the Goddess's names is it now?"

Their gangly little brother sat slumped, tucked into an alcove outside the door to the audience hall. "Saf! Nohra!" he said, looking up hopefully. As usual, his close-fitting robes were untidy. Every day he seemed taller and less dignified, like a lanky colt.

Nohra crossed her arms. "Where's Mytri? Did you run away from him again?"

"The meeting was boring, so I slipped out when a courier left. I'd literally rather practice sums or read Grandmother's diary."

Safiya ruffled his already messy hair. "If you don't want to be found, hide better. Head to the mews. We'll tell him you're at the stables."

Rami beamed. Once he was out of sight, Nohra said, "He can't run away from his responsibilities forever. He's the crown prince."

"He's ten."

"Everyone dotes on him." Because their mother was dead, and he'd never known her. "No one treats him like the king he'll be."

Safiya's expression was pointed. "Ten, Nohra."

"Princesses," the doormen said, bowing their heads as they opened the chamber door.

Nohra and Safiya strode inside. They passed rows of kneeling viziers, scribes, clerks, guards, Merchants Guild representatives, chamberlains, and dozens of other men Nohra scarcely registered. Only one mattered.

Separated from his council by an ornamental grille, their

father sat flanked by his two other Harpy Knights. Through the decorative metal divider, Nohra glimpsed her father in diamond-shaped fractals. His hair was graying at the temples, but new concubines whispered that he was still handsome with his aquiline nose, sharp jaw, and generous smile. Nohra had seen his features in different configurations on her half-siblings, in the mirror, and especially on Rami's face. Wherever she looked, she saw her father.

When he looked at Nohra, did he see her dead mother?

She dismissed the stupid thought as quickly as it came to her.

For his audience with his advisors, the zultam wore a belted brocade outer robe and muslin-wrapped turban festooned with precious jewels. The royal ornaments sparkled in light thrown from a tall window, signaling his station in the room of men. He was Goddess-blessed, and they only wielded influence because he let them.

Calidah stood at attention, scanning the room with inquisitive eyes. Aunt Clemiria had been away in Rayenna for ten years, but her daughter was her mirror image, with the same long hair and thin lips. Cali's skinny fingers curled around the stock of the crossbow *Covenant*. Looking at the glossy hardwood and mother of pearl on the grip made the old wound on Nohra's shoulder tighten.

Finally, Aalya mouthed. The points of the javelins in her scabbard made a crown of steel around her short hair. Her half-sister had blinked awake when the door strained open. Aalya's habit to keep herself from falling back asleep was turning her shield *Segreant* over in her hands. The rearing pegasus moved in and out of view at every flip.

"—attacking farm towns along the Scythe. If their numbers continue to increase, we should send a force to cull the gryphons at the cliffs," an advisor was saying.

"The outlying towns were stronger before so much delegation of the zultam's power," General Fakier retorted. "His new ministers neglect their duty. Now the army should intervene to slaughter beasts? Are you volunteering the funds to move our troops? Lend the man an abacus and show him the crown's accounts."

At the dais, Nohra and Safiya swapped positions with Calidah and Aalya, relieving them from their posts until supper. They settled onto the steps, watching the other two Harpies gratefully take their leave.

Before them spread a sea of patterned turbans and snowy beards, each man with a mouth he couldn't keep shut for long. Safiya rested a hand on the pommel of her sword. The emerald eyes set in the lion's face glinted, a beautiful threat.

Groaning doors interrupted the argument. Nohra turned as Darya and two other servants entered, arranging plates of juicy pickled beets, cheese, dates, olives, and steaming bread in front of seated and kneeling men.

At the intrusion, whispers crescendoed to impassioned shouts, punctuated with flying spittle.

"… is a bigger threat! He's organized several of the steppe tribes over the last couple years. All the other lords kneel for him. They call him the Resplendent Rhah," one young vizier was explaining. "He's caused some trouble in the west, in the kingdoms in Choyanren. I beg you not to dismiss his terms too hastily."

"Barbarian tribes, hardly organized," an older man with a long beard interrupted. Nohra recognized the grating voice of the Minister of Roads. "They're uncivilized men and women eating other uncivilized men, women, children, and horses."

The young vizier, red-faced and flustered, cut back in, speaking with urgency. "If you'll pardon me, Your Magnificence, his soldiers are spreading panic among the farm towns north of the Scythe. He claims his spirit god told him he'll rule Dumakra, the Federated Kingdoms, and both halves of Aglea. Your citizens are desperate and fearful."

Some of the older men scoffed. Nohra scowled, but didn't speak. The Utasoo were famous for their courage and strength. Winters on the red steppe were harsh, and with monsters encroaching each year, ever more dangerous.

Close to the zultam, Grand Vizier Naji stroked his black beard, twirling the end of it around his finger. "This nation won't fall to nomads living among gryphons."

"What word comes from the Federated Kingdoms?" an advisor asked nervously. Dumakra's foreign relations hadn't been strong for decades, not since her father nearly lost the Heartspring and surrendered Keld after the Sunless Months. Now, his isolationist rule irritated his viziers who conducted trade with neighboring countries.

"We've heard that the Tashiri emperor wed one of the princesses to the barbarian king," an older man said. "But a rock-worshiping fool whoring out his daughter shouldn't concern us."

"If the warlord had approached with gentler terms, perhaps some agreement could have been reached, a political marriage—"

"Dumakra will not negotiate her surrender to a steppe lord!"

"He's not invincible," another man interjected. "There are rumors Bataar Rhah is disfigured. My informant says he's got a nasty scar on his face from a loss in Xincho."

The Minister of Education whispered, "Where the hells is Xincho?"

"I couldn't imagine more useless information if I had all day to dream it up," Naji said. "Find new informants."

Nohra had known Yardaan Naji her entire life. He was her father's closest friend, his most important advisor, his shadow. He never leered, never wavered, and he always had the zultam's ear. Wormy voices whispered that he ran Kalafar, and his ministers the other cities. Nohra wished she could tell her father how it weakened him for his people to only catch rare glimpses of their sovereign, to hear his voice always filtered through his advisors.

"It's not—"

"What?"

"It's from fighting a gryphon." The room erupted in laughter. "It is! He fought one as a boy with his bare hands, and now he only has one eye and it glows yellow."

"Sweet, merciful Goddess." Naji bent to whisper something to her father.

"Where's the gryphon hunter now?" the zultam asked. "I'll send two steel battalions to deal with him, and"—he looked at Safiya, then at Nohra—"my sword and scythe."

5

Fields of Red
— Lofri house motto

As Bataar rode through the poppy fields, he remembered Choyanren, where razed farmland had been watered with blood. The sprawling estates of the dragonlords had burned like funeral pyres, and the palaces had stunk of vermilrot. In contrast, the Dumakran minister's crops spread in a blanket, filling the air with a smell that was equal parts sweet and smoky. Beyond sprawling red rows, a thick forest loomed.

"A fine view, no?" asked the man riding beside Bataar. Prince Nassar had long eyelashes and a thin face. His small wrists and narrow waist looked delicate enough to snap, and he decorated himself almost as carefully as Qaira.

"My wife enjoys flowers more than I do," Bataar replied as they approached Lofri's estate.

"I look forward to meeting your wife," Nassar said idly, staring out into the woods.

"I don't. I'm *terrified* she'll be taken with you."

The prince laughed loudly. There was snickering behind them from Tarken and Shaza and some of the men. Tarken's smirk dropped as he lost control of his horse. He'd been struggling with the unfamiliar gait of the Dumakran palfrey since they left town. Its flank twitched, tail swishing in irritation.

"These red flowers are an ornamental strain," Nassar droned. "The ones for opium are mostly white. Indentured farmers grow them in the drier fields and Lofri distributes the seed resin."

High above, Bataar glimpsed the silhouette of Erdene gliding in and out of view. Sometimes he wished he could be above everything like her, higher than political squabbling, intrigue, or war, shooting down like an arrow when there was something he needed to kill. Sharp-sighted, but blind to what dwelled behind the clouds.

He'd never be above the world, but he could be above men.

They dismounted in the outer courtyard of a columned house. Bataar handed his bridle off to his footman, Oktai, Tarken's cousin. He was a tall boy, and he waddled awkwardly in the stiff tunic. The Dumakran style didn't suit him. From the glimpse Bataar had caught of his own reflection in a mirror at the inn that morning, he looked passable. He'd trimmed his beard and hair to attract less attention, but now, he could see his efforts were wasted. The streets of Zeffa were full of foreigners. It hadn't been like that when he was a boy, when they used to come to trade at markets and beg for scraps. He'd stood out too much then. It had almost cost him a hand or even his life.

"I know you told me to wait outside last night," Oktai confessed in a rush, bringing him back to the present. "But Tarken gave me some silver honors, so I paid one of the ladies at the brothel for her time."

"Oh." He realized he should say something more. "Is that so?"

Oktai unclasped Bataar's cloak. "We played Court, but I

kept getting dealt hands of dancers and soldiers, and she had all the lady knights and viziers. She was from Choyanren originally, so I told her about the battles we fought there and she spoke about when she was a child." His eyes glazed over, lost in thought. "We talked for so long the brothel-keeper slammed on the door, screaming we'd gone on for more than an hour."

"You… just talked?"

"Yes, but—well, I also asked her how to *please a woman*, for when I'm married." Oktai ducked his head, blushing. "She knew a lot. She even drew a picture. You think I was a bother?"

"You're a good boy. When have you ever annoyed anyone, except Shaza?"

"I think I'm in love."

He patted Oktai on the head. "I promise you're not."

"My back feels like it's been broken in half," Tarken moaned, coming up behind them and clapping them both on the shoulder. "Shaza shouldn't have bought me that drink, or let me start that fight outside the theater. How'd you two fare last night?"

The Utasoo and Dumakran languages shared several words, so Bataar lowered his voice to talk freely. "The prince told me, 'You can judge a man's character by how he behaves at a Zeffan brothel'. Apparently his uncle wanted him to test my judgment. I think the minister expected the prince would take me to the race track, but Nassar had his own ideas."

They'd met in a secluded parlor at a pleasure house, where a pale Aglean courtesan plied the prince with wine as another ducked bashfully from the drunken kiss Nassar pressed against the column of her neck. It was an insult that Bataar had to debase himself by taking that fool seriously.

Tarken laughed. "I would have killed to see the look on your face."

Bataar grimaced.

"Well, which one will you have?" Neither. *"I can find you a younger one, or a darker-skinned one, or a man—"*

Bataar had pushed iridium blessings into the brothel girls' hands and sent them from the room, straightening their carefully mended clothes. He didn't care for unregulated brothels. Even in Zeffa, on the fringes of Dumakra, where the zultam's laws were suggestions, underground pleasure houses and taverns were still illegal, making life uncertain for workers and patrons. Some pleasure houses worked around the law by calling their girls priestesses, in the way of archaic traditions. This establishment hadn't bothered keeping up such pretenses.

Besides, there was only one person Bataar wanted in his bed.

Tarken prodded him with his elbow. "Well, do you trust him?"

Bataar surveyed the manor belonging to Dumakra's Minister of Commerce. Ivy clung to the columns, curling around arched windows.

"Less than the dragonlords," Bataar admitted. Still, they didn't have endless options. When Bataar had waved away Nassar's offer, the prince had finally sobered up, ready to stop screwing around and discuss their alliance.

Oblivious, Oktai grinned. "I'll have so much to tell my mother. She wanted a good story. Now I have hundreds." The boy wasn't as hardened as the rest of them had been at sixteen. He didn't remember the camp raids and kidnappings, the weddings that became funerals.

"Let's leave everything that happened last night out, alright?" Bataar told him. "And most of what happened in Tanomaki."

Oktai nodded. "Of course. You speak, and I obey."

Tarken flicked his cousin. "Yeah, yeah. Don't get smart."

Bataar faced the procession that waited to receive them.

"My conservator, Ervan Lofri," Nassar introduced, gesturing at the short man with a white beard. "His son, Jawaad." The man was taller than Nassar and thick-muscled. There was a blankness in his eyes that Bataar didn't care for. "And my betrothed, Kasira."

Bataar took her hand and kissed it. He brought her fingers to his forehead the way Dumakrans honored their elders. Red splotches erupted on the young woman's face.

From what Bataar had learned yesterday, the prince had spent much of his early life in a gilded cage, confined to a few rooms at the palace in Kalafar. He'd then been sent to Zeffa to live with Ervan Lofri, a distant relative of his mother. The plan was to marry him to Lofri's daughter, Kasira. But the girl had a fragile constitution, so the marriage hadn't been realized yet. Her skin had a sickly yellow tinge, and her eyes bulged from her small face.

"Come on, boy," Tarken said in Utasoo, pushing Oktai forward. "Do your job."

"*His Eminence.*" He cleared his throat. "I present His Eminence, the Gryphon King of the steppe, son of the Red Mother, the Scourge of Xincho, and Liege Lord of Tanomaki"— he took a gulping breath and rushed on, tripping over his words—"Prince Consort of Tashir, the Conqueror of Choyanren, Bataar, the Great Rhah."

By some miracle of Preeminence, Oktai's Dumakran was worse than his Choyanreni.

"And who might this be?" Lofri asked. "Your sister?"

Bataar looked at Shaza. "One of my commanders."

Laughter made the minister's jowls shake. "A woman commander? You're like the zultam with his Harpy Knights."

Beside him, Nassar looked Shaza up and down with hungry eyes.

In Utasoo, Shaza warned, "I'll geld your little prince if he puts his hands on me."

"You'd gag if you'd seen what I have," Tarken said. "She means it."

Bataar shot them both a warning look. "Stay civil."

Lofri looked between Tarken and Bataar. "You two have the same—" He waved his fingers around their faces, approximating their scars.

"From some trouble when we were younger," Bataar explained. Shaza's scar from the gryphon's claws was out of sight, hidden under her shirt.

"They're gryphon-marked," Nassar explained. "That rumor, at least, is true."

❦

In the parlor, Tarken and Shaza and their men drank Dumakran wine while Bataar nursed a cup of tea. For talk like this, it was better to be sober. Serving girls drifted around the spacious room, depositing trays full of fruit, toasted bread, and dips drizzled with olive oil. Nassar lounged, his folded legs taking up a second seat on the couch. He watched their conversation with offhanded interest, more focused on feeding the golden monkey perched on his shoulder. Minister Lofri's feathery eyebrows fluttered as he spoke, pausing only to take slow drags from an ivory pipe.

"Divide the zultam's troops across multiple fronts, and his advisors will never anticipate your true target," Lofri said, licking his fingers clean. "They're cautious. They'll think Kalafar is too ambitious for you. You'd need a death wish to strike Dumakra's heart, caging your army in at the

Scythe. It's a siege you couldn't win while the surrounding cities stand."

Ervan Lofri had made a thief's fortune smuggling opium to Choyanren and pushing Dumakran contraband in Aglea and the red steppe. He operated out of the illegal port known as West Zeffa, a mess of creaking wooden docks and hovels that reeked of urine, alcohol, and cheap bricks of coffee. There were dozens of wealthy men in the ports running drugs, trading foreigners and the poor as human chattel. Bataar had never cared to learn the names of all the old skeletons. When the zultam had rejected Bataar's terms for an accord, Lofri wasted no time in sending envoys to negotiate an alliance.

What was good for trade was good for Lofri. He wanted open borders and slashed export taxes, unimpeded trade with Aglea, the red steppe, and Choyanren.

"So, you're unhappy with the zultam?" Bataar began. "Don't you believe he's Goddess-blessed?"

"I don't believe that. Some do, but I don't." Lofri put his pipe down, laughing humorlessly. "I've been the Minister of Commerce for Zultam Ramzi's whole life. He's always been a spoilt brat, and now he's the puppet of his advisors."

Once, Zeffa had sparkled like a second capital. Dumakra had been untouchable. Now, its ministers scavenged the zultam's hoarded wealth, and the first to suffer were civilians. Bataar had once almost lost a hand for stealing in Zeffa's markets. Now guards patrolled rationing lines, and the wealth divide was high as a palisade.

"Anyone who speaks loud enough has his ear, and every pretty thing has his eye," Lofri continued. "At least his mother keeps him on a tight leash." But a well-controlled dog was still a dog. "Goddess's misfortune Clemiria isn't a man. Any of Ramzi's sisters would have made a stronger zultam."

67

"Why not put your support behind one of them, then?" Bataar probed.

A silent chuckle shook his beard. "They're all doting and blind to Ramzi's faults. Besides, it's written in the Godsbreath. A woman grasps too much power and she rips her soul in half, declares war, maims her children, seduces a demon, makes *two* hells! Many in Dumakra would prefer a man in charge of the Sister City too—"

Bataar inclined his head. "Is there nothing redeemable about the zultam?"

The minister huffed. "He enjoys his children well enough. Probably because he's always liked looking in mirrors."

"You think your boy Nassar there is Goddess-blessed? He's Ramzi's son."

The prince grinned roguishly at Shaza. When she fixed him with a repulsed look, he turned toward one of the comelier serving girls.

"More importantly, he has Merv's blood." Lofri smiled contentedly. "My cousin's blood. Nothing is worth more to me than my own family."

Merv Attar was the zultam's first wife and only living queen. She was older than her husband by almost ten years and had married him when he was only fourteen or fifteen. Prince Nassar and a younger daughter were the eventual products of that union.

Dumakran kings wished for daughters. It was said the unluckiest zultam would be cursed only with sons: too many heirs who sought his throne and not enough warrior girls to defend him.

Bataar leaned back, raising an eyebrow. The arched windows, painted tile, and velvet couches all spoke of Lofri's wealth. The Attars and Lofris were two of Kalafar's richest families. Their fortunes had built modern-day Dumakra.

Bataar said, "I respect a man who values his family."

Lofri's grin turned cat-like. "If I had another daughter, I'd wed her to you in an instant."

"If only."

"Should we continue this conversation outside?" Nassar interrupted. His pet scampered away. "I'm bored, and the Lofri hunting grounds are rivaled only by the royal woods in Antiria."

Bataar exited into the courtyard first. Inside, suffocation had gripped him, flooding Bataar with the same sense of unspoken danger as this alliance. But even if he would never trust Lofri, Bataar could at least put faith in his self-interest. Beyond trade, their deal would elevate his ward, Prince Nassar, and by extension, Lofri's daughter. Bataar had also promised to name Lofri's blocky son grand vizier, no small honor.

By absorbing the cities and smaller towns and farmsteads of Dumakra, Bataar would continue building an empire to unify the world. One without religious wars, starving children, slaves, and drug dens. A better world.

He couldn't give Nassar Dumakra. The best he'd do was make him a governor, if his conservator proved loyal and cooperative. Name him king of some other city.

"Bring the birds," Lofri called out.

The minister's falconer approached with two hooded peregrines leashed to thick gloves. Some boys still learning to train raptors came from the direction of the mews with sparrowhawks in cages. Other servants brought out barking hounds. Bataar whistled for Erdene. She swooped out of a tree onto his shoulder, screeching so loudly the peregrines' feathers ruffled. The dogs howled, their hackles raised.

"That's quite a bird you have." Nassar sounded begrudgingly impressed. "Thing's the size of a roc. I've never seen an eagle so big."

Lofri's son Jawaad stood beside him, grimacing.

"What's her largest quarry?" the prince pressed.

"A gryphon," Bataar said. "But she's taken down wolves in the winter, and plenty of foxes."

"You're joking."

"I'm dead serious."

The old minister tittered. "Well, we've got red stags and wild boar. Much farther up-mountain, there's goat-antelope and big-horned sheep. Farther south are oryx and Dumakran lions, of course. We've got wild quail in the rice fields down south too, but let's just see what we can catch in these woods today."

Nearby, serving girls crowded around Oktai, giggling as he tried to pronounce complicated Dumakran words. "Tell us more about the Federated Kingdoms," one said, batting her eyes. "I'd like to see the wider world myself, one day."

Oktai grinned, preening at their attention. "The stone crypt cities are like nothing I've ever seen, and the ships—"

Tarken swatted the back of his cousin's head. "Don't go around telling any girl who pouts her lips everything about your life. We're dressed like this because we're trying to blend in. Keep it up, and when we're back home I'll tell your mother what a little pisshead you've been."

"I haven't been a pisshead!"

Shaza pinched Oktai's cheek, pulling his gaping mouth wide. "Hmm… debatable."

"Should we make this more interesting?" Bataar asked, turning from his friends.

Nassar took one of the peregrines from the falcon trainer. "And how do you propose we do that?"

Bataar grinned wolfishly. "We raise the stakes. What should we gamble for? Kasira's hand?"

Nassar grimaced.

"The deed to the Palace of the Heart?" Bataar suggested. The zultam's holiday house in Antiria was famous across the known world for its hanging gardens. "... Kalafar?"

The minister struck Bataar on the back before clasping his shoulder. "You're a very funny man. What about the honor of naming your next son? They say the princess in Tashir is with child."

Bataar almost scoffed. *Who says?* "Done. And if my bird proves the better huntress?"

Nassar smiled. "Name your price, rhah."

Bataar studied him, taking in the oozing arrogance, the flashy belted robe, and the peacock plume affixed to the gemstone pin on his turban. Bataar hummed, rubbing the scar on his chin. "That." He pointed above Nassar's head, where the bauble sparkled.

Nassar's brow furrowed. "I hope your Choyanreni wife will like the name Nassar Zultama."

Bataar watched the dogs flush out pheasants and game birds pecking through the summer foliage. Their silky bodies flashed around the trunks of trees like fish gliding around rocks in dark water.

"Beautiful dogs," Tarken commended the minister.

The dog trainer pushed in to break up a fight between two of the hounds. Their white muzzles were tinged red, a mangled hare strewn in pieces across the leaf litter.

"A dog isn't worth the price of its teeth if it can't come to heel," Bataar muttered.

Lofri laughed. "They're young, still learning. A dog isn't trained in a day. Neither is a man."

"Eventually, a boy becomes man. Better sooner than later, if he wants to amount to anything."

He knew he needed to lay off the stupid prince. Before Lofri's alliance, taking Dumakra would have meant a tedious siege of the nation's capital. All the while they would have been fending off reinforcements sent by the rich fish merchants and mine owners in the port town to the south. If it came to it, Bataar had planned to dam the Scythe to flood the city. It would have guaranteed a surrender, at great cost. With Lofri's alliance, taking Kalafar would be a lightning ride from the steppe, across the desert woodlands, straight into the city.

Shaza sent one of the sparrowhawks soaring into the forest. The hunting party followed the bird's screeches and found it, talons clamped around the neck of a brown rabbit. "I hope you won't mind having a son named Shaza," she told him over her shoulder.

"How about Shazar?" Bataar asked as she knelt.

Under her blade, its thrashing legs stilled. Its soul was a tiny wisp, like hot breath in the winter. She shrugged. "I'll take it."

Erdene squawked sharply. The sound rang in Bataar's ear. He clicked his tongue and she spread her wings, soaring off.

"There!" Nassar shouted, flinging his peregrine up.

The falcon was faster than the eagle, quickly catching up to Erdene. Bataar's bird was trained to fly with other eagles to take down larger quarries. She could stay focused, letting smaller birds flush out her prey. But keeping his eyes on Lofri, Bataar whistled at Erdene, and she whipped around, talons extended, and slammed into the peregrine.

Nassar seethed. "What in the hells, horse fucker?"

"Watch yourself, prince," Bataar said in a low voice.

The two birds wheeled in the sky until Erdene grounded them. The peregrine cooed, ruffling its feathers and flapping feebly. Erdene's amber eyes watched Bataar. She cocked her head. Bataar clicked his tongue, and his eagle dropped the body.

Nassar's eyes widened. "My bird! My Goddess-damned falcon!"

The minister's smile faltered. "Hey now, it's just an animal. Don't say anything you'll make me regret, boy."

Bataar recalled Erdene. "If I have my sights set on something, you'd be wise not to try to take it from me, prince. We'd work better together."

Nassar snatched up his bird and handed it off to the falconer, grimacing and wiping his fingers clean on his linen trousers. There was movement in the peregrine's broken wing. It was in shock, not dead. Erdene wouldn't kill without a command.

"That was unsportsmanlike, rhah," Nassar snapped. "As a show of good faith, let me borrow your bird."

Bataar stared, waiting for Nassar to blink first. "Alright. I see you don't want to lose your pin. Is it from the zultam's collection?"

"No. It's from my mother."

At Bataar's signal, Erdene moved off his shoulder, hopping with outstretched wings onto Nassar's arm.

"What commands does this bird use?" he asked.

Bataar gave Nassar a hard smile. "I said I'd trade birds, prince. If you wanted a lesson in falconry, you should have asked the bird-keeper."

"Heh. Watch yourself. Make your jokes, but remember that my family's connections will win you Kalafar. Have you already forgotten? Lofri's men in the city watch will open the gates for your warriors and take care of the palace guards. Without me, you'll be stuck knocking at the Swan Gate."

"*Your family.*" Bataar stretched the words out on his tongue. "I wonder, will any of your sisters be loyal to us?"

Nassar's lip twitched. "When I'm the zultam, his Harpy Knights will swear their allegiance to me."

"So… no?"

"Not… presently."

"Your conservator has men. Does he have pegasuses?"

Nassar pursed his mouth. "One. It was a gift from my grandfather. But no riders, unless you count Kasira, and that's just barely. Since you have women like that one"—he gestured toward Shaza—"you probably want knights like my father's."

He gave the prince a sidelong look. "It's true then? Only women can ride the winged horses?" Bataar was already running through war plans.

"No man would dare. It's taboo, and people are pissing superstitious. They've got it in their minds that pegasuses don't take male riders because of what was put down in the Godsbreath, and those terror birds sense any hesitation. They're mounts for rich women and occasionally the eunuchs that tend the stables."

"How many eunuchs are there in your father's court?"

"More than there are pegasuses," the prince gritted out. "Find a record-keeper if you want lessons."

Their hunt concluded several hours later, with Bataar killing a number of grouse with one of Lofri's fiery sparrowhawks. The hunting hounds barked and bit at each other's heels on the way back.

"This wasn't fair," Nassar complained. "Your damnable bird only knows how to screech in my ear."

"Erdene doesn't take commands from any man but me. You can keep your mother's hatpin, if your word isn't good for it."

"I'm good for it." A nerve in Nassar's jaw twitched as he ripped the cluster of Noorish sapphires off his turban.

At a rocky stream, the party dismounted to lead the horses over and walked the rest of the way on foot. The minister's stoic son lent his old man an arm when he grew short of breath.

"You're a good man, rhah. I'd like to see our families united in blood," Lofri repeated. "Nassar's grandparents control the Merchants Guild in Marafal. His sister Aalya is heir to feather-iron and diamond mines in the Teeth. I'm sure my cousin would consent to an arrangement."

The prince swatted a bug as he glowered at Bataar. So, the controllers of the Merchants Guild had passed over Nassar to name his younger sister successor. Bataar made a mental note to investigate Dumakran inheritance law.

Bataar nodded. "A princess would be a good match for one of my men."

"Or for yourself. You took a second wife in Choyanren. It's the Dumakran way for the zultam to take two wives, but you follow the rules of the red steppe. A man there can have as many wives as he wants, eh?"

Bataar grinned, all teeth. "*I* can have as many wives as *I* want."

Lofri laughed. "Oh ho, His Eminence follows different rules!"

"As many as my sister wants," Shaza said in Utasoo. Beside her, Tarken snorted.

"If I agree to a match," Bataar said, "is our alliance stronger for it?"

The old man grinned. "I'll have one of my clerks write up a pact. Sign it, and you're my blood."

Nassar looked ruffled but said nothing.

"Two wives isn't enough for you?" Tarken's tone was playful, but the punch that caught Bataar in the arm was a little too hard to be teasing. "Leave some women for the rest of us."

"What woman wants you?" Shaza deadpanned.

"I can think of one." He narrowed his eyes. "Or two."

She shoved him. "Watch your tongue if you want to stay attached to it, louse."

They were almost to the courtyard when the hair on the back of Bataar's neck prickled. Erdene, who had been circling around in the sky, flew down and perched close to the crook of his neck. A twinge pulled at his gryphon's mark, tightening in his chest, before a thunderous pealing filled the courtyard. A quick glance at Shaza's and Tarken's cold expressions told him they were registering the same thing.

"Inside!" Bataar shouted, ushering the old man over the threshold. Erdene swooped through the doorway and landed on a velvet divan, her feathers fluffing and talons digging into the cushions. Nassar's monkey upturned a silver tray running from her.

"What is it? What's that up there?" the minister's son Jawaad demanded, bracing his arms on either side of the entryway.

Bataar shoved him. "Come on."

"The hells?" the bulky man grumbled as Tarken wrestled him inside.

There was a blur of motion and shouts as grooms came running for the palfreys. The Dumakran horses thrashed and reared, pulling their bridles free of grasping hands. Hooves kicked up dust clouds, and frightened noises filled the courtyard with the sound of panic.

"Leave the horses," Bataar shouted at the stableboys. "Shaza don't—" But she was already rushing out, grabbing two of the servants by the wrists and pulling them toward the door.

"Shaza!" Tarken's voice strained.

Bataar locked his eyes with hers, noticing the sweat already sheening Shaza's forehead. A chill pierced his skin when the first shadow dropped from the sky. Its body slammed so hard into one of the horses that bones broke and torn-open veins sprayed showers of red. Bataar had never seen something die as quickly as that horse's soul spurted out of its body.

"Divine Spirit," he swore. Two more gryphons dove into the same horse. A needle of pain stabbed through the scar on Bataar's face, down the length of his neck and across his chest. The sharpness stopped at his heart and twisted. The other loose horses ran, tearing off back toward the cover of the hunting woods.

"Merciful Goddess of peace! What beast of chaos—are those gryphons?" Lofri said, his voice squeaky as he stumbled backward, cowering between servants.

Nassar's mouth fell open. "In *Zeffa*?"

Back inside, Shaza dropped the arms of the shaking stable-hands. The third boy tripped over the threshold and scrambled on all fours into the center of the room.

It wouldn't have mattered if the last one wasn't inside yet. "Shut the door," Bataar ordered, and the hand's-width view of the estate's outer courtyard and the chaos unfolding there vanished.

"Draw the drapes," Tarken yelled at his cousin. Oktai complied, unknotting the tiebacks. One of the servants tottered forward, rushing to help him. As the curtains fell, the shafts of light spilling across the floor were swallowed up by darkness.

In the shadowy parlor, the gryphons' screeches made the servant girls whimper and sink closer together. As Bataar's eyes adjusted, he could make out Tarken's steely expression and the outline of his hand on Shaza's arm. She'd drawn her hunting knife. Bataar unsheathed his own. The tapered blade had killed one gryphon, but that had been mostly luck.

Bataar scanned the room for anything else that could be used as a weapon if the gryphons swarmed in through the windows. There were curtain rods, the legs of the ottomans and couches, and whatever jagged pieces of glass would litter the ground if a window broke. It wouldn't be enough. They needed a ballista. They needed a cannon.

Siege. This was a siege, and Bataar was inside the walls this time. It wasn't the face of Preeminence he saw now, burning behind his eyelids. It was a woman with auburn hair and hazel eyes. The memory of Qaira's voice curled in the shell of his ear. She would tell their children that she'd felt Bataar's soul join with Preeminence, and really mean it.

He imagined her soft touch and breathed in the memory of her edelweiss perfume.

In his most dangerous moments, Bataar's life flashed in front of his eyes in images of Qaira—the first time he'd seen her flush-faced and sweating as she came undone beneath him—her expression twisted in rage, surrounded by blood on the childbed—the beautiful, pitying expression she wore when she reassured Tarken that she'd felt his little brother reunite with Preeminence. After Mukhalii's raids, when mud had streaked her hair as tears trailed her cheeks. She stood in front of him wearing her wedding clothes and a smile that said she knew he was a puddle in her hand. She'd been his, and somehow it hadn't been enough. He must have been cursed. He'd built a home in paradise and still hungered for more.

Bataar blinked, and Qaira's face blew away. The unmistakable beat of gryphons' wings stirred him back to the present. The screeches of the swarm grew smaller, more distant. Someone pulled back the drapes, and one of Lofri's guards took tentative steps toward the window.

"It's clear," the man said, voice cracking like a boy's.

Bataar stepped up to the window casing, looked around the outer courtyard. Thick intestines like strings of sausages were strewn across the dirt, and blood spray painted the cobbled drive. A horse's severed leg lay close to the door, and huge feathers littered the ground.

"Go collect the horses," the minister hissed, gesturing at the wide-eyed grooms. "Or what's left of them. Nuna be damned."

They bobbed their heads, but the tallest one's fingers shook on the door. The smallest boy stumbled back over the threshold, the toe of his boot catching and sending him sprawling again. He vomited, wiped his lips, then hurried after the others.

Ramzi Zultama must truly have been failing Dumakra, his golden age turning to tarnish and rust, for the gryphons to descend like carrion birds.

Nassar barked a laugh. "That was quite good, rhah." His mouth curled like a snake.

Bataar grimaced. "What are you talking about?"

"I don't know what dark alliance you've made with the incarnation of chaos, or if you've just been damned with abominably shit luck, but this works in our favor. I can already see the terror in my father's eyes as the rumors spread that the gryphons will follow their king to Kalafar."

6

Their weapons were first blooded on Vizier Sartarid's men in 360 CE, when the Princesses Safiya and Nohra led the troops that thrashed the Aglean free company in the mountains.[1]

— *A Dark Era*

The men gathering at the northern front whispered and looked up, gazes boring into clouded skies. Over the clang of plate and mail, the same worry echoed on each tongue. *The gryphons are coming.*

From the hills near Mineva, the battleground extended in all directions. The Dumakran war camp was full of banners bearing the royal insignia. The House Zultama, their motto: *Dumakra is our Heart.* In the sea of purple, the tent belonging to the grand vizier stood tall, blue silk patterned with the Naji family's entwined seahorses and castle turret: *We Cut like the Scythe.*

In the far distance, smoke unfurled from the Utasoo cook-fires. The line of white tents looked like the snow-capped peaks of a far-off mountain range. The summer air was wrong, too sweet and damp for a battlefield.

"Let's give the barbarians a reason to fear the skies," Safiya said, coming up behind Nohra and wrapping an arm around her neck.

Saf's voice and smile were all ease, but her eyes sparked with urgency. She shone like her namesake Saffa, one of the Goddess's Harpy daughters who'd been maimed during the godswar. The cool tones in her dark brown skin glowed against her gold armor. Nohra studied their sigil on her breastplate. The pegasus was no gryphon, no true agent of chaos, no creature of smoke and shadow. But they could be monstrous.

Push out your fear.

Nohra clenched her fingers tighter around the hilt of *Bleeding Edge*. The swirls on Safiya's sword shifted and whirled in the gray light beaming down. As Safiya tightened the fastenings on her vambrace, something shone on her wrist, bright silk, like a scrap torn from an imperial concubine's finest robe. In fact, Nohra was sure it was exactly that.

"Zira's?"

Saf nodded. They passed a tent patterned with poppies belonging to Ervan Lofri, Minister of Commerce in Zeffa.

"I've been meaning to ask—pity we don't have the time to gossip like little girls—is there anyone you'll celebrate our victory with?" Safiya asked. She succeeded in looking perfectly indifferent, nothing like when they were little, when Saf would go nosing through Nohra's private scribblings, or hold her down and tickle her mercilessly, wanting to see the contents of Nohra's heart laid bare.

"No," she replied quickly.

Safiya shrugged. "Well, there's Lord Barrister's son. Perhaps you'll be very content with him."

Aglea was a world away, heathenish, beyond Paga's reach. Nohra imagined a stone fortress, furs to keep away the chill of an icy winter. She thought of the songs her mother used to sing of courtly love. If Nohra disappointed her betrothed, he would have countless Aglean women to warm his bed, while she'd be left with nothing but snow.

"What about the southern lord?" Nohra asked, reminding Saf of her own match. "Have you forgotten you're supposed to go to Moshitu?"

"I'm not content to be a political bargaining chip like one of our brothers, to win Father favor with some lesser king. Neither should you."

"I'm not *content*."

"Resigned?"

"Fuck off." Her voice *sounded* resigned, even to her own ears.

They cut through two other tents in the encampment. The white ibex on the Jabour family's black flag stared blankly at them. *Unstumbling Faith*. Another coat of arms depicted Paga holding a diamond, representing the Attar mines. *In Sight of the Goddess*. Perhaps in sight, but the Goddess was deaf when Merv Attar spewed her vitriol.

"Don't be nervous," Safiya said, tightening the straps on her other vambrace. "If we die—"

Nohra smiled grimly. "We die for Dumakra." May the Goddess judge their worth. She pulled up her chain coif and put on her helmet. Part of her wished she had a favor to carry with her.

She reached up, brushing her hand against Mercy's ears. Her eyes landed on the bridle. It was one Fahaad had hand-tooled, not the black one she'd bought at the livestock bazaar. There was a name stamped into the brown leather: *Darya Daheer*. She pressed her fingertips against the indented letters, the corner of her mouth twitching up into half a smile.

"What is it?" Safiya said.

"Nothing."

The last time she'd been on a battlefield this far north, Darya had accompanied them. They'd been girls, pretending to know what war was. All those years ago, when they treated with a representative from the traitor Sartarid family, the situation had demanded the pomp of a full retinue: knights, talmaids, soldiers, guards. This time, the twins, Hana and Syreen, had accompanied them with their own future talmaids. Their younger sisters were eager to impress Saf and Nohra, casting lingering looks at *Bleeding Edge* and *Queen of Beasts*. Nohra remembered the bittersweetness of that ambition.

Darya and Laila, Safiya's talmaid, would be more helpful at the palace than here, buckling armor and washing the blood out of their ladies' hair. Contrary to what Fahaad might think, Nohra could dress herself and tack her own pegasus.

When Nohra, Saf, and the twins arrived at the Hill the night before, they'd taken dinner with the men. Nohra had picked at a stuffed grape leaf, nibbling at the seasoned rice and meat inside it while Safiya regaled the general and his lieutenants with her misadventures in love and battle. The tent had been full of loud laughter, but Nohra had stayed quiet. Before breakfast, she'd visited the sanctium tent to pray for a swift victory. Now there was nothing else to do, no time to fuss with her hair or relieve her empty bladder again.

"It's time," Safiya said.

As Nohra swung into the saddle, she remembered: it wasn't just the pegasuses that the Utasoo feared. It was the Harpies. Her pulse tapped frantically in the side of her neck, fear and excitement bleeding into each other. She wanted to savor the sweetness of adrenaline in her mouth. Already, a divine embrace engulfed her. Paga cloaked Nohra in Her furious righteousness. Nohra would not fail her father. She would not disappoint Paga. Just as the zultam needed a protector, so did their nation. She could be that symbol.

"Hey there, sweet beast." Mercy was the color of midnight, a bluish black so dark his feathers blurred into his fur. He answered by nuzzling her side, teething at the chainmail with his mouth that could snap bones.

Mercy flapped his lips as Nohra settled the saddle pad between his wings and adjusted fastenings. She stroked his neck, feeling the feathers intermixed with hair. He snuffled in the grass, and something hidden in the dirt squeaked. His head tipped up, the tail of a mouse vanishing into his mouth. While he chewed, Nohra put the blinders over his head and pulled the cord, securing the hood.

With his field of vision narrowed, Mercy's ruffled feathers settled. Nohra climbed into the stirrups. In the saddle, she fastened herself in, pulling the bindings flush around her hips and tightening the buckles.

Mercy lifted into the sky in a flurry of black feathers. His massive wings sent up a cold wind that buffeted surrounding tents. Canvas flapped and lines snapped. A page cursed, and a commander shouted, but their words were lost as Mercy climbed above the war camp. At every heavy wingbeat, Nohra's stomach turned until she acclimated to the change in pressure and the unending swooping feeling. Mercy's muscles coiled as his wings flapped, only relaxing when he caught an updrift and could soar.

Underneath Mercy, Safiya's pegasus Prudence glided on a few pumps of his wings and the summer wind. "Ground's clear," Saf shouted up.

Nohra squinted. No ballistae, but they'd still have to watch out for archers. The Utasoo front lines were far enough away that she couldn't be certain, either. The barbarian king had taken

Choyanren, and dignitaries from the Federated Kingdoms had boasted about their gunpowder cannons and fire weapons when they visited the Dumakran court years ago. Now Bataar Rhah would have those, too. But early reports of enemy numbers at the Hill suggested Nohra and Safiya would win a swift victory.

Nohra tangled her right hand in the reins and clenched the fingers of her left around the hilt of *Bleeding Edge*. Her mail rattled, its metal warming the longer it touched her skin.

"Remember the plan?" Saf called.

Nohra looped back and pulled up on the reins. Mercy complied, dropping down and keeping pace with Safiya's pegasus. Prude's yellow eyes glinted molten.

"Circle behind the line. Dive in—"

"—dive out."

Nohra nodded. "Syreen and Hana—"

"Will be fine behind the vanguard," Saf shouted. "Let them prove themselves, like we did."

Men the size of fleas moved on the rocky field below. A sea of purple silk war banners flowed into horse-hair ones from the steppe, red emblazoned with black gryphons. Nohra's gaze flitted over the Utasoo defensive line, an uninterrupted row of round metal shields deflecting volleys of arrows from the Dumakran mounted archers. A few struck, and bodies in leather and steel slumped with deathly finality. When the first wave of Dumakran troops were within range, the Utasoo bowmen returned fire, and shouts exploded into the sky.

Nohra clenched her teeth, spurring Mercy's sides. As he swept low, the sound of the war drums grew to a thunder still slower than her racing heart. The small breakfast she'd managed to swallow in the tent turned over in her stomach. Bile burned in the back of her throat as the cream and bread slunk up. She swallowed and blinked, and the nausea passed.

Tightening her grip against the force of the fast descent, she kept a firm hold on *Bleeding Edge*. This much feather-steel was still heavy, its curving blade unbalanced and difficult to maneuver, but it wouldn't matter. Safiya came hard at the backs of the Utasoo soldiers. Mercy swooped lower. Nohra repositioned her grip as Saf swung her sword at the neck of one of the mounted archers. Gasps and grunts escaped red-smeared lips and steel rang hollowly. Nohra was almost close enough to be splashed with blood when Safiya pulled in her heels and pushed Prude up.

Nohra's fear was short-lived; a thrill spread through her body, settling somewhere in her stomach.

Keeping the reach of *Bleeding Edge* away from Mercy's wing and flank, she braced for the strain as her blade met flesh. The muscles in her arm burned with exertion as the sickle-staff scraped bone. She nudged Mercy, and they sped forward. The momentum helped her follow through on her swing, slicing through tendons, spine. As the man's garbled scream quickly died, surrounding riders turned. His head had been flung off his neck, bouncing and rolling as it hit the grassy slope.

Arrows whizzed past, close to Nohra's face, and the fear returned. She pulled up on the reins. Mercy was low, his back legs stretching to the ground; he reared, kicking up and tucking his inky wings in close. An arrow met Nohra's armor near her collarbone with a dull ring. The spot on her chest where the plate was dented throbbed, and her pulse spiked. She pulled Mercy higher, putting distance between herself and the soldiers.

Chaos erupted in the ranks of enemy troops. Their commanders shouted orders in an unfamiliar dialect, and the formation of archers split. Every beat of Mercy's wings thrashed the air and threw the soldiers below back in their saddles. A sound like thunder made Nohra's ears ring as something boomed out of a cannon. She closed her eyes as a cloud of ash erupted out of the iron barrel.

Safiya dove, her pegasus's wings thrown back like a hawk's. Prudence landed neatly, and Saf jabbed her sword into the soldier closest to her. The man groaned, coughed, spat a glob of blood. Snaring his stomach, she pulled him from his own horse onto her pegasus. Prude's eyes rolled as he reared. The Utasoo soldier slid off the blade, hit the ground, and was swallowed under trampling hooves. As Safiya's pegasus kicked off to regain height, Nohra's breath caught. An arrow clipped the edge of his wing, but Prudence stayed in the air, gaining altitude, neck bending and teeth gnashing for flesh.

Nohra let herself take another breath. Soldiers scrambled back as flaming arrows rained down from the Dumakran bowmen. Most hit their mark, and blazes spread through the lines of fighters. Fire licked through the hot summer brush, and shouts filled the air as men swatted at the flames.

Nohra threw Mercy into a dive. The force of motion pushed her eyes wide open. Gritting her teeth, she dropped her visor down to block out the wind. Before Mercy's hooves could graze the ground, he spread and flapped his wings, sending up a wave of dust and embers.

Sudden drops of rain made Nohra startle. Water pattered against her armor, pooling under plate and cooling her fevered skin.

As Mercy flew up, Nohra swung at a disoriented bowman, slicing through one of his arms. Muscles gave under her blade like flaky meat that had simmered too long in a stew. Blood sprayed up *Bleeding Edge* and splattered Mercy's flank, the rain diluting it as it slid off the steel in watery pink droplets. Back in the sky with Saf, Nohra dropped the reins and pulled back her helmet to wipe the spatter from her mouth. The articulated joints of her gauntlet scratched at her dry lips. Rain hung in the air, beading over their steel and soaking the pegasuses.

There was no time for remorse, no extra seconds for hesitation or regret. This killing was impersonal.

"If there's lightning, we'll have to fall back and keep to the ground," Nohra shouted.

"But there isn't," Safiya yelled back. "We're not grounded yet."

Below, a cluster of shields had been raised to stop the bowmen's volleys. Mounted archers fired up at the pegasus riders. The arrows shot high, shook in the air, and fell back down. Soldiers in the dense cluster of cavalrymen grunted.

The corner of Saf's full lips quirked with an unspoken challenge. *Think you can beat me?*

Both dropped back into the fray. It was easier like this, pretending it was all a game. Nohra didn't have to wonder if the people she was killing had children to go home to or carried favors from their loved ones under their armor. She didn't have to think that they all had names, not when they were just numbers in a bet with her sister. Paga had willed them to die at Nohra's blade.

Prudence's wing slammed a woman from her horse. Before she fell, she hit the juncture of his wing with the butt of her sword. The gelding screeched. Nohra's blood grew cold at Safiya's strangled scream. An arrow must have clipped a weak spot in her armor.

Wordlessly, Saf passed her sword to her left hand. Now she *was* grounded.

"That one, Nohra!" Safiya shouted over the sounds of men and horses dying. Nohra followed her gaze.

A throng of mounted archers and foot soldiers kept close to one man, forming a protective wall around him. At his signals, the soldiers flowed, clustering in new formations. The way the man carried himself reminded Nohra of her father or his viziers. His black cloak swished nobly around his shoulders, and his beard was in the Utasoo style, long and tapering.

Nohra dropped Mercy to the ground and charged the group. He slammed into one of the short steppe horses. Nohra hit a woman's shoulder with a blunt corner of *Bleeding Edge*, and with a groan, the other girl crumpled. Nohra spun the sickle-staff into a second soldier, slicing his leather-and-plate armor. Safiya was behind her now. Her sword met a man's saber with a gritting clash. An arrow scratched Nohra's breastplate, and another struck the side of her helmet. The hit jolted her to the core, cutting through her tired numbness. Her ears rang as she tried to blink away the disorientation.

"Nohra!"

As her senses began to return to her, there was a noise like a peal of thunder as the Dumakran front line swarmed the Utasoo's ranks. Barking dogs raced out of the cluster of soldiers, snarling and lunging at the Dumakran foot soldiers. The commander, who must have been Bataar Rhah, was just out of arm's reach. His eyes met Nohra, and his cold smile chilled her.

He was pretty, almost girlish in the softness of his features, with thick eyelashes and chestnut-colored hair. A thin scar stretched across the bridge of his nose, but how had the vizier's informant noticed something so small? Nohra could only make out the silver sliver now that she was close enough to see his pupils. His eyes were brown, not yellow.

Stupid, to notice that now.

"Ungh—" A sharp pain spread across Nohra's left thigh. She glanced down at the shaft and fletching emerging from her leg. The blood running down her calf was hot and nearly

indistinguishable from the sweat and rain. *No, no. Not now, not now.*

She snapped the shaft in half and swung her sickle-staff up at a soldier. He caught the blade with his saber. She scraped *Bleeding Edge* down the length of his sword until the sickle blade curved around her opponent's crossguard. It gouged into his knuckles, he screamed, and his sword fell.

Despite the pain searing Nohra's body, everything was coming too easily. The rhah's numbers were too few, far less even than the estimates. The fire was quenched, though smoke still danced through the grass. The storm was already slowing, and there weren't any gryphons.

Like most wartime rumors, these must have been lies. The warlord couldn't command Nuna's beasts.

"Saf!" Nohra shouted.

Prudence limped, favoring the wing that hadn't been shot, but Safiya pulled ahead, cutting down the rider closest to the commander. Her sword smashed into the rhah's saber. Nohra shook herself from her stupor, racing to protect her sister from the surrounding soldiers while Safiya dueled. Nohra deflected a man's blade on the long handle of *Bleeding Edge* and spun to redirect it. A crossbow bolt ripped into the man's breast. Nohra turned, searching for her sister. Her braid, loose now from her helmet and the confines of her mail coif, smacked her chin.

Safiya and the commander were both unhorsed. Prude reared behind Saf, his uninjured wing spread around her. Huge dogs snarled, their hackles up. Dumakran soldiers closed in to push back the enemy. The Utasoo commander lunged at Safiya. His blade shed off her sword. She pivoted and struck his back with her pommel. Nohra had been on the receiving end of Safiya's melee—her sister jabbed hard and fast enough to splinter bone. The rhah fell to his knees. He looked up, and his expression changed. His features were uncertain, eyes wide, lips parting.

Nohra fought with the fastenings on her saddle, and free of them, jumped off Mercy. Her boots dug into the muddy ground, and fresh pain burst through her leg. The rest of the battle faded to distant noise.

"I've heard you don't take prisoners," Safiya said, though the king of the red steppe likely didn't understand all her words. "So neither will I."

The rhah tried to scramble to his feet. His fur stole and cape were sopping wet, and mud was slicked up his sides. Nohra swept the handle of *Bleeding Edge* into the side of his knee, and he wobbled back down to the wet ground, splashing into dirt. Safiya snatched up his saber and kicked his chest.

"So this is the might of the Harpies," he gasped. "Impressive after all." He spoke Dumakran fluently, with a strong accent.

Something bothered Nohra. He had brown hair—that wasn't so unusual for an Utasoo man, as far as she knew, but the men at court had mentioned black hair and a scar cutting across his face. A gouged-out eye. One had said the rhah had been attacked by a gryphon at sixteen and fought it off with a hunting knife.

Was this really that man?

Rumors were rumors, but the truth was in front of her, kneeling in the mud.

The soldiers nearest to them halted, some laying down their weapons. Safiya rubbed her sharp blade at the man's neck. She made to swing—

"Stop!" Nohra shouted. "He might just be a commanding officer. He's worth more alive than dead."

Safiya's sword met the man's neck, but she stopped abruptly, sending him reeling back and reaching to catch the blade. His palms and fingers were bloody, pupils blown wide as he locked gazes with them. Between his hands, blood ran down the twisting patterns in the wootz steel, dripping onto blackened grass.

"Your... your rhah," Safiya said, pulling her blade free and prodding his chest with the tip of her sword. "Where is he? Take us to him."

The man's heaving breaths and mumbling voice made him difficult to understand. Nohra read his lips, but what he was saying was impossible. She frowned, lead sinking in the pit of her stomach.

Safiya's face was furious as she met Nohra's gaze. "What? What in Nuna's hell did he just say?"

"Kalafar," the man said. "Bataar is making for your capital."

Nohra's leg throbbed as she stumbled forward. Warm, wet blood squelched in her boot. The rest was forming a weak crust on her thigh around the shaft of the arrow.

Kalafar. Her home, her heart, the last city her mother ever saw. Nohra had grown up watching performers outside its sunken bazaars. She used to sneak away from her chaperones to chase stray dogs and buy candy from street vendors. The capital smelled like tea leaves and bitter coffee, warm bread, sizzling meat. When she thought of Kalafar, she envisioned spires on sanctiums and hammered gold roofs. She saw the faces of its people. Honest, good people.

Kalafar was protected by the wall, by the Wingates. Nohra would send a bird. She'd warn their father to fortify the walls. There was time.

But their army was already spread too thin.

"—surrender, we surrender."

At their commander's order, the enemy soldiers lowered their weapons to the wet earth. White Utasoo peace flags were raised.

Nohra scanned the slope coated in corpses and twitching bodies. Hana, one of the twins, was using red fabric from a banner to bind a soldier's broken leg. An open mouth screamed in agony, but every noise had been reduced to a dull ringing. A pegasus rooted through the bodies, stirring guts with its nose.

Kalafar was—

"Nor? Nohra!" She turned, meeting Safiya's darting eyes. Saf was wincing, fingers pressed around the shaft of the arrow embedded in the juncture of her arm. Her gaze flickered between Nohra's leg and face. "You need a doctor."

Nohra looked down at the puddling blood. "I'm fine. I just need a needle and—" Her own voice sounded faraway.

"No you're not. Sit down. I'll get someone."

All the sound crashed over her at once, flooding back. "We have to *go. Now*."

Behind them, infantrymen at Saf's command surrounded the Utasoo commander and his soldiers, halberds raised. The man who wasn't Bataar knelt in the ash and dirt, watching Nohra.

"You," Safiya said, gesturing with her limp arm to Hana. She was the taller of the twins, willowy and coltish. Her unfocused eyes jumped left to right with a faraway, haunted look. She'd fought before, but never drawn blood to kill, until today. "Tell General Fakier we're turning for Kalafar and drafting terms of surrender on the way. By order of the eldest imperial princess."

Syreen bounded forward, wide-eyed and unblinking and rushing her words. "And me?"

"Syreen, get your pegasus's head out of that soldier. It's Goddess-damned disrespectful to the dead."

Nohra stared dizzily at the corpses on the field. The periphery of her vision darkened as her breaths grew shallow. The carnage stretched up over the hills. The Dumakran tents were so far away she couldn't see them. Nearby, their injured pegasuses scratched at the dirt, huffing. Mercy limped, and Prudence's shot wing was tucked tight against his side. Red fletching stood out brightly against his dark feathers.

"The pegasuses," Nohra muttered breathlessly. "We need to find someone to help them."

She took a step forward, and her leg buckled. Fresh blood leaked from the wound in her thigh, gushing out so quickly the world spun.

"You try to walk back to our lines and you'll die." Saf swayed as she shuffled closer, giving Nohra her good shoulder to brace herself on. "We're closer to the Utasoo war encampment. They have Choyanreni doctors, some of the best in the world."

"And they'll treat us with steel at their jugulars?"

"What other option will we give them?"

The round tents were larger up close, the white canvas glowing as spears of light stabbed through gray clouds. Embers still smoldered in the outdoor cookfires. Dumakran forces milled about the enemy encampment, where prisoners of war cowered in lines and camp followers clustered together, shaking with fear. Bloody smears in the dirt led to the infirmary tent.

Safiya nodded to one of her men, who prodded the captive commander in the leg with the point of his halberd. His wrists were bound, and the blood from the cut on his neck was drying. Soon it would be another thin, silver scar. He tripped forward, fell, and awkwardly picked himself up, grumbling.

Every step was excruciating pain, but Nohra wouldn't let her face show it. The pungent aroma of medicinal herbs struck her as their soldiers pushed into a pavilion, weapons raised.

"Tarken!" a woman with red hair cried out, taking a sudden step forward and saying more words in a rush. Nohra almost caught a few shared words, tilted by an accent that turned them unfamiliar. Safiya tensed. "Your commander surrendered."

The Utasoo soldiers that had been guarding the doctors were at the mercy of the Dumakrans. Still, unarmed and with weapons trained on them, their necks strained and fingers flexed, drawing into fists. They were willing to fight and die for their commander and this woman. The man, Tarken, gestured for them to stand down.

"My sister needs a doctor." Saf repeated herself in Choyanreni.

The physicians in the room looked around with wide-eyed uncertainty, choking on unspoken protests. Bodies shifted in the dozens of cots on the floor. Nohra glimpsed sour bandages and bright poultices spread over bloodied stumps. Her stomach turned at the smell of necrotizing flesh.

The woman who'd cried out met Safiya's eyes and gave a small, firm nod. "I'll treat her."

"I don't need your help," Nohra snapped, as the woman came closer. Nohra was deft with a needle. She could pull out the arrowhead and stitch her leg shut with catgut, later. "My sister and the pegasuses—"

"Let me at least stabilize the shaft of the arrow." The woman had hazel eyes, a brackish green-brown. They were too wide and far set, like a doe. She grabbed a length of muslin bandage and knelt in front of Nohra. "This will hurt," she said, her eye contact unwavering.

A hot flush burned across Nohra's chest. Still riding on the adrenaline of the battle, she flinched at the oddly tender touch. Goosebumps prickled on her throbbing skin. Who was this woman? She didn't look much older than Safiya. She was pretty and well dressed, but she also didn't seem to mind the dirt and blood.

Embarrassment and fascination were quickly forgotten as slender fingers wrapped around the shaft of the arrow. The arrowhead shifted in Nohra's muscle tissue, making searing pain flare down to her toes.

"Paga's ass," she swore.

The wooden shaft snapped. "The head caught on the silk. That's good," the woman murmured. A few of the Choyanreni doctors muttered approvingly, medical curiosity winning out over fear.

Nohra groaned. "*Good?*"

The silk that had burrowed into the wound in her thigh came loose at a sharp tug.

"Yarrow," the woman said, packing the dried herb inside the arrow hole. Each press made Nohra gasp, legs almost giving. Without further preamble, the woman wound a bandage tight enough for numbness to spread. "Wait, for the pain—" She held out a milky red tincture in a glass dropper, but Nohra was already pushing through the soldiers, out of the tent. She needed to find General Fakier.

"*Nohra*," Safiya called warningly. Nohra ignored her, too.

Outside, Utasoo prisoners were being led up the hill. Dumakran soldiers formed ranks as word about Kalafar spread among the men. They'd send birds, warn them to reinforce the Wingates—

Fingers curled around her elbow.

"You've already done your job," Nohra said, spinning around and swatting away the woman's hand. "Go help the other injured soldiers."

Those wide-set eyes blinked at Nohra, expression unreadable. Nohra frowned, looking the woman over. She was dressed in fine clothes. Her nails were neat and clean, and her hair had been meticulously braided. The rest of her skin looked soft... her hands had been.

"You're one of the Harpy Knights?" Her words were

tremulous, like a supplicant in a sanctium.

"And you? You're that commander's wife?" Nohra used all her strength to soften her tone. "You have my word, I won't let anyone touch you."

"Your word?" The woman's voice lowered.

Moans echoed around the encampment, soft like embers crackling in a tired fire. Nohra reached around her neck, taking hold of the cleric's chain and pulling it free. She held it out for the woman, dropping the engraved pendant into her hand. It pooled between her outstretched fingers.

"These are words from our Book. I swear by my Goddess, no harm will come to you while you're under my protection." Nohra would have knelt, if she'd felt certain she would be able to stand back up.

The woman drew herself up. "What's the price for your protection? Will you use me to bargain with Bataar, threaten me, to force his hand?" Still, her fingers curled around the cleric's pendant, stealing the body warmth that had been nursed against Nohra's own skin.

"Are you that valuable? Who are you? His sister?"

"His wife."

The memory of her tender touch soured. "An empress, and you dirty your pretty hands tying tourniquets?"

"And you're a princess wearing just as much blood."

If her father's informants were correct, Bataar had many wives and valued no single life above his own. He didn't negotiate. Nohra had his wife, but if the gryphon king took Kalafar, and the whispers of his cruelty were the truth, she would have nothing over the rhah except for rage.

"I hope for both our sakes that your life is priceless to him."

But Nohra *would* protect her. She'd already given her word and the Goddess's. Her vows were chains no sword could break.

7

A city built by ten thousand hands can be
destroyed by a word.

— Author anon

As Bataar's army rode from Zeffa, shrubland gave way to brackish half-desert prowled by lions and jackals. The thundering beat of thousands of horses pounding iron-shod hooves into the dry earth kept wild animals away, but when Bataar pulled ahead, distant howling reached his ears. At the precipice of the rocky hills surrounding the capital, he stared down at the cluster of glittering lights. Kalafar was laid out before him, a hoard of treasure in the crook of the Scythe. The city on the river was a sprawling expanse of white and turquoise, hammered domes and bone-finger spires, tiled roofs and wide bridges, colleges, libraries, bathhouses, and cisterns.

His soldiers thronged the mountain trail. Bataar clicked his tongue and pulled the reins, leading his horse down the rocky path.

Around the perimeter of the city, the Wingates stretched high into the sky, gatehouses standing like thick-muscled legs, arrow loops like beady black eyes. Lofri said he would have his men on the wall wearing red feathers on their helmets to differentiate them from the others. The city was on guard, but the zultam didn't know that the enemy was already inside.

Bataar hoped.

"Stay back," he warned Nassar, giving a signal to a subordinate. *If we're betrayed, kill the prince.* Erdene shrieked and flapped up, disappearing into the dark sky. Streaks of black clouds obscured Preeminence's open mouth, waiting for Bataar to feed Them.

"Lofri's good for his word," Nassar insisted, pulling his dappled horse back.

Bataar cautiously approached the Swan Gate. An arrow thunked into the ground near his feet. Another. Then a swarm of shadows flooded the wall walk. Bataar's knuckles tightened on the pommel of his saber, anticipating betrayal. He took a deep breath, steadying himself, readying for the worst.

Surprised shouting spilled from the wall. Swords clanged, bowstrings thrummed. Alarm bells rang as dead men slumped, draped over the parapet and speared on iron stakes. Screams filled the air as Lofri's hired swords shoved Kalafar city guards and soldiers down the steep drop. Their bodies slumped in twisted heaps at the foot of the wall.

Finally, the steel grating slowly began to rise.

"Invaders!" a Dumakran screamed. Rows of soldiers waited beyond the grating. "Hold the gate!"

As Bataar's men flooded the city, the alarm bells rang louder, a mournful, desperate peal. Bataar picked out a young soldier with a white feather on his helmet hiding in the doorway of a guard tower. "Lay down your weapon," Bataar yelled.

The boy raised his bow in quivering arms. With a blade at his throat the young archer might have pleaded for his life, but he stilled his shaking and drew back his arm. The bowstring dug deep into a cheek still plump with baby fat.

Preeminence.

In a fluid motion, Bataar pulled his short bow from his back, strung an arrow, and sent it whistling into the soldier's neck. The boy slipped to the ground and dropped his weapon, fingers turning red as he groped at the protruding shaft. Bataar nocked a second arrow, released his bowstring, and sent the young man's soul skittering out of his dead body.

He swallowed the lump in his throat, shame sour in his mouth.

Bataar's soldiers were a surge of steel rushing through the city, breaking Dumakran defensive formations. His and the prince's horses wove around the bodies of the dead and those still bleeding out on the cobbled streets. The strange, ephemeral shapes of the soldiers' souls seeped out of their earthly bodies, undulating in the air above the massacre like silk flags in the wind. Each shape broke into a million tiny leaves and evaporated into the sky.

Inside the gates, ramshackle houses for the poor flanked the wall. Rookeries and stables filled the air with the smell of nervous animals and their feces. The capital's shanty shadow-city edged up to the water, the banks filthy with rotten waste from the tanneries.

"There. Peacemaker's Bridge," Nassar said as they approached the sun-bleached stone.

The bridge connected the east city to the inner city, made up of arches large enough for shipping vessels and sailboats to pass under. Their horses plodded slowly over it. The horsemen in the vanguard peeled around and flowed past, waves breaking around a rock in the sea, picking up force and rushing on to crash against distant shores.

Nassar waved his arm in a sweeping motion, mail clinking.

"This is one of Dumakra's Marvels of Man. The famous Master of Architonics, Shassam Naji, erected the bridge during the reign of Zultam Numa."

How many architects had it taken to build this sprawling city? How many hands to construct the towers reaching greedily toward the blessed sky? How many men would it take to break Kalafar?

Bataar knew the answer to that last question from conversations in his war pavilion. What he didn't know was how long it would take to rebuild once his army was done.

Unification. An end to senseless wars and oppression. No more violence toward religious dissenters. No more trade bans with the Utasoo tribes or oppression in the south. Bataar's world would be one connected, under the leadership of a man who'd fought for it, earned it, deserved it.

Don't get lost in your head, Tarken would have told him, but Tarken wasn't here. He'd arrive with reinforcements in a day or less. Tarken would return with Qaira, and once the zultam surrendered the capital, and the surrounding cities fell in line, they could send for the children.

Right now, Bataar couldn't afford to dwell on any other outcome.

Nassar's features were partially shrouded by his helmet, but he wrinkled his nose, probably at the iron smell hanging over the rotten-egg stench of the streets.

Wolf-sized war dogs with rugged coats raced through the carnage, shaking the dead bodies, mouths foaming, aching to bury their teeth in flesh. Two dogs nipped at each other, snarling over an arm separated from its body. Up ahead came a whistle, and dozens of amber eyes snapped toward the sound. At a second, higher tone, the dogs sprinted on. Bataar motioned for his men to follow.

With a battle cry, a small Dumakran force seeped out of one of the alleyways. The enemies brandished halberds, cudgels, and short bows. An arrow flew by and glanced off Bataar's armor, swatting the flank of his horse.

"Close up!" Bataar signaled. A fight in such close quarters would end with more deaths than necessary. They could put distance between themselves and take out some of the Dumakran cavalrymen by feigning a retreat. "Fall back!" His soldiers spurred their horses away, but Nassar remained behind.

"Stop! Lay down your weapons for your new zultam," Nassar commanded. The Dumakran soldiers' steel and bows remained in hand.

"*Divine Spirit*," Bataar swore. Turning to his men, he gave the order, "Attack!"

His soldiers opened fire, raining down a volley of arrows. When his horse was almost abreast of the enemy forces, Bataar drew his saber and plunged it into a soldier. The long blade slid into a weak point between two pieces of Dumakran plate. It sank in smoothly, parting neck and shoulder, and the man screamed, his arm hanging uselessly.

"You'll die now, barbarian scum," an older fighter seethed, swinging for Bataar's neck.

The street corner became a battleground as men fell around the prince. A child cried inside a house. Somewhere, a woman screamed, over and over. An old man had been cut down, and lay half out of his open door, watching the skirmish with unblinking eyes. Bataar couldn't unsee him as he deflected soldiers' blades, the woman's desperate noise stabbing his ears. The prince swung his sword with the stiffness of someone taught to fight for show. When they finally circled and routed their attackers, a few made a clumsy retreat.

"Don't let them go," Bataar said, nodding to his men.

"Bataar—" Nassar started, sounding almost apologetic.

"Listen when I tell you to do something, would you?" Bataar snapped. "I'll defer to your expertise in a brothel. In battle, you'll follow my lead."

The prince nodded, finally rattled. Ahead, a sanctium with red spires stood out against the bleaker-colored, shorter surrounding structures. A loud whoosh blew through the cobbled streets as the sanctium went up in smoke. Its windows exploded, and shards of colored glass struck the road, smashing and ringing out like bells. The flames grew quickly, creating a column of smoke above a beacon fire.

Dark clouds were moving in. The rain might contain the blazes.

The prince's unease turned to fury. "Control your men," he snarled. "They aren't a barbarian horde anymore. You can't let them leave Kalafar a smoldering heap of ash."

"Maybe you're unfamiliar with how a city's sacked. One fourth of the zultam's wealth, including holy relics in the public sanctiums, are to be divided equally among my men, and the widows and orphans of my soldiers."

Nassar blinked. "You can't be serious. Nuna's infernal tits, it will!"

Bataar tried to muster up some diplomacy. The middle of a battle was a bad place for it. "I've given orders to not harm any priestesses, if that's what you're worried about."

"I don't give a cup of piss about the priestesses!" The prince's face went red. "There are always more girls who'll come to the faith, but it takes a damn sight longer to build a sanctium. This city has *history*, and my father's wealth belongs to me, not your sons of horses bastard soldiers. What in hells' terms did Lofri agree to?"

A scream interrupted their argument. One of Bataar's men

swung his saber at a man running toward them. Blood sprayed. Black gurgled down his chin. His soul seeped out as his legs buckled. In a halo of torchlight, Bataar saw that the attacker was a civilian wearing roughspun, not a soldier in armor. The dull blade looked like something that had been collecting dust on a wall.

"Fucking twats," Nassar swore. "Everyone's gone mad as donkey balls."

❧

The Rutiaba Palace was the suspiciously calm eye of a storm in the middle of the city. A gray-bearded man had been thrown from the guard post, his legs, arms, and neck bent at unnatural angles. His blood ran in rivulets down the cobbles. They continued forward, passing through wide-open gates. The grounds and gardens were tossed with corpses of Dumakran and Utasoo men and horses.

"Gryphons?" asked a soldier, pointing up at the churning mass above the palace. Bataar's mouth went dry, heartbeat jumping, but his scar didn't tighten.

"Pegasuses," Nassar said. "It'll be a bitch getting them back down."

Several palace guardsmen were dead, their bodies strewn about the courtyards and causeways. The rest of the palace's servants and guards stood or knelt near the hedges, trembling as soldiers trained weapons on them. In an inner courtyard, armed men stood near a group of kneeling serving girls. One woman numbly held her torn bodice shut.

"You. Where's the general?" Bataar said, dismounting and approaching one of Shaza's higher-ranking commanders.

"Outside the audience hall. The zultam's locked himself in," he huffed.

Bataar gave him a short nod, gesturing for his soldiers to move forward.

"Wait!" the man said quickly, forgetting his rank in his impatience. "What should we do with them?" He nodded toward the mass of soldiers clustered around the servants.

Most of the kneeling women were barely older than girls, their sleeping gowns painted with rain-watered blood, speckled with pieces of meat. On some, the fabric was slick, like they'd butchered a goat and bathed in the gore. A few flinched, straining their necks to avoid meeting Bataar's eyes. One met his gaze and held it. Her linen dress clung to her thick waist and ample hips.

Bataar shook his head. "What is this?"

Confiscated weapons were heaped in a pile in front of the maids. When Bataar scooped up a sheath and pulled out a dagger, turning it over in his hands, the woman with the unflinching stare staggered to her feet. Her hand twitched, reaching out. Soldiers pushed her back, tension etched in the lines of their bodies. But there was no fight in her obsidian eyes. She trembled.

Bataar glanced down. The blade was black, and diamonds glittered on the hilt. It weighed less than air. *Feather-steel.*

"These palace girls are dangerous, Your Eminence," the commander stammered. He motioned for a soldier to grab the one with the torn bodice. She strained as a fist tightened around her hair. "We shouldn't let them live."

Embarrassment burned the back of Bataar's neck. "You're afraid of them, of *this* woman? You should fall on your sword and spare yourself further humiliation."

"You don't understand." His hand tightened on the pommel of his saber. His throat worked as he swallowed over and over. "They submitted willingly, but the mess we found them in—at least three of our men slaughtered. We need to make an example of them."

"Kill," a voice croaked, hoarse and fragile. It was the girl who'd grasped out reflexively for the diamond-studded knife. "Kill me, not her."

Blood pounded in Bataar's ears. He leaned into the commander, stirring his breath. "Do it then, you weak little gryphonshit. But you'll answer to Shaza for *everything* that happens here."

Metal scraped as the commander drew his saber. His elbows shook from either exertion or fear as he raised his blade.

"No! Don't!" begged a man with short hair and dark skin. This servant thrashed against the soldiers holding his wrists. The woman with the torn bodice whimpered, then cried, sobs turning to hiccups, but the one about to be killed didn't cry. Her stunned eyes were vacant, mouth slack in shock.

Speaking languages came easily. Deciphering script was more challenging for Bataar, but there were words embossed on the expensive-looking knife. The Dumakran characters shared few similarities with Utasoo script. "Nohra. Who's Nohra?" he asked Nassar.

"One of my sisters," the prince said, examining his clean nails. He was watching the short servant girl through his fingers with an unreadable expression. "Her mother was an Aglean slut my father took a special liking to. Enough to marry her, if you'd believe it."

Bataar didn't have time for any of this. "Is Nohra one of the Harpy Knights?"

"Yes. She's got her mongrel hands on *Bleeding Edge*."

All my heart, Nohra. Bataar squinted at the constellation made by the fingernail-sized diamonds. He recognized the shape. Dumakrans said it was the leash the chaos incarnation of their goddess had tricked the Demonking, a djinn general, into wearing. A symbol of servitude on a priceless gift.

"Stop!" Bataar shouted at the man about to deal the killing blow. When the blade stalled, Bataar focused on the woman. Her trembling had stilled. She didn't even appear to draw breath. "Are you close to her? To one of the Harpies?"

"I-I k—"

"She's Nohra's talmaid!" the dark-skinned man answered for her, voice strained.

"Then tell your mistress I spared your life," Bataar said. The man slumped with relief, but the woman didn't so much as blink. Bataar faced the commander. "Keep her with the others." His gaze flitted toward the one holding her dress closed. "And don't let your men lay their hands on the palace girls. They're the zultam's pets, for rich men to marry. Tell your soldiers to keep a grip on their swords, not their cocks. Craullstreet has dozens of pleasure houses if they get desperate."

One of Lofri's boys waved Bataar's retinue forward. "This way."

Bataar fastened the leather sheath to his own belt and sunk the talmaid's knife inside. They passed by the clustered women and the soldiers, taking sharp turns on covered walkways. The cool summer air carried grayish flecks of ash and distorted screams from the fighting and looting in the city.

"The audience hall is just through here," the soldier said.

Bataar stepped out into carnage that made the contents of his stomach curdle. "Preeminent Spirit," he whispered.

"What in the hells?" Nassar swore, paling as he covered his mouth and gagged into his palm.

The soldiers' bodies had been moved, but pieces of them were still there. Chunks of flesh splattered the columns and dripped from the roof of the walkway. Bataar stepped carefully around the sticky puddles. The scene painted a picture of the terrible fervor and desperation that must have overcome the palace girls when they'd been attacked by the soldiers.

"Unlucky sods," Nassar muttered. "Of course my sisters would turn half the palace into maniacal killers."

Maybe Bataar should have let that sword fall. No. He'd given the Preeminent Spirit enough souls to feast on tonight, and he'd offer up more before sunrise. When all the dust had settled and the blood had dried, he would figure out what exactly happened in this courtyard. Shaza would want to know.

They continued on. Inside the palace, soldiers ripped down weavings, pried gold faucets out of the walls, and carried off copper washbowls.

"Do you know the history of this palace?" Nassar hissed. "The furnishings aren't just shit we bought at the bazaar last week. Those sconces, Omaar the Peacemaker—"

"Educate me later," Bataar interrupted.

Close to the grand audience chamber, a cluster of soldiers standing outside double doors turned to Bataar, bowing their heads. Shaza was among their ranks, her cheeks speckled with blood. "Stand back," she warned.

Two of her soldiers pulled at the heavy doors, groaning from the effort. "Barred from the other side," one said.

"I don't know how many spearmen he squeezed in. Twenty, thirty? More?" Shaza muttered to herself. "He's probably been holed up since the birds from the Hill came."

"From the Hill?" Cold dread stabbed Bataar. "What happened on the Hill?"

His army had struck on three fronts, spreading the Dumakran forces as thin as Bataar dared. The Hill was the northernmost battlefield they'd chosen, for their smallest force. Tarken was commanding, and Qaira had gone with him.

He shouldn't have let her go. He also knew he couldn't have stopped her. Shaza studied him, her expression steely. "A courier arrived. We won at Zeffa, but two Harpies went to the Hill. They swept Tarken's battalion. The princesses are king's guards, not brutes. They'd take prisoners for leverage."

Leverage was never his nor Shaza's first thought on a battlefield.

"It isn't like when Mukhalii took Qaira," Shaza said, then repeated, as if by making it a mantra she could convince herself, too. "And Tarken knows when to surrender."

His mother's death and Qaira's abduction during Mukhalii Rhah's raids had started Bataar's conquest of the steppe. This war couldn't end with Qaira and Tarken gone. But if they were dead, Bataar would know. He'd feel it—at least, that was what he told himself.

Bataar curled his hand on the pommel of his saber. "Break down the door."

They struggled to force the battering ram into position. The first connecting hit shook the floor and surrounding tile loose. Lacquered wood strained and trembled. As soon as the doors splintered open, the spike of a halberd pierced through an eye of one of the men holding the battering ram. Before Bataar could blink, a flurry of arrows knifed into an enemy guardsman's chest. Someone swung a curved sword at Shaza. Bataar pushed in front of her, parrying with his saber. Their blades met with an ear-splitting clang—and Shaza fired an arrow through the man's throat, blood burbling around its shaft. Terror flashed in the guard's eyes as he collapsed to the floor, spasming feebly. The palace guards pressed closer, bottlenecking their advance.

Shaza gestured forward. "Those must be his Harpy Knights."

On a dais, two figures in gilded armor stood close to a man with a short beard. One of the Harpies raised a crossbow. A bolt blew past Bataar, piercing through the leather breastplate of one of Shaza's commanders.

"Agk—" the officer grunted, light quickly fading from his eyes. He made a second sound, as soft as a sigh, and his spirit blew out of his body in a cloud. Men pushed in front of Bataar, raising shields and obscuring his view of the winged throne.

"Push left," Shaza shouted, and the troops broke through, encircling the zultam's guards. More fell to steel bolts, and three were impaled with javelins thrown by the other Harpy. Soldiers swarmed and surged around Bataar. The sensations were dizzying, nauseating, intoxicating. For one horrible moment, he thought he tasted blood in his mouth, and he looked down, expecting to see the handle of something jutting from his body. Nothing.

"Stay back," he shouted at Nassar. To his soldiers, he ordered, "Form ranks around Prince Nassar. Mind the women over there." Concubines and their handmaidens clustered near the dais. "And the crown prince," he added, noticing the young boy standing among the women.

Prince Rami. The child had lighter skin than most Dumakrans, and fairer hair. But he had the same dark eyes as the man who sat on the throne.

"Damn the kid," Nassar said.

Bataar's protests were swallowed up by clashing steel and aborted grunts. When he was close enough, Bataar grabbed the boy from the concubines and dragged him back from the fighting, pushing him into the arms of one of his men.

"Take him!"

An old woman—probably the esteemed queen mother— swiped at Bataar with a hooked knife. Her blade closely missed catching his vambrace and caught the neck of a nearby soldier. Tripping back, Bataar watched the man's fingers constrict around his own throat, face reddening as frothed spit seeped from his mouth.

Her karambit was laced, likely with venom. The vipers that Dumakrans called "Nuna's whips" were fast killers.

"Watch yourself," Bataar warned Shaza's men.

The Harpy with the crossbow had emptied her quiver. Bodies piled high enough that the soldiers flooding into the room had to climb over corpses. The zultam drew back behind a circle of guards. Bataar's soldiers cut them down.

The princess throwing the javelins collapsed back, groping at an arrow in her neck as Bataar's men broke closer to the throne. The second Harpy Knight dropped her crossbow and knelt beside the other, stabilizing the shaft with bloodied hands.

"Calidah, on your feet!" the zultam shouted at her. Her wide eyes flashed to him, mouth twisted in horror, and then her face turned back to the other girl.

The Utasoo soldiers pushed around. Bataar stumbled back as the zultam raised a heavy-looking cudgel and swung. But Ramzi was aiming for Nassar.

Bataar's blade clashed against the thick handle. "Step down now, and I'll make sure you die with dignity later. Call off your men."

Zultam Ramzi ignored him, leering at his oldest son. "I should have had you put down like a dog when you were a sick, hacking, useless child."

"I was never your son, was I?" Nassar's voice rose. "You never saw me as anything other than a threat."

"Dumakra will never be yours." His spit hit Bataar in the face. "And she will never kneel to a barbarian king."

"*Stand down*," Bataar ground out.

"You're a puppet king," Nassar shouted. "Your weakest advisors keep you like a gelded horse, hiding you like a woman from your own city." He shoved forward toward his father, saber drawn, spots of color high on his cheeks. "Damn you, I'll kill you myself."

Without the prince, Bataar's hopes of holding Dumakra could collapse. "Get back!"

Something shifted on the older man's face. The zultam stepped away, holding up one hand. He still gripped the cudgel in the other, but it was a gesture of surrender. Bataar almost relaxed—when the zultam swung. He was going to bludgeon his own son's skull open.

Bataar reeled forward, arcing his saber. The tip of his blade slid across the Dumakran king's throat, opening a second, bleeding mouth. Something spilled out, grayish white and smoky. It climbed Bataar's sword in grasping tendrils, stopping shy of touching his fingers before drawing back and joining the other souls evaporating at the domed ceiling.

A woman whimpered.

It was over.

Bataar's eye twitched and pain spiked inside his head. It wasn't supposed to end like that.

Nassar tripped away, his boots slipping in a red puddle. His breathing came fast as his gaze shifted away from the zultam, toward the Harpy Knight lying at the bottom of the dais and the one kneeling over her.

"Stay away," the crouched woman with the crossbow growled, shoving the prince's leg. She was gaunt and small, but Nassar was bloodless enough to stumble back.

"Calidah?" Ignoring her protest, he moved closer, kneeling and pulling back the visor on the unconscious woman's helmet. "Aalya. Shit."

"Escort the women from the room," Bataar told two of Shaza's subordinates. His voice was dead, devoid of any emotion. A few of the women and servants who had sheltered in the audience hall were wet-eyed and trembling. Others wore steely expressions as their fine clothes were frisked for more weapons. "Take Prince Rami to his quarters and watch the door."

He didn't trust Nassar or Lofri with the boy.

"Stop!" the Harpy Knight, Calidah, yelled, flailing against the soldiers who grabbed her by the arms and dragged her up. "Don't touch her!"

"Aalya. That's your sister?" Bataar said, stepping closer and looking at the blood-smeared face of the girl sprawled on the floor. He knelt and touched her face. Under death-still lids, her eyes had rolled back to the whites.

Nassar's shaky expression pulled into a grimace. "Your little deal with Lofri was to marry her, not kill her. If the diamond mines pass over her, they go to some second cousin, not me. A Dumakran prince can't inherit anything except Dumakra."

The girl's chest still rose and fell in weak movements. "A physician for the princess," Bataar shouted. Doctors rushed forward.

"Take the bodies to the yard," Shaza ordered. The remainder of the zultam's people were herded up; resisting prisoners were bound at the wrists.

With the corpses gone, there were still scarlet puddles on the tiled floor and the metallic odor of blood. Despite the smell, part of himself settled back into his body. Bataar's breaths came easier now, more level. He could finally see the room. A depiction of paradise spanned the domed ceiling, overcrowded with fruit trees and white buildings. Bataar tore his eyes away from the murals. The velvet-cushioned, lion-footed throne sat empty now, framed by four lacquered wooden wings.

Nassar grumbled to himself and stalked toward the throne.

With a heavy sigh, he sank into the cushions. Bataar couldn't tell if the prince was unsettled by his own father having almost killed him, if the straight-backed bravado and a swaggering step masked his unease.

The prince's actions in the throne room had nearly cost Bataar everything. They still could. His plan had required the zultam alive, surrendering the country before a trial.

Bataar unsheathed his saber and twirled it offhandedly. "The people of Kalafar need a face and a name they recognize, a strong figurehead governing the capital to put them at ease. You drawing steel on your father jeopardized that. We can't let it get out that you tried to kill the zultam—and worse, failed."

"Not just Kalafar," Nassar said warily, picking the wrong thing to focus on. "All of Dumakra looks to the zultam who rules from this city."

Bataar said nothing.

"But it doesn't matter. When I'm crowned, I'll be named Goddess-blessed, and everyone in Dumakra will rally behind me."

"You can call yourself king of Kalafar. Call yourself whatever you want. But I'm placing my own men in command of the other Dumakran cities. You'll pay tribute and tax as a vassal of my empire."

Nassar sprung up. "Wait, wait, wait. What're you saying? You can't be so slow as to think I'm not going to succeed my father. I risked my life—"

"To nearly ruin everything because your bapa didn't love you enough," Bataar said darkly. "I've been patient, but I could have you trampled to death under my horses for publicly challenging me."

Apprehension flashed across Nassar's face. "You can't be serious. Trample me? This isn't insubordination! It's a conversation between allies. You know my worth. You killed my father to protect me."

"A moment of brainlessness I'm sure I'll regret for years to come." Bataar nodded to his guards. "Restrain the prince. He's exhausted. Take him to his quarters to get some rest."

"I said wait a moment, rhah." The prince's manic smile wavered. "We're not done talking."

"You favor your right hand. That correct?" Bataar tilted his head, considering Nassar's long fingers.

The prince's dark brows pinched. "Yes, but what—?"

"And you're literate."

"Well, obviously."

"One eye and one hand are more than enough to govern a city. Your tongue I could do without." Soldiers grabbed Nassar, pinning his arms as he thrashed. Bataar stepped close enough to smell last night's camp dinner on the prince's breath. "Or can you keep your mouth shut?" he whispered.

Nassar grimaced, his lips a tight line.

Bataar smiled. "Now *that's* a good boy."

Oktai burst into the room, panting. Scanning the carnage, his face paled. "Battalions are storming the city gates. The Harpy Knights are leading them. They want you on the wall."

❧

The climb to the top of the guard post on the Swan Gate made Bataar's thighs burn. Archers ran around him up the twisting stairs, bows raised and arrows nocked. Soldiers carried steel ballista bolts, two men for each heavy rod and hooked arrowhead. Men hauled up cauldrons full of burning sand and bubbling pots of oil.

"Heave!" a commander shouted.

Kalafar was theirs. If the zultam's daughters wanted it

back, they would have to take it by siege. If he were the general outside the walls, he would have reclaimed Zeffa first, then pinned the capital in properly with reinforcements from the south. But Bataar wasn't the one outside.

Atop the Wingates, the walk was slick from the misty sheets of rain. Preeminence's greedy gaze burned. Officers shouted to be heard over whooshing white noise.

Bataar squinted into the blackness. "Where are the reinforcements?"

A soldier lit an incendiary arrow and fired it to the foot of the wall, illuminating rows of Dumakran military units.

The ballista operators swung their equipment around, pointing the bolts up. They aimed the frames at the storm clouds, into the rain. If Bataar had blinked, he would have missed the black horse that swooped out of the sky. Something long and red flashed; a boy screamed, a deep gouge splitting his arm open.

Bataar scrambled back from the arterial spray, blinking in confusion. He reached for his saber, unsheathing the blade. "Form tight ranks!" he shouted. If their formation was loose, the Harpy could pick them off in the darkness.

The metal grating on the gate shook as something pounded against it. Men shooting at the crenels fell back from burning arrows. The Harpy Knight dropped out of the sky, swinging out of the saddle into the crenelation and running at Bataar. He tried to anticipate her swing, but he didn't account for the reach of her staff. Its blade was cold against the side of his neck.

"Your wife, for my father," she hissed.

Her proposal hung between them in the thick air.

The sickle's sharpness stung at every beat of his pulse. *Qaira. Tarken.* The battle on the Hill was supposed to be a quick sweep. But the capital had fallen quickly. The zultam had diverted too many soldiers north.

"Your father's dead," he said, parrying his saber against the long handle of her battle scythe. He feinted back, out of its reach.

Around him, men fell, blood gurgling in their mouths as they clawed at arrows protruding from their chests. The Harpy slammed into Bataar's side, knocking them both to the ground. With a grunt, he threw her weight off him. Their armor rattled, metal clanging against steel. Her helmet flew off her head. Tangled hair tumbled out around her chainmail coif, brown like dead leaves, unbrushed and matted.

He scrambled up, but she was already back on her feet. Grief and savagery flashed in her eyes. Her voice was a snarl. *I'll kill you.*

She reeled back and then lunged, swinging wildly. A strangled yell tore from her throat, as loud as the screams of the archers, louder than the boy holding his bleeding stump. It didn't matter. Without the flying horse, Bataar could outmaneuver and overpower her. In a few swings, she was gasping for breath. She favored one leg—he could use that against her. Her eyes were bloodshot and sweat ran down her face. A nerve pulsed on her forehead as spit flew from her mouth.

Bataar let her wheel the scythe around again, sidestepping her blows. A wave of calm rushed over him. His breath came evenly, his heart pounding steadily. When exhaustion curled at the princess's mouth, he stepped close, slamming the pommel of his saber down against her fingers and shoving her to the ground. He pinned her down, and she lay under him, gasping and bucking.

"Lay down your weapon," he said.

She wriggled a leg free and kneed him weakly in the side. He readjusted his knees on her thighs. Her mouth opened in a silent scream.

Bataar grimaced. "Surrender, and I spare your life."

"Rot in holy hells," she hissed. "My sister will take Kalafar back, whether I live or die."

"I have your little brother. The zultam is dead, but Rami isn't. Yet. Will your sister let him die? Will you?"

Her eyes met his. A tiny flicker of understanding pulled at her brow. Her squirming stilled, and her grip on the red weapon loosened. It hit the stone and wobbled, settling with a metallic scratch. When numbness spread over her features, he climbed off her. She lay frozen where he'd left her, staring up at black clouds.

8

Be it a meter on the battlefield or a city yielded, stand your ground. Nothing relinquished willingly is ever easily reclaimed.

— Obeyd's *Wartime Strategies*

In the struggle at the palace, hanging plants and topiaries had been sliced through, flowering bushes flattened. A hollowness filled Nohra as she was led through the wreckage. Her home wore the golden light of day like a funeral shroud.

In the central courtyard, the statue of the famous Dumakran queen Roksanya, Nohra's great-great-grandmother who'd died a century ago, was broken. The top half of her stone body crumbled into a tiled pond, crushing lily pads and displacing water. Guards grunted as they fished out a bloated corpse floating face down in the pool.

"Inside," a soldier grunted, shoving Nohra.

When Bataar's men shut the door to her rooms, reality set in harder and heavier. Books had been tossed, drawers thrown open and weapons pilfered. A dresser lay on its side. Her gowns in the armoire had been rifled through. Half of them were missing. Her natal-day rings were probably gone.

A statuette of Paga still sat on the vanity, scythe and smooth, featureless face all captured in bluish-gray feather-iron. It must not have been worth stealing last night.

The wound in her left thigh radiated pain. The rhah's wife had closed it with catgut, but the surrounding skin had been feverish for several hours, ever since their fight, when Bataar wedged a knee into Nohra's stitches. Her leg finally gave, and she collapsed into the clean covers, inhaling the scent of lavender and milky soap. Something caught in Nohra's throat. She tried swallowing it down, but her eyes burned and her vision blurred as she buried her face in a pillow and let the tears fall. They kept flowing until her stomach ached enough to throw up.

Over ten years ago, she'd been powerless to keep her mother alive. She could never have stopped the internal bleeding, or put the lost blood back in her body. But had the Goddess willed it, Nohra could have saved her father.

She didn't know who else was alive or dead.

The bedclothes smelled like Darya. Her friend might be gone, and when her scent faded from the sheets, that would be it.

After the surrender the night before, they'd separated Nohra from Safiya. Inside the room they'd locked her in at the Swan Gate, Nohra had shaken with anger. Now, her ferocity had faded.

Outside her bedroom window, the sky darkened. A guard cautiously opened the door and slid a tray of food inside. Nohra didn't get up or think to pray over it, to thank the farmers who'd brought in the Goddess's bounty as she normally would. She blinked bleary eyes, keeping them open as long as she could. When sleep hit her, all her dreams were nightmares.

She relived that horrible moment over and over, Safiya

yelling at her not to fly to the wall, the rush of adrenaline as she picked off that first boy and cut his arm.

She'd been untouchable until *him*. The fabric of the world seemed to bend around Bataar Rhah.

They were too late, and she was too sloppy.

Unlike the reality of that night, her dreams ended with Bataar's blade slick with red. She woke from fitful sleep feeling like she was choking on blood. He hadn't ended her. Somehow, that made her want to kill him more.

⌒◦⌒

A knock at the door made Nohra sit up, swiping at her sticky cheeks. Light fell in strips across the floor. She caught a glimpse of her reflection in the polished mirror on the dressing table. Her eyes were puffy and red-rimmed, her skin splotchy.

"A moment," she said. The guards didn't wait, pulling the doors open.

Nohra wasn't sure who she expected to see; not Darya, but that was who ran toward her, falling into her stunned embrace and pulling her close.

"Are you alright?" Nohra asked, grasping Darya by the arms.

She drew up her talmaid's sleeves and grabbed her chin, twisting her face left and right. No bruises or bandages, but there was red-brown crusted under her nails. And her smell was wrong, fire and iron, like she'd slept curled by the kitchen hearth, too exhausted to change out of blood-soaked clothes.

Darya pulled back, slipping like smoke through Nohra's fingers. "I'm fine."

"You'd swear it? On the Godsbreath? No one touched you?"

"No one touched me." Darya's fingers flexed toward her hip, where she kept her sheath. It was gone. It must have been confiscated.

"Did you get one of them?" Nohra asked, wanting to draw Darya closer when she nodded. She laughed shakily. "So the kitten has claws, after all. Tell me everything."

"Fahaad is alright, and your cousin Calidah wasn't hurt." Her words were measured. "Rami's being watched by the rhah's guards."

Nohra let out a heavy breath, letting a wave of relief wash over her. "Paga hasn't forsaken us, then."

"A lot of servants were killed, and palace guards." Darya hesitated. "Captain Mady, Kaatima, from the kitchens, and Aalya was—one of the archers... at least Laila heard... we don't know for certain."

Fear snaked between Nohra's ribs. *Aalya*.

"What are you saying?" Nohra's voice wavered. She didn't want to think it.

"She's alive. One of the girls took breakfast to the physicians. Aalya's in the infirmary. The wound won't stay closed, and she's too weak to wake up."

But she's alive. Nohra stood, moving toward the window. Through the gauzy curtain, her view of the grounds looked the same as always, though the causeways were emptier. "Where are they keeping the servants?"

Darya came to her side, hands on Nohra's elbows turning her to face her. "We slept on cots in the second receiving hall. Tonight, we're allowed back to our quarters. Where were you?"

"The first night, they locked me in a room at the Swan Gate. I was so worried. I should have been here with you all. With Father." She'd been hasty, and still too late. She remembered Safiya's furious expression of disapproval as she took off for the wall in the storm. But Nohra had thought she could use Qaira, the rhah's wife, to bargain with him.

"They asked me to get you dressed." Darya surveyed the

clothes strewn over the floor, her gaze lingering on the flies buzzing around the untouched dinner.

Nohra scowled. "What do they want?"

"You're supposed to go to the audience hall." Darya's eyes had never looked so remote, so vast. "Bataar Rhah is in council with your father's viziers. They're negotiating the terms of the surrender. I think they're hoping you, Safiya, and Calidah's obeisance would send a good message, especially to the Sister City."

"To *Clemiria*?" Nohra was too surprised to keep her voice down. "He thinks my aunt cares if I swear fealty to a barbarian king? Now that she knows what to expect, they won't be able to take Rayenna from her."

The nomads who lived in the red desert to the east said that Rayenna was a city built by djinn, that it disobeyed human maps and moved with the shifting sands. The city walls were the color of bone, made from an unidentifiable material that predated Dumakra and its feather-steel. It was mythic, impenetrable. Bataar couldn't take Rayenna. No one could.

"He spared my life." Darya winced slightly, like the words had claws, climbing up her throat. "He told me to tell you that."

Nohra had stopped Safiya from killing Bataar's general. She'd made sure his wife was safe on the ride to Kalafar and that no man touched her. She would have scraped out the eyes of anyone who looked at her wrong. And he'd still killed her father. Bataar owed *her*. She wouldn't forget that.

"There's something I think I should tell you. Something happened when I—" Darya started.

Nohra was already walking past her, distracted with thoughts of what demands Bataar would make. She turned back, and Darya hesitated.

"It's not important. I can't give you more grief to carry."

"Did you kill someone?"

A small nod, her lips parting in misplaced fear of judgment.

"Your life is worth more to me than a million of Bataar's men." Nohra made a grabbing motion at open air and drew her closed fist to her chest. "I'm stealing your guilt. It's mine now. You can't have it back, even if you want it." Grief and guilt would fuel her vengeance.

Darya snorted out a soft laugh. "You would have been disgusted. Terrified of me. I was a monster."

"Nothing you could do would make me see you as a monster." Quieter, Nohra added, "But I'll make sure you never have to do it again."

❧

In the audience hall, the zultam's throne was gone. That was the first thing Nohra noticed. She stood numbly as Bataar's female general checked her for weapons. Nohra refused to put on a pretty dress to be gawked at, so she'd let Darya help her into some plain linen clothes.

"I've got nothing," Nohra said pointedly.

The room was full of men in silk brocade, their earrings and brassy bangles jangling. Bataar stood at the end of the room, poring over documents while mavens from the Conservium read aloud over his shoulder. He looked like a big black wolf that had stalked into the palace, circling on the dais where her father's throne should be, watching the room with untrusting eyes.

Nohra could kill a wolf.

Viziers argued with Utasoo generals between aisles. Scribes wrote dizzyingly fast and translators mediated with red faces, their voices spilling over each other. So many words flowed out of silvered mouths, all as empty as air.

Traitors.

Grand Vizier Naji knelt nearby on the low seats on the left side of the aisle. Tarken, the commander Nohra had spared on the Hill, crossed his legs on the right, inspecting his saber. Ignoring the gazes that tracked her, Nohra took her place beside Safiya and their cousin.

Calidah's eyes were red and shadowed. There was so much they should say, so much they couldn't say, that words couldn't mend. Instead of uttering meaningless platitudes, Nohra squeezed her cousin's hand, once, twice, and then let go.

One vizier's wrinkled face kept dropping forward, neck lolling as he fell asleep. The man snorted awake, blinking and adjusting small spectacles on his long nose. A pang twinged in Nohra's chest. Such a simple, stupid thing made her think of her sister Aalya, always falling asleep in the sanctium.

Nohra's eyes landed on her little brother, kneeling beside a dark-skinned man wearing a turban. "Why's Rami here?" she whispered. Her brother blinked slowly, his big eyes reminding Nohra so much of their mother. She did a double-take, finally recognizing the man dressed in velvet and crepe. "And what's Fahaad doing with him?"

"Ramman Mytri was killed during the invasion," Calidah replied quietly. Her voice was fissuring glass. "Fahaad's kept close to Rami the last two days. Everyone says he'll be named head eunuch."

Nohra's skin tingled. "But he'll be needed in the stables."

Fahaad was always with the horses, and when he wasn't, he was asleep in the loft above the stalls. Nohra had never seen him dressed in court clothes. He looked… handsome, and oddly at ease.

"Who's that?" Nohra asked. A hunkered old woman stood on the stairs to the dais, stirring the contents of the pouch at her hip. A sound like rocks clacking punctuated the arguing.

"Bataar's shaman."

Nohra squinted. "Looks like a regular old woman. She has magic?"

"Could you focus?" Saf hissed. "Who made the formal surrender?"

Nohra had thought it was Safiya.

Cali crossed her arms. "Grand Vizier Naji helped Rami press your father's seal into the wax."

"Who killed Father?" Nohra asked. "I want to know whose sword he died on."

"*Bataar.*"

"The full account of the lands in Dumakra that belong to the zultam, repeat those," Bataar commanded, voice bellowing over the others. The edges of Nohra's vision blackened as her gaze focused on the dark-haired man with the sable cape.

A scribe shuffled papers. "The ports in Marafal," he read, "the Palace of the Heart in Antiria, the Rutiaba Palace in Kalafar, two feather-iron mines in the Teeth, Anhabar—"

"*Anhabar?*" The scar cutting across his face wrinkled when he furrowed his brow. Without it, he might have been truly handsome. The admission made Nohra's gut clench.

"An old city. It's in disrepair now." A cleric in loose robes spoke—the Minister of Faith, some old goat from the Jabour family. "The palace was abandoned after the vermilrot outbreak, hundreds of years ago. The ruins are cursed. The most dangerous job for my order is maintaining the sanctium there."

"Because of... ghosts?" The edge of Bataar's mouth twitched in amusement. His men snickered, but Dumakrans were superstitious of the former capital with good reason.

"There's no denying it's an accursed place, haunted by the unrestful dead. The Nights of Flame marked an unholy end to the Zultama reign in the Impasse. The desert is perilous.

Heretic cannibals live in the waste around the ruins, picking off stragglers from Rayenni caravans to sacrifice in their rituals, just like the cursed rites that made the disease."

When Nohra and Safiya had helped escort Aunt Clemiria east a decade ago, they'd briefly glimpsed Anhabar carved into the mountain. Nohra remembered the unease that had spiked in her heart and made Mercy flatten his ears.

Bataar leaned forward. "By heretics, you mean exiled religious dissenters: Dumakran preeminists and followers of the Dyad sect, is that right?"

The cleric minister averted his eyes, dabbing at his damp brow. But a few outcast clerics from a schismatic denomination didn't change the fact that there was greater religious freedom in Dumakra than anywhere else on the continent.

"Your Excellence," the scribe butted in, straightening the deeds to the properties. "There are also the public lands in Rayenna, the Sister City, uh, as I'm sure you already know."

Bataar raised an eyebrow. "Will Queen Clemiria honor the surrender?"

Nohra blinked. He was looking at them. She prodded her cousin.

Calidah stiffened. "My mother is loyal to the Sister City. She'll act in its best interest. I could go with the envoy and speak for you."

"You'd be more useful at the palace." He meant she'd be more valuable as a hostage.

Nohra prepared for talk of public executions, for a decree that her father's concubines would be given as gifts to Bataar's commanding officers. She held her breath, waiting for those words to fall.

When they didn't, she murmured to her cousin, "Why isn't this bloodier?"

Calidah wrung her hands. "Look at history. They're always gentler when there's a wedding. He's marrying Aalya. This peace agreement's been sealed with their marriage pact."

But Aalya was unconscious. She could die.

"Bataar," a lofty voice called out. "May we speak privately?"

A tall, slim man reclined close to the grand vizier, leaning against a pillar. Something wound around his neck—a golden tail. The macaque twisted its head in Nohra's direction and screeched. The man who wore the monkey like a stole had Queen Merv's thick eyelashes.

Bataar waved a hand. "After the rest of the terms are read, Nassar."

The last time Nohra had seen her half-brother, he'd been a scrawny little boy crying for his mother. Safiya had once locked him in the circumcision room while Nohra wore a white shroud and pretended to be the ghost of a prince who'd died under the surgeon's scalpel. He'd peed himself and cried so much his nose bled. He'd grown into a courtly man, with smooth, unscarred skin. His sweat probably smelled like roses.

"For Ervan Lofri's loyalty, he will receive a quarter of all public lands in Kalafar," a mediator read. "Prince Nassar is to be instated as king in Kalafar until such a time as Dumakran succession can be reevaluated."

"*What?*" Nohra said, voice strangled.

Safiya shook her head warningly. "Don't start. Not here."

"In a show of good faith," the mediator continued, "His Eminence takes the former Crown Prince Rami to ward."

For less than a second, Bataar's eyes met Nohra's. Indignation sparked, growing into rage. She swallowed it down, unable to ignore how badly it burned.

༺⚬༻

Nohra crouched in the courtyard as advisors slowly filed out of the audience hall. The summer air was dry and hot, but at least outside she wasn't suffocated by the viziers' oud colognes.

She jumped at a light touch to her elbow. "Calidah went ahead to the infirmary to sit with Aalya," Safiya told her. They shared an intense look. Their new guards watched warily from a few yards away. Quieter, Safiya tacked on, "Mind what you say here. The three of us can talk later."

Nohra nodded, already thinking of plans to slip away from her escorts. "Should I come to your quarters?"

"No. To the wharf house. I'll explain more when I can."

The wharf house?

Nohra was suddenly engulfed by a cloud of the same musky perfumes that lingered outside pleasure houses.

"I'm glad you've been let out of your rooms, sisters," Nassar called, approaching them. Their brother spoke with unwarranted familiarity, like they hadn't taunted him mercilessly as a child for picking on Darya and the other servants; like he hadn't helped Bataar take Kalafar. "Though I see you're not wearing mourning colors for our father."

"Excuse me?" Nohra's voice was low and dangerous as she stood. Her hands shook. Fury emanated from her in white-hot waves.

A cluster of women followed Nassar, the Dowager Queen and some girls wearing gaudy jewelry. Merv Attar looked as haughty as she did unsettled. Her kohl was smudged, silver-striped hair disheveled. Her son was practically the zultam, but her husband was dead and her only daughter was unconscious, fighting for her life.

Too bad Nohra didn't have an endless well of sympathy, or every cold-hearted bitch could drink.

Nohra walked forward, not sure what she was going to

do, just that it would be bloody. Righteousness cloaked her like she was striding onto a battlefield.

"Don't step any closer," said someone behind her. Nohra recognized that low, sardonic voice—Bataar. Moving nearer, he signaled for his men.

She sneered. "Why are you calling for guards? I'm unarmed. All my weapons were confiscated at the Swan Gate."

"My friend, what's the meaning of this?" Nassar laughed. "Stand down, rhah."

"If you know what's good for you, step back," Bataar said firmly, positioning his body between Nohra and her half-brother. His black cape swirled around his legs, and as his lip curled, the jagged scar across his face tightened.

Nassar smiled. "Are you worried about Nohra and Safiya? They're my sisters. I know they were only fulfilling their oaths by trying to serve our father. I won't hurt them."

The world went white. Nohra lunged at Nassar, arms raised to rip his throat out. The reddish-gold monkey around his shoulders shrieked and jumped away, skittering across the courtyard toward an olive tree.

"That's enough," Bataar warned.

Large hands caught Nohra and held her back. As she thrashed, her elbow connected with the side of Bataar's head. He swayed but gripped tight, enveloping her in arms that smelled like sweat and pine resin. But Nohra was close to Nassar and struggling too fiercely to be dragged back by one man. She pulled free, and her brother screeched as she sank her teeth into the meat of his shoulder. First her gums met silk; then she tasted iron.

Her stepmother released an ear-splitting scream. The girls that had been following Nassar dispersed like birds. He screeched as blood oozed down his white sleeve, hot in Nohra's mouth.

"You bitch!" Nassar floundered like a fish, fists landing weak punches. Bataar's arms were around her again, his chest warm against her. She tried to reel her arm back, to strike him with her elbow, but he held her firmly.

"Murderer!" she yelled at him.

"Nohra, calm down," Saf said, her voice hardly reaching Nohra over the angry drumming of her pulse. "Think before you lash out; have just a second of consideration for yourself and all of us. We can't afford any impulsive mistakes."

Finally, two guards pulled Nohra from Bataar's arms and dragged her away from her wounded brother. "Blood treason warrants death," she snarled, spitting a glob of red onto the paved pathway.

Safiya crossed her arms and sighed. "Now's not the time or place for that kind of judgment. You don't really want to kill him. You'll regret this when you're calmer."

Nohra wheeled her head around, glaring at the ministers, chamberlains, viziers, and military officers who'd stopped to gawk. Who cared if she was a spectacle to them?

"Send for help!" Merv yelled, her normally satiny voice raw. "Someone, help my son—don't just stand there!"

"I'll help him," Safiya said impatiently. She walked over and took the prince's shoulder. Looking steadily at Bataar, she added, "I've received some training in medicine at the Conservium."

Saf's eyes flashed to Nohra's. A vicious smile pulled at the corner of her mouth. With a jerk, she wrenched the prince's shoulder up and out of its socket.

"*Spirit*. Grab her," Bataar yelled, wincing and rubbing his jaw.

Nassar whimpered as his arm fell slack. Safiya punched him, once, twice. There was a wet crunch as bones in his face smashed.

The courtyard filled with curses, the mumbles of old men and shouts of guards. Nassar's party squealed as his courtesans flitted around in a brightly colored, jingling flurry. The monkey screeched in the olive tree, and an eagle screamed as it wheeled in the cloudless sky, its shrill vocalizations echoing like mocking laughter. Hands slipped off Safiya, and every kick turned head-splitting.

"Don't you dare touch me," Saf growled, kneeing one of Bataar's guards in the groin.

He grunted, and the other guards edged back. When the courtyard quieted, the only sounds were Safiya's and Nohra's heavy breathing, Nassar's pathetic whimpering, and the groans of the injured guards. Probably, Nohra would need to pray for exoneration, but right now she felt only relief. Nassar's face dripped blood. He wobbled as he stood, squinting accusingly at Bataar.

"We could have killed him," Safiya said to their stepmother. "Remember that." She turned to Bataar. "You too."

Nohra smiled, baring blood-stained teeth. One of the Utasoo guards shook her roughly, and the feral grin fell.

When both were restrained, Bataar gave the order, "Send for a physician, and escort the princesses back to their quarters. Lock them in. I'll call for them when the funerary procession starts."

9

Souls scatter like ash on the wind to be
rewoven into the web of all things.

— Utasoo saying

Funerary bells pealed as Bataar squinted up at the domes on
the sanctium. The hammered bronze trembled in the sweltering
heat. Dumakra had him longing for the cool breezes that rolled
off the mountains in the west. Kalafar's streets were littered
with rubble, and the smell of smoke still lingered, almost a
week after the invasion. Wells had been damaged, sanctiums
pillaged. In the aftermath, homes and businesses had been
looted.

Soldiers tried to keep the peace, but rioters had stolen
weapons from one of Lofri's units four days ago. The next
night, civilians broke curfew to flock to mob executions.
Vigilante justice was bloody and inexact. More bodies hung
in the squares to be cut loose each morning, mostly captured
soldiers and prisoners—rapists and murderers who'd escaped
from the Forked Tower in breakouts the night of the invasion.

"Orders, Your Eminence?" a faceless voice in the line of
armed men asked.

"Watch the crowds." Excitement thrummed through the crush of people squeezing into the sanctium courtyard. Peeling off from the line for the charity kitchen, everyone clambered for a glimpse of the royal family, or Bataar.

He motioned for the soldiers to carve out a path for the women. Eunuch guards formed a close perimeter around the concubines and royals. The zultam's family quickly ascended the steps to the sanctium, casting nervous glances at the streets not yet clear of rubble. The old woman who'd caused him more trouble during the invasion than any of the princesses, the queen mother—Ramzi's mother—stepped unhurriedly, chin jutted up as her narrowed eyes scanned the crowd. The harem flocked around her in a blur of gold, Dumakra's mourning color.

By now Bataar knew most of the women's names, especially one. The woman who'd rushed to fight him on the Wingates. Nohra Zultama wore a jacketed dress embroidered with black filigree. Her chainmail veil obscured her nose and perpetual grimace. She turned on the stairs, her amber-flecked eyes trained on Bataar, a shrike regarding a mouse.

Oktai nudged her forward. The boy shrunk back when she twisted to direct her glare at him. One of Lofri's men grabbed her elbow and shoved her toward the open doors.

Bataar spared another glance at the ebbing crowd on the street. Dead eyes stared up at him. A summer breeze rippled through his hair as he reflexively rubbed the old scar that cut through his stubbled chin and disappeared under the high collar of his Dumakran tunic.

"Let me escort the princess," he called, ascending to offer Nohra his arm.

She scowled, taking it with reluctance. "I don't see your wife, or your generals."

Inside the antechamber, her hand quickly dropped away. Cerulean-colored tiles surrounded the carpeted vestibule. Everything was so blue, as if the sky had been pulled into the sanctium.

He tried to smile, put her at ease. "This is your mourning day, not ours."

"And yet you're here, making a mockery of us. I'm not a tool for you to win approval. Don't try using me again, or you'll regret it."

Around them, women removed their slippers to wash their hands and feet at a burbling fountain. Everyone had overheard her. They just pretended to be busy.

Bataar grabbed her arm, wrenching her closer. Through clenched teeth he hissed, "Don't threaten me, princess. You'll find I'm not like your half-brother with his stupid monkey."

Nohra's eyes were focused on the talmaid's black knife in its sheath on his belt. "That's not yours. The women in my family need their weapons back. They're not safe around your men. You should return them."

"I'll consider it."

Their gazes were locked, but her arm shot out, moving for the jeweled hilt. He caught her fingers, pinning her hand. Her fingertips were cold. Through her chain-link veil, her lips were cracked and bloody.

"I'm going to pretend I took your hand to comfort you," he murmured. "We're at your father's funeral, and you are an unmarried woman in my care."

He uncurled his fingers, and her hand slipped free. Brows pulled, she shrunk back. The veil jingled, a harsh sound, unlike the ornaments Qaira sometimes wore in her braids.

"Keep her close," Bataar told Oktai. "Don't let your guard down for a second. She and Safiya aren't allowed near the rest of the harem. Those two are in isolation until I say they're not."

The boy nodded. Bataar looked around and copied the harem. He knelt to wash his feet, then stood, splashing his face and hands with the cool water. Two little princesses giggled, rushing by in a gust of gilded silk. His heart ached for Ganni and baby Bato. It could be another week before he saw his children. He wanted to welcome them to a safe city.

A mural above the fountain depicted the Dumakran goddess's two incarnations—one bat-winged and shadow-cloaked, the other wielding a red scythe like a farmer bringing in a harvest. Neither had discernable features: one's face a spiky star and the other's an indistinguishable smear.

It was a private comfort, for a god to not have eyes to watch him.

"Your Eminence." Bataar dimly remembered that toneless voice from his audience with the viziers: the cleric who'd been in the audience hall for the councilors' meeting. Majeed Jabour stood near the fountain, staring intently. "Did you know I personally oversaw the design of this building, with the Minister of Architonics, some twenty years ago? It was difficult sourcing a blue that matched—"

Bataar sighed. "Please make sure you're telling me pertinent things."

"Of course!" The Minister of Faith had the drooping eyes and scraggly white beard of an old goat. When he bobbed his head, his jowls jiggled. "Today, I would be pleased to be Your Eminence's guide to Dumakran religious custom. Please follow me."

Bataar jolted as carpet gave way to cold tile underfoot. Blinking away his discomfort, he clenched his fists to keep from curling his toes. In the inner sanctium, ornate sarcophagi glittered in the light filtering through tall windows. A strong smell radiated from the incense diffusing in hanging burners. On a raised platform, a cleric in gold-trimmed gray stood beside priestesses wearing elaborate headdresses.

He picked through the crowd for the individuals he knew. The queen mother, Safiya, Nohra's talmaid farther back with the servants, and Nohra. When Nohra knelt in front of the dais, she winced. Qaira had mentioned dressing a wound for the princess at the Hill. If it had opened during their fight, a physician would need to clean and redress it, but she'd dismissed the doctors he'd sent to her rooms.

"Let them in now," Bataar ordered the doormen.

The Minister of Faith stepped forward. "Your Eminence, if it's pertinent, the harem never prays with the commoners at Thora's Sanctium."

"Why?"

The old man looked taken aback. "Well, safety, most importantly. And unsanctified eyes profane the Goddess-blessed."

"Form a line behind the harem," Bataar ordered his soldiers as the crowds from the street began filtering into the building.

He counted all the princesses and Zultam Ramzi's respected concubines, a few old enough that their hair was graying, their faces lightly lined. Others were so young the zultam hadn't shared his bed with them. Prince Rami stood among the women. Bataar recognized his golden-brown hair and startled calf's eyes.

"His Excellence," the minister said reverently, bobbing his head in front of the most magnificent of the caskets. His gaze kept darting between the worshipers thronged in the outer ring and the glittering gold lid carved to look like Zultam Ramzi.

The face wore a peaceful expression, nothing like it had looked twisted in anger as Bataar cut the man down. Ramzi had lived as a king and died fighting. Now his spirit had taken wing, off to some other place, and the king of maggots would eat his body in his subterranean tomb. In Ramzi's face, Bataar picked out Nohra's brow, Safiya's smirk, and Nassar's curling hair, all captured so realistically he could breathe to life at any moment.

They stepped back, finding their places, and knelt.

"The gold was melted down from the possessions of Aglean lords," the minister said. "Claimed following the first battle for the Heartspring in one forty... hm... nine. Ramzi had this casket made years ago, the same time as Thora's."

"He must have cared for his wife deeply." This was the mausoleum of a woman whose husband he'd killed. But Bataar couldn't muster much regret in such an ostentatious monument.

"His heart died the day Rami was born," the minister said, features twisting with remorse.

"She's with Preeminence now," Bataar said somberly. He blinked, remembering he was talking to a Dumakran cleric. "Or, uh, paradise."

The old man didn't seem to care. "She was foreign-born, hailed from Pagaskeld. Ramzi held the city until 340, when Aglea took it back during the Sunless Months. Do you remember that time?"

Bataar didn't remember, but he knew the stories. Ash in the air from a volcanic eruption in Moshitu had blocked out the sun. "Hardly. I was born on the last day. You remember so much," Bataar cajoled. "What can you tell me about the Harpy Knights?"

Dull eyes brightened. "Which are you inquiring about, Your Eminence? Your betrothed, the princess Aalya?"

Around them, women in the inner ring sobbed. From the outer section of the prayer hall, there were excited murmurs and grunts as the crowd flowed forward and was pushed back. Bataar was a king they could see, one almost close enough to touch. His aid would rebuild the city stronger than it had been in decades.

"All of them."

"Safiya is Dumakra's daughter, Ramzi's firstborn. It was such a joyful day when she was presented at the palace gates, squalling and kicking and full of fire. She plays the harpsichord beautifully. Aalya dances... danced passably well. Calidah is pursuing mavenhood at the Conservium—"

This wasn't what he'd had in mind. "Tell me how they fight."

"Ah, you want blood? The viziers whisper that Nohra is Paga reborn with a bloody scythe. She killed an assassin on that very dais when she was freshly fourteen. Sworn in at fifteen, after her wounds healed. Her and Safiya's first battle... there was some disorder in Marafal. Vizier Sartarid entertained treasonous thoughts in an alliance with an Aglean lord."

Bataar hadn't met a representative from the Sartarid family yet. "I don't know that name."

The minister pursed his lips, his tone grave. "News didn't spread. A small battalion put down the Aglean forces. Safiya and Nohra led them." He stroked his thin beard, brows pulled. Whispering now, "There were rumors one of Ramzi's cousins was a co-conspirator. Muraad wanted the throne, so he questioned Ramzi's legitimacy. He also spread salacious lies about Princess Clemiria. He said her daughter, Calidah, was conceived out of wedlock, fathered by a low-ranking soldier. It must have been eight years ago. Nohra was something like sixteen then. No, seventeen. Hm, no, Safiya was—"

"Never mind precise ages."

"Sartarid's lands were seized, his titles revoked. He's an honorless beggar, and his men are dead."

"And what of the cousin, Muraad, and the legitimacy?" Bataar pressed.

The minister blinked, looking like the conversation had either turned very stupid or very dangerous. "It's said Grand Vizier Naji urged Ramzi to kill the blood traitor, but the zultam was forgiving. He wouldn't kill family, even if he was betrayed first. Kalafar moved on from the insurrection and the false claims were forgotten."

Remembering what had happened with Nassar in the throne room, Bataar identified some improbabilities in the minister's events. More likely it was Grand Vizier Naji who had told Ramzi not to kill his cousin for some unsubstantiated rumor of a rumor.

But Nohra and Safiya had put down a traitor's rebellion. Kalafar was their first defeat. Safiya was hard to read, but her bullheaded sister seemed straightforward enough. Nohra had the courage to be a skilled fighter, but she was too impulsive to be a good soldier.

Bataar's recent visit to the stables had been disappointing. Palace records indicated fewer pegasuses had been born in the years since the Sunless Months; however, the beasts that weren't brittle-boned were powerful weapons of war. The Harpies' trust would be hard won, but if Bataar made allies of them, he could rule the skies. Was Safiya their leader, or Nohra? Who was their father's favorite, Dumakra's darling? Which did the zultam's generals most respect?

Safiya had looked to Nohra in the courtyard. Her mercurial rage influenced the other Harpies. Bataar needed to learn their strengths and weaknesses. He asked, "Which is the most dangerous on a pegasus?"

The old minister shrugged. "No woman flies better than Nohra, probably because no one else is as willing to fall."

Bataar's chest clenched. Tarken would call him a fool, tell Bataar he was always too quick to respect brainless bravery. "Tell me more."

From the glint in the minister's eyes, it was clear he read Bataar's curiosity as attraction. "You may want to know she's engaged to a South Aglean lord's son. An ambassador from Hythebryde proposed the match to His Majesty to strengthen relations with the north. And she's very close to her servants. Her talmaid, who bakes a splendid syrup-soaked cake that could make angels cry. There's also a eunuch stablehand—"

Bataar rubbed his mouth contemplatively. "A eunuch stablehand?"

"Your Eminence, a eunuch is a man who—"

"I don't require an explanation, minister, thank you. This stablehand, he…?"

"Grew up at the palace as a servant-ward. He's some Moshitu warlord's son."

Bataar raised an eyebrow. "A warlord's son, a ward of the zultam, and he was castrated?"

The minister laughed. "Harem eunuchs take an infertility tonic. Other than preventing accidental children, the drug makes men clearer of mind, free from desires of the flesh. The *old* methods aren't practiced at the palace anymore."

"And outside the palace?"

A conspiratory smile quirked at the corners of his mouth. "We can't know everything that happens everywhere in Dumakra."

Bataar's lip curled. "Try."

The ceremony began. Soon, the excitement of a royal marriage would replace the grim veil of death. Bataar's life had been a series of sporadic weddings and funerals, and sometimes weddings that turned into funerals. When he pictured

Nassar's little sister Aalya as a bride, he only saw a too-young girl with a bruised, bloodied face. The miniature in the locket Merv Attar wore wasn't enough to make a concrete impression. If the princess woke up, perhaps Bataar could marry her to Oktai, partially fulfilling his promise to Lofri. He and Nassar were already tense about the king-in-Kalafar business.

"The zultam's heartbox," the cleric announced, holding out a small, ornate chest. He looked left and right, scanning the mourning supplicants.

"I accept it for my father," Rami said, standing up. His skinny arms bowed under the weight of the box.

"What will you do with the crown prince, Your Eminence?" the minister whispered. "He's your ward now."

Bataar shrugged. "Find him a suitable marriage match. Teach him how to hunt. I don't know."

Bataar needed to meet with the Minister of Treasury about minting virtues with new molds. Since Ramzi was dead, a new face needed to be pressed into gold coins. The Minister of Education wanted to discuss damages done to the Conservium's library during the invasion, and there was even more Bataar needed to hammer out with Grand Vizier Naji.

"When we've stopped the riots in Kalafar, I can worry about the zultam's heir," Bataar said. Right now, he was more concerned with rebuilding and strengthening public works: Kalafar's aqueducts, cisterns, and wells.

The minister was solemn. "Of course."

The cleric intoned his holy words, but Bataar couldn't focus. The room was closely packed, full of coughing and whispering and the reek of too many bodies, so many variations of sweat and musk. His eye twitched; he swallowed down the stiffness that clogged his throat and made it difficult to breathe.

The sanctium was suffocating, like the press to get into

the zultam's audience hall during the invasion. The incense smelled like the herbs the field doctors in Choyanren worked with. Bataar's mind strayed to that first night in Xincho, when the fields blazed. Then he was fourteen again, watching a little boy's funeral pyre smolder.

"Your Eminence. That concluded the ceremony."

Bataar blinked, clearing his blurring vision. Tendrils of smoke snaked out of the sides of the coffin. The silent chaos priestesses in their half-veils grasped the handles and lifted, conveying it away. From the back of the room, the city watched.

It was over. They needed to move.

"Clear a path," Bataar shouted, "and keep the crowd back. No one touches the harem."

The people packed into the outer sanctium shouted and grappled for a better look at the zultam's family. In the vestibule, children in rags stood in the fountain, laughing as they fished coins out of the water. A woman skimmed a bucketful of soapy water off the handwashing fountain.

"Palace gold! It's Goddess-blessed!" a man with enough teeth to count on one hand said deliriously, pushing little boys out of the water and grabbing fistfuls of gold virtues.

"Get back," a guard yelled, prodding the sharp point of a halberd into the fray.

"Wait," Bataar ordered, wincing at a shout. Wide eyes tracked him, shocked to see a king not partitioned behind a metal screen. Anger, confusion, and wonder all warred on the shifting faces. Even for those who'd had little love for Ramzi and his tarnished era, Bataar's sack of the capital had made life more precarious. Lifting rationing and promising prosperity wasn't enough.

Soldiers shoved men and women out of the sanctium, onto the crowded steps. Screams were answered with fearful squeaks from the women and girls huddling close together behind the guards.

It happened in an instant, a man surging around the armored soldiers to take one of the young concubines by the wrist. She groaned, trying to twist free. A hand swiped close to her face and something fell to the floor. Her broken earring hit the carpet, and a bead of blood welled at the concubine's ear.

"Zira!" a woman yelled, voice shaking.

Bataar drew his saber and was upon them just as a rush of men and women surged around the guards. Beggars on hands and knees scrambled to grab the sparkling Noorish sapphire. He slashed at the man's forearm and wrenched the concubine away, passing her back to one of the guards behind him. The man he'd struck screamed out, cupping the gouge with his other hand.

"You shouldn't draw blood in the house of the Goddess," the Minister of Faith warned, dabbing with an embroidered kerchief at the sweat dripping from his brow. "But this is certainly an unusual circumstance."

"Keep the princesses close," Bataar ordered, ignoring the old man. "If any of them have a scratch on them before we've got them back to the palace, I'll have your hands for it."

❦

Bataar stopped in the doorway to the infirmary. Faced with more pressing concerns, yesterday's funeral felt like a distant memory. In one of the beds, Aalya's chest rose and fell in shallow breaths, her eyelids closed as if in sleep. She'd suffered blood loss from the arrow wound and fractured some vertebrae in her neck when she fell off the stone dais. Over the week, she hadn't stirred.

A physician employed by the Merchants Guild had arrived

days ago but proved insufficient. Bataar had brought in mavens from the Conservium, Xincho doctors, and his shaman Boroo, who was skilled in natural medicines. The first night, Boroo had burned a witching pyre in the courtyard outside the sick room, interpreting smoke signals from the Preeminent Spirit to determine what to add to her tinctures and compresses.

The young princess still slept like the dead.

Bataar pushed past the door guards and folded his arms. "I've come to relieve you of your watch," he said.

Calidah was slight and shorter than her cousins. Her hair fell in a lank, unbrushed sheet. She squinted, looking at something in her lap through glass lenses on a wire frame.

"I didn't know your vision was impaired," Bataar commented, surprised. Her crossbow aim was deadly.

"I'm farsighted. I'm fine at a distance." She held up a weathered tome. "I need the lenses to read."

A silence passed between them, neither meeting the other's eyes. The infirmary was quiet except for distant birdsong and children's shouts.

"You've been the zultam's ward since you were eight years old, but you didn't join the funeral procession yesterday."

Calidah turned to him, gaze suddenly cold and sharp. A nerve in her face twinged. Bataar's guards stiffened, but he waved for them to stand down. "I've never cared for funerals," she admitted. Her expression turned distant, looking at something beyond the cots and trays of gauze and containers of bitter herbs.

Bataar crossed his arms. "Where's Nassar?"

The physicians had plied him with analgesics after the fight in the courtyard. The prince had a bruised eye socket, broken nose, cracked tooth, and dislocated jaw. They'd put a gold crown on the molar, set his nose, and cleaned the bite marks.

"Convalescing in his own quarters. Thank the Goddess for that. I couldn't read with him moaning."

"Go read in your apartments. I told you, I came to relieve you."

Her frown never wavered. "I can't leave my unmarried cousin without a chaperone, even if you're betrothed."

"I'll sit with him," Qaira said, sweeping into the room trailed by one of her handmaidens, her face a solemn mask. Calidah stood stiffly, nodded, and took her leave, still grimacing like the decision was painful.

Qaira's smile faltered as she leaned forward and wiped Aalya's brow. "Her hair's so short. Did the physicians cut it?" She traced the scabbing wound stretching from the girl's temple back behind the shell of her ear.

"It was like that when we took the audience hall. It could be common for girls her age here," he replied gruffly. "She's only seventeen, Qaira."

"You were seventeen at your first wedding." Her voice was unreadable. "You were so young to be starting a war."

And stupid.

The deals Bataar had struck with the rhahs created such a convoluted web of debt and alliance that a Dumakran royal genealogist wouldn't be able to untangle it all. Dozens of rhahs ruled the steppe, each with their own titles and way of ruling. A marriage, or the promise of one, was always the strongest assurance of allegiance, but there were other bargaining prices.

Bataar had promised his daughter Ganni's hand to the grandson of the Blood Rhah before she'd even been conceived, before he'd been wed himself. In contrast, the Rhah-kha's alliance had been cheaply bought: a hundred ermine pelts. The man was just hungry for war. Then, when the Blood Rhah's young grandson had been trampled in battle against Tobukaah Rhah, Bataar had promised his daughter to Rhah-cal instead.

Bataar had been young, putting victory first and burying his new, almost unignorable feelings for Qaira. He'd offered himself for an alliance, since thoughts of marrying for love felt like childish dreams. But in the middle of his hand-binding ceremony with the Blood Rhah's daughter, their wedding had been ambushed. Tobukaah's grieving brother shot Bataar's almost-bride through the throat. Bataar had stumbled back as her body slumped onto him, her silver hair turning red. With their wrists bound, he couldn't stop the bleeding. Horses had exchanged hands, and Qaira's parents took Tobukaah Rhah's two orphan sons to ward. Eventually, all the steppe kings swore fealty, freeing Bataar to wed Qaira.

Bataar looked at this girl Lofri wanted him to marry. They'd both had childhoods marred by blood and war. The difference was, her blood was on his hands.

Qaira straightened out a length of cloth secured in her embroidery hoop. She slid a thin needle through the eye of a brightly colored bead. Taking her cue, Bataar smoothed out the rumpled parchment he'd brought and pulled over a quill and inkpot.

"A letter?" Qaira asked.

"For Ruo." His Choyanreni characters were clumsy, but he didn't trust the scribes to faithfully translate his message to the empress without snaking their own meaning onto the page. "You never have idle hands, do you?"

"It's for Ganni's ninth natal day." She held up the headdress. "If your letter can wait, will you hold this?"

He obediently lifted the beaded cloth.

"Aalya isn't the only suitable match you could make here," Qaira murmured, her words measured.

147

"Most Dumakran wealth is in the mines her mother's family owns. The rest comes from fishing, which the Merchants Guild oversees, and smuggling, which is her Uncle Lofri's business. The only rich family she isn't connected to is Grand Vizier Naji's."

"I had coffee with Naji's wife. She told me his great-grandfather constructed the Conservium and his father designed Thora's Sanctium. Some great-great-uncle was the architect who designed Rutiaba and the Palace of the Heart."

"Their money built Kalafar when the capital relocated." The elites had fled the old capital, Anhabar, when vermilrot broke out. It had been a stumbling start to the city on the Scythe, but one better than the pandemonium at the mountain, poor souls subsisting on the bodies of their own diseased dead. Poor management of a bad strain by a weak regime had rendered the rot uncontrollable, impossible to treat. Superstition that the place was haunted—or at least plagued by heretic desert tribes—had persisted ever since.

"Well Naji's wife spoke as if she personally built all the Marvels of Man. She's proud of her husband's family and of her daughters. She wants me to suggest you betroth Prince Rami to her oldest, but she wouldn't just come out and say it."

"Really?" It wasn't a terrible idea. "You hear things I never would."

"It's called listening. It isn't a divine gift. Does this look alright?"

He squinted at the thick knob of threads. "It's a dog?"

"A pegasus." She turned her project over and started ripping out her sloppy stitches. "A match with another Harpy could also be useful, like Calidah. Queen Clemiria might be persuaded to swear fealty if her daughter is a queen."

"Well, the Minister of Faith"—Bataar blinked; had the

princess's fingers twitched?—"told me he'd never seen a brother and sister as close as Ramzi and Clemiria. I stole her brother from her. She'll think I'm trying to take her daughter, too."

Bataar focused his attention back on the letter. The Choyanreni characters looked slightly off, his handwriting clumsy as a child's. If he used the formal punctuation marks incorrectly, Ruo wouldn't let him forget it.

"Hm," Qaira mused. Her needle dipped in and out of the taut fabric, pulling through with a ribbony whisper. "You could marry Safiya, or Nohra."

Bataar turned, a brow raised. "Former concubines' daughters? They have no wealth outside of their father's, no family connections."

"They're well-respected. The people's admiration is priceless. I was taking tea with Himma, the queen mother—"

Bataar nearly choked. "What? That old bat laced her karambit with venom from a Nuna's whip viper. Don't you dare drink anything she gives you. I don't care how well you usually get on with old women."

Qaira tossed her head. "Left to your own devices, you'd make enemies of every woman at court. Let me win their favor."

She had a gentle power of persuasion. When Mukhalii kidnapped women and boys to sell in Zeffa, it was Qaira who'd kept the prisoners calm until Bataar and Shaza could free them.

"Your Eminence," the Utasoo door guard interrupted, stepping into the sick room. "One of the Dumakran priests is here."

Bataar recognized the slender man with his peppered beard from the funeral. "I ask your blessing to pray over the princess," the cleric said. "If it pleases you."

He waved his hand. "As you'd like."

The man pulled the stopper out of a jeweled flask. Liquid

sloshed inside. "From the Heartspring," the cleric explained as ruby-tinted water glugged out onto a rag.

Bataar jumped up. "I gave you leave to pray over her. What are you doing?"

A physician's assistant traipsed into the room and stopped dead. His gaze flew over the unfolding scene, head jerking left and right. "You can't be in here without the mavens' approval!"

The princess's lips were unmoving as the cleric wrung out the cloth. Red droplets slid into her mouth. She didn't swallow; her throat was still. Seconds passed. Then, Bataar stumbled back, shaking his head, fighting a bark of laughter. The princess's throat bobbed, and the tips of her fingers twitched.

Wars had been fought for the Heartspring, though the water was just colored by iron deposits. Bataar had once killed a man standing knee deep in diluted runoff from that muddy-red pond. His opponent had gurgled blood from his mouth and stomach as he drowned. The spring didn't pour from a Goddess's huge body or a demon's vein, as some people claimed. It came from the earth like all other water.

It didn't contain miracles, but sometimes miracles happened anyway.

10

As Paga cleans the pus from Her daughters' torn-off wings, does She remember wading in the river when Her soul was whole, when everything was still good and gleaming and new?

— Author anon

The baths were empty when the guards shoved Nohra through the dark doorway.

"His Eminence wants you to bathe." The voice belonged to the Utasoo boy Bataar had following her, *Oktai*. Something in his features, the shape of his eyes, his chestnut-colored hair, reminded her of Tarken, the commander at the Hill.

Nohra had cleaned herself for the funeral, but that had been days ago. Now the dirt crusting her body was like a snake's papery shed, and no one came to refill the washbasin in her room. She kept waking up covered in cold sweat from nightmares where she was entombed at the palace in Antiria, folded in the wall with her father's embalmed heart.

"Hurry up, or I'll drag you in myself." This was one of Lofri's personal guards, a tall man who spoke unaccented Dumakran. Nohra's heartbeat spiked at his rough tone.

Both men looked expectantly forward. In the cavern-like darkness, water dripped. Nohra's cheeks colored from the steam. "Where's Darya? Who's going to bathe me?"

"Yourself." The Utasoo boy tried to sound firm. "Princess."

A leer spread across the face of Lofri's man. Nohra would have knocked out his teeth, but she needed Bataar to trust her, to think she'd learned her lesson and would behave.

She had to lose her guards so she could visit Aalya. And she needed to meet Safiya and Cali at the wharf, to plan their revenge. It almost made Nohra regret starting the fight in the courtyard. But in the moment, nothing could have eased her grief more than that taste of revenge. Nothing could have been sweeter than her brother's blood on her teeth.

"Don't worry," Oktai told her, "we'll keep watch. Bataar—His Eminence—would be angry if anything happened to you."

She stalked past them, throwing cautious glances over her shoulder, and stripped out of her clothes in the most shadowed corner of the room. To Grandmother Himma's chagrin, Nohra didn't teeter around on sandalwood slippers. She was used to getting her feet wet, and if Lofri's man grew bold, she could use the slippery tile to her advantage and crack his head open. The thought was comforting.

Covering herself with a towel, she climbed the steps and then descended into the warm pool. Minerals in the bathwater stung her thigh, where Qaira's poultice had dried and was now flaking off around the ugly stitches. The water unwound the knots in her joints, but the bundle of nerves in her head wouldn't untangle.

The last time she'd bathed here, before she left for the Hill, Darya had scrubbed Nohra's back with a crocheted cloth as the two sat submerged to their waists in the steaming, soapy water. Dripping candles in lamps had cast a golden glow over the faces of bathers and illuminated the mosaic at the bottom of the pool: the royal crest, a winged horse rearing. Now, alone in the dark, Nohra's eyes strained to make out the image.

Naji family wealth had been used to tap into the mountain hot springs, so the pegasus was entangled with the coiling bodies of their sigil's two seahorses. Nohra absently traced one curling, serpentine tail with the tip of her toe. The rest of the room was still, the shadows unrumpled.

"Is it alright if I join you?" said a silhouette backlit by the far door.

Nohra jumped, scrambling away from the edge of the pool, clutching her sopping towel tight around her. Large hazel eyes blinked at her as Qaira took a few steps closer and knelt, the tips of her red hair skimming the edge of the water. Nohra hadn't seen her hair down before, free from its elaborate braids, hats, and ornaments.

"I'm sorry for disturbing you," Qaira said, her smile conveying how perfectly at ease she was. "You looked so peaceful."

She wore a silk robe that was coming open at the chest. A delicate chain dipped over her collarbones, pouring down. The cleric's necklace Nohra had given her? Nohra kept her gaze firmly on Qaira's round face, willing herself not to look lower. It would be rude, even if she was curious.

"I can't say I thought this was a good hour for a bath." Qaira spoke like they were friends, talking with her hands. "But I sent one of my girls for water, and Oktai told her you were alone."

Nohra gripped her towel tighter. "Well, I'm fine. You should leave." Her voice came out low and raw.

Qaira looked at Nohra in disbelief. She answered, in a clipped, measured tone, "Of course," politely bobbed her head, and turned to leave. "I won't bother you."

The steaming water was usually full of laughter and light, so many smiles and relieved sighs and stretching arms, the smell of herbal salts and oils. The baths were normally alive with whispered gossip, mothers groaning that their daughters had gotten too fat or too skinny. Without all that, in the dark, imagining Lofri's guardsman ogling, Nohra was—*no*. She wasn't afraid. This feeling was something else.

Inexplicably, she reached out. "Wait—!"

Qaira turned. After the battle on the Hill, she'd put her faith in Nohra, entrusting her with her own safety. On the ride to the capital, Nohra had watched Qaira's back. Would it be so bad if Nohra asked Qaira to wash hers?

"You can join me," she blurted, holding herself still as death. "If you'd like." Why hadn't Bataar's wife just sent a servant? That would have been easier.

Qaira wiggled her fingers. "Help me in? I'm afraid I'll slip."

Nohra obligingly eased her into the bath. The silk robe spilled open, falling off Qaira's shoulders. It splayed around her on the surface of the water, tickling Nohra's elbows.

"Sorry," Qaira muttered, pulling the edges closed.

Nohra quickly looked away. "It's alright." But she couldn't unsee the soft curves and silvery stretch marks that seemed to glow in the dark. Qaira was entrancing. A woman like her had to be, for a king to always want her by his side.

"Then"—Qaira shrugged out of the dressing gown—"let me help you out of that. Women in Dumakra bathe without their clothes, right? Bataar said it's just the men who wear towels in the public baths."

Gentle fingers loosed the wet fabric and laid it out on the edge of the pool. Qaira leaned close, reaching around Nohra and pulling her braid down before combing through the brown hair with her fingers. Her touch tingled. She smelled like flowers, ones Nohra didn't know the names of. Nohra herself reeked of salt and iron, sweat and blood. Qaira's thumb brushed tenderly against Nohra's jaw.

She jolted and waded back, eyes wide. "What are you doing?" Qaira was close enough to slit her throat if she'd been armed. She'd stupidly let her guard down.

"You had something on your cheek. Here." Qaira tilted her head. Her touch seared Nohra's skin, her trailing fingernails like the tips of knives, pressing more gently than a blade ever had at Nohra's throat.

"You know..." There was the hint of something Nohra couldn't identify in her voice. Qaira lathered a washcloth. "I'd like us to be close. We might be sisters soon."

Her tenderness dissolved in the hot water. She didn't owe the warlord or his wife anything; not kindness, not favors. "Because of Aalya?" she spat venomously.

The doctors said Aalya was recovering quickly, but she might never walk again. Nohra knew they were wrong, even if she hadn't been allowed to see Aalya yet. Bataar's invasion had taken so much, but not her life. With Safiya and Nohra helping her, she'd walk and fight again.

Qaira's words reminded her that Aalya's life, like all of theirs, belonged to Bataar.

"She's getting stronger," Qaira mused, seemingly oblivious to Nohra's brewing anger. "I've been visiting. Her body's fighting the infection, but her speech is still slurred, and she's confused. She's so young. I wish there was some other path for her."

At that, knives twisted again in Nohra's gut. "You just don't want her in your husband's bed." Perhaps Qaira could be an ally in her anger. Surely she'd harbor resentment toward her husband for taking a younger wife. Qaira was stunning, but

Aalya would be a new toy. "I doubt you enjoy the thought of Bataar sleeping with someone else, keeping so many wives."

Dark amusement hid in Qaira's smile. "A man doesn't need a wedding to do that."

Nohra burned at her tone. Men could treat their wives like they were less than people, things to be owned and bedded and replaced by a new one or a courtesan. That was Aalya's future. It might have been better if she hadn't woken up. How could Qaira be alright with a life like that?

How could Nohra have resigned herself to the same thing?

"But if a woman's unfaithful, it'll be her head," Nohra seethed in a low voice.

Qaira reclined back, regarding her with half-lidded eyes. "Can't a queen in Dumakra take a consort?"

She moved closer, using the crocheted cloth to rub soap against Nohra's shoulders, her collarbones, down to her chest. Goosebumps prickled on Nohra's skin. Fire coiled in her stomach and slithered low.

"Why do your guards and servants take infertility tonics, if women aren't expected to have those kinds of desires?" Qaira asked, seemingly oblivious to Nohra's discomfort.

"Bataar would let you take a consort?" Nohra squeaked. Her face was hotter than the water.

Qaira smiled. "Why would he object to what brings me pleasure?"

Nohra numbly let herself be pulled to the shallower end of the bath where they sat, waist-deep. The cool air against her breasts made her whole body stiffen. Qaira's hazel eyes flashed down, then back up, a cursory look so fast Nohra might have imagined it.

Nohra reminded herself to breathe.

What was she saying? Did Qaira patronize pleasure houses

looking for pretty, perfumed men? Did she seek rough suitors among the ranks of Bataar's soldiers?

Or among his wives...

Qaira's lips parted, her fingers splayed on Nohra's thigh. "*Hm.*" She cast her gaze down, into the rippling surface of the bath.

She was so close. If Qaira had any weapon, even a hairpin sharpened to a needle point, Nohra would be done for. She could cut open her jugular and bleed Nohra out in the bathwater.

Her throat ached like she'd already done it. Nohra's mind was unraveling, lightheaded from imaginary blood loss. Women like Qaira didn't have to draw blades when they wielded soft touches and honeyed words like steel.

"No." Qaira tutted. "This isn't good enough. I can't tell. Can you sit on the edge?" Seriousness whetted her features. "I'd like to take a closer look at your leg. I heard you sent the palace physicians away yesterday."

"It's healing fine," Nohra said quickly. And she prayed every day for it to heal faster. "Your poultice was good."

Qaira blinked up at her through dark eyelashes, her gentle rasp becoming a purr. "If it's healing well, then you won't have a problem with me examining it, will you?"

Rising to the bait, Nohra stuck out her chin and pulled herself out of the water. "I don't." She sat on the edge of the bath as Qaira gently rubbed off the flaking poultice and inspected the arrow wound. Her fingers were firm, pressing into the meat of Nohra's thigh like the flesh was wet clay. Nohra let herself melt into that unyielding touch, let herself be pinned to the edge of the bath as if Qaira's hand was a spear.

She bit her tongue trying not to think about how close their naked bodies were. If she'd been embarrassed in the pavilion at the Hill, now she was mortified. Qaira had at least some cover in the water. Nohra drew her legs tight and focused intently on the swirl of Qaira's hair.

Qaira whispered something in another language, possibly Choyanreni. "I wish I had some light, to see you better," she muttered, when she noticed Nohra staring at the top of her head. She grinned, flashing teeth, and Nohra's skin prickled at the suggestion. But Qaira was somber again. "There's some pus, and I'd like to know the color of it. The Xincho doctors taught me the importance of that. These stitches can be pulled, but your skin's feverish. That's worrying."

"I'm fine. It's… from the hot water."

"You use this leg, I assume. I'd like it very much if you could keep it." Qaira's fingertips pressed down hard, and Nohra winced. Qaira smiled sheepishly. Her grip softened, spreading as she absently rubbed gentle, widening circles. Her touch was maddening. "You should go with your escorts to the infirmary tomorrow, let one of your physicians take a look, if you'd be comfortable with that. It is such an intimate place."

Nohra dropped back into the bath, splashing them both, thankful her legs didn't buckle embarrassingly. "If I agree, will you stop prodding me?" It was good to be back in the warm, lapping bath, less exposed.

Qaira laughed. "Maybe. Lean back. Let me wash your hair."

"You shouldn't." Nohra shook her head. "You're not a servant." But at Qaira's insistent touch, she obediently lay back. Gentle hands worked over her scalp, lathering the soap. Nohra unthinkingly leaned into that touch, relaxing under Qaira's commanding fingers.

"Wash my hair in return," Qaira said, humming while she combed through to the tips, teasing out the knotted tangles. "We'll be each other's servants tonight."

That was a dangerous, strangely thrilling proposal. The

world became goat's milk and honey. This wasn't like Darya deftly washing her. This touch was snowmelt and hot wax. Nohra wanted to fall asleep, to keep Qaira's hands in her hair forever. Nothing had ever been so private in a family as large as hers; no secret moments, no darkened rooms. Seconds existing for no one else's eyes, in the shadows of after-midnight. Nohra almost let out a soft moan—

"Your hair's so long," Qaira murmured. "When was the last time you cut it?"

"When I swore my vows. My mother was buried the next day." Her braid had gone to the crypts with Thora, coiled around her wrists like bracelets or handfasting ribbons.

"The color is pretty, but I think silver would suit you, one day."

Nohra wasn't sure if she'd live to see her hair lighten to silver-white. She'd always been the girl with a broken bone to set or a cut to stitch shut. Once, she'd fallen from a pegasus and knocked out half her baby teeth. Another time she'd had so many sprains, she'd been in bed for a month.

Qaira looked like a woman who would live to meet her grandchildren. Her hair would turn steel-gray, and her face would line gracefully as her body shrank and sagged. She'd be like Nohra's grandmother, who still possessed the beauty that had captivated the old zultam.

"What's that, on your belly?"

"When I was fourteen, I was stabbed by an assassin in a sanctium."

"And this scar? What's it from?" Her fingertips skimmed up Nohra's ribs, to the juncture of her shoulder.

No prodding, Nohra wanted to protest.

"My aunt shot me with a crossbow. Same day, same sanctium." A pause. "It was an accident."

"You're braver than I am. I'd never go back to a sanctium." Qaira pulled away, her face no longer hovering over Nohra's. "Should I call in my handmaiden to help us dress?"

Her fingers trailed over Nohra's shoulder, down the length of her outstretched arm. If she wasn't so hesitant, Nohra could interlock their fingers, and *then what*?

Qaira climbed out. Nohra was suddenly untethered without her touch. She didn't bother hiding her stare. Even in the darkness, every droplet of water was visible. They dripped down the silhouette of Qaira's breasts, running over her stomach and hips before disappearing down her legs. It would have made leering men gape.

"You—your handmaidens have been here this whole time?" Nohra stammered.

"Waiting outside with Oktai and the minister's man."

"You, but you said—I was going to wash your hair."

She laughed. "Next time?"

"I can dress myself," Nohra said stiffly, turning away to dry off and wiggle into a nightdress and pants. The linen shift clung to the moisture on her skin, and though she twisted her hair up in a thin towel, water still dripped down her neck.

Don't turn your back for long. Nohra spun around, conditioned to expect a knife at her throat. There was no blade, just Qaira, unassuming and smiling and oh, so coy.

Unthinkingly, Nohra reached out, straightening Qaira's damned robe and belting it tighter to preserve some sense of modesty. Qaira's eyes widened before she quickly turned foxish.

"I heard your talmaid isn't allowed in your quarters right now. Do you need a bedmate?"

"No!" Nohra replied, too quickly.

Qaira's smile fell, her face becoming shrouded. "Oh. Otherwise I would have asked one of my ladies to stay with you tonight. Maran's a very good girl. She never snores, and doesn't toss. But the nights aren't so cold in Kalafar. I wouldn't want you to work up a sweat when you just got clean."

"I rarely get any sleep anyway." Recently, the nightmares came unbidden.

Qaira's fingers brushed the dark circles under Nohra's eyes. "That explains these."

That touch was too intimate, like her mother smoothing those same shadows. Nohra balked, lost for a moment in Qaira's brackish green stare.

Finally, she pulled back and mumbled, "Who taught you Dumakran?"

The smile was back and bright as stars. "One of the language instructors from Xincho, if you'd believe it. Is my pronunciation poor? I don't pick up tongues like Bataar. Our languages are cousins, so it was just a few new words, really."

"No, it's good."

Qaira's brows knitted. "Did your mother teach you her language?"

Nohra stiffened. "Only a few words of songs. Father made all the musicians visiting court play ballads for her, chivalric romances between knights and maidens." Bitterness roiled in Nohra's gut, blotting out any embers of arousal. Her brother Rami had never known their mother, and now he'd lost their father too. He would never love those melodies like Nohra had. His entire childhood would be marked by war. Bataar's war.

The pink tip of Qaira's tongue flicked out. "I'd like to hear one, someday, if you were the one singing for me."

Nohra swallowed what felt like a fat slug creeping up her

161

throat and said nothing. Sealing her lips to keep from blurting out something she might regret.

Walking with Qaira was preferable to being dragged or jabbed forward with the butt of a weapon. As they crossed quiet corridors, Qaira whispered stories about her two children, mostly her daughter, Ganni, who was apparently a menace whenever she wasn't as shy as a sanctium mouse.

"We're always finding toads and tadpoles where they shouldn't be. Tarken should have checked before he drank from that cup."

Beside them, Oktai tried to keep a serious expression, but the corner of his mouth twitched a little.

"He must have swallowed five before he realized," Qaira continued.

It was endearing how Qaira's face scrunched up when she laughed, before she was halfway through a story. With her, Nohra didn't have to pretend to smile. It all came dangerously easily.

"They arrived safely in the city?" Nohra asked.

"Yes. And they're getting along well with the little princesses, who've been borrowing Bato to dress up in their doll's clothes. Ganni's taken with the pegasuses. But I'm terrified to let her try to ride."

"She's... eight? That's plenty old enough to learn. If Fahaad isn't at the stables, send for me, and I could teach you both."

What in hells was she saying?

"You would?" Qaira smirked. "Can a pegasus saddle seat two?"

Nohra started to reply as her guards opened the door to her quarters. But it had already slammed shut behind her. Qaira was gone, leaving Nohra blinking in her wake.

Qaira said something, her voice muffled. It sounded like she was scolding Oktai. Nohra discerned his sheepish defense. He used a different word for door, but Nohra had heard it yelled at the boy often enough to have learned it quick.

The sounds beyond her room faded. Nohra wrung out her hair and climbed into bed. She stared into the dusk, feeling a flurry of emotions.

She buried her face in the pillow that still smelled like salty tears. She couldn't become Qaira's friend, even if her laugh made traitorous warmth bloom in Nohra's chest. Even if she hadn't felt a touch that gentle since her mother died. If she was going to crush Bataar, Nohra couldn't be afraid of hurting his wife or his children. She didn't need misplaced sympathy or any other feelings clouding her resolve.

Bataar was the open-handed slap across her face, hard enough to crack teeth. Qaira was the gentle caress, meant to ease and soothe the hurt. They were working in tandem to break her will.

She couldn't want Qaira's affection, her company, her touch.

The linens were suddenly stranglingly tight and hotter than the sun. She stripped them off the bed, barely resisting the urge to tear off all her clothes and rip out her hair. Her heart still raced and heat still pooled and her mind still traced crescent-moon curves in the dark.

Stupid fool. Nohra intoned verses from the Godsbreath in her head to distract herself. The words rolled off her tongue and flooded her ears. The price of vengeance, the cost of war, the value of duty.

Starting tomorrow, Nohra would earn Bataar's trust with good behavior and visit Aalya. She'd finally meet Saf and Calidah at the wharf. Together, they would figure out a way to take back Dumakra. It didn't matter if she had to cut down everyone Bataar loved to do it.

11

Reaping what the Goddess Sows.
— Shaam house motto

In the palace kitchens, servants hauling iron cook pots out of storage pushed around Bataar. Men grunted as they pried open and unloaded fealty presents: fruits and nuts from the farmers along the Scythe; honey in glass jugs from the apiarists in Antiria; ice cream from Mineva packed between slabs of mountain ice; and seafood from Marafal so fresh that tentacles still wriggled in the salt-crusted crates.

Everyone worked methodically, emptying and dissembling barrels and boxes, flowing and breaking around Bataar as if he were an expected fixture in the kitchens.

Girls spread syrup over the long sheet of apricot cake as a man candied dates and figs on a stove. Across the room, a group of women with muscled arms upturned steaming pots of stuffed grape leaves onto long platters, and boys plastered flatbread dough to the sides of urn-shaped clay ovens and retrieved the cooked bread with long iron hooks. One servant carefully picked the juiciest mussels out of a box and trundled off with a cask of wine and a bowl of lemons for a stew.

Bataar searched the kitchens, looking for the faces he'd recognize from the courtyard the night they took the castle. Hands that had worn the blood of Shaza's soldiers were also decorated with burn marks and calluses from the ovens and knives.

"Is everything to your liking?" asked a woman standing on an empty crate. Wood creaked as she stepped down.

Bataar blinked, surprised to see Nohra's talmaid Darya. "Why aren't you with the princess? She's supposed to have all her servants back." For their recent good behavior, he had allowed Safiya and Nohra to move freely within the Rutiaba Palace, but he still had eyes on them.

Darya started, "Since the invasion—"

The girl carrying the shellfish and wooden bowl jerked, her shoulders stiffening as black shells clattered across the tiled floor.

She apologized profusely, even as Darya reassured her in that toneless voice of hers that no harm had been done. They both knelt to pick up the mussels and lemons. When their fingers brushed, the girl jerked back. The tight knot between her shoulders didn't ease, even after she'd been told a dozen times it was alright.

Bataar glanced around. "Where's the head of the palace kitchens?"

Eggplants boiled down with herbs in pots hung above the stoves as salads were ladled into tureens to be served with heaps of bread and bowls of hummus and peppery red muhammara. All this was something Qaira would usually oversee.

"Cut down that night, Your Eminence," Darya murmured, straightening up.

"You…" He cleared his throat. "You must have been terrified. All that blood." He'd offered a reward for answers, but so far no one had come forward. Bataar couldn't blame them for protecting one another.

"I was frightened, but not for myself." Her unnerving black eyes watched him, unblinking. "I hope it won't happen again."

"It won't. I've been meaning to return this to you." Bataar unfastened the leather sheath on his belt and held it out.

In Dumakra, all the palace girls carried weapons. Qaira said he should allow that tradition to continue in Kalafar. What had transpired in that courtyard was almost inhuman, but things had been quiet, and he couldn't afford to appear frightened of servant girls like this pudgy-armed maid who wasn't tall enough to look him in the eyes without craning her head up. He couldn't truly fault the palace staff for their ferocity, for fighting to live then and continuing to live now, as if none of their friends had been killed.

"It's a fine knife your princess gave you."

It looked awkward in her hand, as if she didn't know quite how to hold it. She blinked down at the dagger for a few seconds before finally threading it through the waistband of her skirt.

Bataar remembered the flecks of flesh splattered on the columns. These girls had slaughtered their men like pigs. He shook his head. If anyone else was hurt, he'd re-confiscate all the weapons and punish perpetrators without holding back.

The tile on the kitchen walls and floors clouded over from the steam rising off the simmering pots and smoking meat. A bead of sweat ran down his face. He grunted and nodded. "I'll leave you to it then, Daheer."

❦

That night, servants carrying trays of food and handwashing bowls poured inside the zultam's suite alongside viziers and their families. Clothing sparkled as silk caught the light, embroidery and beadwork glittering. Bataar stood stiffly in the center of the entertaining quarters, bobbing his head in greeting to the advisors. This was the foyer where the zultam broke his fast in solitude guarded by his armored daughters, where he'd entertained only his most important guests.

Heavy drapes were drawn over the windows, making the fringes of the room darker and even more constraining. Guests gasped at fire-eaters swallowing lit torches and contortionists firing bows with their feet. The beat of goblet-shaped drums and tambourines swelled. It had been almost a month since they took Kalafar. Bataar wanted to smile and laugh and drink himself into a stupor, but he couldn't relax entirely.

He crossed his arms, uncrossed them, picked at a loose blue thread on the hem of his tunic, and tried to stretch his toes in his too-tight silk boots. Beside him, Nassar's head craned forward, his long, sticky eyelashes framing bright eyes. Ervan Lofri took a drag from his pipe. A few women wrinkled their noses at the smell, at once bitter and cloyingly sweet.

"I wanted your wives to be here," Lofri said, "so the performers could dance for their fertility." He smiled wryly. "May these women just dance for your pleasure, then, eh, friend?"

"To *our* pleasure!" Nassar corrected, laughing loudly, pupils blown wide.

Lofri had demanded this victory party, a feast to celebrate ushering in a new era, and Bataar was stuck hosting it.

A musician played a few ghostly notes on a flute. At that cue, women wearing modest dresses stood and began dancing for the seated guests. Gold virtues sewn onto their long skirts jangled as their hips shimmied and their arms wound through the air. Some guests let out scandalized gasps. Dances with female performers were normally reserved for all-women audiences, but Lofri liked spitting on tradition.

"You look well," Bataar commented, nodding at Kasira, Lofri's daughter. "Did you arrive today? I'm pleased you made the trip. Are your quarters to your liking?"

"I did, and they are," the young woman squeaked, her cheeks coloring. "Your Eminence."

Her skin looked less sallow, and her hair was braided in a way that made her face fuller. A thin rim of kohl sharpened her dewy eyes.

Nassar looked between his betrothed and Bataar and snorted. Jawaad, Lofri's son, stared forward, his gaze trained on the dancers. His blockish shoulders obscured the performance from the row of guests seated behind him. A man of few words, he said nothing, as usual.

"Where *are* your wives, Your Eminence?" Kasira asked. "I'd hoped for their company."

Ruo was in Choyanren, so who were these "*wives*"?

"The princess Aalya is no one's wife yet." Nassar's young sister couldn't walk or say more than a few words at a time, or remember her name, or eat without someone holding a pearled spoon for her and reminding her when to swallow. "Though she's improving faster than anticipated."

Nassar nodded along to the music. "I told you my sister was strong. You doubted me, but I knew. Mark my words. She'll be weddable in no time."

"And your Utasoo wife?" Lofri added.

"The Dumakran water doesn't agree with her. She's had loose stool for days. She can hardly keep bread and yogurt down." Actually, Qaira had just wanted to spend time with the children, now that they were in the city. She begged him to make a good excuse.

Lofri and Nassar made faces. The minister's daughter turned a mortified shade of red. Bataar had spoken like he would in a war tent. Sometimes he forgot how touchy people could be when you took away the blood rage and scrubbed away the grime. He looked pointedly at the prince. "Where's your, uh, companion—?"

"Abayae? I didn't know you'd grown so attached to my monkey." Nassar let out a bubbling laugh. "He's an endearing little thing, isn't he?"

"It's an interesting choice of pet," Bataar muttered. He'd gotten used to listening for the monkey's screeching as an early alarm for Nassar creeping up.

The servants worked diligently. Flaky date pastries, pistachios, apricots, and sweet oranges were speedily replenished whenever a tray was picked over. Bataar kept reaching for cubes of jelly flavored like roses and pomegranates. The sweets were covered in powdery sugar that stuck to the roof of his mouth. It was damned good.

Nassar wore a wolfish grin. The prince's face was still discolored by fading bruises, his nose set with a plaster. "Say, is your woman over there married? Your soldier."

"She isn't." Bataar followed the prince's line of sight, knowing Shaza was the object of his interest. Kasira ducked her head, hiding behind her hair. Bataar couldn't tell if her tiny sigh was one of relief or resignation.

"Would it offend you if I approached her?"

"You have good taste, my boy," Lofri said, chest shaking with laughter.

As valuable as Nassar's marriage into Lofri's family was, the minister never betrayed any hint of offense at the prince's games. Already, he was more of a son to Lofri than his own children. The straight line of Jawaad's mouth barely cracked at Nassar playing in the face of his sister.

Bataar considered them all. "It wouldn't offend me... but let me warn you, I held your sisters off, but I won't restrain Shaza if she's offended by your advances."

The prince's turban pin, won in their hunt, dangled from Bataar's hat, casting a spray of light. Nassar would lose more jewels if he tried touching Shaza.

Nassar's crowned tooth glittered. "Does she not like men?"

Kasira, flushing, busied herself by cleaning her hands a second time. Jawaad's scowl deepened, but he didn't grunt a word.

"She likes men well enough." Bataar sniffed the steam rising off his cup of coffee. "She just doesn't like men like you." The dark, swirling liquid was nutty and rich, strong enough to almost mask Nassar's cologne and the smell from Lofri's pipe. "*Princes*, she doesn't like princes," he added before Nassar could bristle. He lifted the copper coffee pot and served Kasira himself. "Sugar?"

"I don't like it so sweet," she squeaked.

The prince waved a hand. "Perhaps I should set my sights on one of the dancers. Or an acrobat."

Bataar's eyes fell on orange yolks glistening in bread boats full of melted cheese. "Truly an important conquest. I couldn't imagine a purpose you could better apply yourself to this evening." He wiped his hands clean on the napkin slung over his shoulder.

Across the room, Tarken drunkenly swayed in time with the drums. Bataar could practically smell the alcohol on his breath, layering the usual scent of cinnamon. Shaza smacked the back of their friend's head when he fell on someone else's shoulder.

"Watch it, woman," Tarken barked, slurring his words.

"You shouldn't have shaved the beard," Shaza grumbled. "You look like a girl now."

"Shove off. You like my face."

He pushed her, and she kicked his legs out from under him, and they both fell in a tangle of limbs. One of the officers under Shaza's command whistled. Two dancers giggled, pulling Tarken off Shaza and leading him up to the front of the room. A brown-haired girl rolled her hips, gesturing for Tarken to copy her. He did, laughing. His cheeks were flushed from the liquor; Shaza's face was red with fury that softened quickly in amusement. The idiot was only looking at her.

Nassar remarked, "Your friend is enjoying making a spectacle of himself."

"He always does."

Bataar craned his neck. Toward the back of the room, the Dowager Queen Merv sat in terse silence beside the queen mother. A servant read shapes in the coffee grounds at the bottom of Merv's filigreed cup. From the razor glare the old woman was leveling at her, it would appear Nassar's mother had a dagger in the back in her future.

Before she'd been escorted from her quarters, Bataar had Queen Mother Himma frisked for weapons. Her small pout did nothing to disguise her contempt for the room.

"We need to discuss something," Lofri said, drawing Bataar back. His smile didn't touch his eyes. "My son, when will he be elevated to his new position?"

Bataar worked his stiff jaw. "When Naji resigns in two years, I'll instate Jawaad as grand vizier. In the meantime, keep your son at court. He and Nassar should stay close to Naji and learn from him."

Lofri's smile dropped. His wrinkled fingers trembled on a spoon carved from boxwood. "Yardaan Naji has made it clear he doesn't want my son around him."

"Really? That surprises me." Actually, the grand vizier hadn't hidden his disapproval of Ervan Lofri at all.

"His daughters are unwed and unspoken for, but when I proposed a match to my son, he said he wants to betroth his eldest girl to Prince Rami." Lofri punctuated each word with a spray of spit. "The boy's less than eleven years old."

Bataar looked at Jawaad, who couldn't be younger than twenty-four. "Isn't Naji's daughter thirteen?"

"And she'll be sixteen when her husband's only thirteen! She'll need a man to father her children, not a boy."

Bataar didn't have to review Dumakran law to know what Lofri was saying was dubious.

"The hells does he want his daughter married to Thora's son for?" Nassar sniffed, taking a fistful of shelled nuts and stuffing them into his mouth. "Did someone tell Naji that Rami's not the crown prince anymore? Who would even arrange the match? My *sister*?"

"The boy's my ward now," Bataar spoke with finality. "I made the match."

Rami wasn't the crown prince, but neither was Nassar. Not yet, despite Lofri's badgering. Nassar was even more deluded drunk than sober.

Lofri took a long drag from his pipe. "Have you decided on a face for the gold virtues? There's talk you're considering putting Prince Rami on the coin. Silly rumors, I'm sure. Ramzi's choice of heir isn't something you'd want to honor. Nassar would be far more suitable as king in Kalafar. Or Your Eminence, undoubtedly."

"I haven't given it much thought. Perhaps Princess Aalya, if she'd want that."

He balked. "A woman has never—not even Queen Roksanya, may her heart rest—"

"I wanted to speak with you regarding the curfew," a vizier with a dark beard cut in.

Lofri stood and ordered, "Bring in more tables. Start the dinner."

Bataar nodded to the counselor who'd spoken up. "I'll hear you out."

"It's damnably difficult to impose a curfew when so many people are on the street now after the fires. Families are camping at the wharf, building cookfires from broken crates, interrupting commerce at the fish market."

"But the riots!" another man interjected.

More petitioners appeared in front of Bataar, arms outstretched like they wanted to place pleading hands on him.

"*Your Resplendentness*, a merchant boat expected today hasn't arrived up the river from Marafal. Can you do something about that?" asked a third vizier.

"One of my men, Tamyr Ali," another vizier interrupted, "my emissary in Halamut, reports half the town was wiped out in an attack."

That caught his attention. Halamut was one of the villages down the Scythe. "Who attacked?"

"Goddess-damned gryphons. Killed Diaco Shaam's youngest daughter and the pegasus she was riding in the courtyard outside their manor. Snapped her and the horse right in half."

Bataar's stomach turned over. "Diaco Shaam. His father is the Minister of Agriculture, isn't he? What does he need? I'll send battalions to help evacuate the town." He'd declare war with the beasts if he had to.

This was like Zeffa all over again. At least those gryphons had moved on quickly. What in Preeminence was driving them into these smaller cities? And how long would it be before they descended on Kalafar?

"There's nothing left of Halamut. The gryphons have all flown off. The survivors are in Ditria and Marafal. The port towns can't support this many refugees, and leagues of farmland have been abandoned." The man started to shake. "Olive orchards, apricot groves—"

"Quite the feast," Lofri said, nodding his head and smiling at the table.

The golden lantern light was growing disorienting. Bataar blinked, shook his head. "Bring this matter before me tomorrow in the audience hall."

The vizier nodded, his mouth a grim line.

Servants pulled back the rest of the covered lids on the platters, but Bataar had lost his appetite. Over the mountains of yellow saffron rice, pyramids of flat metal sticks were stacked tall, stuffed through chunks of chicken marinated in yogurt and handfuls of grilled lamb mince. Less than half the room observed the Dumakran faith's diet.

"Magnificent," someone said appreciatively.

Empress Ruo's chefs from Choyanren had prepared cuts of lamb in a gingery sauce. The plates full of dumplings and hand pies filled with meats and cheeses smelled like home, like growing up in the shadow of the mountain. All day, whole goats had rotated on spits erected in the courtyards, marinades blackening on burnt flesh. Now gaping eye holes stared.

"A most impressive display, rhah," a minister decreed, tipping his glass.

Bataar nodded, smiled. All eyes were on him. He looked to the person who tested his food. Minutes passed, and the young man nodded his assent. "Believe it's safe, Your Eminence."

Everything was generously garnished with parsley or cilantro and swirls of olive oil, pinches of sumac, or a bright dusting of paprika. Bataar took his first bite, relishing the flavors of cinnamon, cumin, and coriander. The low tables were full of glasses of tart yogurt drinks, mint lemonade, cinnamon milk, jasmine tea, and pomace brandy.

He blinked. A shout, a crash, and ayran spilled across the table in a frothy white river. Drunken laughs answered as servants rushed to mop up the spilled yogurt and pluck up shards of glass.

Bataar caught a girl by the arm. "Could you please tell Darya Daheer to—"

"She's not in the kitchens, Your Eminence. She stepped out after we made the desserts, summoned to the Princess Nohra's quarters for supper with her."

"Yes, of course," he said. Princess Safiya wasn't in the room either, or Calidah. Enough of the harem was there that it didn't matter. This was Lofri's spectacle, not the Harpies'.

Lofri's meek daughter Kasira stole a hit off his pipe while her father was distracted. She slumped, sighing.

"This is straight out of Mineva, isn't it?" Nassar hummed. "Tastes like mountain snow."

Scoops of ice cream sat unmelting in copper bowls, topped with chopped pistachio and drizzles of honey. In others, sugared raspberries had been mixed into cherry ice cream. The red syrup dripping onto his finger reminded Bataar of blood seeping out of a puncture wound. Even as that thought flipped his gut, he licked his fingertip.

It was sweet, piney and resinous. Chewy from the mastic.

Men in robed gowns replaced the dancers. They moved in a flurry of color, winding around each other in steps so small, it was as if they floated. Time seemed to spin with the whirling performers. Sounds in the room grew and ebbed.

The indulgent feast turned over in Bataar's stomach as the tempo yawned, stretching low and morose into a historical ballad. A hush fell over the guests, as if the musician were reading funerary rites, and any chatter would be an ill omen.

> *"High on the hill when red tears spilled*
> *Queens fled with coin and kin*
> *Lowborn alone fed on rot and char*
> *Until all that remained were haunted halls*
> *—blood-stained walls, and*
> *Ashes over Anhabar."*

Just as the last performance was beginning, the city bells began to ring.

"What in hells?" a minister muttered.

A wave of concern washed through the zultam's entertaining quarters. Oktai rushed in, interrupting the panicking party. "Your Eminence? There's a disturbance in the city."

Bataar made to stand, but Lofri put out a hand.

"Leave it for the Kalafar guard," he said. "Wael Bahdi's a capable captain. I picked him myself. His father was the head of my personal guard for thirty years." He shrugged like he'd settled it. "Some misunderstanding about the curfew shouldn't concern you, rhah."

"*Your Eminence,*" Oktai repeated. He looked away, back to Bataar, then quickly away again.

Bataar winced. "What is it?"

"You said everyone was supposed to stay on palace grounds, but none of the Harpy Knights are here except the princess in the infirmary. Not Princess Safiya, or Calidah. I even checked the palace sanctium for Princess Nohra."

"I would have thought she'd give up the zealot act when her mother died," Nassar snarked with an offhand wave. "All the prayers in Kalafar didn't save that northern whore."

Bataar ignored the prince. Cold dread settled in the pit of his stomach. They couldn't be caught up in a riot in the city, could they? He'd loosened their leash. He would have permitted them to leave the palace before curfew—but that would have meant telling him where they were going.

"Rhah," Lofri said around a mouthful of food. "I'll send some men to find them. Calidah's probably holed up in the library, and Princess Safiya is"—he lowered his voice—"likely with one of her women. Princess Nohra spends more time at the stables than she does in her own rooms. She's obsessed with pegasuses." He made a flippant gesture. "If she isn't there, she's embroidering."

"Embroidering?" Bataar blurted. "Nohra?"

"Her stitchwork is beautiful," Kasira whispered. "She has great patience for it, and decorated the loveliest dress, which her mother wore when they entombed her body."

"Her mother was my father's second wife, rhah," Nassar cut in drunkenly. "Mine was his first wife. The order is important."

Bataar clenched his fists. "I don't have a tit to give about all this right now."

Lofri sighed. "If I had to bet my life, I'd say they're out riding, so—"

"Prepare the horses. Shaza, can you ride?"

Shaza nodded. "My bow."

Her footman rushed to fulfill her order. Standing, she pushed Tarken's head off her lap. He protested tiredly, reaching out for her, his cheek smooshed against the marble floor.

In a low voice, Lofri hissed, "If they're conspiring, stamp it out in the morning when they're back. Lock them in their rooms and throw away the keys. Send them far away. Put them to the sword, if you feel it's right. If, for Goddess knows what reason, you're worried about them, know this: in a fight, they won't need you to save them—"

"*That's enough.*" Bataar put enough venom into his voice that the minister flinched. "Oktai, have ten men meet us at the palace gates."

"And me too?" He looked too hopeful, too excited, bushy and wide-eyed. That immediately made Bataar want to leave him behind, safe at the palace. But Oktai had been watching Nohra closely.

"Do you think you have an idea where they might have gone?"

The boy nodded, sheepish. "They've talked about the wharf, but I didn't figure it was important."

Bataar choked back a frustrated groan. "What's happening in town?" If there was time, he could change into riding clothes and boots. He frowned, touching the hem of his silk tunic.

"People are screaming about a monster."

His head shot up. "A gryphon?"

The boy shook his head. "I think it's something else."

12

Kalafar at night is a city of spectacle. Hagglers argue
prices with merchants at canopied stalls, and exotic
women dance through clouds of sweet-smelling smoke.

— A traveler's account of Dumakra

Fahaad's things were neatly organized in his bedroom loft
above the stables. Nohra sifted through one trunk, looking for
bulky, plain clothes that could disguise her and Darya. She
picked out a purple tunic with knobby silk and gold embroidery on the sleeves, which had been balled up at the bottom.

Nohra tutted. "This was a natal-day present." She took
it out and smoothed it down. It was in Zultama colors, with
stitchwork by the palace dressmaker. She threw it back and
covered it up with the roughspun and undyed linen.

A wedge of light slanted in through a small window, illuminating every dust mote drifting above the worn floors and
battered old trunks. Nohra had less than an hour before her
puppyish guard grew suspicious that she wasn't still in the
baths. For her good behavior, she was permitted to roam the
palace grounds, though her "attendant" was a reminder that

Bataar was constantly watching. Oktai was easy to distract, but she needed him to be completely unsuspecting tonight. She'd find clothes, get Darya from the kitchens, and sneak them both out while everyone was distracted with Lofri's party.

"Paga's ass!" Fahaad swore. "What are you doing in here?"

Nohra turned, looking him over. "Oh, that would work well."

"*What?*" His lip curled. "I haven't seen you in weeks, except when we pass in the hall and you're being hauled off by guards, and now you're kneeling on the floor in my room?"

"Take off your clothes, Fahaad."

"Excuse me?" His voice cracked.

"I'm not trying to take your virtue. I just need to borrow some clothes."

"My virtue? Just because it wasn't good enough for you, doesn't mean someone else wasn't happy to take it!"

"Can we talk about your unresolved feelings another time?"

"*Tch*, don't flatter yourself."

"Do you have something else I can take for Darya to wear?"

"You're not roping her into this." He stalked over the threshold and snapped open a second trunk.

She gaped. "Holy Hell, you have a lot of clothes. And 'this'? Do you even know what 'this' is?"

"I can tell by that look in your eyes that you're scheming. Darya's been through enough."

Nohra recoiled. "'*Scheming*'!"

He held out a neatly folded tunic and some fraying pants. "Be careful. Traitorous talk can be a game for noble women like you, but for some of us, it's our lives on the line."

Nohra's smile fell. She hadn't even realized she'd been smiling. "Nothing matters more to me than..." She trailed off.

"Than Dumakra? Family?" he prompted, slamming the trunk shut and hauling it onto his back.

"Than family. And you and Darya *are* family." The room looked emptier than she remembered, except for some yellowing manuscripts strewn across the bed like Fahaad had been studying. Bedlinens pulled painfully taut meant Darya had recently straightened his room. The new, fiery smell of her hung in the air too—or perhaps that was the scent of singed wood. Ash smudged the floor as if Fahaad had knocked over a candle. Nohra's eyes narrowed on the lacquered chest. "Where in hells are you going with that?"

"I'm taking it to the Head Eunuch's quarters in the palace. My new rooms are in the same wing as yours. Apparently, Bataar likes my counsel." His brows drew together. "Or he'd like me to advise Nassar. Or Rami. I don't know."

Nohra's chest tightened. "You're giving Bataar advice? He's seeking your counsel?"

He stiffened. "Why does that surprise you? Darya and I had the same tutors you and your sisters did. I took classes at the Conservium. I'm not daft."

"It's not that," she blurted. It stung to realize Bataar had elevated Fahaad, while her father had kept him lowly in the stables. She shielded her hurt with anger. "You're my friend. How could you be comfortable giving him counsel? What's he asking about?"

"Moshitu, history, other things he thinks I'll be knowledge-able about." He sighed. "Almost all of Dumakra is a part of his empire now. It's the new order of things. I've got bigger concerns than answering his questions about pegasuses." Quieter, he added, "Let me know if you need to borrow anything else. I won't need the riding clothes in that extra trunk."

The chasm between them seemed to widen every day. She

cast a look over the strewn parchment on his bed: illuminated pages from the Godsbreath, ones about the chained Demonking and greater djinn. Fahaad hadn't been to a sanctium of his own free will in a decade. Her Goddess wasn't his, and she'd always figured he thought the spirits in Moshitu were folk-fables too.

Fahaad seemed to search her face for something as he watched her shuffle the fragile documents. His eyes deadened, and he turned away without offering any explanation.

"Thank you," Nohra added, before he could disappear.

His reply was tired and punched out. "For what?"

He'd been so gentle with Dar, fragile as she'd been since that night. "For taking care of Darya, and getting the horses back down after the invasion." The attack had sent the pegasuses into a frenzy, battering the stall gates and breaking loose.

"Looking out for Darya isn't some favor I do for you." He frowned, his mouth a line carved in marble. Sometimes, Nohra thought Fahaad had never been in love with her; he just only let himself want what he couldn't have. "And you clearly don't understand those monsters your family hoards. They came down on their own. I just waited and was there to bridle them."

❧

As Nohra pulled Darya through the palace grounds, the sounds of Ervan Lofri's party faded to a distant hum. The night sky was dark and overcast, dotted with stars peeking out behind gray clouds. Large moths flapped around the lantern light, their wings rustling softly. At the end of the walkway, Darya skidded to a stop, fussing with the hood on her cloak.

"Wait!" She pulled her wrist free when Nohra started tugging again. "Slow down. These boots are loose—"

The sound of rustling silk and clumsy footsteps reached

Nohra's ears. She threw a hand over her friend's mouth and dragged her off the paved path into the rose bushes and trees.

"What is it?" Darya's voice was muffled against Nohra's palm. Thorns caught on their cloaks and hair, pinching fabric and scratching needle lines on Nohra's skin.

"Someone's coming," Nohra whispered as two men turned the corner.

The pair of viziers' sons laughed loudly, stumbling, drunk on brandy from the zultam's private stores. One man slumped over and hung limply off the other.

As they'd left the harem wing, Nohra and Darya had passed by some man collapsed in the gardens, his eyes clouded over, unseeing, mouth lolling open. The sour smell of opium hung over him. Everyone was having a good time, it seemed, except them.

When Lofri's guests were out of earshot, Nohra pulled free of the ensnaring thorns, smoothed out her flyaways, and tucked her braid back in. "Alright. Take my hand and try to match my pace until we're clear of the gates."

"We're leaving the palace?" Darya's mouth fell open. "What about the curfew?"

"I'll explain at the wharf. Cali and Saf are already there."

She shook her head. "The wharf? What aren't you saying?"

"There are things we need to talk about that we don't want anyone to overhear," Nohra hissed. "Plans we need to make."

"'Plans'?" Darya's luminous eyes hardened. "You aren't talking about a feast, or anything I'd know about. What help would I be?"

"You hear and see things at the palace that we don't. You aren't watched like us. You can go where we can't. We need someone like you."

"I don't think I'm what you need. Lately, it's been taking all my energy to just *be Darya* and not… something else. I've only just started feeling normal again."

Nohra knew how difficult that first death was. Regret was a swift river that weathered mountains, with an undertow that dragged the guilty down. "I just want you to keep an ear out for us, let us know what you overhear." After tonight, Nohra could protect her from the more dangerous parts of their plotting, shelter her from the war to come. "We may need you to send a letter to your grandmother—"

"Shhh, guards are coming," Darya whispered, taking Nohra's hand and pulling her forward. They stumbled out of the bushes, over the covered walkway, across the lawn. Nohra turned, catching a glimpse of the glow of an oil lamp.

"Bataar has soldiers posted at the main gate," Nohra explained, retaking the lead. "But no one's gotten to that hole Aalya found when she was little, those loose bricks near Roksanya's fountain."

"*That's* how we're getting out?"

Nohra squatted near the wall, prying white blocks free and stacking them behind a tree. "Yes."

"Can we still even fit through that? We're not little girls anymore."

"It'll be a problem if one of us gets stuck." Nohra picked up a long strand of hair that had caught on a brick and examined it. "Cali squeezed through. She hasn't grown in ten years, but I still think we'll make it." Cali's talmaid must have wedged the bricks back into place behind her.

Darya didn't appear convinced, the furrow between her brows refusing to smooth out. "Did Safiya get out this way?"

"Saf snuck out some other way hours ago, before sundown. One of the chambermaids has been covering for her all day with Bataar's guards." Nohra squinted up at the palace wall.

This side was smooth, but there were barbs under the crenelations on the outward-facing length, six yards off the ground. "You go first, and I'll push you, if I have to," she said, dropping low. The ground was wet and soft, spongy against her palms.

Darya squeezed into the hole. They needed to crawl about two yards in the dark, push out the bricks on the outward-facing side, and they'd be through.

"I'm stuck," Darya whispered.

"What, already?" Nohra squeezed forward, shoving her friend. The bricks on the other side scraped. Some clattered down the hill, crumbling like chalk. Nohra and Darya tumbled out, catching themselves on splayed hands before they could hit the city street.

Darya crouched, collecting the broken pieces of stone. Together they awkwardly filled in the Nohra-and-Darya-sized hole in the palace wall. Their effort was passable, in the dark.

Nohra stood and brushed the dirt and dust off. "We should hurry. That little steppe rat is probably already searching for me."

Close to the palace, the streets were quiet, empty and unlit except for the patrols. Lanterns moved in the darkness and footsteps echoed in patterns Nohra committed to memory as they kept close to the wall. More noise came from deeper in the city, and yellow lights shone in the distance. Nohra's pulse picked up. She squeezed Darya's hand tight as she tugged her up a tight flight of stairs wedged between two buildings. Dar's heart beat in her palm.

"What happens if a patrol finds us?" Darya asked.

That was an easy question.

"We run."

Darya dug her heels in, pulling them both to a halt. When had she gotten so strong? "This is too dangerous. Even for you.

The fact Aalya's awake is a miracle. You could be endangering her life, or your little brother's. Or *yours*."

"Well, it's too late for you to go back now, Dar. Not alone."

Up ahead, shouts came from a crowd of men packed tightly into a small courtyard. The Forked Tower loomed against the murky black sky, the prison's stone walls desolate, its barred windows dark.

Darya pursed her lips, her brows knitting. "I thought there was a curfew."

A prickle of fear gnawed at Nohra's stomach. "It's probably just some demonstration. The people are restless. Don't get separated from me and you'll be fine."

"I'm not worried about *me*."

Men in cloaks dragged a thrashing man through the street. "Please, no!" he yelled. This must be the vigilante justice the viziers were so afraid of. In the middle of the square, in view of the prison tower, someone read out a list of crimes. Bataar's conquest had stirred up the city's seditiousness. Now every man wanted to be a revolutionary.

The cloak's fastenings dug into Nohra's neck at a sharp tug. She met Darya's eyes and was surprised to see a fire in them. "It's not too late for us to go back," Darya growled. "If you give this up, Safiya and Calidah will. And if your cousin acts obeisant, Queen Clemiria might—"

"And then everything will be alright?" Nohra interrupted, her last dregs of patience evaporating like smoke. "It won't be. My father was killed by the man who plans to marry my sister. She was gravely wounded in the conflict *he* instigated. She can't even remember her own name!"

The sparks of flame in Darya's eyes died with a whoosh of wind. "Nohra—"

"No, no, don't *Nohra* me. When the barbarian bastard

finally moves on, *Nassar*, my dog-brained half-brother—may Nuna take his piss-reeking soul—will command Kalafar with that opium-addled skeleton Ervan Lofri. Everything will be far from alright."

"Nohra!" Darya snapped, not loud enough to be a shout, but firm enough it hurt like she'd thrown a rock. Her black eyes widened, as if she'd surprised herself. She'd never raised her voice, not in as long as Nohra had known her. Ducking her head, Darya swallowed, clearing her throat. "What exactly would be different?"

Nohra snorted. "More than you could imagine. My mother died to put Rami on that throne. I won't let her rot for nothing."

You know that's not true. Would she have wanted a zultam for a son, or to keep being their mother?

Nohra didn't like Darya looking at her like that. Pityingly, like she was a beetle squirming on its back.

"I know you loved your parents, but it makes no difference to concubines if they're visiting Nassar's bed or your father's. Fahaad, Laila, all of us still have to wake up and get to work, no matter who's sitting on the throne. Life at the palace doesn't stop, even when our lives stop."

Nohra straightened up. "Isn't there anything in your life worth fighting for? Didn't you like the way things were?"

"I did!" Darya lowered her voice. "Or else I wouldn't have... I have you and Fahaad and Grandmother's letters. I've always had things worth fighting for. People, not thrones."

"Are you saying you'd fight for me?" Nohra pressed. "Kill for me?"

Darya trembled. Nohra couldn't tell if it was from rage or fear or annoyance. "I've always been fighting for you. Can't you try to be happy? Everything could be normal again, if you just let it. We can pretend like it never happened. Bataar can dissolve your marriage contract and you won't have to go north. You belong in Dumakra, in Kalafar, with us. Your heart belongs to this city."

For a second she was the Darya Nohra remembered, the one she'd left in the capital when she went to the Hill. Blood rushed in Nohra's ears. Ahead, a man groaned, a choked sound in his death throes.

A chasm yawned open between them that Nohra couldn't reach across. She couldn't pretend she was ever getting star-watching nights with Fahaad and Darya back. She couldn't choose happiness with them if it meant not avenging her family. Bataar hadn't even let them entomb their father's heart. Her vows meant her life would never belong only to her.

"Get back!" shouted a man wearing the dark gray uniform of the city watch. "Break it up, back to your houses. Clear the square or *he* won't be the only one hanging today." The soldiers backing him up were tall and broad-shouldered. Their cloaks swished, the steel in their hands glittering dangerously.

A man rushed from the shadows, jostling Darya. His arm reeled back and swung forward, smashing into the chin of a guardsman.

"Die too, pig!" he yelled, thrashing the uniformed man.

Darya stumbled, her eyes wide, oil-slick moons. Another man piled on, pinning the guard's hands behind his back.

"Goddessless fools," Nohra swore, as more officers of the city watch joined the fight. The small crowd swarmed around them, sweeping Darya into their riptide.

Unhesitating, Nohra plunged into the swell, which reeked of manure and sweat and alcohol. She shoved a man off her and redirected another's stray punch. She reached for Darya's collar, but the press of bodies kept pulling her deeper. Nohra slammed her elbow into one man's temple. She threw her fist into a second person's ribs. Fire from a lantern blazed close to her face. One of the guards fell, and the licking flames spread through the screaming crowd.

In a small gap between recoiling bodies, Darya was crumpled on the cobbles. Nohra yanked her away from the fray, toward a narrow alley.

Fahaad's tunic and trousers were too long on her. Nohra stepped close, re-knotting and tightening the rope belt. "Are you alright?" she asked. "Keep your head down and stay close to me."

"Nohra, I—"

"I'm sorry."

"No, I was out of line... I was wrong." Darya's voice was so weak it was difficult to pick out against the shouts and screams and sounds of fists cracking against faces, boots kicking into stomachs, and sabers cutting back the crowd.

How could either of them really be sorry, except for hurting each other? They'd said the words that were really in their hearts.

The noise swelled. A cat hissed, and stray dogs barked. If Lofri's and Bataar's boys couldn't maintain a curfew in Kalafar, at least they had no hope of bringing the Sister City and its Harpy queen to heel. Nohra and Darya pressed close to the shadows when reinforcements from the watch ran past, brandishing curved swords.

Their destination was a house less than a kilometer from the docks, so close the sharp smell of fish from the merchant ships carried. The door was cracked, its paint worn and peeling.

"Someone lives here?" Darya was making a show of gasping for breath as she nodded toward the drawn curtains. There was no way she was that exhausted.

The door squealed open and Safiya's face emerged, backlit

by the faint glow of a taper candle. "Come on, inside before the watch circles back." She grinned. "*Darya*. I'm surprised she convinced you to come."

"Princess." Darya bobbed her head politely.

"So this is the place you sneak off to on market days?" Nohra asked. There must be a comfortable bed up the skinny stairwell.

Saf shrugged. "It's not to your tastes?"

Nohra glanced around, her eyes adjusting to the darkness. The floor jutted sharply to the right, and the sunken ceiling bowed. Water dripped from a stain on the roof, clinking into a bucket. Nohra pulled off her cloak and hung it up.

"When it rains, the ceiling leaks for weeks," Safiya told them. She held her candle up to a sconce, lighting it and then another. "Are you sure you weren't followed? You have an ever-persistent shadow these days."

"If we had a tail, we definitely lost them in the fighting near the prison." Nohra craned her head, peering around the room. "You know, it honestly doesn't look that bad." A mosaic spanned the space above the clay oven. A lace tablecloth covered a sturdy table with carved legs— "*Cali!* You scared the piss out of me." Her eyes fell on a folded paper in front of her statue-still cousin. "Is that the letter? You haven't opened it yet?" The rectangle-shaped seal wasn't the red one that had adorned so many letters her father used to receive. Nohra snatched the parchment and cracked the wax.

Calidah folded her arms. "We were waiting for you. Are you going to read it out loud? I intercepted the bird carrying it today. It's from Mother."

"If it's from the queen, why in the Goddess's names is it addressed to me?" Darya asked, neatly folding her cloak as she peered around Nohra.

"I thought Bataar's men would probably read anything coming from Rayenna," Calidah explained. "I figured correspondence between you and your grandmother would seem less suspicious."

"Sorry, Dar, you were our cover." Safiya stood on her toes to look over Nohra's other shoulder. "Pegasus shit. Well, that's what I expected, honestly."

Cali's face pinched. "She's furious, isn't she?"

Nohra skimmed a paragraph where Clemiria called Aalya a "new encumbrance" and said it was their duty to find the shield *Segreant* a wielder who wasn't bedridden and name an able-bodied Harpy. Cruel words were the only ones her aunt ever bothered with. Clemiria had once called Nohra a half-breed. Albeit, it wasn't as bad as Merv calling her the daughter of an Aglean whore. She'd pretended not to see Nohra when she'd said it. Clemiria's disgust was at least undisguised.

She was wrong about Aalya, but they needed her ruthlessness now.

"It's good that Clemiria wants to fight," Nohra said. "If she didn't, we'd have to convince her before the emissaries reach Rayenna."

Nohra hated her aunt. Clemiria stuck to Father's side like a burr on a pegasus. But if she could be useful now, none of their family drama mattered.

"Fighting might not be our best option," Saf said.

Nohra glowered. "What other options do we have?"

"The sky's the limit." She shrugged. "If your mind isn't made up, I was thinking of leaving the capital."

"Run? Why would you run away?"

Safiya suddenly seemed very focused on the leaking roof. "Zira's expecting."

Nohra swallowed. "It's Father's?"

"Well, it's not mine, Nohra," Saf snapped. She took a steadying breath. "The zultam always gets the last word. One last prince or princess will be born in Kalafar."

Nohra's fingers tightened around the letter. "Are you going, then? You're going to run away with her? Abandon us?"

Darya laid a hand on Nohra's arm.

"*I want to.*" Saf's voice was a desperate whisper, her small smile listless. "Goddess, Nohra, I want to. But I won't. It's not because I think we can win this fight; my conscience would kill me if you died alone."

Nohra would be angry about that slight later. Concubines who gave the zultam a child were rewarded with a fine house and retinue of servants. They were sent away, where they couldn't conspire for power. When Suri, Safiya's mother, had left, she made her promise to take care of Nohra, still fragile from mourning. And now, at this moment of fresh grief, Saf was threatening to leave, too.

"We need to destroy this." Nohra stalked to a cabinet and rifled through Safiya's things. When she found the tinderbox, she struck a piece of flint against the firesteel, lighting the char cloth and then the logs in the fireplace. She held a corner of the paper in the flame and let the fire devour it.

Darya spoke up. "What did the queen write? I'm not following what you're saying."

"She wants war," Saf explained. "And Nohra does too. Aunt Clemiria won't accept Bataar's terms of surrender. She's going to declare Rayenna an independent city-state."

"So Bataar would go to the city and fight her?"

Cali's face fell into her hands. She groaned, lightly hitting her head. "I'm not ready to die. I have another year at the Conservium before I'm finally an inducted maven. We just need to think of something."

Nohra pulled out a chair and sat, grabbing a pen and reaching for the inkwell and parchment.

"Can you wait, Nohra?" Calidah snapped. "*I'm* not done thinking yet, so I know you haven't even started."

"This may surprise you, but I don't need a Conservium education to write a letter," Nohra shot back, already scratching words onto the paper.

"Nor," Safiya cooed. "Let's not throw oil on the fire. You may not get along with our aunt, but you two sure as hells have a lot in common as far as your personalities are concerned."

"What's *that* supposed to mean?" The quill nib screeched to a halt, sending a spray of ink across bone-colored parchment.

"Let's allow our more even-tempered cousin to draft a letter. Then we can read it and make sure it's completely diplomatic and conveys our level-headedness." Saf pried the pen out of Nohra's grip. "First, we need to consider all our options. We should be three steps ahead. We devise a plan and a backup plan, and a—"

"Give the pen back. I already have a plan." Nohra's chest rattled at the ragged breath she drew in. They'd ask Clemiria to march her troops on Kalafar before Bataar could move for Rayenna. Their aunt's forces would help them take the city back.

"Our best approach is subterfuge," Calidah said. "We don't have an army, so we should play into what Bataar wants, earn their trust. We ask my mother to settle on temporary terms with him. If we play this right, we won't need to fight now."

"That isn't a game I want to play." Nohra clenched her fingers to keep her hands from shaking. "I want Bataar dead. I want his blood on my hands and his head on an iron spike. I want Rami on the throne, not as king of Kalafar or some other stupid made-up title. I don't want Aalya to be the gryphon king's third wife." She slammed her trembling fist down, rattling the inkpot.

Calidah slumped. "If you would wait for me to finish. In the time we buy, we'll make alliances. There must be steppe lords who don't want to continue to swear fealty to Bataar. There's Tobukaah Rhah's sons. They probably want revenge for their father's death, just like you. There's those dragonlords Bataar terrorized in the west. And some of our viziers might benefit from having Rami on the throne instead of Nassar and Lofri. We could even form alliances in Aglea! With your marriage pact with Meric Ward's son, we could secure the allegiance of most of the Aglean lords south of Barrister's Bridgewall."

Nohra shook her head. "So I marry his son, and we get an Aglean army. Is that right, more or less?"

"I thought you didn't want to marry the northern lord's son," Darya said. "Don't you want to stay in Kalafar?"

Nohra ground her teeth. "I don't *want* to marry him. I *have* to. It's what my father wanted, and it's what can put Rami on the throne."

Safiya squeezed Nohra's shoulders. Nohra wanted to bite her sister's fingers. "Our father is dead. You can put his plans to rest, too. Don't waste your life on his approval now. Your duty's done, and your life can be your own."

The words didn't make sense to Nohra. She was a Harpy Knight. They'd sworn vows. Failing didn't render those oaths meaningless.

"Think. Does Rami even want to be zultam?" Saf asked.

"Excuse me?" Nohra turned and blinked at her. "Why wouldn't he?"

"He's just a little boy. He likes writing poetry and hunting and watching the sailboats at the wharf."

"And? Many kings are skilled calligraphers. Zultams have hundreds of sailboats."

"Unless you're starting a war or opening a trade route, no one needs an entire shipyard. He could be happy with one little boat. But he can't stay here. As long as Nassar breathes, Rami would be safer anywhere but the capital."

"What are you saying? We all run away like scared dogs, or else we kill Nassar?" Nohra had wanted him dead in the courtyard, but he *was* their brother. Now that she was cool-headed, she couldn't plot to murder him.

"Were you thinking if we took over, we could just exile him?" Safiya sneered. "Maybe we could send him to Rayenna and see how long he'd last in their fighting arenas. I wouldn't bet ten egos on him."

Nassar probably didn't think anything of betraying their father, but Nohra wouldn't spill more of her own blood.

A tense silence descended. Nohra shivered, chilled despite the summer heat and crackling logs. There must have been a draft. Muffled through the thick door, yelling and the thunder of boots hitting the cobbles echoed through the streets. A thump, and someone's body slammed into the window, rattling the panes.

"What's happening?" Safiya stalked over and pulled back the curtain. She squinted out at the darkness.

"Vigilantes killed a man on Larcstreet and were attacking some city guards," Nohra explained. "If we take the route that loops behind the prison, we'll avoid the fighting on our way back."

Darya squeezed in beside her and pressed her cupped hands against the glass.

Safiya drew back and crossed her arms. "Half the city's running away from one fight? They're not coming from Larcstreet."

"What're you talking about?" Nohra put down her crumpled letter.

The crowd outside all ran in the same direction, downhill to the east. Lights glowed in neighboring homes. The frantic press of bodies clothed in rags swelled against a cracked door. The door gave and men pushed their old mothers and waved children inside to safety. *Ding, ding, ding*, the city bells started chiming.

"Are the soldiers doing something at the docks?" Nohra asked.

"Let's go see." Safiya reached behind the hanging cloaks for *Queen of Beasts* in its sheath.

Darya drew herself up, but Nohra steered her aside and grabbed a cloak folded on one of the kitchen chairs. "Stay with Cali. We'll be back soon to take you back to the palace. That's an order, Dar. Don't follow me."

Outside, the sound of the alarm bells pierced the night. Nohra and Safiya plunged into the fray, but moving toward the docks was like swimming against the Scythe's current. Elbows stabbed Nohra's ribs, and she had to spread her sliding feet wide to keep her footing.

Nohra caught and steadied a woman holding a swaddled baby. "Come on, then, you get inside," she muttered, her words barely audible above the distant shouts of city guards. The girl in her grip breathed raggedly as Nohra guided her to Saf's house. Suddenly men crashed against Nohra with too much hope trembling in their eyes.

"Please, my wife can't run!"

"My son's bleeding!"

Saf grumbled and waved refugees from whatever disaster had occurred into her lopsided wharf house.

"You'll be alright?" Safiya asked. Cali and Dar stood over a flock of civilians in tattered, stained clothes. They looked like two dogs guarding sheep. Calidah gave a firm nod.

Nohra loomed over a gasping young man. "What happened?"

"We were attacked at the docks," he wheezed out. "It came from the water."

Prying anything clearer out of the evacuees was impossible. In the chaos of night, they hadn't fully seen what had descended on them, cutting them down and stealing their children.

Nohra and Safiya would have to see for themselves.

"You shouldn't go." Darya's voice sliced through muffled cries and panting breaths. Her face was contorted like the sounds were all too much.

Nohra smiled. "I can't start listening to you now; I'd be breaking tradition."

"If guards come, escape out the back, into the shared courtyard," Safiya warned. "If it's anything else, cover the windows, smother the lights, and barricade the door with any furniture you can move."

After securing shaky promises, they left.

The thinning crowd cleared the closer Nohra and Safiya pushed toward the wharf, until only straggling city guards stood in scattered formations around the river harbor. The water was high, lapping at the stone steps down the floodwall. Fish bones, piles of nets, and pieces of broken crates littered the ground on the riverwalk. The shadowy masts on the moored ships swayed like trees.

Usually, the fish market was full of the sounds of bartering, the flop of dead fish being poured out into display trays, and merchants from Marafal drunkenly humming rowing songs. Ropes tying off the cargo boats groaned as river vessels bobbed against the planks of the pier. The cobbles were wet, but some of the puddles were too dark to be water. Smoke wafted off smoldering cookfires near pots and pans full of burnt rice and white beans. Stained bedrolls and makeshift tents made a maze Nohra and Safiya had to duck around.

From the stone ledge dropping down into the water, piers stretched out, crowded with river boats and more broken tents. One of the merchant ships moored there bobbed erratically, its prow scratching against the side of the pier. The bow slammed against the metal cleat its line was tied off to. Wood splintered, and a noise gurgled. It was taking on water, fast.

Fear prickled Nohra's chest, poison in her heart.

"Paga's sweet lips," Safiya hissed. "What's that?"

Nohra blinked, uncertain if her eyes could be trusted. The shadow of a cloud passed over the moon, and silver light beamed down on the docks, illuminating the hulking shape coiled around the mast of the merchant vessel.

Nohra's blood ran cold. "They're not supposed to be in Kalafar," she whispered.

Seahorses were creatures from the Thirst. Most gray-bearded fishermen in Marafal had never seen one. There was story of one swimming up the Scythe when the capital was still under construction, hundreds of years ago, an account so old it was probably urban legend told to children so they wouldn't swim in dirty water.

"It doesn't look anything like the picture in the bestiaries," Safiya said. In the illustration in *Beasts of Land, Sea and Sky*, the seahorse had frilly fins, a flowing green mane, and a curling, serpentine tail.

"The Naji family sigil didn't get it right either," Nohra noted, her voice sounding faraway, even to her own ears. A gray horse's head bobbed up, tiny ears twitching on the sides of a hairless neck.

Nohra stepped back, tripping over something round and wet. She put her arms out, catching her balance. Her stomach turned. The dock was littered with metal pots, rag dolls, and other objects people had rescued from their burning homes during the invasion. But beside her foot was the head of a guardsman, identifiable from the conical shape of his helmet. The metal and his skull were sunken on one side, skin broken and dented like a smashed melon. Arms, legs without bodies, and a torso with the ribcage peeled open were splattered around, unmoving and still. Bone, blood, parts of organs crunched and squelched under her feet.

The seahorse's tail constricted around the mast of the boat. The batten sail bent at an awkward angle, folding in on itself as the mast snapped in two. The seahorse's bulk shifted and the ship groaned. A percussive sound shook the air, coming from deep in its throat. Eyes rolled toward Nohra as the creature's head cocked to the side. It whirred and clicked, vocalizing in a keening, high-pitched whistle.

One of the guards spotted Nohra and Safiya. He yelled, "Get out of here!"

The boat bumped the edge of the dock as the seahorse slipped into the water. Nohra glanced left and right, gaze boring into the blackness for any sign of movement.

Safiya drew her sword. Nohra searched her peripheral vision for metal hooks, a fishing spear, a rope net that wasn't torn. Her sister had *Queen of Beasts*, but lugging a huge, ruby-encrusted sickle-staff into Kalafar would have made borrowing Fahaad's clothes pointless. She patted her pockets. Surely Fahaad had a paring knife or his damnable horse whip. Her hands closed around a cold shape that warmed to her touch.

She pulled out an onyx-colored dagger and turned it over in her hands. Darya's blade. Goddess's grace, she'd grabbed the wrong cloak.

"Do you have any idea how to calm this thing down if it comes at us?" Safiya asked. "You know horses."

"This isn't a normal horse, Saf."

"Neither is a pegasus!"

She was right. Pegasuses were dangerous monsters, but their family had tamed them. Now their sisters, little girls, soared high in the sky on the backs of raptors. They might not have to kill this beast, either.

"Back up," Nohra said, grabbing and pushing Safiya behind her.

Ward us from agents of chaos, she recited in her head. The words came instinctively. *Protect us from misfortune and injury.*

May the Goddess see their worth and not expunge their light. This beast was Nuna's. Paga's absence ached like phantom pain, but Nohra needed her faith to steady her.

Screamed orders, heavy splashes, and strangled yells reverberated around the basin, resounding off the ships docked along the pier. The seahorse's hooves scrambled on the stone ledge. It rose up in front of them, moonlight catching its body. Water glistened on its pebbled skin. Its eyes were smaller than a horse's, beady and black on the sides of its head. Rows of sharp teeth gleamed in its open mouth. *Thurup-thurup-thurup.* The clicking echoed in the back of the horse's throat. Nohra went lightheaded as she adjusted her grip on Darya's knife, fighting to keep her breaths even.

One of the city guards lunged forward, jabbing with his halberd. The seahorse's wide tail whipped around. Its fluked fin connected with the man's body. The long wooden handle of the weapon splintered first, then the man's neck snapped.

Nohra and Safiya ran, scrambling over the rubble at the wharf until they were pinned in, backs to the floodwall. Wood cracked and ropes groaned as the seahorse dragged its body over the debris.

"Get behind me!" Saf shouted.

The seahorse lunged, pink spittle hitting Nohra's face. She looked down its lines of sharp teeth, staring into the darkness at the end of its throat. Her body flinched, preparing for a shock of pain as she feebly raised the knife. The shouts, the gong-like bells, all of it was eclipsed by the erratic thump of her heart. The monster's hot, fetid breath dripped with rot and fish.

Air whistled past Nohra's cheek. A blur struck the seahorse's neck, and the creature reared back, snout swiveling toward the fletching lodged deep in blubber. Froth seeped from the wound.

Nohra spun around. She recognized the arm outstretched to her. Those same arms had dragged her off Nassar in the courtyard.

"Give me your hand," Bataar said. Clasping his wrist, she let him pull her up by the shoulders onto the raised platform bordering the docks. Balsam surrounded Nohra, nose-wrinkling in its tangy sweetness. The person who'd saved their lives was the one she most wanted to kill.

13

The sea-horse is exceedingly swyft and shy, with the head of a horse and tail of an eel. It rides the crests of ocean waves and is the bane of lone sea-men.

— *Beasts of Land, Sea and Sky: A Children's Bestiary of Fantastic Creatures*

Bataar's soldiers fanned out around the wharf, weapons trained on the winding sea beast as the city alarm clanged. A monster like this didn't belong in the middle of the Dumakran capital. Of course he'd find Nohra and her sister in the center of this chaos.

"You alright?" Bataar asked, twisting Nohra's head around to get a look at her. "You've got both your eyes and all limbs?" The seahorse's teeth had gnashed so close to her face.

Nohra shook free, swaying back on trembling legs. Her voice came out hoarse. "I'm in one piece."

She wore a man's tunic and a ratty cloak streaked by horse manure. Thankfully she hadn't been in her armor. Nohra was tall for a woman and lean-muscled. Even if it was Dumakran feather-steel, the plate and chain would have made it more difficult to pull her over the floodwall.

Bataar tugged his palfrey's reins. "You ride," he told Nohra, holding the mare steady while she swung up into the saddle.

Behind him, Shaza's horse whickered nervously as she nocked and loosed another arrow. Her hit landed, the shaft shooting into and disappearing inside the seahorse's body. Keening, it twisted its head. They had it surrounded, but the soldiers' horses reared back from it. Without warning, the seahorse let out a shrill whistle like a hot kettle and disappeared at the water's edge in an explosion of foam.

"Now what in Holy Preeminence was that?" Shaza swore. "Is it going to come back? Bataar, what's your order?" She dismounted and stalked toward where Nohra's sister Safiya crouched, looking ashen and uncertain for once.

"Spread out and search the water," Bataar called, keeping a wary hand on the reins as his gaze passed over the faces of his mounted soldiers and the haggard city guardsmen cradling their bleeding arms. "I'll pay a king's ransom to anyone who kills it."

Shaza rubbed the back of her neck. "What should we do with our princesses?" She extended her other hand out for Safiya's sword.

"Have someone escort Princess Safiya back to the palace. Double her guard."

"Excuse me!" Safiya's voice was sharper than her lion-headed sword.

Shaza nodded. "And the other one?"

He could try to provoke Nohra to talk. "I'll keep her close and take her back myself." He pointed to five soldiers and jerked his head left, where the floodwall and riverwalk edged tilting rowhouses. He ushered his horse around, walking it down a slope to the waterfront. Nohra sat stiffly, her shoulders pulled back and taut.

"What're you and your sister doing out here?" he deadpanned. "Violating curfew, evading your attendants?"

Oktai trailed, darting glances between the two of them. Bataar made a cutting motion to tell him to shove off and give them some distance. *With Shaza*, he mouthed. She'd be annoyed and send him back, but maybe he'd get some answers from Nohra while they were alone.

Nohra whispered, "Can you blame me for wanting to see for myself how bad things are in the city?"

"Ask politely, next time, and I'll escort you. Your talmaid is notably absent. Where is Darya Daheer? And your cousin?" Bataar needed Calidah alive more than any of them.

Irritation colored her tone. "They're somewhere safe. Saf and I saw the crowd running from the docks and went to investigate alone." Her leg brushed his side and went rigid at the contact.

Bataar didn't want to lean into her touch either. This night smelled like treason. "If you want to take a piss without armed guards breathing over your shoulder, you'll tell me where they are."

What were they doing? Inciting riots? Sowing unrest? Whatever their precise aim, the Harpy Knights had wanted to talk away from listening ears. Away from Bataar.

"If you're trying to start an insurrection in Kalafar, those fires don't need tinder to keep blazing," he told her.

She stammered. "I wasn't—"

"It's dangerous out here. The purpose of the curfew is to keep people safe. Your family is under my protection, including you. Your death would have been on my hands."

She stiffened. Any tauter and she'd snap. "Don't worry

about protecting me." The flare of her anger scorched him. "In Kalafar, the Harpy Knights keep the people safe."

Glass shattered, and a door thudded inside one of the houses above. He motioned for two of his soldiers to peel off and investigate the sound.

Bataar watched the dark water as he led the horse forward. The river was quiet, bobbing up and over the cobbles, its distant bank stretching a black ocean away. The seahorse was gone, but he hadn't seen its spirit when Shaza shot it. Even gryphons had souls. The whole situation left him eerily hollow.

Though Their face was obscured, the Preeminent Spirit panted hungry against Bataar's neck. Before they'd come upon the princesses, the cyclone of color above the docks had filled him with such primal dread he could have vomited.

Near the water's edge, something white flashed in the moonlight.

"Stay here," Bataar said.

Nohra bristled. "That an order?"

"No, but don't go riding off."

His last two soldiers looked between them, uncertain without a direct order. The alarm bells kept ringing. Already a headache stabbed behind Bataar's twitching eye.

Nohra's boots hit the cobbles, her dark silhouette stalking toward him. "What're you looking at?"

The other two soldiers dismounted. One took up the reins of Bataar's palfrey. They hung back, away from the water, blurring into the shadows near the wind-battered houses.

"If you see it in the water, get back," Nohra warned. "Unless you're interested in rejoining your Encompassing Spirit."

"Preeminent," Bataar corrected distractedly, gooseflesh prickling despite the hot, thick air. "It's Preeminent Spirit."

Nohra pressed in close. "Are you sure it isn't Encompassing? Maybe you've gotten the Dumakran word wrong."

"I don't think I have." Bataar knelt and grabbed a handful of the foam at the water's edge. He pressed the bubbles between his gloved fingers and kept a hand on his sword, in case Nohra reached for it like she had the knife in the sanctium, or anything surged out of the water. "It must have gone this way. How many people do you estimate it killed?"

She shook her head. "I'm not sure. There were pieces of a city guardsman, at least one, but I think the mob might have killed him. I don't know… three or five that I saw. But those were just the ones there were still parts of."

Bataar had seen the bloodied limbs, the nosed-over carcasses with torn-open chest cavities empty of organs. Was it glutted, its hunger sated?

He stood, dusting off his legs. "Now that it knows Kalafar has so much food, I don't think it'll go back downriver." Animals went where the meals came easiest. He'd learned that lesson young. "I'll have the Scythe blocked off, post guards at the waterfront and double at the dock. I'll send someone to inspect the grating at the mouth of the river in the southern port. More won't be coming once this one's dead."

Nohra folded her arms. When she spoke, her tone was accusatory. "And what about the people who live in these buildings and the refugees? Where will you house them? And the merchants who use the docks, what about them? You want to suspend trade for however long it takes to find it? If you let the fishmongers continue selling, you're inviting it back to the market for fresh breakfast."

A gurgled exclamation fell from dying lips behind them. It was barely audible, but Bataar spun around. Shapes pulled away from the shadows. His two soldiers slumped, their mouths darkening and slick. The attackers were armed with sharpened stakes, twisted pieces of iron that might have been rail posts, and dull-looking knives. Two disarmed the sagging bodies of the soldiers, unsheathing long swords.

Bataar drew his saber, putting himself in front of Nohra as the thugs peeled away from the darkness to surround them. The horses tossed their manes, nostrils flaring in agitation as the soldiers collapsed prone in the street.

One of the shadows spoke up. "That's some nice clothes, mister." His gruff voice cracked like a boy's. "I've never seen silk so fine in my whole life. And that shiny thing there." He stepped forward, flicking the bauble Bataar had won off Nassar. "Looks like it belongs on one of the princes."

Bataar smacked his hand away with the flat of his blade. One of the other boys snickered. There were four of them, all wearing undyed linen, all with nondescript faces. None of them could have been older than twenty, but they were muscled instead of gawky, with facial hair that was full rather than patchy, and bulbous, broken noses.

It was an advantageous night to be a thief and a murderer, looting the dead and killing when monsters hunted. But riches wouldn't matter to corpses.

Neither Bataar nor Nohra were wearing armor. He was adorned like a Dumakran prince, and she was dressed like a stable boy. They were outnumbered too, but they weren't unarmed. Bataar flexed his fingers on the hilt of his saber. Nohra drew something from the pocket of her cloak. Darya Daheer's knife. The dagger in Nohra's hand bent the night around it, black steel glinting ominously.

She'd been a menace with her scythe on top of the Swan Gate, but Bataar had no idea how well she could fight with a smaller blade. His saber was balanced in his hands, though he would have been more comfortable with his straight knife or bow. He didn't care. He could cut enough of them down that it wouldn't matter how Nohra fought.

"Why don't you come with us, dove?" one of the other boys said. "You look like one of the king's Aglean girls." He stuck the iron bar he was holding into a crack in the cobblestone street and leaned against it. "We'll treat you good. Dress you up like a *real* lady and then fuc—"

Nohra kicked him, knocking out his breath before the rest of his words could fall. As he stumbled, the butt of her knife cracked against his temple. His eyes rolled back, eyelids fluttering shut as his legs foundered.

"Hey, you crazy witch," another one said, jumping forward with his stolen saber drawn. "What in hells?"

The princess feinted back, sheathing Darya's knife and pulling the iron post out of the crack in the cobbles. She shifted it in her hands, testing its weight, then spun the shaft against the man's legs. He groaned and fell, catching himself and limping back. Another gangly attacker was already in his place, slamming his saber against Nohra's iron rail post as the fourth thug circled around her. That one grabbed her by the hair and pulled her head back, knife pressing against her exposed throat.

Bataar had been toying with the boy with the cracking voice, but now he shoved him and sent him sprawling. Clearing the distance between them, Bataar tore his saber into the back of his neck. The hand holding the knife against Nohra went slack, and he coughed, spraying blood onto her hair. She grabbed his knife before it could hit the cobbles and pushed him off her.

"Die, you donkey's bastards!" the one with the blade cried, lunging.

His shiv nicked Bataar in the side. Turning, he grabbed the boy by the wrist, twisted until his fingers spread wide and the knife fell and clattered against the street. The other boy with the cut-open throat gurgled pitifully on the ground.

It happened in an instant, something swelling out of the water, scraping up onto the shore. The two remaining muggers screamed, falling back and disappearing into the shadows between buildings. Nohra grabbed the one she'd knocked unconscious and hefted him onto her shoulders as the seahorse slid forward, pulling itself toward the one Bataar had stabbed. The dying boy's fingers seized as he tried to scramble back.

The first beast at the docks had been larger, darker. The color on this one was more diluted, mottled gray instead of black and white.

There was more than one monster in Kalafar. The realization chilled the blood in Bataar's veins.

Scarlet spread across the prone boy's chest. Strangled screams died in his wet mouth as the horse's snout sunk into his chest. His spirit scampered out of his mouth like a fat rat. Clouds parted, revealing the moon, and the jaws that never shut yawned even wider.

"Drop him and get behind me," Bataar commanded.

The horses whickered their nervousness. Nohra groaned as she lifted the unconscious boy up and laid him down over the back of the palfrey.

A nerve in Bataar's face spasmed in annoyance. He shifted his saber to his non-dominant hand. "I didn't say put him on the horse."

"This one's just a boy."

"A boy who killed my men. He threatened you." Bataar grazed his hand over the nick in his side. His fingers pulled away red.

"Because your men have given these people good reason to trust them?" She was spitting her words now. "You have no idea what your soldiers might have taken from him the night of your invasion!"

Hoofbeats cantered closer, a rhythm against the cobbles that made sense, not the tap-tap-*drag* of the seahorse pulling itself across the embankment. Bataar's tongue was dry.

"Your Eminence?" Oktai said, finally sweeping up behind them on his horse. "What should I do?"

Bataar's fingers were slippery with sweat on the hilt of his saber. "Shoot it, Oktai."

"Wait!" Nohra started, frantic. "With a net we could—"

The seahorse's head shot up and twisted in her direction.

"With a net *what*? What in Preeminence's true name do you need a net for?"

Her eyes were wide. "To—"

She had to be joking. Her will was almost impressive. "*To catch it?* This isn't one of your pegasuses! You won't be able to break this one. I'm not keeping this abomination at the palace." He didn't need any more unpredictable appetites in an already insatiable court.

Nohra met his gaze and held it. "Why can you only think about killing it? Is that your answer to everything?"

Bataar remembered a gryphon eating a little boy. "Yes, usually," he snarled. "I thought we had that in common. Fire, Oktai."

"Don't! You've been assigned to guard me, to listen to me."

The boy's face twisted. "I'm sorry, princess. I have to listen to Bataar first."

The first arrow shot forward, thwunking into thick blubber, then another. Nohra spun on Bataar, holding up one of the thieves' discarded weapons. Her hands on the wooden pike shook. "Are you not listening to me, rhah? Less than a dozen people have ever seen a seahorse and lived to describe it to mavens at the Conservium. If our scholars could understand it, if we could catch it alive, then we could tame it!" Her shouts and the creature's keening echoed off the tall houses edging the waterfront. Fervor trembled in her eyes. If he was just a bit stupider, more naïve, his spirit would have bent to hers. That thought was terrifying.

"Kill yourself over some monster another day. I left the palace with the intention of bringing you back alive."

The seahorse writhed, twisting its neck and gnashing toward the shafts of the arrows. It vocalized in splintering clicks and whistles. A noise answered it, or maybe it was just the first sound reverberating. All the shouts and screams were dulled by the alarm bells clamoring. Bataar's stabbing headache grew.

"I think it's calling to the other one," he realized as Shaza's officers rode up. "Don't turn your back to the water."

"*Another one?* Do we fire, Bataar?" Shaza asked, her bowstring already drawn taut.

"Kill it."

Blood burbled out around the shafts of the arrows as more sunk into thick flesh. The seahorse wobbled, screeching so sharply Bataar's ears stung. He couldn't look at Nohra's mouth twisting in horror. When the seahorse finally fell forward, its body began to melt into a pinkish puddle of seafoam and jutting bone. Its soul burst out, crashing over Bataar like an ocean wave.

14

They say a woman should sew, dance, play, sing, ride and proficiently wield a blade, but there are only twelve hours of daylight, and I strain my eyes embroidering by candlelight.

— Queen Roksanya's diary

Nohra was sent to her room and locked in with double the guards outside her door. At the threshold of her quarters, Shaza confiscated the dagger as officers shoved past, dumping out boots and patting down the cloaks and tunics hanging up in the dresser. They overturned Nohra's plate armor, checking every crevice and crack.

"Keep looking," Shaza ordered. When all Nohra's weapons were piled in the center of the room, the commander nodded, and a soldier carried it all out, metal clattering and clanging.

Nohra shook free of the men holding her arms. "When can I leave?" Her blood still thrummed from the scrape with the seahorse at the wharf. She hadn't been that close to death in a long time, and the sight of its carcass has felt like hands scraping out her guts.

Shaza regarded her with narrowed eyes. Was this really

Qaira's little sister? "You can leave when Bataar says you can."

"And when will that be?" Should she plan on being entombed in her quarters? How far could she push Bataar before the warlord took her head? The gryphon king took no prisoners, suffered no losses. Breaking his rules should be suicide, but Nohra kept crossing the line. "Are Darya and my cousin safe?"

The door slamming shut was Shaza's answer. It was better than being thrown into a cell in the Forked Tower to wait for morning. Fingers of light reached through the curtains. Dawn was close, and Nohra's eyelids were heavy, but she was too stirred up to sleep. Rows of teeth kept flashing through her mind.

Blinking away the dryness burning at her eyes, she brushed dust off the cover of Obeyd's *Revised Wartime Strategies* and cracked open the spine. The pages smelled new. The text had been meticulously transcribed in legible writing, probably by a zealous Conservium student, someone like Cali.

All the neatly printed words tilted and spun around, becoming unreadable nonsense in her head. She flipped toward the blank endpapers and ripped them out. If a servant brought Nohra a pen, she could finish the letter to Aunt Clemiria and start one to Meric Ward. Shaza and Bataar probably wouldn't trust her with so much as a nib now.

Nohra remembered the volley of arrows blasting into the seahorse, its body exploding into mincemeat and bloody foam. Like an idiot, she'd fought *with* Bataar, not against him, swinging the fishing spear into the robbers by the wharf. The Goddess would smite her for brainlessness.

Nohra folded up the blank sheets of paper. She read and reread the same page of her book, considering throwing it at the wall. Tiredness slammed into her, and she fell asleep unexpectedly, cheek pressed against a window pane, the book on tactical theory still spread open on her lap.

"Bataar said you embroider, so I thought I could sit with you," a softly rasping voice said.

Nohra jolted awake, blinking in surprise. Her head connected with the corner of the window frame, and two Qairas blurred in her vision.

Her disoriented mind swam. The doors were still shut, but Bataar's wife hovered over her, wearing a robed gown belted with iridium blessings. Morning had turned to midafternoon, and the sun was bright enough to scald.

"My handmaiden, Maran, has no patience for this sort of thing," Qaira explained. "It bores her." The pauldrons on her shoulders were shaped to look like snarling wolves' heads. What hair didn't hang in braids was wrapped around horn-shaped hair ornaments.

Nohra marked her page in the open book with a finger. "I'm not interested." Her mouth was cottony, voice hoarse from sleep.

"Oh, you can keep reading." Qaira waved her hand. "I called for tea. Or would you prefer coffee? You must still be rattled. Would you like me to help you change?"

"What?" Nohra stared down at the clothes she'd borrowed from Fahaad. Dark stains from last night had made the fabric harden.

Qaira didn't look bothered. "I can call for one of your servants, or Maran, or I could help you dress, if you'd like," she said, reaching forward. She started unbuttoning the top of the tunic before Nohra lurched back, her face hot.

"What do you think you're doing?" she snapped.

Qaira blinked her doe eyes. "I only wanted to help."

Nohra's nerves were coiled as tight as a spring. "Did Bataar send you to try to get information out of me? Or Shaza?"

After all, they were sisters, even if they seemed nothing alike. Shaza was tall, with hair so black it almost bent light like Darya's knife, and a personality that made Saf seem sweet.

"No. But Bataar *is* increasing the number of palace guards on watch so no one breaks curfew again. He may have mentioned you're deft with a needle, but he didn't ask me to come."

Nohra hopped up and stalked toward her armoire. Her eyes latched onto a pale blue dress. Fahaad's words came to her. Her treason could get Darya killed. Nohra murmured, "Tell Bataar my talmaid is innocent in what happened last night. I should never have made Darya violate curfew with me."

Keeping her back turned and wary of her reflection in the large mirror, Nohra stripped off the shirt she'd borrowed from Fahaad. Qaira's curious gaze seared her exposed skin, surveying old scars and new bruises. Before meeting Qaira, Nohra had never been shy or ashamed of her body. Why would she be? She was a princess.

If the rhah's wife was going to look anyway, Nohra wouldn't slouch.

Silk rustled as the chemise fell over Nohra's head. She wrapped herself in the jacketed dress, squeezing to fasten the buttons down her bust. The old gown clung tight to the lines of her torso, snug around her waist, its waterfalling sleeves draping her arms. Finally, she shimmied out of Fahaad's trousers and turned around, skirts swinging.

Qaira's gaze roved up and down. "Silk suits you almost as well as steel." The flirtatious gleam in her eyes was quickly smothered, and she became every bit Bataar's wife again. Pulling herself up, she patted the space beside her on the window seat.

Nohra wobbled as she tucked her legs carefully under her

215

body. They sat in silence for a moment. She reread the same sentence at least five times. "What are you embroidering?"

Qaira was humming softly to herself. "Ganni's natal-day headdress." She held it up. "Are you interested in having children?"

Nohra's cheeks warmed. "When I marry, I'll perform my duties as a wife," she stammered. "My mother told me that in Aglea, there is a saying that the childbed is a woman's battleground."

It wasn't a field Nohra had any experience fighting on. Many concubines never bore a zultam any children, but expectations were different in Aglea. A man had one wife and as many lovers as he cared for, but illegitimate children were shunned, and a wife who didn't bear her husband heirs could be put to the sword.

Qaira wasn't a soldier, but she'd seen war, and more battlefields than just the childbed. The corner of her lip twitched, but her faraway look was troubled, as if the adage unsettled her. "Does your mother live far from the palace?"

Nohra kept her expression shrouded. "She died ten years ago."

Qaira didn't wince. "I'm sure she's very proud of you. I'll never stop loving Ganni and Bato, even when I've rejoined Preeminence. My children brighten this life in ways I can't express."

"You're their mother," Nohra snorted. "You have to pretend you like them."

Qaira put down her sewing and looked at Nohra levelly, with false sincerity. "I'd tell you if they were little demons. Sometimes Ganni is."

Nohra had glimpsed them around the grounds, usually being led by one of Qaira's handmaidens, or carried by Tarken.

The fat baby Bato was always squirming in a maid's arms while the young girl tugged at Qaira's skirt, watching with wide hazel eyes. Ganni usually shrunk back when the children in the harem ran past but always chirped excitedly to Bataar when he stopped to scoop her up and spin her around.

Nohra's stomach churned.

A few of her sisters had their own children now, curly-haired squalling babies toddling around on fat legs, not out of dressing gowns and cloth diapers. Nohra had decided on marrying Meric Ward's son, and she knew he'd want to put a baby in her, but somehow, she hadn't pictured being a mother. She was a sister, a knight, a daughter.

No one had taught her anything else. Unlike Saf, she'd never been good with kids.

"This is an Utasoo natal-day headdress?" Nohra reached out, stroking the stitchwork. "In Dumakra, at court, girls usually get jewelry for their birthdays. My father gave me rings as natal-day gifts until I turned fifteen."

"Rings?" Qaira's warm fingers ghosted over the tops of Nohra's knuckles, tapping each one. "I haven't seen you wear them."

Heat prickled in Nohra's chest. "They were stolen during the invasion." It hadn't been the worst thing taken from her that night.

"I'll see if I can do something about that." Qaira leaned in and blinked up at her, almost batting her eyes. Her eyelashes were a darker brown than her reddish hair. "Bataar already found a merchant selling vases from the palace and bought them back."

"It's—it's fine. I wasn't that attached to them." The rings had stopped coming when her mother died, souring her opinion of them. And she didn't want Bataar finding them for her. "After that year, Father just gave us money to buy what we liked."

"Oh? Tell me. What do you like?"

"Uh, I," Nohra stammered, trying to think of an answer that wouldn't make her sound vain or childish. "Sugar animals," she blurted. Nohra always tipped the candy vendors so well their carts stayed off the street for months.

Qaira cocked her head. "Sugar... animals?"

Nohra's face was on fire. She focused her attention on the tiled wall. "They're these, uh, sweets, obviously, shaped like gryphons or..." she choked out, "seahorses or pegasuses. Street vendors sell them to children, and confectioners come to the palace for parties." The sweet makers erected sculptures as tall as peacocks and as realistic as living animals. Nohra couldn't shut up. "When I was little, at Nassar's circumcision party, my stepmother slapped me for sticking one shaped like a turtle to her silk coat."

Qaira's bubbly laughter erupted out of her pursed lips. She was so close now that Nohra could almost taste her breath. It smelled like candied tansies.

"I remember I ran crying to my father, and he pulled me up in his arms—" She stopped, tongue leaden.

"You must miss your father. That wound is so fresh."

"His heart should be entombed. I wish I could at least give him that." Nohra clenched her lips sealed, though there was no hiding that her voice had wavered with hurt.

At her sudden shift in tone, Qaira's smile faltered. "Of course you should give him his final funerary rites. I'll tell Bataar." A knock at the door made her eyes widen. She pulled back. "That must be the tea."

Nohra smoothed down her rumpled skirts as servants carried in the service on silver trays. Qaira would think she was weak, close to crying over her father.

Qaira took a small sip from her cup. "I can try to read your tea leaves, if you'd like. Bataar might have told you I do that. I'm not very good at it, though."

"Really?" It was dangerous how Qaira could steer a conversation. "Darya can read shapes in coffee grounds... but she says it's all superstitious drivel."

Qaira tucked a braid over her shoulder. There was a freckle on the shell of her ear. "She doesn't believe in those things?"

The Goddess could slip meaning into anything. "Do you?"

"I believe the Preeminent Spirit sometimes communicates in signs"—Qaira's little finger traced the rim of the cup—"and some people can read those portents."

"Like your husband's shaman?"

"Yes." Qaira straightened and nodded. "Like her. People with gifts."

"Are you one of those people?" Nohra looked Qaira over. She had a dreamy, far-off look in her green-brown eyes. She was so beautiful, like a character in a myth. Beauty and kindness could be both burdens and blessings.

"I fear I'm not that interesting." Qaira looked out onto the courtyard. "I wish They had given me some useful gift. One like yours, or Shaza's."

Nohra balked. "What gift do I have? Whoever told Bataar I was skilled with an embroidery needle was grossly exaggerating." It was probably Ervan Lofri's moon-eyed daughter. The Minister of Commerce and his family were stuck to Bataar like fat leeches.

"You can fight. You're courageous, daring. Everyone knows it. When I was a little girl, I'd shake whenever I saw blood."

"You just embody the Goddess in a different way." Catching herself, Nohra balked. Qaira had her *Encompassing Spirit*. "Sorry. I didn't mean..."

She hid her smiling lips demurely behind her fingers. "It's alright." Suddenly, those hands were moving down, slipping into the neck of her dress.

Nohra's throat constricted. "What are you doing?"

"You kept your word," Qaira said, pulling out the cleric's pendant. "You kept me safe. I've been meaning to return this."

"Keep it." Nohra pulled back, but Qaira was already reaching around her, pushing the chain over her hair. Against her neck, the metal was as warm as Qaira's skin.

"Thank you. For what you did at the Hill. And now, for continuing to humor me." Qaira tilted her head and flexed her fingers on her knees. "Could you help me? I know I said you didn't have to, but I fear this looks nothing like a pegasus."

Nohra pursed her lips, squinting at the white blob. It looked more like a dog than a horse with wings. "Here," she said, taking the needle and silk thread.

She tried to match Qaira's style, a sort of squarish translation of flowers and animals and flourishes. Nohra worked quickly, making neat, precise stitches. It reminded her of sitting at her mother's bedside, before Rami was born.

After Nohra had returned from escorting Clemiria to Rayenna all those years ago, the physicians had put Nohra's mother on bedrest. Since the injuries to Nohra's stomach and shoulder were still healing, she'd sat in beside her mother as she described patterns she'd seen when she was a girl in Aglea. Nohra copied them from her mother's descriptions. She covered the bodice of one of her mother's gowns, then the panels of the skirts.

While she sewed, her mother sang songs. Nohra had treated that dress like an offering, and when she was done it had been fit for a goddess, but the prayers she stitched into the silk hadn't kept her mother safe. It was still the most beautiful thing her bloodied hands had made, and thinking of it filled her with soured pride and bitterness.

At least she'd had that time with her mother. Even as her father's guard, she'd spent less time with him.

Qaira pulled Nohra from her confusing memories of a calm before the storm. "Your skills weren't exaggerated at all."

"You flatter me." Nohra resisted the small smile that tugged at her mouth. She tied off the thread and cut it with her teeth.

A voice called out, muffled beyond the doorway. The only word Nohra understood was "children," and then suddenly Qaira's daughter was bursting inside, her baby brother dangling by his underarms like a limp kitten. The little girl froze, eyes widening when they landed on Nohra.

Little brat thinks she owns the palace already.

"Be polite. Say hello to the princess."

Ganni put Bato down and turned even more sheepish, rocking on her feet and hiding her face behind her hair.

"You like the horses?" Nohra asked. A tiny, jerky nod was Ganni's answer. Nohra turned to Qaira, poised to test if her authority was as good as Bataar's. "With you as my chaperone, do you think I'd be permitted to leave my quarters?"

"Oh?" Qaira purred. "Where would you want to go?"

⌒⌒⌒

Bataar must have ordered the guards to follow Qaira's orders because with questioning glances and resistant stiffness, they let them leave. The scent of fresh straw blanketed the stables. The slick floors had been freshly scrubbed after a feeding. Above each stall, a pegasus's name curled in wrought-iron letters. Inside Faith's compartment, her foal dangled in a sling, head bobbing as he reeled his legs.

"When its feathers come in and its wings grow, he'll be

221

able to fly normally, just without a rider," Nohra explained, modeling for Ganni how to pet its patchy mane. "Even one as small as a little girl."

In the stable's main corridor, Bato wriggled in the arms of Qaira's young handmaiden. The fat little toddler made grabby fists at the fountain, and giggled at the spray of light from the chandelier sparkling in the burbling water. All Qaira's ladies clustered around, cooing at him and petting his hair. It was auburn like his mother's. He had her smile too, but the little boy would soon be groomed to be a tyrant like his father.

At the tack room, Nohra lorded over a copper-skinned stablehand, pointing out all her gear. Fahaad would have always had it ready for her. "And that one." She gestured to a child's saddle stitched with protective prayers and tiny birds. It was hers from long before she'd had Mercy.

Out in the yard, Nohra steadied Ganni in the saddle. The pony pegasus's lead was staked to a chain in the ground. When Ganni could sit up without curling forward and puffing out her cheeks like she was about to puke, Nohra stepped back and let them circle, three yards off the ground.

"Do you want down?" Nohra called out.

"No!"

"She's strapped in tight," Nohra reassured Qaira, who jerked forward at every wobble and delighted squeal out of her daughter's mouth. Nohra ripped a handful of grass from the ground, tore the blades smaller. "I promise. She's having the time of her life; there's nothing like flying." There was nothing closer to the Goddess.

Ganni pitched forward and steadied herself. Qaira gasped and grabbed Nohra's wrist so tight her fingertips whitened.

After last night, Nohra needed to ease her own troubled mind. "Come on, let me prove it to you."

She tacked Mercy in the palace's finest saddlery, nothing that had seen blood or reeked of war. Nohra lifted Qaira by the waist, sliding her hands down to her hips, thighs, the swell of her calf, folding her leg and guiding her slippered foot into the stirrup. Qaira's hot skin quivered through the layers of fabric, and her belt jangled.

What in hells are you doing?

Nohra had a rebellion to plan. There were alliances to forge, and none of them included Qaira. All this could end with Bataar's precious children at *Bleeding Edge*'s blade. Not that she wanted that. She should be alone now, reflecting. Praying, if Qaira would take her to visit the palace sanctium.

She climbed up into the saddle, a specialized one, elongated for two riders. "That thing's going to poke my eye out," Nohra grumbled, as Qaira lifted a hand to support her pronged headdress.

Nohra resigned herself to being whipped in the face by Qaira's braids and leaned around her for the reins. They were flush, back to front. Qaira's heartbeat stirred her honeyish perfume. Sweat leaked through their bodices, and the press of shoulders dug the cleric's necklace into Nohra. The force of their bodies would impress the shape of a chain and flower plaque into her chest, and the sear of Qaira's flesh would brand her.

Goddess.

Bataar probably had Qaira trying to earn her friendship to stave off insurrection, to soften Nohra and make her loyal to him. And Nohra was doing the same, batting her eyes and using a teary voice to manipulate like weapons never had. As they peeled out of the stable and Mercy leapt into the sky, Nohra's pulse was hammering.

15

Don't rob the gryphon's nest near the
cookfire you fry eggs on.

— Moshitu proverb

When Bataar crossed the threshold into the zultam's parlor, Fahaad was already seated at the serving table, tipping the contents of a blue vial into his cup. Behind him, the zultam's bed was obscured by the gauzy canopy draping over the four posts. Chandeliers hung like huge clusters of crystal grapes. Marble, tile, and giltwork covered every centimeter of the walls and floors. It wasn't to Bataar's tastes, but it would only be his room for a few more months.

He nodded for his guards to stay by the door. "Do you play?" He took his seat and began setting up pieces on a glass board.

"Only passably." Fahaad winced as he took a gulping sip.

Bataar squinted at the medicinal tonic. "Is that bitter?"

"As an orange peel. Coffee masks the flavor." Fahaad's flat, empty smile didn't reach his eyes. "I remember sobbing and choking when Ramman Mytri first forced it down my throat."

Bataar took it as a good sign that Fahaad was being so open.

He ran his tongue against his teeth. "You were just a boy when you came to Dumakra. You've lived at the palace most of your life as a servant, a hostage, a prize. You must carry so much animosity."

Fahaad's expression grew more guarded. "I used to be angry."

"You're not anymore?"

He shook his head. "The Head Eunuch's dead now. Besides, Mytri was a boy once too, dragged kicking and screaming to the Dumakran court against his will. Someone else made him swallow from the same vial."

"So stop taking it now," Bataar said with a shrug. "You can't be Head Eunuch, but I'll make a new title for you. How does Ambassador to Moshitu sound?"

"Tempting."

Bataar waved at the set board. "The first roll's yours. I didn't ask, is lions fine?"

Fahaad wordlessly took up the ivory dice and shook them. They clinked like the bones in Boroo's bag of runes. In Eagles & Lions, the first to conquer the board won, which meant rolling to move each piece and rolling again to fight to claim your opponent's. Each animal-shaped token had different weight.

"You must miss home. Moshitu. The plains, the Bloodmount."

"I miss my mother more than some mountains." Fahaad took Bataar's roc piece. "I'm sure you miss home too. Everyone does."

White-capped red peaks filled his mind. "My home *was* a mountain." Of course he longed for the day when he could rule from the red steppe, back with Tarken's parents and Qaira's, who'd become his family.

"But you left of your own choice."

Needles prickled Bataar's chest; a sharp, brief pain shot across his face. "Only because Mukhalii Rhah struck first, kidnapping women from our camp." He shook his head. "Making the great rhahs kneel and swear fealty was a lifetime ago. I was just a boy pretending to be a man."

Now *he* was being vulnerable.

"Your first war lasted half a decade." Fahaad threw again. A bad roll, but he didn't frown as he lost the low-value piece. "You were a man when you beat Mukhalii Rhah at the Heartspring. You took the Federated Kingdoms more quickly." His voice turned carefully disinterested. Maybe they were playing the same games. "Must have been easier."

Bataar grimaced. Reliving it was like reading someone else's story, old history. "There was a blizzard at the start, and another freeze the next winter. The islands were fighting us as hard as the battalions." Messy sieges, burning fields. In the stone city, Bataar had gawked at the granite statues of gods and thought their fingers moved. His mind had been fragmenting, cracking apart.

"Did you face less dissent there after you took the cities?"

"No. After Tashir, the dragonlords tried retaking Tanomaki. There was a rebellion and public executions." Bataar rolled to capture one of Fahaad's leopard pieces. "A council member was plotting to assassinate the empress."

"And you removed them from the council?"

Laughter streamed into the room through the thrown-open windows. Children were playing on the lawn. Bataar's daughter was probably with them. She was shy but growing braver.

"I stabbed the councilwoman at a tea ceremony in the card house," he deadpanned. As Councilwoman Yeeon had stumbled back, her blood had dripped over a tray of sweets, speckling flower-shaped rice cakes red.

Fahaad pursed his lips.

"What?" Bataar prompted. "Speak your mind."

"Is it true your Choyanreni empress wife is with child?"

"No, that's almost impossible." He tried and failed to picture a baby half-Ruo and half-him. If he were a boy, he'd be a menace to his tutors. If she were a girl, she'd be worse, dangerously intelligent and cutting as a knife. But Ruo was even less interested in having sex than Bataar was in sleeping with her.

She'd confessed to him that she'd sat in on consummation nights out of curiosity and found herself entirely apathetic. '*If you're interested in coupling with me in the usual manner, I could research which position would be the least trouble in one of the books in the palace collection,*' Bataar remembered her saying as he'd choked on his tea one morning.

"Her council wants an heir," he finally said. He'd failed to see her the way he saw Qaira, to feel the stirrings of want, but appeasing them was important. They'd need to do something, eventually; acquire an orphan, perhaps.

Fahaad's brow furrowed. "Is she hideous? Why haven't you given her one?"

"Portraits don't do her justice." The empress had sleek brown hair and powdered skin. Citrusy, jasmine perfume from orchid sachets clouded around her, and she wore face paint neater than any doll's. "My bride cares more for poetry and hawks than desires of the flesh."

Quietly, Fahaad muttered, "It's... interesting that you care what she wants." He lost both his cats, pawn pieces, and captured one of Bataar's eagle tokens. "I do miss Moshitu. I speak the language clumsily. Sometimes I practice with concubines and courtiers from there. None of the palace chefs know any recipes from that far south." He took a long breath that shook his shoulders. "But I don't hate Dumakra. I've made a home here."

Bataar leaned in. The Minister of Faith had said something in the sanctium that needled at him. "With the princess?"

Fahaad stilled, fingers hovering over the double-level playing board. *"Nohra?"*

He still needed to understand the Harpies. Safiya was deceptively easygoing when her sisters weren't spurring her to violence, with a secret, tender side that she showed around her lover, Zira. Calidah cared more for books than people and was determined to keep attending classes at the Conservium. Nohra was impulsive, but she wasn't dim or vain enough to be easily manipulated with the right promises, like Nassar and Ervan Lofri were. Bataar had to break them, for the same reason he'd tamed Erdene as a boy: so they'd fly for him, kill for him.

Of all the Harpies, Nohra stuck in his head. He remembered the fire in her eyes when she loomed over him on the Swan Gate before he'd pinned her down. Her goodwill and loyalty wouldn't be easily won.

She's always at the stables. For the horses, or…?

"You're close with her." Bataar kept his voice light, clipped. "You and her talmaid are her best friends, her only friends, except for her sisters."

Fahaad's gaze darkened. "I haven't spent much time with her since the invasion. Since we were children, really."

If Bataar wanted the Harpies in line, he needed to possess them completely. There couldn't be any fear they'd betray him. Nohra was fiercely loyal to her family, born to guard her father. Bataar needed to earn her trust and assert his dominance. If he got her on his side, she'd be his Harpy Knight. Safiya and the rest would follow.

If it wasn't Fahaad, then Darya Daheer was the key. "Her talmaid, then—"

The panic that flashed in Fahaad's eyes was quickly smothered. He dropped the dice, recovered by feigning interest in the half-assed roll. "I've heard rumors of what happened yesterday at the fish market," Fahaad redirected. "Was Nohra there? Is that why she's been confined?"

Dressed in men's riding clothes. Bataar eyed Fahaad's linen tunic dubiously. So, he didn't want to speak about Darya. She might be the key to more than just Nohra's allegiance.

Bataar smiled crookedly as he claimed Fahaad's lioness token, sliding it carefully out of the lower board. "What are the servants saying happened?"

Fahaad leaned back. "The stuff of legends, stories torn from the pages of some fantastical adventure chronicle. A seahorse at the wharf, attacking the displaced families camping on the piers." He lost his tigress piece, then rolled and stole Bataar's kestrels. They each had a small menagerie of the other's animals. "That's why you've generously opened the grounds at the zultam's second palace to the unhoused. The kitchen girls are whispering that a monster wiped out the Kalafar city guard, but you saved the princesses and killed it."

"What do you know about seahorses?"

"That they're supposed to live in the Thirst, if they even still exist, or ever did. They're as skittish as wild horses, and no one's ever gotten a clear look at one."

They kept playing, but Bataar wasn't seeing the boards. "What else do you know?"

"You won."

"What?"

Fahaad waved at the serving table. "The game, you won. You should have proposed a bet." He'd thrown it, Bataar was sure. He'd blown his lead with calculated sloppy moves at the end. Fahaad must have learned to keep favor at court by making sure no one saw him as a threat. He continued, "If I knew more, I'd tell you. When I started as a servant in the stables, I learned how to tack and brush down pegasuses, how to feed them without getting my fingers bitten off, but I'm as ignorant about seahorses as anyone. If anyone should know about monsters, it's you. You're gryphon-marked."

"Just because I killed a gryphon, doesn't mean I know what they think. I don't know why they started coming up the steppe all those years ago. I don't know why seahorses would start swimming up the Scythe." Mostly to himself, he grumbled, "Divine will?"

Fahaad drummed his fingers, bouncing his leg. "If you want religious explanations, talk to Majeed Jabour, or your shaman, or Nohra, even. I don't believe in goddesses or any of the Moshitu faiths. No god's hand guides the monsters that live in our world."

"What do you think, then? No myths, only facts." Bataar finally took a sip of his coffee. It had gone cold.

Fahaad's leg stilled. "The old accounts say seahorses are emotionally intelligent animals. Some at the docks say that the Merchants Guild in Marafal sells seahorse meat. It's supposed to be briny and spongy. They have to be lying, though."

Markets in Choyanren made similar boasts, saying that the long, silver-scaled bodies hanging at stalls were water dragons instead of oarfish. But the only dragons left in Choyanren were the dragonlords breathing out clouds of opium smoke.

"Not even inducted mavens have seen a seahorse," Fahaad continued, "so I don't know how fishing ships could catch them."

"But if the rumors were true... are you suggesting they could seek revenge?"

"Animals can be very emotionally complex." He nudged his cup around, and then his eyes flickered up to meet Bataar's, sparkling with thinly veiled excitement. "You want another possibility? The neck of the Scythe is crowded with shipping vessels. There are more boats in the Thirst than ever, and more salted and smoked fish is sold in the towns upriver than even in Omaar the Peacemaker's time. Less fish in the Thirst, less food for the seahorses. If they're hungry, they might follow the merchant ships, and eat what falls off."

"That's not a bad explanation," Bataar conceded. "What about gryphons? Do you have theories about them?"

Fahaad shrugged. "Habitat loss from mining in the Teeth could have disrupted their migratory paths. The increasing attacks could be the result of food scarcity. They were likely as affected by the Sunless Months as anyone. I really am only truly knowledgeable about pegasuses—"

"Then tell me about them." Bataar had expected enough flying horses for an army. Instead, he'd gotten a half-full stable and servants stuttering about brittle foals.

"They're unnatural beasts." He hesitated. "Some monsters are born, and others bred. The wild stock, the beasts they breed in Antiria, aren't what you'd expect, and their offspring don't always come out looking... right."

"I don't understand."

"As much bird as they are horse, with a face you'd recognize better than I do."

A hippogryph? Was that the name of the creature in the bestiaries?

"If we found a better way to breed pegasuses, could battalions ride them?"

Fahaad snorted a laugh. "You'd have an army of women, or an army of eunuchs. Men don't ride pegasuses."

"Don't, or can't?"

The rectangle of light falling across the marble floor cast the room in a warm glow. "I'm not the best person to consult about breaking tradition. Rami's probably done with his lessons. I should go. Pity you'll miss my thoughts on overhunting in Aglea. Or my theory that rocs are the common ancestor of both pegasuses and gryphons."

"Rocs? Those massive birds?"

"They keep to the aeries. You'll see them from a distance if you move on the Sister City, but their population is shrinking. The desert has little to sustain raptors the size of houses. These days, they pick off the smaller caravans, usually targeting pack horses. Bird-horse, bird-lion: the common denominator is—" He clicked his tongue, letting the rest hang unfinished. Bataar winced at the mental image. "Problem is, it doesn't fit neatly with the story in the Godsbreath. If you'll excuse me."

"Of course. Come back tomorrow." Bataar smiled, and meant it. "I'll find us something stronger to drink. Less bitter."

Fahaad bowed his head and left. Bataar waved for his guards to step outside the double doors to the zultam's quarters. Alone in the huge rooms, the sounds of children's voices carried louder from the grassy courtyard outside. The trilling melody of birdsong spilled on the air, soft and cheerful.

It didn't change that Bataar was sleeping in a dead man's room.

He walked to the windows. Clenching his fingers around the frame, he breathed deep, steadying himself. With a creak, the doors opened. No one announced themselves, but the guards had let the person pass without a word, and he knew the sound of her slippers padding across the checkered floor. Hair picks made plinking sounds as she pulled them out. Heavier metal scraped against one of the tables as hair rustled. Something obscured the smell of edelweiss flowers: steel, blood, sweat, and...

"You smell like hay," Bataar hummed as she wrapped her arms around his middle. "Did you go to the stables?" Nohra had smelled like that last night, at the docks. Bataar held Qaira's hands on his waist. Slowly, he pulled them off, turning and looking down at her.

"I was with Nohra."

A knot formed in his stomach. "What's your aim with her?"

"You think I have ulterior motives?" Qaira tilted her head. Her hair flashed in the beams of sunlight, glowing like embers. Her laughter was music, his favorite melody.

Bataar buried his nose against her cheek, the corner of her mouth. He inhaled black tea and salt sweat.

She parted her lips and breathed him in. "Is that jealousy I smell?"

Her every exhalation was a pant. "I'm not jealous. If you want the princess, have her. I trust you. I just don't trust Nohra."

"You wound me," she taunted, playfully clutching her chest. "She helped me at the Hill. I want to help her now, if I can, be a friend to her. I think she needs one. And along the way, if I make an ally of her—"

"She might get the wrong impression."

"*This* is how I'd seduce someone." Her fingers undid the pearl buttons on his robe and then her warm mouth traveled down the gryphon's mark across his chest. The trail of her tongue burned with want.

Heat spread down his body, his blood pounding. His trousers were too tight, all his clothes too restrictive. "Should

I help you out of your dress?" Bataar said in a rough voice, forgetting all about the damned Harpies.

She fanned herself with an open hand. "Please. It's so hot in here."

He jerked the drapes shut, and Qaira dragged him toward the bed. He let himself be pushed down and she climbed over him, snaring his hips with her thighs as he unfastened the closures on her dress. She tugged her chemise up over her head. Her bare skin glowed golden-white from her neck to her navel.

"You haven't had supper yet?" Qaira asked. The dishes rattled on their tray as she pulled them onto the bed. A silver lid scraped against its round canister. "*Mmmm*, this is delicious. Want a taste?" She leaned in close. Bataar slid his tongue into her mouth, tasting honey on her teeth.

He breathed her in, running fingers down her bare back. The necklace she'd been wearing recently was gone. Gooseflesh prickled on her skin, though the room was sweltering. Her hands traced his other scars; the dent in his collarbone from an old fight with Tarken, the puckered knot where he'd taken an arrow to the abdomen. He gripped the stretch marks striping one of her hips. She pushed into his hand. With his other, he traced the curving side of her body up.

"I want you," he said. *That's all*.

Her breaths came faster. "Luckily I don't already have plans to sleep with any princesses, or I'd have to regretfully decline."

They threw off Bataar's clothes and upturned the silver tray. Like their wedding night, they competed to lay claim. He grabbed her by the hips and flipped her over. She grunted in surprise, wriggling underneath him. Molten iron crept through his stomach, hotter than the sun. Her arms and legs enveloped him, drawing him in, and he swam in her breath against his neck. Bataar winced when her fingertips skimmed the plaster on his side, covering the cut from the boy at the docks.

"Sorry," she hummed.

They drew lines on each other's scars and threw off the sheets. When they were together like this, he couldn't tell where her body ended and his began, only that it filled him with a sense of rightness. He'd never belonged anywhere more than he belonged close to her heart. Home wasn't in the Red Mother's shadow, it was where she was, warm and laughing. When he sank into Qaira's embrace, he let her devour his soul like the Preeminent Spirit.

He'd been almost nineteen when they married, and she was more than a year older. On their consummation bed, the whole world had sparkled. Light had radiated from Qaira's smile like lightning bugs, fallen stars. Her touch was electrifying. It was still fire and ice, almost a decade later.

Before Bataar, Qaira had been with two boys in their camp and one girl. It didn't bother him that she'd slept with other people. Qaira was good at things like this. Once, Rhah-kha had sent a naked girl to Bataar's tent to pleasure him. Bataar had been seventeen, drunk and uncomfortable. He'd thrown up, and the girl fled in tears. Bataar wasn't meant for this, at least not with most people. It was different with Qaira. He *knew* her.

When it was the two of them, he didn't remember cannons or ash falling like fat flakes of snow. He didn't breathe in blood and rot, only flowers and her. She moaned into his mouth and raked nails down his back. She shook under his fingers, his breathless tongue. When they were both finally spent, darkness bled through the heavy drapes, bathing the zultam's room in bluish shadows. Every bit of her was pressed against him. He

235

traced the arc of her ear absently with his free hand. Her chin was propped up on his chest, and her hazel eyes watched him, like a cat's eyes flashing in the dark.

"Untie me?" Bataar asked, testing the binding taut around his other wrist. She'd tied his red silk belt like a mooring line. The bedframe groaned.

Qaira pouted. "I like you like that."

"I can't wage a war strung to a bed." He flexed his hand. It was starting to go numb.

She pulled out the slipknot and settled back down, cradling his wrist.

"What is it?" he asked, watching her expression shift.

"You shouldn't make those girls prisoners in their own home." Her words were measured as she entwined their fingers. "You should let them finish burying their father, in the mountains."

"If you want that."

She pursed her lips. "Now you. Tell me what's weighing on your mind. I see it on your face. I'm supposed to share your burdens."

"I need Rayenna," he said. He kept his face still, watching her expression intently for any flicker of emotion. "If Clemiria continues to deny me, I'll have to take the city from her."

It wouldn't be tomorrow. It might not even be in a month's time. Kalafar should be under control first. He had to solidify his claim here. A wedding would help with that, more pacts and land divisions.

Smoky night air floated languidly through the zultam's quarters. "Then, I'll move on Aglea." He held his breath. If she said to end this, he would. When he'd been younger, he couldn't just stop. Wheels had been spinning, and if he'd tried to stand in front of them, the war machine would have run him over. But he wasn't a boy anymore. The machines of war didn't move without his word.

Knowledge and resources shared and traded freely from Kalafar all the way to Choyanren would be enough. He wanted a world where families didn't go hungry in the winter, where little boys weren't devoured by gryphons, where girls weren't torn from their families in the middle of the night. This empire could be enough. Ramzi's sister could keep Rayenna.

Qaira's voice was low and raspy when she finally answered, touching his eyelids tenderly. "Is this what They compel?"

How could Bataar ever hope to know what that horrible face wanted? The universe craved carnage and rebirth. He hated when she looked at him like he'd been singled out by the Preeminent Spirit, his ability to see souls an indication of Their favor. If she knew exactly what he saw in the sky, he wasn't sure she'd ever smile again.

"I think so." *Something* possessed him to constantly want more.

Her nose wrinkled. "Then the world belongs to you."

He'd have to be an idiot not to see the pain twisting her mouth. Qaira knew the cost of winning a war. She was the one in the triage tent, covered in blood, collecting final words. She wanted an endless spring for Ganni and Bato to grow up in.

But Bataar knew the price of peace.

"And your love?" he asked.

"It's yours. It's always been yours."

The world was massive, and Bataar was miniscule. He needed to be the force that controlled the tides, not the ship dashed against a rocky shore.

If Clemiria resisted, he'd take Rayenna. Then the rest.

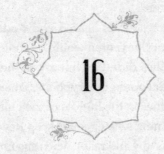

16

Chasms of my heart a vault I'm locked in.

She wants tears to water the roses,

rage to rattle a kingdom.

— "Ties of Blood", a poem

Nohra kept a close eye on her little brother during the carriage ride to the mountains. The heartbox was balanced on his knees, Rami's touch on its corners feather-light. At every bump in the unpaved mountain road, Oktai lurched forward, ready to catch it if it slipped through her brother's fingers. Nohra's thoughts were too distracted to be annoyed that Bataar had sent his ears with her to Antiria.

Her father's heart had haunted her troubled dreams. Entombing this last part of him was long overdue.

The grand vizier's daughter, Mahveen Naji, sat beside Rami, pressed up against the opposite window, as if she couldn't be far enough away from the prince's unkempt hair and rumpled clothes. Her hands were folded primly on her lap, and a shawl modestly covered her shoulders and head.

"It doesn't smell bad," Rami observed, voice mild and toneless. Up until then, the thick silence had been broken only by the sound of misty rain pattering on the carriage windows. Mahveen made a face.

"That's because it's preserved like the bodies in the crypt," Nohra explained, "with scented oils."

Her brother blinked up at her, once, twice. "I know how embalming works, Nohra. I'm not six." He was already taller than most of her half-brothers had been at his age. He knew a little algebra and was a fast reader, but he didn't care for lessons as much as he enjoyed riding his pony and hunting. Nohra's heart tugged. He would have been a good king.

No. He would still be the zultam.

Oktai's annoyingly steady gaze burned the side of Nohra's face, like the stupid boy could hear her thoughts.

Nohra forced a tight smile. "After we visit the vault, Saf can take you hunting."

Rami twisted to stare out the other carriage window. "We didn't bring Snowy. I don't want to fly another bird."

Nohra nodded at the grand vizier's daughter. "You hunt?" The girl shook her head. The glittering embroidery on the cuffs of her long sleeves caught Nohra's eye. "Do you sew?"

"She can play the lyre," Rami said absently. The older girl looked down, cheeks coloring. He added, in a mean whisper, "She's alright at reading music, at least."

"Then you'll have to play for us after supper."

The girl squeaked her acquiescence. What a meek little queen she'd be. Maybe their exchange would be less stilted if Nohra and her guard weren't riding with them. Nohra had been spared the awkwardness of a childhood betrothal. On the way back, she'd ask her grandmother or Darya to play chaperone.

Their coach rolled to a stop. "Are we there?" Rami asked.

Nohra unlatched the window to crane her head out. The stagecoach drivers shouted at a merchant carriage with a wheel stuck in the wet dirt. The horses whickered, swishing their tails in agitation.

"Come on, Nohra. Let's help," Saf said, climbing out of one of the carriages stalled behind them. She was dressed like a prince in men's clothes. As her boots sloshed through the mud, she pulled back her thick hair and tied it up.

"Wait, princess, I'll go—" Oktai started, nearly bumping his head on the roof as he hopped up to get the door.

"Stay there," Nohra ordered. "Watch the prince."

She jumped down and trudged forward, grimacing when dirt splattered up her pants. The hills surrounding the palace were full of fields of wildflowers, thick forest, and brick houses. The people of Antiria were mainly beekeepers, craftspeople, and artists, but large estates outside of town belonged to rich families who visited in the spring, when the hanging garden flowered at the palace. Cool mountain mist covered the ground in clouds. After hours cramped in the carriage, it caressed Nohra's skin like an icy kiss. The air carried the scents of nectar and petrichor, and light bathed the village, casting it in an otherworldly glow.

She took a long, deep breath and strode stiffly toward Safiya and the harem guards crowding around the stuck merchant cart.

The back of the apiarist's covered carriage contained row after row of jars filled with honey and pieces of waxy comb. Wicker baskets in various sizes, shapes, and colors tottered in stacks. The couple driving the cart accepted their help with stuttered apologies. Safiya wedged a broken board under the stuck wheel and pushed with the grooms and guards while Nohra coaxed the mule forward.

A crowd of villagers gathered to gawk and whisper.

"Our daughters won't believe it when I tell them what

happened," the apiarist gushed, pushing jars of pale, creamy honey into Nohra's and Saf's hands. One of the harem guards shoved the man back, making space between him and the princesses, but Safiya waved their valiant protector away.

"That's alright," she said, sounding more amused than annoyed.

"And to carry them," the man's wife said, thrusting the handle of a splint basket at Nohra. "Woven by our oldest. The willow branches were soaked in the Heartsvein that feeds into the Scythe."

"What will I do with a basket?" Nohra whispered when the couple had left, their cart rolling on its wobbly wheels down the muddy road.

Safiya shrugged. "Give it to Darya. You'll need to find something for her natal day soon anyway."

Nohra's face heated. "I was going to give her something better than a basket."

She'd bought a bolt of cobalt-colored silk at the textile market and was embroidering pink lotus blossoms on it. Her sewing instructor would have sneered at her attempt at beadwork, but the real problem was that she hadn't picked up the project since the invasion, except to check it was still hidden in her chest.

"That shawl you're working on is too showy. You know our little kitchen mouse wouldn't wear something like that. She prefers being invisible."

"Don't you think that color would look good on her?" Nohra fired back.

"You're not subtle. Everyone knows Fahaad's favorite color is blue." Safiya gave the jar of honey a shake. "You know, I've actually thought about keeping bees. Zira loves the palace gardens, so we've talked about finding a cottage, planting roses and crocuses and orchids, something like Mother's house. Somewhere where there'd be no one around to bother us." Safiya threw open the door to the carriage and swung herself up.

"Your Highnesses," Oktai stammered as she squeezed past.

"Could you ride with the grooms?" Saf asked, sliding open a viewing window. "You can keep an eye on us through here. Please, Oktai, there's not enough room."

As her guard climbed out, Nohra's mind went numb at the thought of Safiya leaving their family forever to keep *bees* like an old man.

Rami brightened, leaning toward Safiya as she climbed in across from him. "What were you talking about, Saf? You're going somewhere? I'm allowed to come visit you, right?"

She punched his shoulder. "I'm sure you'll have much more important things to do than visit your *ooold* sister," she said in her best impersonation of Grandmother Himma, who was probably grumbling about the delay in one of the trailing carriages. Naji's daughter shrunk back, grimacing and keeping the hem of her dress away from their muddy shoes. "Life's too short to worry about getting your clothes dirty, Mahveen," Saf teased.

At the colonnade in front of the palace doors, Safiya helped Mahveen down. Then she goaded Rami into jumping the steep drop while Nohra held the heartbox. Nohra absently stroked the smooth mother-of-pearl inlay. When she died, it would probably be on a battlefield. The carrion birds would pluck out her heart before it could be preserved in a pretty jeweled chest.

Rami landed, legs buckling as he pitched forward. He got up and rubbed his scraped knees. "*Saf,*" Nohra chided.

"It's just some fun," Safiya said, walking to the next carriage and putting out a hand for their grandmother and each of the concubines. The last out was Zira, wearing earrings even larger than Nohra's. The glossy folds of her dress billowed as she hopped and Safiya caught her around the waist.

Zira had bright eyes, not as black as Darya's, and deep brown skin. Her thick hair was fastened back with golden bands in a style popular to the south, on the islands that traded with Dumakra. The small swell of her belly was mostly hidden under her skirts. Her hand lingered for a second on Saf's glove; then she swept past, bustling off toward the other concubines. Safiya's eyes stayed locked on Zira's fingers as they slipped through hers.

How could their father have not noticed the gentle touches and lingering smiles? Maybe he had known, and he'd liked holding power over his unruly oldest daughter.

No. Their father could be cold, but never cruel. He had loved Safiya's mother Suri. He would have married her if she'd accepted the Goddess. He wouldn't have knowingly hurt Saf. It was just unkind fate. Nohra shook her head, banishing the thought.

Butterflies flitted between flowers, probing at the jasmines, and spiderwebs stretched between the bushes, glistening with dew. The hanging gardens blanketed the building in green ivy. Some younger concubines and handmaids stretched to pull down white flowers to tuck behind their ears. Nohra had once thought this palace was paradise on earth.

"The box," Rami said, putting out his hands for it after he'd swiped all the dirt off his clothes.

"Go get dressed, and we'll visit the tombs," Safiya told him, ruffling his hair. "Can't have you looking like a wet rat in front of your mother."

Rami swatted her hand and rolled his eyes.

Nohra's hands were empty without something to hold. Home for the next few days would be the Palace of the Heart, a sprawling vacation house with hundreds of rosy granite pillars, dozens of fountains, and pools full of pink lilies.

As morning turned to afternoon, the smolder of the sun fought the crisp air coming off the mountain, but in the shade cast by the leafy veiled walkways, the late summer breeze turned refreshingly cool.

She matched Saf's pace, walking beside her through the winding inner gardens as Oktai trailed behind. Servants who'd arrived yesterday carried trunks and stacks of clean sheets and buckets of hot water. Clouds of lavender-scented steam poured out of the bathing rooms, and maids passing by giggled and smiled. It was all wrong. Nohra instinctively grabbed the chain around her neck, twisting it between her fingers.

"After you, Your Highness," Safiya said, bowing dramatically. Oktai stood stiffly at attention outside the threshold, grimacing as Saf shut the door behind them.

She hadn't led Nohra to the Harpies' quarters where they'd stayed that spring. This room was trapped in time, looking the same as it had a decade ago. Their childhood quarters at the Palace of the Heart had a worn quilt on the bed and sunny yellow tile on the walls. The lacy curtains rippled.

"These are still here, too," Safiya said, kneeling down and prying up a loose board on the floor.

She pulled out two wooden play swords covered in scuffs and splintered edges, a diary, and a doll. Nohra reached for the leather-bound journal.

"No you don't." Saf pushed the doll at her. "This one's yours. Sixteen-year-old Safiya's innermost thoughts aren't allowed to see the light of day. Play with this creepy thing instead."

The porcelain doll's hair was spun gold, and its eyes sparkled like Noorish sapphires. After her mother died, Nohra had worried its delicate body would shatter, so she'd found a safe place for the doll and entombed her. Now, she sat her on the dressing table by the bed.

"Please tell me you aren't going to let that watch me all night," Saf moaned, tossing off her dirty tunic. She threw open her trunk, and bright velvets spilled out.

Safiya had set her jar of honey from the apiarist on the dresser. Nohra stared at it until the edges of her vision blurred, resentment swirling inside her. "So you're going to leave us and sell honey," she finally blurted.

"Sure. Every bird flies the nest someday. Why can't I?" Safiya squirmed into her chemise.

"Because we have responsibilities here! Oaths we swore. Duties to our family."

Nohra's mother and father were gone. Suri leaving had felt like losing her own mother all over again. Losing Saf too would be unfair.

"You think I'm running from my duties?" Safiya's brows pinched together. "I'm here, aren't I?" The dress she'd picked fell fluidly down, swirling around her bare feet. It had been ages since Saf wore a gown.

"Have you even tried to bring anyone to our cause?" Nohra whispered. Her voice was barely louder than the sound of rustling fabric as she stripped off her clothes.

Saf glanced between Nohra and the shut door. "I found a family who might support Rami." Her voice was low, barely audible. "The Sartarids."

"No." Nohra tugged on the doll's hair. "That's not even a good joke."

"Does it look like I'm trying to be funny?" Safiya was unsmiling. "You can give them back some of their lands in Marafal, the ones Father gave to Lofri, and they'll give you their support. Their youngest son's been fighting in Aglean tournaments and winning. You could use a fighter like that."

Nohra gaped. "A tourney fighter? They're all flash. And their father"—she lowered her voice even further—"challenged Father's legitimacy. *Our* legitimacy."

"Yes, well, yesterday's enemy is tomorrow's reluctant-yet-willing ally. They have nothing left to lose. That's the only kind of people you can rally."

"There's no one else?"

Saf smiled sweetly. "Meric Ward, if you'll put on a wedding dress and a fur cloak, and ask Darya to pack your things."

She pulled Nohra's jewelry out of her traveling trunk. Inside the box, all fifteen of Nohra's natal-day rings were tied into the velvet lining. That had been Qaira's doing. She'd made Bataar track them down and buy them off the man who'd trashed Nohra's room. Blinking at the rings, the edges of Nohra's vision swam with white.

Safiya took out a pair of earrings and held them up to Nohra's ears. "Where is Darya? She really should try to do something with your hair."

Nohra winced, bending her arms over her head to pull her hair through the collar.

They both jumped at a knock at the door. "Sorry about the mess," Safiya's talmaid Laila said, poking her head in. "We only aired out the rooms we thought we'd need. Dar and I didn't think you'd want to stay here tonight. I'll fetch fresh linens and a broom to beat the dust from the rugs."

Saf laughed radiantly and threw herself onto their childhood bed. A cloud of gray blew up from the quilt. "I like the dust. It smells homey, like being a little girl."

"Listen," Nohra said crossly. "If we need *friends* and are having so much trouble finding them, our aunt is the answer to our problems—"

"Not right now, Nohra," Safiya sang, sending her a warning look. Oktai peered into the room, flushing when he spotted Nohra still half-undressed in her chemise. He hit his shoulder against the doorframe as he ducked back out.

"Apologies! I thought you'd be ready," he stammered.

Bataar hadn't come with them to Antiria, but he'd probably sent more than one pair of eyes to watch her. Oktai was a thorn in her foot Nohra would be glad to get rid of.

If they needed allies, they should just spur their aunt to action. They wouldn't need the Sartarid family or Meric Ward or anyone. Clemiria wasn't just the queen of Rayenna, she was a Harpy queen. She was worth a dozen stupid jousting knights. If she moved her army on Kalafar, they could retake the city.

"I'll help with your dress, Your Highness," Laila said, standing on tiptoe to reach.

"Have you been alright? Since…" Nohra trailed off. Outside, rose bushes stretched as far as she could see. The royal woods beyond the gardens made an impenetrable wall of larch, fir, and pine.

Laila swallowed, a thick sound. "Safiya took me to the training grounds at the palace to practice with my knives. I froze up that night, when one of the soldiers grabbed me."

Nohra laid her hand over Laila's small freckled one. "It's a reaction anyone could have. No one's disappointed in you. Thank the Goddess you all could protect each other."

The talmaid's fingers twitched. She nodded quickly. "Darya." She choked on her name. "I think we all would have died without her. She was…"

Probably indispensable in evacuating and keeping everyone calm.

Saf squeezed Laila's shaking shoulder. "You would have done the same for her, for any of the girls in the harem."

Laila's smile was so small and brief it could be mistaken for a spasming muscle. "I couldn't have done that. I'd never seen Darya like that, you wouldn't have believed—" She bit her lip to cut herself off, face reddening. "Forgive me!"

A rush of adrenaline could be more powerful than even the most fastidious lessons, Nohra knew. It was almost as frightening to see someone you love become a monster as it was to strike the killing blow yourself. A thrill of pride tightened her throat that her Darya had protected the other girls.

Saf clapped her hands. "Are you ready? Rami has the box. We should go to the vault."

⚮

The story went that when Queen Roksanya died, the king sent her body back to North Aglea to be buried in a grave at her family's fortress. Her husband wanted to be entombed beside her, but a zultam's casket couldn't be removed from Dumakran soil, from Kalafar, so he kept her embalmed heart in a wooden box and built a mausoleum for her in Antiria, where she loved to watch winter turn to spring.

It was a romantic story. Nohra didn't believe in sentiments like that anymore.

The temperature dropped several degrees as they descended the winding stairs into the vault. Darya walked solemnly ahead, lighting the way with a lantern. They'd been distant since the wharf house. Darya had never been so close yet so out of reach, as though if Nohra were to stretch out her hand, her fingers might pass through the spectral shape of her.

Firelight flickering on the wet walls reminded Nohra of the cisterns in the capital that were connected to the aqueducts, and subterranean pools full of pale, blind fish.

Most of the concubines had come with them, and almost all

Nohra's sisters, except for the little ones and Aalya. Missing was Nassar—the treasonous snake had stayed in the capital— and their half-brothers who were wards of families in distant parts of the country. Queen Merv was also absent. She'd stayed in the port town, squabbling over the mines and money Aalya was to inherit.

Nohra was sure Merv wouldn't have been pleased anyway to watch her husband's heart laid to rest in the dual crevice beside his second wife's.

Grandmother Himma tightened her grip, her fingers digging into the meat of Nohra's upper arm. Her other lightly wrinkled hand snared Saf so she could walk between them.

"How are you, Grandmother?" Safiya asked.

Grandmother Himma hmphed. "What mother wants to entomb her son?"

Nohra grumbled, "Calidah should be here." Their cousin had stayed behind to keep Aalya company.

Their grandmother regarded Nohra with an arched eyebrow. "Well, it's not like he was her father."

"But she was one of his Harpies."

"And what does that mean anymore?"

"I'm surprised any of us are allowed to come," Safiya said, leaning around to watch Nohra with curiosity and a hint of amusement. "It was very generous. Surprisingly generous. Did you do something?"

"No," Nohra answered, too quickly. She thought of the natal-day rings, of Qaira's kindness, too warm to trust. A word from her meant everything to Bataar, and she'd spoken for them, for Nohra. "I might have expressed a little regret to the rhah's wife."

"I wonder what other suggestions you could convey to Bataar through her?"

"Suggest that he should try wearing a Nuna's whip as a necklace," Grandmother Himma hissed.

Saf laughingly patted her hand, steadying her when she teetered on a step. "Now, now, Grandmother. It's dark, but the spiders and scorpions are still listening."

Heat boiled up in Nohra's chest as she stared down at her grandmother, and Himma met her gaze, fire with fire. She didn't know how much influence their grandmother had at court with their father dead, but the queen mother was the most well-connected figure at the palace. Her venom belied her usually perfectly polite facade.

Rami pulled ahead, walking down the rows of stone niches toward Thora's heartbox, as if he'd memorized the way. He couldn't possibly remember where it was. Nohra had taken him down here once on his sixth natal day and hadn't bothered dragging him back again on the following anniversaries of their mother's death. Instead, every year, Nohra let Safiya and their father take Rami hunting in the woods for his birthday while she stood down in the cool, damp hall, staring at the box in its cubby on the rock wall, trying not to shiver.

Nohra handed off her grandmother and lifted the hem of her dress to walk faster. Her earrings jangled as she picked up her pace, overtaking her little brother's strides. "It's that one," she told him, pointing at the empty spot beside a silver heartbox, but he'd already stopped.

He did remember.

Wearing the same blank, disinterested expression he'd had in the carriage, Rami pushed their father's chest into the open space. His unreadable gaze flitted briefly to Thora's spot before moving on, into the darkness. "You all can say the words now," he said. "If it's alright, I'll go to my room."

17

Omaar ruled the newly formed capital city with a firm hand. His prison tower casts a longer shadow than Peacemaker's Bridge.

— *Making Kalafar*

The cobbled road stretching toward the prison tower was packed with carts, horses, and pedestrians. Bataar had dressed in plain clothes and brought few guards. A large retinue would attract attention, and he meant to judge the streets by daylight, without crowds cowering back and parting for him. At the road's fringes, a few fruit merchants argued with hagglers and a vendor peddled sweets in the shade of a tree. A smoky, caramelly scent and the sound of chattering academics wafted from one of the sunken coffee houses.

Somewhere, something was dying. Every second of every day, a life ran out. Faint ephemeral shapes danced in the air. Stronger than the gazes of random passersby, the weight of black sun eyes bore into the back of his head. Preeminence drank in the day.

Wael Bahdi, the captain of the city guard Lofri had appointed, grabbed Bataar by the shoulder and pointed. "Would you look at that?" He tossed a copper ego into a metal bucket. A girl snapped finger cymbals while a man loomed over a small animal beating a drum. "It's amazing what a man can make a monkey do in Kalafar."

Bataar was sick of monkeys. He made a face and brushed Wael's hand off. "There weren't any disturbances last night?"

"The city's not as restless anymore." Wael fussed with the sleeve of his tunic. He was a broad-shouldered man with a face like broken knuckles. "The mob's been slavering like dogs at the public executions, but there's order. It's *our* executioner's block they're crowding around. Better the king's justice by the light of day than some butcher-boys in the middle of the night." He glanced at Bataar like they shared a secret. "Things have been a lot quieter after we caught the last one of *those things*, and dragged it downriver to the Conservium, like you asked."

Bataar rubbed his neck. "It didn't burst into seafoam?" Perhaps it *could* be useful, like Nohra had wanted.

"Nah, screamed like something awful though. We couldn't keep it quiet. Probably no one in the wharf houses could tell what the boat was pulling, I'd bet. It wasn't a sound I'd ever imagined an animal could make."

"I'm impressed your men caught it." The monkey had stopped beating the drum and was now waddling with the donation bucket toward the gathered crowd.

Wael's laugh fell like coins. "Yeah, well it was distracted. Found it with its face buried in a girl's guts."

Concerned faces flashed to them. One man put a protective arm around his son, and a towheaded foreigner looked over with brows drawn, as if his passable grasp of the language must have failed him. Bataar steered the captain away before his words accidentally incited panic. His own fingers still smelled metallic from picking up copper pieces, handling and approving the new die at the royal mint that morning.

The grand vizier stood up ahead, stroking his neat beard. "Your Eminence," Yardaan Naji said, waving a hand at the stone prison. At the top, the Forked Tower jutted in two directions, ending in tall arches supporting conical roofs with gold finials. The music of the sanctiums' afternoon bells filled the sky, dispersing flocks of pigeons, but the prison stretched taller than the holy buildings.

The entrance was up a winding flight of stone stairs. Guardsmen stationed on the landing straightened and acknowledged them stiffly.

"Grand Vizier, Captain Bahdi, *Your Eminence*." The last, spoken like foreign words, rough on their tongues. Four more city guards sat on crates playing Court with worn cards, while another sharpened his sword against a whetstone, watching the unassuming crowds on the street with a mistrustful look.

Compared to the chaos after the funeral, Kalafar had mellowed. More food was flowing into the city, and Bataar sent representatives into sanctiums to inform citizens of new public works plans. Whispers about the gryphon king were turning reverent.

Darkness fell as they passed through the threshold, round gray walls illuminated by the light of only a few sconces. "There are more cells on the basement levels," Naji said, "but for most of them, we'll need to go up. The more dangerous or important the prisoner, the farther their cell is from the ground floor and mezzanine." A creaking wooden staircase coiled up the tower, jutting from the rough brick without any guardrails.

"I would've worn looser pants if I'd known I'd be walking all over Kalafar," Wael Bahdi complained. "When we get to the top, I might jump and save myself the trouble of stumbling back down all the damn stairs."

Naji glared, conveying that he thought it would also save the rest of them some fuss if the man took a long fall and splattered himself all over Larcstreet. Bataar couldn't help but concur. The captain of the city guard was in Lofri's pocket. That concerned Bataar, though the man was irritatingly capable when he wasn't soused.

Grand Vizier Naji explained the history of the building as they climbed up the first few flights. "The open upper floor is the highest point in Kalafar, other than the mountains. City guards use it as a vantage point to watch for fires. Not that it was helpful during the invasion."

Yardaan Naji's great-great-grand-something, Shassam Naji, was Omaar the Peacemaker's architect and later Zultam Numa's Minister of Architonics. The grand vizier was probably a trove of knowledge about all the secrets hidden in the capital's old buildings, if Bataar could wheedle them from him. This business with the assassin was disquieting. If there were secret rooms and passageways in the Rutiaba Palace, Naji might know of them.

How much higher? Each flight seemed like a bolder challenge, trespassing on Preeminence—

"Thank you for proposing the match with Rami and Mahveen, Your Eminence," Naji said, wrenching Bataar from his thoughts. "My daughter has a particular fondness for the young prince, and I think their temperaments complement each other."

Bataar glanced down at the blackness at the foot of the spiraling steps. "It's a strong match." Clearing his throat, he tried to keep his voice from cracking. He'd needed to throw Naji a bone, and apparently Rami was sufficient.

"I think it's wise to unite the families, especially now." He paused, seemingly mulling something over. "Bataar, you have a daughter yourself."

If Bataar never struck another marriage match for Ganni, it would be too soon. The words to shoot down whatever Naji was proposing sat on the tip of his tongue.

Captain Bahdi had fallen behind, almost a flight below them. He stopped and hunched over, hands braced on his knees as he gasped for breath.

Bataar faced the grand vizier, tilting his head. "Speak freely."

"I've known Ramzi's daughters since they were little girls," Naji murmured, his voice barely louder than a whisper. "I stood outside the birthing room with the zultam when Safiya was born. I bounced Nohra on my knee during councilors' meetings when she had the gripes as a baby. Little Aalya, taking in all those mangy cats—she's as dear to my wife as our own daughters. I care about those young women. And even Calidah, she used to read books to my girls in the courtyard."

Dread swirled in Bataar's stomach. "Alright. What are you trying to say?"

Naji looked down at his boots as the platform leveled out. "There's disquieting news from Rayenna." His voice was even lower now, almost inaudible. He took a shaky breath. "Queen Clemiria will move on the capital, and when she does, I fear the Harpy Knights will take her side. When they fail, it will be too late for my words. My silence could mean the death of them. If you interpret this admission as treason, I'll walk to the cells gladly, but show mercy to those girls."

The chill making Bataar shiver wasn't just from the cool stone walls, and his spiked pulse wasn't from climbing the stairs. Suspicion stabbed him. "How'd you come by this knowledge? Someone entrusted you with it willingly?"

"One of the concubines has Princess Safiya's ear. I've paid her to keep an eye on the girls for over a year now, at Ramzi's request. Zira comes from one of the island pleasure houses, and she's very comfortable living at the palace. She'd do anything to stay here. When she visited me after the invasion, I told her to keep watching Safiya. I was worried about something like this, and I was right to be. Zira intercepted a missive from their aunt."

The eyes Bataar had watching the former courtesan hadn't noticed she was in the grand vizier's pocket.

"You could stop them," Naji insisted. "If you march on Rayenna, you can blot out the treason before it's begun. This wasn't their idea. They're just so loyal to Clemiria—"

It was difficult to focus on the grand vizier's whispered pleading with the realization of sedition making Bataar's blood pump so loud.

"Right this way," Wael interrupted breathlessly, leading them toward iron bars.

"We'll discuss this matter later," Bataar promised, his mind racing.

The floor was covered with soiled straw. Metal pans to piss in were scattered around, but a few prisoners in the communal cell must have missed, because the whole level of the tower reeked of urine. The chamber pot was full and covered in black flies. Two men sat near a stinking pile of feces, wearing glazed-over expressions.

Bataar jutted his chin at them. "They're assassins too?"

"A couple of thugs enjoying their last day with both their hands," Wael explained. "I thought they could keep *her* company. Bring her over."

Bataar looked at the woman slumped against the wall, revulsion turning over in his stomach as he took in all the blood. The jailer unlocked the cell and dragged her through the straw, pushing her down in front of Bataar. As she stumbled forward, the chain attached to her shackled leg rattled.

"We knocked out a false tooth." Wael tapped his own mouth. "Might have gotten a bit ahead of ourselves, 'cause Zareb pulled another one too, except it didn't have a cyanide cap, and then her mouth was full of blood and she couldn't say anything."

The woman's nails were cracked and crusted with brownish-red flecks, and the faces of the men in her cell were raked with bloody streaks. Some of her fingers ended in freshly cauterized stumps, and her face was swollen from a black eye. One of her arms bent at an unnatural slant; yellow bruising encircled her swollen ankle. Her lip was split, and bruises made a chain around her neck above the collar of the torn tunic they'd dressed her in. She shook, but met Bataar's eyes with a steely gaze.

"Here's the fake tooth," Wael said. "And we've got all her things on the first floor: poisons in bottles, knives and hidden blades and thin picks. She snuck in through the Swan Gate without papers and landed on Craullstreet. You wouldn't believe me, but she was a perfectly pretty thing before yesterday."

Naji cut in. "The woman who supplies Prince Nassar with courtesans acquired her and directed her to His Majesty. A maid became suspicious and riffled through her personal belongings—"

"You have one of them in your employ, too?" Bataar guessed. "I'll bet she was curious because you're paying her to be."

The older man shrugged. "I make it my job to know what's happening with the zultam's children. The girl reporting to me is dead now, but at least Nassar isn't."

"He was her mark?"

"Or the Dowager Queen, or—more likely—you."

Bataar swallowed thickly. "She confessed that?" Since they'd removed her poison-capped tooth, they'd stolen her painless way out.

Wael Bahdi scoffed. "After the tooth, she bit off her own tongue."

"And she's definitely one of Clemiria's? She looks Aglean."

The captain grabbed a fistful of brown hair and twisted her head around, exposing a small red tattoo at the nape of her neck. "A Nuna's whip. That viper's a symbol of one of the guilds in the Sister City."

"Light-colored eyes are common among the Qadishal people in Rayenna," Naji explained. "I'd wager she's got some of that ancestry."

Bataar sighed, rubbing his temples. "The woman supplying Nassar with girls had to have seen the mark. She knew then, if she didn't already. She's as guilty as Queen Clemiria."

"Yeah, well the old bat fled last night." Captain Bahdi crossed his arms and leaned against the open door to the cell. "Got my men out looking, but she's probably snuck outta the city."

"And this woman is going to be executed tomorrow?"

The captain drew a line with his thumb across his throat. "We can have her head tomorrow or when the rest of the Harpies are back. Might send a stronger message, a united front. Until then she'll be plenty comfortable here."

The Qadishal woman stared at Bataar through blood-crusted lashes. Outside, below on Larcstreet, children licked candy animals. There were rocks in Bataar's stomach. Gravelly bile burned up his throat, but he choked it down. Quickly, he unsheathed his knife and, kneeling, reaching around her neck, he stabbed into her spine. Her spirit sighed out of her, unspooling onto his lap. He could almost feel its weight, could have cradled it in his hand. She fell forward into his arms and bled out, limp and unfeeling, slumped against him.

❧

"If you want to disrupt the Harpies' plan, you should move on Rayenna," Naji repeated as they passed through the palace gates. He paused, building to something else. "And when you send troops across the desert, your caravan should stop at a critical old waypoint, to replenish water and rest."

The shirt Bataar had bought at a bazaar stall was stiff and scratchy, too hot for the waning end of summer. But he'd been even less inclined to wear the tunic the jailer offered, covered in sweat stains, than he was to keep wearing the one dyed with the blood of the Qadishal assassin.

His scar itched. Shaza would smack his head and say he was too soft on women. "What waypoint?" he asked, trying to rub all the blood off his hands before—

"Bapa!" Ganni yelled, running through the lawn toward him. Her brother toddled behind her. When she crashed into Bataar's legs, he hesitated to lay his hand on her dark hair. What if the smell of iron never washed out?

It was all in his imagination. His hands were clean, he'd scrubbed them raw in a sanctium fountain.

"Anhabar is midway between Kalafar and the Sister City," Naji explained. "I could go ahead with a small retinue, if it pleases you, to make arrangements to house the soldiers and confirm the water's potable. Most caravans circumvent the ruins out of fear, but it presents an invaluable shelter against storms and is potentially the only source of water for the second leg of the journey."

Bataar dimly remembered learning about the abandoned city in the audience hall when the terms of surrender were read almost two months ago. Most Dumakrans balked at the mention of its name, as if merely intoning "Anhabar" would summon specters and cannibals.

He scooped up Ganni. Every day she got taller and heavier. Near one of the bathing pools, Qaira waved at him.

"Would that be necessary?" Bataar was ready to be done with Naji for the day. This man would betray the zultam and his daughters; he had even less reason to be loyal to Bataar. "Doesn't the High Sanctium assign a cleric to care for the temple there? Surely the water's drinkable, at least, if that man's alive. I don't see why you need to go."

Yardaan Naji was the son and great-grandson of some of the nation's most accomplished architects. Anhabar was Dumakra's preeminent Wonder of Man—a city carved into a mountain, with a palace and temple worthy of kings and gods.

"Ramzi was superstitious," Naji explained. "He didn't like when I brought up this idea. Kalafar is finally calm—but imagine the favor you'd win if you reclaimed the old capital and banished the superstition. The flight west was centuries ago. You'd be the one to take the mountain back. You could host a magnificent wedding there, after you take Rayenna."

The generals would want Aalya wed before they went east, to strengthen the alliance, but the girl was weak, and her mother was still in the port town, arguing for her inheritance. Bataar had decided he'd marry her to Oktai. His bloodsworn brother's cousin was Bataar's blood too, and the boy was overdue to take on more responsibility. If Lofri objected, Bataar could always kill the old man. He could marry them in the old capital, after they took Rayenna.

"You're not afraid of Anhabar?" He was still mistrustful. Ganni snuggled against his shirt. "You think it's possible to rebuild?"

Naji stroked his gray-streaked beard. "I can't be sure. The temple's the only part that's inhabited, and it's inaccessible to the public. But Anhabar only fell because of disease. Structurally it should be sound. I can take some scholars from the Conservium and assess its stability. Many will want to study the ruins."

"You smell like the copper pieces we were throwing into the wishing fountain," Ganni said, blinking up at Bataar. "Look what me and the baby found in the garden." She pulled a fat, wet slug out of her pocket and pushed it in Bataar's face.

Eight years old was getting to be too big to spend all her time playing with toads, slugs, spiders, and bugs with thousands of legs, but he couldn't tell her that.

"Ah." Bataar nodded, appraising. "That's a handsome one."

"Did you want to see?" She shoved the slick-looking creature at Naji. His nostrils flared.

Little Bato was still teetering halfway across the lawn, but Qaira was already past him. Ignoring Ganni's protests, Bataar put his daughter down and caught Qaira in his arms. She laughed like bells chiming as the force of her momentum swung them around. The world blurred and he fell down, her body firmly on top of his.

"No fair. You didn't spin me," Ganni grumbled. Behind her Bato stumbled, rolled forward, and began squalling.

Qaira nuzzled Bataar's face, inhaling the scent of him. "You smell like blood," she whispered, and the summer day was less golden. "Did something happen? Are you alright?"

He leaned forward and swung them both up to their feet. "I'm fine." Bataar smiled unconvincingly, aware he wasn't showing his teeth. "Don't I look fine?"

She smoothed his cheek, her thumb smudging something off. "You've looked better."

Naji cleared his throat. "Remember your promise."

Bataar nodded. On the way back, in hushed tones, the grand vizier had elaborated on Clemiria's plot. If Bataar cut off their aunt, tightened the Harpies' leash, anticipated their moves, and kept them in line, he wouldn't have to execute them for treason. He didn't want more blood on his hands. But he wouldn't let them stab him in the back, either.

"Bapa! Let me braid your hair," Ganni said, tugging on his leg.

Around the grassy courtyard, little princesses and their mothers stared at him with wide eyes and quickly looked away. These girls were too young to visit the vault in the mountains with the rest of their family, so they'd been left behind. His daughter pulled him into the center of the women. Bataar remembered being fourteen, watching Qaira braid blossom circlets for the children in their camp and thinking he'd never seen anything more useless than a crown made of flowers, but also that Qaira's hair was pretty when the sun hit it and it lit up like flames.

A needle of warmth pricked his chest.

Bataar sat on the lawn while Ganni tied his hair in knots. He tried not to wince at the strain on his scalp as he bounced Bato in his lap. When the children got up to play, Bataar looked dazedly at his idle fingers, imagining red stains.

Qaira wet a handkerchief in a drinking glass and gave it to him. "What happened?" she murmured.

He shook his head and chose his words carefully, to put the minds of any listening concubines at ease. "Carrying out a king's duties. That girl in the tower I was visiting… she died."

All hells had broken out when the guards crashed into Nassar's quarters yesterday, interrupting the prince entertaining his courtiers over coffee. That morning, the halls at the palace had been eerily quiet. Bataar had been expecting to walk back into rooms clouded with apprehension and fear, but Qaira had worked her magic, and now all the women were laughing and smiling.

"Also, they caught that… creature," he added cryptically. "The rioting's under control, but the city doesn't feel any safer."

His wife turned his fingers over in her hands. "You can be a great king, the best to ever breathe, and the world will still be a bad place. You can try to make things better, but you'll only ever be one man."

She was looking at him like he was a man now, not a god, not the saber of Preeminence's will.

He wasn't just a man, though. That was the problem with being a rhah. He'd brought war to Kalafar, just as Aglea started a religious war to take the Heartspring, and Ramzi brought that war back to Keld. Like how the steppe kings brought a war to the mountain, and Bataar had taken that war west. Kings were worse than gods.

Ganni picked up Bato by his arms and dipped his feet in the water on the shallow end of one of the swimming pools. He screamed and splashed. When she dropped him, he crawled out and chased her through the yellowing grass.

"We have to march on Rayenna," Bataar told Qaira.

Her voice was soft, mild. "Now?"

"Three weeks, maybe four."

She nodded. "Mmm."

"We can't bring them with us. And you should stay with them." A line of black ants paraded toward a tray of sticky sweets and raisins. "Or we can send them back to your parents."

"They'll be fine with Maran for a few weeks." Her tone became cheery. "Ganni's even made a friend. Look, one of Lofri's daughters." A gangly young girl had their daughter by the hand, dragging her across the lawn. They were playing Queen and Lady, Ganni using a stick as a bow. Their laughter was a foreign sound, one that belonged in a time before wars, or after them.

Bataar let out a sigh that loosened the tension coiled in his arms and chest. "I'm tripling the guards at the palace, then." He'd take the Harpies and Nassar, anyone he didn't trust, and keep them close. Leaving them behind would only spell trouble for the capital, for his children.

His hands twitched. He looked at Qaira's lap, full of brightly colored clippings. More flowers were stacked neatly on gold platters. Blankets and pillows littered the lawn, keeping the ladies' silk slippers safe from the wet grass.

"Want me to give those hands something to do?" Qaira asked, noticing Bataar absently picking at an unraveling thread.

The final knot between his shoulders loosened. "I can't promise I'll be a perfect student."

Her smile was a sky full of stars. "I'm not a perfect teacher."

Qaira's warm knees pressed against his thigh as she guided him through the correct motions to weave the green stems together. Someone had filed each rose smooth, except for one hooked thorn. Bataar sucked his pricked thumb and cursed.

"It's bad isn't it?" he said, holding up his work. The stems made a distended braid that sagged and bulged. Around them, concubines giggled demurely behind henna-stained finger-nails, too polite to be honest.

But Qaira wore the chain of roses in her hair for the rest of the evening, to supper with the viziers and their wives. Bataar watched the yellow petals slowly wilt, curling at the edges. Her smile remained as vital as spring.

18

They warned me that no woman is as ruthless as the zultam's Harpy daughters, capable of brutalities beyond imagining, but my husband's sisters have been so kind.

— Queen Roksanya's diary

Back in the capital, Nohra waded through the musky cloud of sandalwood and patchouli incense that hung in Aalya's room. Wisps of white smoke curled off the wood shavings in a burner on the table. Weapons with jewel-encrusted blades were mounted on the walls, and glass dolls on shelves stared with beady black eyes. Their grandmother's eyes watched her too, following Nohra as she crossed over the threshold.

A cat lay curled up at the foot of the bed, its whiskers twitching while it slept. At the sound of the doors shutting, Queen Purri yawned awake with a meow, unsheathing her tiny claws.

On the vanity, sapphire and ruby necklaces spilled out of a jewelry chest, all presents from Aalya's other grandparents who controlled the Merchants Guild in Marafal. The table was crowded with other treasures too, bottles of perfumes and cloud jade eggs on footed stands. There had been even more before the looting.

Nohra used to be jealous of all her things. Now, none of that mattered.

She kissed Grandmother Himma's hand. Her rings were skin-warmed pressing against Nohra's forehead. Bony knuckles and Noorish sapphires rapped against Nohra's face. "Alright, stand up. Gentility doesn't disguise the way you hobbled in here." Grandmother Himma regarded Nohra and Aalya both. "Only stupid girls get themselves shot."

Aalya cracked an eye open and sighed. "Should we get on with it then?" Her shield, *Segreant*, had been dragged onto her lap, and Aalya held it like a child clutching a blanket. Separating her from it would be a cruelty.

A weak breeze stirred the smoke. Someone had opened the windows. Nohra tilted her head, addressing Grandmother Himma. "Has the Head Physician been by?"

"Adeem Aden, or the one my grandparents sent from Marafal?" Aalya replied.

"You're doing better if you remember that gloomy goat's name," the queen mother said.

Nohra couldn't help the smile that split across her face.

In her letter, Aunt Clemiria had urged Safiya to retire Aalya, to repossess *Segreant* and name a new Harpy Knight. Cali's faraway looks suggested she agreed with her mother, at least on this, but she had no authority to challenge her older cousins.

Nohra and Saf should have been with Aalya the night of the invasion, defending their father, not playing into one of Bataar's diversions.

Aalya's short brown curls looked glossy and recently brushed, and color had returned to her face. The sickly shadows under her eyes had been smoothed away. Nohra stepped closer, then recoiled from her own reflection in the mirror. She self-consciously touched a strip of lank, greasy hair with her callused fingers, ran her tongue over her cracked lips. Was that really what she looked like? But a bath, a full night's sleep, a glass of water, those things could wait.

She pulled a second chair over to the bed. "Do you want to practice your balance?"

Aalya's grip tightened on the steel shield. "Well, I suppose I can't do anything else until I can stand properly."

Nohra helped her sister sit up and go through the chair exercises. The physicians said these would improve her balance and rebuild her core strength, but the best medicine was time. Aalya's arms and legs shook from strain as she worked through the simple movements. Their grandmother tutted around, judging her form and rearranging everything in the room, her embroidery hoop orphaned on the bed. Aalya's eyes kept flickering to the open window, where the curtains stirred and the sound of happy voices poured into her sick room.

"I can take you outside to sit," Nohra suggested, pulling Aalya's cheek.

"How?" Aalya swatted her hand weakly. "The mavens aren't done making the chair with the wheels."

"I could carry you."

She recoiled. "That's alright." The cat leaped down and padded over to mewl at the door. "I don't think my pride could take that."

"Just lean on me."

She let out a shaky breath, an almost-smile flickering at the corners of her lips. "Fine."

Nohra unceremoniously pulled her sister out of bed, and with Grandmother Himma a counter-anchor on her other arm, they limped awkwardly onto the outdoor walk. As they crossed the lawn, the sun burned the back of Nohra's neck. Sweat dripped down her face and slithered between her shoulder blades. Fluffy little Queen Purri kept close at their heels.

Wincing, Nohra asked, "You alright?"

Aalya nodded. The muscles in her arms and back had gone as soft as her legs. Aalya used to be able to hurl a javelin almost fifty yards. Now, most of her weight slumped uselessly against Nohra's side. Where blood had pooled out onto tile in their father's audience hall, a dark pink knot on Aalya's neck remained to mark the arrow's entrance. Nohra had her own scars. They all did. The mostly healed wound in Nohra's thigh stiffened the surrounding muscle, making their walk clumsy when Aalya's knee knocked against her.

With a squeal, one of their half-sisters ran past and dove into a pool. The day was sweltering, the bathing ponds full of splashing children. A few women basking on the tiled edges of the pools watched them pass. Their eyelashes fluttered prettily as their long legs stretched out, skirts pooling around their knees.

It must be nice to be so carefree.

"I suppose I should thank you," Aalya groaned, easing onto the bench. She flexed her toes in her satin slippers, stretching her fingers in the bright light. A look of contentment softened her face, revealing a rare glimpse of her crooked bottom teeth.

"Don't thank your sister for doing her duty," Grandmother Himma griped. "Serving your family is no favor."

"We'll go on another walk tomorrow," Nohra promised. "You'll get stronger soon. You can already talk, and your memory's returning."

Aalya's reply spilled out slowly, "But what if I don't get better? Nothing's promised. That's written in the Godsbreath. I might never be able to walk on my own."

"You will."

Grandmother Himma feigned interest in the bathing pool and the harem guards in the distance. She'd never been good at reassurances.

Aalya's face turned pleading, mouth twisting. "You don't know. Don't make it hurt us both worse by believing in something that may not be possible." Her soft breath wavered. "Even with the memories coming back, it feels like I'm learning about someone else's life, like I'm only pretending to be *her*."

"The rest of your memories, your balance, all of that can come back, in time." Hopefully some of the death and blood would stay forgotten.

"You were already a burdensome brat," Grandmother Himma said, without any venom. "You can't get worse."

Aalya straightened up, turning smug. "I'll have them make me a feather-steel cane with a grip shaped like a pegasus, out of the biggest chunk of Noorish sapphires I can buy. It'll make Saf's *Queen of Beasts* look like a child's toy."

Grandmother Himma snorted.

"You're definitely Aalya." Nohra laughed.

Her confident smile wavered. "You're the only one who thinks so. Everyone else treats me strangely. The physicians, the servants. Saf and Cali. Everyone's on edge around me. Do you know what that's like? To know your name is on everyone's tongue?"

"Self-pity is a sin," their grandmother scolded.

Squeals and childish laughter veiled the courtyard with noise. It wasn't just that everyone was walking on gryphon's eggshells around Aalya because of the injury. It was the threat of the betrothal. Before the year ended, both Aalya and Nohra would be wed to men they didn't choose.

Dizziness washed over Nohra.

"Rami visited me," Aalya added. "I know he was there, the

night I was injured. He said our father died on his throne, that the rhah killed him in the audience hall."

Grandmother Himma craned her neck, probably checking to see who was close enough to overhear. "My granddaughters will be the death of me," she muttered.

"Everything Rami told you is true," Nohra said.

"Yesterday, Saffy came to see me with some woman, one of our father's wives, I think."

"One of his concubines," Grandmother Himma corrected. "He only took two wives. One died."

Aalya squinted, her mouth silently moving as she seemed to remember something, then mumbled to herself, "Thora died." She looked at Nohra. "Your mother. I remember her entombment day, and Father crying, and her face carved on the lid of the coffin. You didn't cry."

"She's… in paradise now." Nohra's voice was hollow. She found herself scratching at her nail beds and forced herself to stop before she tore skin.

"Did you cry when Father died?"

"I didn't." At least, no one had seen her. "Not at his funeral, and not when we buried his heartbox at the Palace of the Heart in Antiria. By Mother's."

"And Thora wasn't *my* mother. My mother went to Marafal."

"Because your grandfather is sick," Nohra explained, trying to be judicious.

"Well I'm sick. She should be here with me."

That sounded like the girl Nohra knew. Grandmother Himma snapped, "Don't complain, child. We're all here with you."

Aalya's other grandparents doted on her. She was the darling of the Merchants Guild. Her mother Merv was just a vulture hoping her own father died quickly so she could claim his mines in Aalya's name.

Aalya pouted. "But some days *you* don't come, Nohri. You were gone for a week."

"If I could come every day, I would." She tried to smile, but it was brittle. "You're my favorite sister."

"I bet you tell all our sisters that." Aalya sulked, crossing her arms. "Saf told me the same thing."

She pinched Aalya's cheek. "Really? I thought I was her favorite."

"Safiya would trade both of you for a night with a courtesan," Grandmother Himma huffed.

Nohra grunted. "And Cali would trade us for a book."

Seconds passed. Aalya looked so innocent, so young. Nohra remembered her face padded with baby fat, slumping while she slept in the sanctium. Watching her, the guilt grew crushing.

"Did I let Father die?" Aalya asked, slowly, like she was afraid of the answer. "Was it all my fault?"

Grandmother Himma took a sharp breath and turned away, leveling a look more piercing than an arrow at a twittering songbird.

Nohra shook her head. "It wasn't a fair fight in the capital. Saf and I were at the Hill near Mineva when Lofri made his first move, attacking from inside the walls. His soldiers let in Bataar Rhah's. You, Cali, and Rami were all with Father, barricaded in the audience hall."

Aalya's brows scrunched. "Ervan Lofri? But he's my mother's cousin. My brother's conservator. *Nassar* betrayed Father? Why, that shit-eating dog—"

Grandmother Himma glared.

"Aalya, mind your words," Nohra whispered. "He's king in Kalafar."

"He's *what*? Who appointed him to this made-up office?"

"Your betrothed." She blurted it without thinking then slapped her hand over her mouth.

Aalya's mouth dropped. "My *what*?"

By now the engagement was probably official on paper if not before paradise, but Nohra still choked saying it out loud, like there was a knife to her throat. "Your mother and uncle arranged the betrothal."

"Well, is it a good match?"

Grandmother Himma sneered and prodded Aalya between her slumped shoulders to get her sitting straighter. "Practice sitting upright."

"It'll be very important to your family that you marry him."

"Who is he? This oh-so-important man?"

Nohra released a strangled breath. "It's Bataar. You're engaged to wed Bataar Rhah. You'll be his third wife."

"But—but he killed Father!" Her voice cracked. She looked everywhere but at Nohra: at a child chasing a dog with henna-stained ears, at the silhouette of a pegasus drifting in the sky. "I'd rather marry the Demonking. He practically *is* a demonking!"

"I hate him too," she whispered, "but lower your voice. Please."

Aalya fixed her with those dinner-plate eyes. "Would you marry him?"

Nohra snorted humorlessly. "I'd rather shove a hot poker up—"

"Then help!" She grabbed Nohra's arm, her lip wobbling. "You're my big sister."

"If I could undo all this I would." Nohra covered Aalya's hands with her own. "Believe me."

"Then undo it! You *can* undo it. If anyone can, you can. You'll fight."

"There's already a plan." But it would only end Aalya's engagement if Clemiria marched on the capital soon.

Her sister brightened. "Really?"

"Half-baked and poorly proofed," Himma hissed.

The Goddess's incarnations were evidence that women were to be feared, to be worshiped and revered, forces of creation and destruction. At the snap of Nuna's fingers, the bone-white gates of Her hell could open and Her demon army could launch an attack on mankind. So why did Nohra feel so small?

Tonelessly she muttered, "These marriage matches are important to our families." At worst, Aalya would only be married to Bataar for a few months. Clemiria's soldiers could be in the city sooner than that.

An eternity of time stretched in front of her.

Their father had arranged Nohra's betrothal to Meric Ward's son. It should have been his place to pick a match for Aalya, with his advisors' input. Their engagements weren't equivalent, no matter how hard she tried to rationalize it all. What had Calidah said at the house near the docks? *Try to earn Bataar's trust.* Nohra had been so furious at the idea she hadn't been paying attention to whatever asinine plan her cousin had cooked up.

No one was on Aalya's side, not her mother or brother or Queen Clemiria, so Nohra had to be. She looked left and right. The courtyard was empty except for the harem and their eunuch guards, keeping watch at a distance.

Nohra's fingers scratched her thigh, like she could work the stiffened scar tissue open again.

"Does Lord Ward have a daughter?" Nohra asked in a low voice.

Grandmother Himma scoffed. "Why would I fill my head with northern genealogy?"

"He does, doesn't he?" Aalya said. "Two daughters. One visited court when I was younger, with her brother and their tutor and a small retinue. The girl was my age." She puffed up, looking proud of herself for remembering.

"You're right!" Nohra forced herself to quiet her voice. "You're incredible, Aalya. Is she betrothed?"

"Well, I don't know that."

"*Rami*. He can take two wives if we need him to. I'm sure Ward would rather have his daughter be the queen of Dumakra than marry his second son to *me*."

Nohra could break off her betrothal, and they could keep their alliance in Aglea—if Rami married the northerner's daughter. That would free up Nohra to take Aalya's place.

"You impulsive, foolish girl," their grandmother murmured.

"I'll be the fool who takes him down."

"You'd try."

She could grit her teeth and bear it for a few months. Besides, this was an opportunity for Nohra to have Bataar close and unguarded, naked in front of her. Who else had access like that other than a wife, a lover? If she could somehow earn his trust while she organized the revolt, she could defeat him on all fronts, break down his defenses, rip out his *Goddess-damned still-beating heart* in their bed if she had to.

Nohra scanned the grassy courtyard. Bright insects and birds darted around the flower bushes. Women reclined at the bathing pools, and children giggled as they ducked around yellowing lily pads withering in the water. Summer was dying.

The issue was that Bataar got something out of a marriage to Aalya: the Merchants Guild in Marafal and her family's feather-steel mines in the Teeth. The match solidified his alliance with Ervan Lofri and Nassar.

He wasn't marrying for lust or attraction. If he'd wanted the prettiest of her sisters, he would have picked Safiya, or perhaps one of the twins, Princess Hana or Syreen, but he hadn't. Bataar wasn't in love with Aalya. He didn't even know her. When he did, he wouldn't like how spoiled and childish she could be. If someone could offer something as precious as Aalya's inheritance—like the unwavering loyalty of the Harpy Knights...

"I shudder to think what's running through your head," Himma said.

"A plan."

What else could a bride bargain with? Nohra's father had looked at Thora like she was keeping him alive. As though the rest of the world could be on fire, but as long as she was alright, everything would be fine. A light in his eyes had died the day Nohra's mother was entombed. Few men gazed at their wives like that.

Nohra could try to inspire that in Bataar. Her smile fell. That seemed impossible, after everything.

A hush descended over the inner courtyard. The women at the wading pool started to whisper instead of laugh, shushing the children. Splashes and shrieks quieted. In the distance, on the training yards, steel had clanged, soldiers had grunted. Those sounds faded too.

"What in the Goddess's names is happening?" Grandmother Himma asked, stiffening.

Nohra instinctively checked the sky for dark shadows and the walkways for armored shapes. She hadn't earned any of her weapons back. If they were attacked, she couldn't defend anyone.

The silence transformed into a low, excited buzz. Soldiers jogged past, cutting through the harem's private wing to the outer courtyards.

"Hey! You can't be here!" Nohra shouted. Only a few of

them even looked at her. Behind her, mothers fished their naked babies and children in soaked chemises out of the water, bustling them inside.

"Go," Grandmother Himma told Nohra, laying a shielding hand on Aalya's leg.

Nohra stood, approaching the soldiers to pull a young man out of formation. "What is this?" she demanded. "Are you practicing drills?"

"P-princess!"

"What's happening?" She said this slower, carefully enunciating every word, since he appeared to be dense.

Starry eyes blinked at her. "They said we need to be lined up at the training yard, as quick as possible. I know we aren't supposed to-to—so I wasn't looking! I was averting my gaze as the Goddess would want."

"Fine. I don't care about that right now. What's all this about?" For good measure, she shook his shoulders. His owlish eyes widened even more.

"Orders, Your Highness. We're heading out. To…"

"*Yes?*" She gave him one last good jolt.

"To Rayenna."

Rayenna. It echoed around in her head. She let the boy go, stumbling back. The paving stones winding through the courtyard wobbled, snaking into new, wrong patterns. Dizzily, she counted the days on her fingers. How could Bataar's envoys be back already?

They weren't back. They wouldn't be coming back. Clemiria must have sent a bird. The pigeons from the Sister City were white with smoky red breasts. One of them must have carried the message. Queen Clemiria would not bend, would not waver. If Bataar wanted Rayenna, he would have to take it from her.

But what had forced his hand *now*? His own pride?

Their plan to take Kalafar was crumbling, brick by brick. A crazed smile broke across Nohra's face. She wanted to laugh. She started to, soldiers stopping to stare at her.

"Princess?" the one she'd grabbed asked.

"Go on. Get to the armory," she snarled. "Follow your commanding officer's orders. May the Goddess spare your souls. When you die, may you rest eternally in paradise and not writhe in hells."

"Y-Your Highness." The boy's voice was so small.

Something tugged in her chest. "What?"

"I have family in Rayenna, a brother. I didn't get schooling, so I go to this girl, at a house. She writes missives for two coppers. I don't know if I can…"

Families like this boy's sold their sons to the army when they were barely old enough to toddle on chubby legs, so young he probably couldn't remember their faces. His girl was writing letters to ghosts in Rayenna, a phantom family who'd long forgotten the boy they traded for a fat sack of coin.

"I'm afraid. They're saying we'll shelter in Anhabar. What if we die like the old kings in the songs?"

Garrisoning an army in the former capital? That couldn't be true. But it would be impossible to reason with the scared boy.

Nohra thought of Saf reverently touching Zira's handkerchief at the Hill. Soldiers could be made braver if they were sent off to battle with tokens. She leveled her expression. "Would a favor ease your mind?" She reached into the neck of her dress and pulled out the cleric's unfurling flower pendant. The necklace pooled in his outstretched hand. Ever since Qaira gave it back, the silver chain had burned against her neck. "Take this. I hope it fills you with strength."

His voice was worshipful. "Your Highness."

Nohra turned from their stunned faces. They'd blocked

up the causeway and collected a crowd of impatient soldiers. There were grunts as someone shoved the line forward.

"What was that? What's happening?" Aalya asked, standing clumsily.

Nohra caught her as she teetered. "I need to get you both inside. They're marching on Rayenna."

"Who is? *We're* marching on Rayenna? But it's our city! It's part of Dumakra. It's always been Dumakran, since—since before Anhabar."

"Not anymore," Nohra muttered. "Clemiria must have declared it an independent city-state."

"My stupid daughter would rather slice Dumakra in half than give it to Bataar." Grandmother Himma sounded begrudgingly impressed.

Nohra grimaced. "She could have waited, like Saf and Cali wanted, until we had an alliance with Ward."

They'd lost the advantage they would have had in Kalafar.

"I always hated her," Aalya said. "Now I'd just hate to be on the opposite side of her huge wall."

A new plan was beginning to form in Nohra's mind. Rayenna was an oasis in the red desert, so fortified no one had ever taken it, and Clemiria knew those sands. Bataar had the numbers, but he was overestimating his abilities. They could help her crush Bataar's forces in Rayenna.

ᑲᐧᐤᕓ

Nohra tore into the kitchens. Steam rose in waves off boiling pots of milk. Trays clattered onto countertops. She grabbed the back of the tunic of the first person close enough to ensnare, some servant making cheese.

"Where's Darya?" Nohra demanded.

"Probably visiting the stables," replied the smallish girl

with a port-wine stain on her cheek. Whey dribbled through the muslin in her fist.

What business did Dar have with the pegasuses if Fahaad wasn't the stablemaster? Unless he was meeting her there, for Goddess knows what sort of dalliance. They'd been close and secretive since the invasion.

She also needed to find Safiya, and of course Calidah. It would be easiest if they left Kalafar now, to beat Bataar's forces to Rayenna. Cali would have to lead them. No one else at the palace had made the journey between the capital and the Sister City as many times as her.

"—her flagship waits in Marafal. Send a bird and move Ruo's fleet east to seal Rayenna's ports," an accented voice suggested.

Nohra took a corner too quickly and slammed into someone, some clerk or scribe. The hawkish boy fell back, parchment, quills, and a pot of ink all skidding and spilling over the floor. Shocked gasps punctuated their collision. Important men with graying beards began mumbling, Utasoo generals among them. Shaza sneered. Beside her, Tarken looked steely, his arms folded.

Watery black ink glugged out of the cracked inkwell, puddling. Nohra stumbled, the heel of her slipper sliding against a leaf of paper. She reeled, squeaking in surprise, and flung her hands out. Her fingers brushed the front of the collared robe belonging to the Minister of Faith.

"*Princess*," Bataar said, and suddenly she wasn't falling. He wasn't even a full head taller than her, but his shoulders were broader. His arm caught her and wrapped around her middle, unbending, like the bough of a tree. Under his resinous balsam cologne, Nohra breathed in the floral scent she'd come to associate with Qaira brushing past her in a room.

Of course the smell of her would linger on *him*.

"Your Eminence," she said shortly. She found her footing and politely stepped away from him.

Bataar leaned down and hauled the scribe up. "*Nohra*. Why are you in such a hurry?"

She squatted to collect the papers and shards of glass. Bataar used her first name so flippantly, so familiarly, like they were friends. It made the hairs on her arms stand up.

She gritted out, "I was just going to retire to my quarters, Your Eminence."

The small smile strained his jaw, and his eyelid had twitched when he said her name. His fingers stretched toward the knife sheathed on his belt. Idiot. Nohra wouldn't kill him here. She wouldn't have stabbed him in her mother's sanctium, either. She was impulsive, maybe, but she had a sense of self-preservation.

She didn't *want* to die.

Had she really thought she could seduce this man? Make him fall in love with her? At least now, unless he pushed it forward, there wouldn't be a wedding, only more war. She wouldn't have to take Aalya's place.

The worst part was, Bataar wasn't hideous. Nohra begrudgingly admired the way he commanded a room, a wolf everyone was wary of prowling the corridors. Under vastly different circumstances, he might have been a good match for her fire. She could admit that, and still hate him.

Bataar cocked his head to the side. His shaggy black hair flopped. "Did you not receive my summons?"

Nohra looked away. Something in his gaze was too unnerving to meet. "Summons?"

"I need you, Princess Safiya, and your cousin in the audience hall for a war meeting with my close council."

"You want us with your advisors?" Shock and fury battled

inside her. She ground her molars to keep from biting off her tongue.

His voice didn't waver. "I want you commanding troops at Rayenna's gates. Besides, Rami will accompany me, and I'm sure you'd want to be by your brother's side."

She blinked. Her head was suddenly empty, more half-formed plans unraveling. Every game they played, she lost. He'd make Rami his captive, and she'd be disarmed again, before she even raised her blade.

"If we may," the Minister of Faith said, waving forward sanctimoniously.

Nohra sneered. "What does any of this have to do with *you*? Aren't you a cleric? Shouldn't you be in a sanctium?"

He coughed. "Excuse me, princess—"

"Are you anticipating this fight will take a divine turn?" The fool king was planning on sheltering in Anhabar's bloody halls. Nohra barely suppressed a shiver.

Bataar pursed his lips. "*My lady*." He held out his bent arm for her to take.

It was the same as outside Thora's Sanctium, a show for the viziers, the men who thought she was worse than a feral dog in a dress, yet who would be happy to marry her to garner more influence.

Nohra could play her part. It was like Saf had said: she had to think three steps ahead. Losing this game didn't mean they'd lose the war. Nohra would devise a plan to sabotage and outmaneuver him at the front, to break away and join Aunt Clemiria.

Swallowing her pride, Nohra smiled. She met his eyes and held his lording gaze, looping her arm through his. She dared the gryphon king to look away first. "Your Eminence."

19

AUTUMN, 368

In the final weeks, order in Anhabar dissolved. No laws or morals were enforced. As the bloody rot spread unchecked among the impoverished masses, wealthy families fled west.

— *Making Kalafar*

As the war caravan crossed the desert, hours rolled together like the red dust blowing atop the dunes. Coarse grains scratched inside Bataar's clothes, gritted between his teeth, and stung his eyes. Erdene had been a fleck in the wide sky, flitting through the clouds as the army passed the farm towns, defiant of Preeminence's hungering gaze.

Their caravan had started on the merchants' road to the southern port town, diverging east at the stone marker for the old Anhabar trail. The ancient road to the city had been swallowed by the sand tides, reclaimed by prickly saltbush and capers. The soldiers cut through the eastern desert toward Rayenna and would stop in Anhabar to replenish their supplies before carrying on to take the last city in Dumakra that still resisted.

The thought filled Bataar with tension, tinged with relief. It had been weeks since Grand Vizier Naji spelled out the Harpies' treasonous plans. Bataar couldn't let himself relax until he was sure he wouldn't have a knife in his back.

"Storm ahead," the haggard guide warned.

At first, the horizon was nothing but red mountains of dunes like waves of blood. As they traveled deeper into the desert, the sky was flooded with crimson sand. With a screech Erdene plunged, disappearing into the storm, a feather carried on the wind. Bataar hiked his scarf up over his nose.

"The horses can't continue," shouted the guide, an elderly cleric who was duty-bound to maintain the mountain sanctium for the next five years. It was a thankless, lonely, and dangerous job, if any of the rumors were true.

"What about the carriages?" Bataar asked, turning and wrestling with the reins of his horse. Gusts of sand engulfed the caravan, splintering the glass windows of one coach. The drivers struggled with the doors, bracing their legs against the undercarriage. Bataar hastily dismounted, pulling with the men until his arms ached. "Oktai, help."

The boy trudged forward, bracing himself beside Bataar. With a jolt, the door flung open. A gust of wind caught it, snapping it off its hinges. Sand flooded in, lapping at the women's ankles and spraying against their veils like sea mist. Bataar held out his hand, took Nohra by the wrist, and lugged her out. He only had a moment to fully savor how wide-eyed and pale she looked, fearful for once, before she drew her veil, hiding her face.

"You should have ridden ahead with the other generals," Bataar muttered. The blade of her sickle-staff glinted, a dangerous smile haloing her head. He lifted Qaira out of the carriage with more grace. "And you should have stayed in Kalafar."

Bataar wanted distance between Qaira and Nohra, but his wife had waved away his worries. "It would look suspicious if I suddenly stopped speaking to her," she'd said. "Besides, how can you trust Naji is telling the truth? Trust me."

It wasn't Qaira he didn't trust. She was perceptive, smart. As he'd lifted her into the carriage that morning, he'd whispered a warning: *"Don't play dangerous games with her."* When Bataar was young, he'd thought Qaira was too kind, and the world would crush her. But the truth was she could play with the best of them. In a game of Eagles & Lions, Qaira *always* won. She didn't need a knife to cut to Nohra's heart.

His horse's tail disappeared as the mare startled into the sandstorm. There was a flurry of movement up ahead, visible in fits and bursts, but the only things Bataar could make out clearly were his own hands held up in front of his face, and Qaira, if he kept her in arm's reach.

Nohra stumbled forward. "The pegasuses—I have to help Fahaad. I'll be back for Rami."

"Take Qaira with you," Bataar told her, before the princess could vanish into the curtain of red. "I'll ride with your little brother."

Nohra faced him, her expression shrouded.

"If you're flying, you can't take him with you anyway," he pressed. "Unless you think it wouldn't draw attention, in the storm."

She paused, as if weighing danger against the damage to Rami's reputation. Nohra couldn't risk publicly emasculating the boy she wanted to put on the throne. What a stupid custom.

"No, he's never ridden before." In a clipped voice, Nohra warned, "Take care of him." She entwined her fingers with Qaira's and pulled her away.

"Take my hand," Bataar ordered, extending an arm to Rami,

who blinked up at him. He scrambled, boots cracking the carriage window as he braced against it. He kicked the velvet seat cushions, pulling himself up and sliding down the side of the carriage, landing beside Bataar without ever touching him. "Which way did my sister go?" Rami asked, as if Bataar were some nameless guide who gave directions in the desert. "Oh, I see her!"

"No you don't." Bataar took hold of the boy by the shoulders. "Your usual keepers aren't here, so you're staying by my side, understand?" He'd already lost a horse. He didn't need to lose Nohra's little brother.

And Rami wasn't much older than Ganni. Bataar was good with children that age.

The storm lulled, subsiding just enough for Bataar to glimpse his surroundings. The nearest carriage was half-overturned. The spokes on one wheel were broken, and another wheel was buried in ruby sand. The people who'd been riding in it stood huddled. Ahead, the pegasuses were a blur of white or black wings. The hoods over their eyes didn't seem to calm them. They reared, straining at their leads. Fahaad stood among the women, helping them onto the backs of the winged horses and fastening them into flying saddles.

Bataar's heart spasmed in his throat. Qaira was going to be up in the air, flying above the storm. Fear prodded him. Nohra lifted Qaira up and Fahaad fidgeted with straps around her hips. Qaira's body lurched forward as the pegasus pulled at its lead, flapping its huge wings.

Rami tried to shake off Bataar's hand. "My sister told me not to leave her side, and that if I do, I need to be with Fahaad."

Bataar tightened his grip. "Well, they're both unavailable. I swear you'll be safe with me." Regiments of soldiers fanned out, standing in large groups, jostling to hear shouted orders.

Bataar's eye twitched. Unthinkingly, he rubbed the heel of his hand against his chin, scratching his old scar through the linen scarf. His beard was thicker now, and coarse. "Come on, Rami, Oktai."

In the distance, the camels stood in a cluster, whinnying and shaking their humps as they were fitted to ride. Saddles swayed on their backs, large platforms draped with thick canvas curtains to block out the sand and sun. Their Anhabar guide alighted from his horse to hoist a nimbler-looking young man out of the sand.

"How long do the storms last?" Bataar asked, taking the fallen page's other hand. The storm covered Preeminence, but Bataar still felt Their unearthly, elemental weight.

The old man wore a cleric's gray robes and draping habit, a scarf wrapped around his face to keep the sand out of his mouth. He raised a hand to shield his eyes as the storm blew back to life. "What?" he shouted.

The grainy roar persisted. Bataar yelled back, hardly able to hear his own words. "I said—"

The man nodded, reading his lips through the blur of red. "It could be hours, a day, or a few more minutes!"

It was hard to believe this hunched old man was the sole caretaker of the abandoned sanctium. Most Dumakrans were too superstitious to even speak of Anhabar. The cleric's wrinkled fingers shook on his cane as it sunk into the shifting sand. Bataar took him by a sagging arm and grabbed the young prince by the other, hauling them both through the storm toward saddled camels. He and Oktai helped the sanctium-keeper up. Then Bataar moved to lift Rami onto another large platform. The prince craned his head, searching for his sister.

"You'll ride with Oktai," Bataar said firmly.

Golden-brown hair whipped in every direction. "I'm only supposed to ride with Fahaad or Nohra."

"Alright. Then I hope you won't mind my company." Bataar pulled himself up. The strange saddle wobbled. Rami twisted around, watching him with wide, unblinking eyes. "You're safe with me," Bataar repeated.

Safe as a grave. Bataar's grave, if he let Nohra's little brother perish in the desert.

"My sister's gonna be mad," Rami grumbled.

Looking at the boy, anyone would see Ramzi. The prince was the spitting image of his father with lighter hair. The months had transformed this child's features into the death mask that haunted Bataar. His gut clenched. To take Dumakra, he'd left this boy without a father.

The thought didn't sit easily. A vermilrot outbreak had killed Bataar's father when he was young, and Bataar's mother had died in a raiding. The world took and took, but Bataar's hand had held the blade that cut Zultam Ramzi's throat. It wouldn't matter to Rami what had motivated his father's murderer.

The prince squirmed, complained, and shrunk back.

"Do you want to see a knife?" Bataar asked, playing his last card. Rami spun around, fidgeting hands clasped in his lap betraying his eagerness. Bataar handed him the straight-edged knife in its sheath. The boy's eyes glowed as he slid it in and out. "Don't cut your fingers off."

He couldn't afford to regret what had happened with Ramzi in the throne room. Bataar's hand had been forced. The zultam would have caved Nassar's head in with his lion-paw club if Bataar hadn't swung his saber, and his alliance with Lofri would have ended just as swiftly. Only time would tell if he'd miscalculated.

Rami turned the blade over. "Is it very sharp?"

"Enough to kill a gryphon."

"*Really?*" A hint of skepticism colored the prince's voice. "I'd thought those stories about you were embellished." *Embellished.* Such a big word for a little boy. He stared owlishly at Bataar. "Is it true that you can command the gryphons? They say you can set them on your enemies like war dogs."

"That's just a story." Bataar had fought the zultam *in front of* Rami. He'd killed Ramzi in front of his son. Had the prince screwed his eyes shut? Had he seen Ramzi rushing at Nassar? Bataar couldn't remember.

He was still young. If Bataar earned Rami's favor now, he wouldn't pose a threat as the avenging son later. He'd need to gauge the boy's feelings, try to ascertain what he knew and what his sisters had been telling him.

The camel's swaying stride churned Bataar's stomach. He pulled himself up in the cumbersome saddle and peeled back the canvas drapes that curtained the wooden frame. Ahead, the caravan slowly stretched into an impenetrable wall of whipping red dust. One camel in his line of sight bore a tower of wooden crates, chests, and rolls of canvas. It lumbered forward, then was swallowed up, consumed by the storm. Only the lead connecting their camel to the ones in front and behind kept Rami and Bataar tethered to the caravan, safe from drifting out into the sea of sand.

❧

That first night in the belly of the desert, they made camp on a rocky outcropping. Below, the red dunes rolled. Sand skated across the tops as the wind blew. Hyenas whooped, and a desert wolf howled, the sound carrying in the dry air. Everyone beat out their sleeping rolls, a precaution in case scorpions or spiders hid inside. Collected sand tumbled out in clouds.

Bataar kept smacking his sleeping roll long after others had thrown theirs onto the hard-packed ground. The last thing he needed was bugs climbing in his mouth.

He tensed to keep from shuddering.

Glancing over the sprawling camp, Bataar made a mental inventory of the caravan. Nassar and Jawaad Lofri sat on crates near the main fire, surrounded by their house's guards. Women clustered together drinking hot tea. Qaira sat among the princesses, laughing at something Safiya said. Of the faces he knew best at the palace, only the aged queen mother and Princess Aalya had stayed behind.

In the distance, Utasoo and Dumakran soldiers stood around fires, their sleeping rolls laid out in unending neat rows behind them. Tension dulled their chatter, but Bataar's efforts to reduce fear of the old ruins had been mostly successful. The Dumakran forces were split between those who were cautiously superstitious and the soldiers who thought they could fight the Goddess and a whole army of cannibals.

Closer, stablehands threw raw meat for the pegasuses. The horses whinnied and nipped at each other's ears as they pushed their heads down, nosing through the chunks of organs and ropes of sheep entrails.

Bataar peeled cooked meat off the bone as he ran through their plan for the thousandth time. Before the caravan marched on the Sister City, they would replenish their water reserves in the mountain ruins. Anhabar could become a base of operations and defense against the east, if they needed one. Grand Vizier Naji and a retinue from the Conservium had gone ahead, ignoring the Minister of Faith's protests, to begin preparing the abandoned town.

"That's a very nice bird," Rami murmured, ogling Erdene.

Bataar swallowed, licked his teeth clean, and grinned. "You

have a gyrfalcon, is that right? I've seen you with the falcon master."

"Snowy." Rami eyed Bataar uncertainly. "She was a gift from Saf for my tenth natal day."

The hyenas had finally stopped braying in the distance. "Are you close with Safiya?"

The prince shrugged, nibbling a date-filled cookie. "Saf takes me hunting every winter at the palace in Antiria, just the two of us, and…" He trailed off. Fondness softened his tone. "Just us."

"Is she your favorite sister?"

At that age, children were always picking favorites. Ganni loved the kind of mushroom that looked like teeth covered in beads of blood, all the world's wartiest toads, prickliest flowers, and her Aunt Shaza. Her love for terrible things was something she'd learned from her mother. Bataar only wanted what was luminous and good, beauty for marred fingers to stain.

"I like all my sisters equal," Rami said, giving the diplomatic answer and watching Bataar with a guarded gaze. "Even Aalya, when she rumples my hair in front of Grandmother."

"Is there anyone you don't like?" Bataar asked, expecting Rami to name him.

The prince blinked. His mouth was a straight line. "Mahveen Naji."

Bataar let out a wheeze like he'd been kicked in the gut. "Grand Vizier Naji's daughter?"

"I heard her talking to her father." Rami pursed his lips. "She said, 'Betrothed to Prince Rami? He's just a child'. Well, she still rides the pony pegasuses that little girls use for lessons. And she reads slower than my baby sisters. I read as fast as Cousin Cali, and I do sums quicker than the maven who teaches us, I swear on Paga, and Nohra tells me never to swear on the Goddess's names."

Bataar couldn't stop the laughter that came spilling out of him. How had he misread the boy so badly?

"*Bataar*." Nassar sneered from behind a wall of Lofri's soldiers. Jawaad stood behind him, a boulder with unreadable, droopy eyes. "You look like you're enjoying watching the kid. Just remember who helped you take Kalafar."

He wiped the tears out of his eyes, sobering. "I haven't forgotten."

Nassar glared daggers back. If he had an opening, Nassar would probably shove Rami out into the sand and be done with the threat to his succession. All the more reason to keep the boy close.

Soon, Bataar would solidify his alliance. He'd elevate Lofri's blockish son and ease that family's worries. He didn't like that he had to contend with Nassar's paranoia, but what alternative did he have? Put Rami on the throne?

It could keep the Harpies... well, at least Nohra in line. But the necessary political maneuverings would be convoluted; it was only feasible if Nassar was dead.

Bataar could rectify his mistake in the throne room.

"Let's get you to your sisters for the night." He steered Rami toward the huddle of laughing women. "Tomorrow you'll ride with me again."

Nassar be damned, he needed the boy close. As long as Bataar had Rami, he'd keep control of the Harpy Knights.

❧

Bataar's eyes were bleary and burning days later when Anhabar shimmered like a mirage on the horizon. The tall mountains were a part of the Impasse range, but unlike its arm in the north, there was no snow capping them, even on the highest peaks. The ancient city was etched in relief on the side—massive pillars, open doorways, and countless windows all carved into the crimson stone.

"This is Anhabar," the old cleric informed Bataar, pointing straight ahead.

"I assumed."

His camel loped over the sand and dirt, grunting as it batted thick eyelashes. They'd made good time. Less than a week had passed since they'd veered away from the farm towns. The drapes on his saddle were drawn back, and no wind blew.

Bataar's waterskin was empty, down to the last drop. He wanted water, to gurgle and spit out everything red and gritty in his mouth.

The line of camels plodded past the sanctium. This structure put the ones in Kalafar to shame. Its doorway was thirty yards tall, flanked by giant carvings of the two incarnations of the Dumakran goddess, each wearing identical beatific expressions. The reliefs were so detailed that the folds of their dresses looked soft enough to ripple in the wind.

"It's unconventional, I know," the cleric said contemplatively. "Modern interpretations of the Goddess respectfully omit Her unknowable faces."

Here, Nuna and Paga had parted lips and bold eyes. They were nothing like the unnerving bleary smears and pointed star-faces on the murals at the palace. The camels moved on, padding feet kicking up orange-red clouds and stirring saltbush.

Past the sanctium, abandoned buildings stacked into the sky. Wide staircases jutted from sheer rockface, life-size carvings of lions roared, and water trickled out of statues' gaping mouths. A gust of wind blew sand off part of the sprawling mosaic spanning an outer courtyard. Bataar made out the curve of a cheek and a nose, but the piles would need to be swept to reveal the complete image.

All around were carvings and statues of gryphons, pegasuses, and the giant birds, rocs. It made Bataar feel small to stare up at it all, like he was a boy again, standing at the foot of red mountains.

Gaping, Rami exclaimed, "It's huge! I've never seen anything so tall. And this was once my family's house?"

"It's just ruins now," Bataar explained, "but Grand Vizier Naji proposed restoring it as a wedding present for your sister."

Rami's shoulders slumped. "Aalya? She'll lock herself inside with all her cats." The prince twisted, turning to look squarely at Bataar. His brown eyes were almost as coal-black as Darya Daheer's for a second, clouded over by a flicker of resentment. The boy blinked, and it was gone. "I don't think Aalya would like getting sand blown in her face for so many days. You might want to get her a different present."

Bataar snorted. "It'll be difficult to get Naji to abandon his restoration project."

Naji had sent a bird three weeks ago to a vizier in Sinnobad where Bataar's caravan first stopped to be housed by the town. His letter described plans to sweep out rooms on the lower levels and clear collapsed passageways. Apparently, the springs were still feeding into the salt pools, and some of the mosaics on the walls inside the palace were restorable. They'd been mostly shielded from the sand blasting through the other carved houses. Using special vessels, the water could be heated and made potable, a boon considering the next oasis waypoint would be a week out from Anhabar.

A little curiosity spiked, hot in Bataar's blood, at the prospect of exploring the "haunted" ruins.

"Nohra says we're going to see Aunt Clemiria," Rami said. "You want to fight my aunt's men with yours and change her opinion."

Bataar shook his head. A siege in Rayenna wasn't a happy place for a ten-year-old boy. He would witness bloodshed and depravity. "It'll be good for you to get an idea of war." Even if he was young. He'd keep the boy safer than he'd be back at the palace, unattended with Lofri's jackals.

He dismounted and helped Rami down. A page pulled fabric coverings off bird cages. The pigeons inside them cooed, downy white feathers floating through the metal bars.

"Is there even a coop in Anhabar?" Tarken complained, coming up behind Bataar. "A mews for the hunting birds? A stable for those—" He nodded toward the pegasuses wheeling in the sky, circling lower and lower. "They go in stalls, don't they?"

"They don't just fly around."

Tarken closed his eyes and rubbed his nose, scratching the thin silver scar. "I didn't know if they roosted or something."

The women alighted from the backs of their winged horses. The sound of Qaira's laughter rang the clearest.

"Fahaad can watch Rami now," Nohra said, her clipped voice niggling at him. She was quickly upon Bataar, glaring up at him.

He arched an eyebrow. "He has the pegasuses to watch. Fahaad's other duties come second while we're here."

"Don't you have a Master of Horses? You Utasoo are famous for your little ponies. Have that person handle the pegasuses."

His smugness dropped away as he eyed the pegasuses, wary. "They eat meat. Those aren't normal horses."

"Then ask your Master of Hounds to feed them and brush them down." Nohra gestured dismissively at Tarken, her irritation mounting if the spots of color on her cheeks were any indication. "Come, Rami."

Tarken grumbled, his usually rigid posture slumping at the new humiliation of being "Master of Hounds."

The air was quiet. Water poured out of the carved faces with whispery splashes. If he focused, Bataar could make out the sound of it trickling over the cliff face and dripping into puddles, collecting in cracks. The sand blew, whooshing. Erdene made a shrill noise and landed on his shoulder.

"Where's Grand Vizier Naji?" Bataar asked.

Soldiers and servants unloaded the pack camels, unfastening trunks, pots and pans, and bundled bed rolls from the saddles. They stacked the supplies out in the courtyard in pyramids.

Bataar took Rami's hand instinctively, tugging the boy forward.

"Where do you think you're going?" Nohra asked, stomping after them.

A breeze snaked through the outer courtyard, blowing through the pile of sand on the large mosaic. For an instant, the image could be made out completely. A woman's face materialized, her black eyes penetrating, her large breasts bare. A goddess, or one of Dumakra's giant demons—a djinn? The sand drift spilled back over the mosaic, hiding the entity from view.

The wind also exposed arching bone, a skeleton too large to be human—a camel with a few strips of leathery hide still clinging to the sun-bleached spine. Could it have been one of Grand Vizier Naji's pack camels?

"Your Excellency," the old cleric called. "Before you enter, please listen to a few rules I'll need you to abide by—"

"Later." Bataar pushed the old man's entreating hand off

his arm and stepped over the puddling sand toward Qaira, who was dressed in her riding clothes. The hair on Bataar's neck was already prickling, standing on end. Heat crept up his skin, fire in his veins, a burning itch coming from the mark that cut down his face and across his chest.

"What is it?" Qaira asked, smoothing out his fingers. He'd been scratching the scar without realizing. What had appeared at first to be a partially disassembled supply crate was really broken wood, the damaged content strewn across the sand and swallowed.

Bataar gently brushed Qaira's hands away, maneuvering Rami in front of her instead. "Something's wrong. Naji wrote to me. I thought he'd be ready to receive us." He scanned the ruins, running through the list of possible threats. "Vermilrot?" he whispered. That was what had ended the city, but the infection would be dormant after hundreds of years.

"*Vermilrot?*" Nohra repeated, sounding incredulous, like she'd rather believe in ghosts.

"No." He pulled down his scarf to rub his neck. The scar seared. "The zealot cannibals living in the canyons. Could they have attacked?"

"You mean the *heretic* cannibals? Just because their priests wear clerics' robes, doesn't mean they're true devotees of the Goddess."

He waved his hand. "Fine, whatever. Go get me the guide. The sanctium-keeper who took us from Sinnobad. Ask him how many camels Naji had."

"'Get you—'? Do I look like a servant you can just order around?" Her sickle-staff glittered dangerously on her back. Its meter-and-a-half long jewel-encrusted snath was gaudier than the holy relics in Kalafar's sanctiums. The blade kept mocking Bataar, a curving red smile.

"You look like my subject, like an officer under my command." He didn't bother with politeness. "Fetch him. We can speak with him, construct a sequence of likely events."

Her face turned blank, and she nodded. "Your Eminence."

One of the stable grooms shouted as a pegasus reared up, its hooves reeling in the air, wings blowing up gusts of sand. The rest of the pegasuses started jumping, flapping around and straining against their leads. One pulled a boy off the ground. He let go of the rope with a scream. The camels panicked, making noises that had Bataar wanting to cover his ears.

Erdene signaled.

What do you see? He followed her line of sight toward the stone palace and the city on the rockside. Faces watched, but they were all carved from stone. Dark red gryphon statues stared straight ahead, out onto the courtyard. Compared to some of the blockish carvings, these were so detailed they seemed to be breathing.

Their eyes moved. Bataar shouted.

20

The griffyn is a creature with the mane, arms, and tufted tail of a lyon and the taloned feet and beak of an eagle. Found where misfortune is frequent, it tears to ribbons creatures alive or dead.

— *Beasts of Land, Sea and Sky: A Children's Bestiary of Fantastic Creatures*

For a beat, the gryphons watched like vultures, still as statues. Then, stretching awake, they shook off the red dust and dove like hawks, pulling away from the mountainside.

Soldiers standing in scattered clusters ducked as shadows shot overhead. "Get down!" someone yelled.

Screams turned into shrieks, a battle of noise too loud for Nohra's pulse to drown out. *"Take cover!"*

"Don't break formation!"

"Ready armor-piercing arrowheads," Shaza shouted. *"Hold until you see their yellow eyes!"*

Nohra searched for the faces she knew, the ones she needed to protect. Safiya stood in front of the pegasuses. Her sword looked molten, full of rivers, hungry for blood. Fahaad and some stablehands stood behind her. Fahaad's grip strained on one of the leads. The pegasuses whickered nervously, feathers bristling.

Nohra reached for the cleric's pendant, but her fingers didn't find the chain. The boy wearing her necklace was somewhere in the mass of thousands of soldiers.

"Where's Calidah? I need to find Darya—" she started to say, but she couldn't leave Rami. Hazel eyes flashed toward her. Qaira. Nohra snarled in frustration. She couldn't leave her unprotected, either.

"You're not leaving!" Bataar's voice was husky, clipped and clumsy with desperation.

Bataar's commanding officers flocked toward him, cutting Nohra off and forming a protective barrier between Bataar, Qaira, and the gryphons. Rami would be safer with them in the defensive circle than with Nohra.

"*Nohra*," Bataar growled. So much for the fearsome gryphon king.

She pressed through the crowd, drawing *Bleeding Edge*, and Bataar swore, wrestling through bodies with an arm thrown out to reach her.

"Protect them!" she yelled at him. "Not me."

Nohra needed to find Darya. The sky was full of wraith silhouettes. An inky body landed heavily in a sand drift, and Nohra adjusted her grip on the snath of *Bleeding Edge*. The gryphon's hackles were massive, its large paws disturbing the shifting red piles as it stalked forward. Nohra could count each rib pressing through its feather-fur hide. A string of slaver hung from its beak as it stalked toward the pegasuses.

Fahaad's eyes widened, and Safiya's hold on *Queen of Beasts* tightened. "They don't look like the picture in the children's bestiary either," Saf hissed.

The gryphon had banded back legs like a bird's and bare purplish patches on its wings. It was even larger than the lioness Nohra had seen once in a vizier's menagerie.

It prowled closer to Fahaad. Safiya cut in front of him, and Nohra ran forward, skidding through the sand. Once she was close enough, she lifted *Bleeding Edge* high, her arms burning with exertion as she swung. The gryphon's tail lashed the air. She cut it off in a clean sweep. The gryphon spun on her, screeching. It writhed, claws unsheathing, and threw its head back, screaming louder. Some of the other gryphons answered with shrill calls.

"Get back, you idiot!" Safiya yelled.

"Paga's ass," Fahaad cursed as the pegasus he was holding reared, its shoed hooves swinging a breath's distance from his face. Mercy's black flank rippled. The ears poking out of his hood twitched.

Nohra grimaced as she stepped back, leading the gryphon away from Fahaad and the horses. It swiped for her, making a noise between a hiss and a screech. She fell back farther, keeping just out of reach.

"Uh-uh, eyes on me, bird." Saf kicked up a spray of sand with the tip of her sword. The gryphon spun, shrieking.

A second gryphon leaped forward. The roaring screams around her dulled. Nohra's sweaty hands bathed the jewel-encrusted snath of *Bleeding Edge*. She willed her fingers not to slip. Swung, missed. An arrow whizzed past, sinking into the gryphon's shoulder. Then another, and another. It slumped, slowing with a shrill noise only after several quivers had been unloaded. Nohra turned and met Shaza's gaze across the courtyard.

"Move!" the general yelled.

If a seahorse was comprised of ocean foam, a gryphon

was made of smoke. Its heat oozed out around the wooden shafts, dissipating in the air. Fahaad wrestled to keep his hold on Mercy's lead. The gelding whinnied and tossed his mane, muscles twitching and ears flattening.

"Launch a second volley!" Shaza shouted to her soldiers.

All around Nohra, men were underneath gryphon's bodies, screaming until voices died and thrashing stilled. Some of the gryphons were brown like Bataar's golden eagle, others more reddish. They seemed slightly smaller than the inky-black ones. Many had blurry eyes, and they all looked ravenous.

Two of the pegasuses' tails swished in agitation, and they pawed their hooves into the sand, backing up to Mercy. They keened in strange tones, nothing like horses.

"Fahaad, watch out!" Nohra blurted as Mercy tried twisting and biting his fingers.

He glared. "Don't worry about me. Find Darya. Keep her calm."

"What do you mean—"

"I'll protect Fahaad and the horses," Saf promised.

Nohra's thoughts were a whirlwind as she spun away from them. Her clenched hands were white-knuckled on *Bleeding Edge*. She'd have blisters tomorrow, if she lived. Two of the pegasuses opened their wings, blowing up a gust of sand. Fealty, a large, mottled gelding, leaped up. His rope line hung in the air behind him as he became a small gray spot in the sky.

A gryphon hunched over a body on the ground, pulling wet, purple ropes out of it. Another rooted through a pile of supplies, crushing crates and casks. Two screeched as they each clamped their beaks down on the arms of one limp soldier. His body ripped open down the middle in a shower of red, intestines stretching between the two halves.

A hailstorm of arrows pounded down, close enough to Nohra that she ducked, fell. They thunked into the wood and pinged off metal. The gryphons screeched and took off. They shouldn't have come to Anhabar. This was divine punishment. The incarnation of peace wouldn't bless this path Nohra was on.

Darya, Cali. Nohra would let the Goddess abandon her, if she found them.

She crouched, then slowly stood, straining to see through the sand clouds filling the courtyard. Her vision was all red, peppered with black and brown feathers. She stumbled through the cloud of dust for seconds that dragged into desperate minutes, or maybe hours.

"They're fleeing!" someone shouted.

Nohra yelled hoarsely for Darya. She wasn't sure she'd be able to identify her friend in the puddles of blood soaking into the sand, in the miscellaneous gore scraps left behind.

How many of the limping, groaning men were gryphon-marked now? By tomorrow, if the stories were true, they'd be battling fevers and gasping feebly, close to death.

A face materialized out of the dust clouds. A short dark beard, those unnerving, severe brown eyes. "I found your talmaid and your cousin." Bataar extended a hand for her. A spray of blood spatter made a sharp line across his face.

Nohra's whole body went numb. Through the blur of sand and screams, the bottom steps of one of the carved staircases set into the mountainside became visible. "Where's Rami? Your wife?"

"Inside the mountain, under guard."

She turned, relief freeing her to finish what they'd started here. "If they're safe, we should—"

"It's over. The ones that aren't dead are running away. Reach out your hand. There's a rope railing."

Reluctantly, she grasped it. The rest would be gryphon sickness, cleaning up, and burying corpses.

The rope was worn, petrified by the years and now as unyieldingly firm as stone. She tentatively tested her weight, and it didn't budge. She couldn't see far enough in front of her to glimpse more than Bataar's arm. He grabbed her wrist like he was leading a child.

His raw voice rasped, disembodied. "When I tell you to jump, do it. There's a missing step here. Rami almost fell—"

"*What?*"

"But I caught him. Now jump."

Having *Bleeding Edge* strapped to her back threw off her balance. When her feet hit the stone step, she slid, almost pushing Bataar over. He grunted under her weight, steadying them both. She considered hooking her leg around his, unbalancing him. He'd smash his skull in the courtyard below. But the rest of him had slowly taken shape; the white tunic, red sash belt, fur-trimmed boots, his loose black hair blowing around in the wind. In the courtyard below, the dust was clearing. Now, in broad view, she couldn't make it look like an accident.

One gryphon limped, spreading its wings and lifting up into the sky. There were only a handful of dead bodies tossed around the sand and several more unmoving gryphons. Amid the carnage, the soldiers had re-formed ranks.

Nohra whispered, "Do you think Naji's retinue was killed by the gryphons?"

The grand vizier always wore a pleasant smile. He was kind to his wife and gentle with his daughters. More than his advisor, he'd been her father's closest friend, his only true friend.

She heard the frown in Bataar's voice. "I'm not sure. It should have been easy to fortify a section of the city, but he and some of the Conservium mavens were going to map the rooms for a future restoration project. His last missive came the day before we departed from Sinnobad."

Nohra hesitated. "Surely there'll be something of Naji's to identify?"

"The gryphons never leave bodies, but there might be bones in the mountain if they were nesting here."

She dug her fingers hard into the rope line, tight enough to burn her calluses. "That's unlikely. Surely the sanctium-keeper would have noticed?"

The stairs had almost leveled out onto a wide platform when Bataar wobbled. With a loud crack, the step above them fissured and split. Nohra tightened her grip on the guide rope. Without thinking, she readjusted her grasp on Bataar's hand too, grabbing higher and wrapping her fingers around his forearm. He braced himself, clasping her arm and stumbling back onto the last stable step.

"Thank you," he muttered, sounding surprised.

Her nostrils flared as she released him. "Watch where you're walking." Divinity must have cursed her to be so monumentally idiotic. But no—just killing him wouldn't be enough. If Bataar died now, command would fall to Tarken, Shaza, or another general. And fat-headed traitorous Nassar would probably gain even greater control of Kalafar.

Arched entrances led from the platform into a towering open-air anteroom. Blue sky stretched over the red stone, bright as sapphires.

"Down there," Bataar said. A wide staircase descended into dimness. He seized a lit torch from a metal sconce. "After you."

Boots had trodden through the piles of dust, leaving prints. "If the mountain isn't safe, we shouldn't risk staying here." Nohra was unsure how much her word mattered, but he *had* made her a general. Persuading most of the Dumakran soldiers to shelter inside Anhabar would be like coaxing a horse to walk down stairs.

"There are hundreds of rooms, space to house all the soldiers. We need to replenish our water, regroup, and take inventory. Most importantly everyone needs rest, and we're safer with walls than we are in tents out on the sand. We can barricade the exterior doors, post guards outside the main rooms, place sentries, and have a rotating watch for attacks."

The rough stone corridor constricted tighter the deeper they descended.

A hunkered shape came into focus in the dark. Nohra stiffened at the sight of talons and feathers.

"That one's dead," Bataar said. "Your cousin and my guards killed it."

"Calidah? Was anyone hurt?" Her gaze reflexively flitted to the mark across his face.

"Everyone's unscathed." He scratched the back of his neck. "Nassar might have pissed himself, though."

Nohra steadied her breathing, trying not to cough. The hairs on her neck and arms prickled. She reached for *Bleeding Edge*, then relaxed. Finally, the fear and adrenaline were fading. They'd survived.

Two doormen kept watch outside an open archway leading into a large chamber. Soldiers squeezed around Nohra and Bataar, lugging trunks and crates of supplies. The cavernous stone room was lit with oil lamps, illuminating the servants moving through the wreckage on the floor. Nohra's eyes fell on Calidah first.

Her cousin moved toward her, clutching her crossbow *Covenant* in a strangling grip. "Saf's alright? And you're not hurt? I should have come back to help, but—" She looked pointedly across the room. Nassar stood with Lofri's son and their household guards, brushing off his white trousers and collared robe. "Someone needed to watch the room."

Nassar met Nohra's eyes, baring his teeth, and quickly looked away. She sneered, her pulse spiking. "You couldn't hold a sword, brother?"

"The fighting was mostly over." Nassar's voice was brittle. "The rest is for the servants to clean up."

Rami huddled next to Qaira, hugging her as she rubbed his shoulder. His face was flushed red, and tear tracks glistened on his cheeks. He looked so much younger than ten. He wriggled free, rushing to Nohra. She put her arms out, catching him and holding him tight.

"Was there trouble?" Nohra asked.

Rami's hair fell in his eyes when he shook his head. He pulled away. "If there was, I could have protected everyone." His fingers moved to the straight-edged knife in its sheath hanging from his belt.

Bataar's knife.

Girls sorted through broken crates, laying salvageable food out on clean fabric. Darya jerked out of the flock, straining the arm of one of the girls, Safiya's talmaid Laila. Dar's brown hair was sweat-sticky and mussed, billowing around her flushed face as her lip curled. Her skirts were stained with spatter, colored by red dirt.

"He told us he'd find her and bring her back!" Laila said, screwing her eyes shut and clutching desperately. She spread her legs to keep her balance. "Fahaad would want you to—" Her hands seized when Darya's struck out and ensnared both her arms.

"Laila, let me go, or I'll break your ribs," Darya whisper-snarled, her voice more guttural than it had ever sounded.

Is that really Darya?

Laila released her, hands flitting to her throwing-knife sheath. Her whole body shook. Darya already had her black dagger drawn. Nohra didn't know who'd returned it last time, or when. There was a fearsome gleam in her eyes. But when she turned, her expression softened. She sheathed her knife and stumbled forward, slowly at first, then faster. Nohra swept her friend close and hugged her tightly.

"Dar?"

Her hair was scented like the smoke from last night's fire, like damp shadows, and warmth that smolders deep underground. Darya gasped a ragged breath that might have been a sob. Her grip bruised. "Don't let me go."

Nohra's racing thoughts froze like winter ice. She held Darya as if she were glue fusing her together. She'd promised Fahaad she'd make sure Darya was okay. She hadn't been, until Nohra got here. She rubbed circles between the flare of her shoulder blades, like bird wings. Knobby silk gritted under her fingers.

She met Bataar's gaze over Darya's head. "Where are Naji's supplies? What rooms were they staying in?"

"I don't know," he told her. "Now that the gryphons are gone, we'll search the upper levels, establish a guard schedule, make sleeping arrangements."

"Alright. I'll take a group to—"

He shook his head. "You and your cousin can stay here and help with inventorying supplies."

"You made me a commanding officer and you want me to count crates?" Nohra shot back, untangling herself from Darya. "Should I help prepare supper and mend uniforms?"

Nassar's short snort of laughter made her want to turn her murderous anger back on him.

"That's enough, Nohra," Bataar barked. "I don't have infinite patience. And unlike you, I don't make idle threats."

Killing him would be so satisfying.

❧

Nohra tossed on her sleeping roll. The floor under the canvas was cold and bumpy, impossible to get comfortable on. Her stomach growled. Shaza had ordered the gryphon meat field-dressed and cooked. Even some Dumakran soldiers who didn't adhere to the faith's dietary restrictions were leery of gryphon meat, fearful of eating Nuna's beasts. Nohra had said a curt prayer over a hunk of cheese and some bread and tried not to feel nauseous at the sulfurous scent rising from the cookfire.

Her reflex when she couldn't sleep was always to prowl in circles like a leashed cat. To seek comfort in the palace sanctium, where the specter of her mother's memory lingered. She wasn't sure she'd find even that peace in Anhabar.

Bataar's search party had turned up the rest of Naji's pack camels dead in the outer courtyard. Their supplies, ruined and rooted through, decorated the inner rooms, and a few bloodstains marred the red stone. The rest of Naji and his Conservium scholars were probably melted in gryphons' stomachs or already excrement. If they'd found anything while dressing the meat, Bataar had said nothing. Without their supplies, they'd be dead in the mountain. Better the gryphons had been quick and thorough.

Nohra climbed to her feet. Around her girls tossed, chests rising and falling deeply. Through small windows in the rock wall, bluish moonlight leaked over sleeping faces. The women's quarters were under heavy guard. Bataar had made it clear he didn't want her exploring the ruins, but something had been thrumming in Nohra's bones since they got here, a restlessness that had her aching to wander, stronger than her fear.

Ten years ago, when Nohra helped escort her Aunt Clemiria east, Anhabar had been nothing but distant ruins, a strange mountain that the caravan veered sharply around, giving it a wide berth. Something still haunted these halls, a bloody history that lingered with dust and debris and old bones. When she was afraid, her instinct was always to fight. Seeing Anhabar with her own eyes would settle her, and she would find peace in the sanctium.

The guards at the door stiffened, barring her from leaving. Oktai sat slumped against the stone wall. He straightened, blinking away his tiredness and swiping at sticky eyes.

"Where do you think you're going?" a guard grumbled.

Nohra didn't have *Bleeding Edge* to brandish at him.

"Princess?" Qaira said, suddenly at Nohra's side, threading their arms. Nohra could hardly make out her face, but she smelled of the flowers she wore in sachets on her skirts. Their perfume lingered on her thin sleeping clothes.

"I wanted to visit the sanctium," Nohra blurted. "If you would accompany me."

"We'll bring a guard." Qaira led her out into the dark corridor. "Oktai, walk with us." To the other guards, who watched warily, she added, "Not a word to Bataar."

One man opened his mouth, lurching forward to protest, but she batted her eyelashes and smiled. He shuffled back and buttoned his lips.

"Are you alright?" Qaira asked Oktai, who was shuffling behind them.

He juggled his saber to his other hand and rubbed his thigh. "Bataar has me standing on duty all night. I wanted to sit in on the war meeting—oh, *oops*."

War meeting? So Bataar was planning things without her and her sisters. But that didn't explain why Qaira wasn't there. It seemed he esteemed her opinion above any other. Probably she was tasked with watching Nohra, and she'd done her job.

Qaira ducked her head, and they walked in silence past guards posted outside other rooms. Inside one, rows of soldiers slept, snoring loudly. The men standing outside the doors watched them pass with disinterest. After the chaos, the mood in Anhabar had settled.

In a farther room, Nohra knew the wounded screamed and shook. But she couldn't hear them here.

She raised her arm over her chest, suddenly aware of how revealing her sleeping clothes were. "It's freezing. We should have worn coats," she muttered.

Before the mountain city was abandoned, there would have been coal braziers and plush carpets. Its halls weren't hospitable to people now, only ghosts. Qaira cuddled closer, her body pressed hot against Nohra's side, arm hooked around Nohra's elbow.

"Better?"

Against her better judgment, Nohra leaned into her warmth, softening.

They took a sharp turn, past dark rooms with fewer guards at the open doors. Nohra freed her arm to pry a lantern off a carved sconce. The rest of the hall petered into blackness. Shadows spilled out of an open arch in front of them.

The three of them were completely alone now.

"We should turn back," Oktai said. The closest guards were posted so far down the hall, all that was visible was a dim glow, and the only audible sounds were whispers distorted by the stone walls.

"This must be the passageway to the sanctium." Nohra was

breathless. Her stomach fluttered and her pulse spiked, blood rushing so loudly Qaira could surely hear her heartbeat. Bataar had cleared this floor, and the sanctium had been maintained by the old cleric. It was the house of the Goddess. If any part of the mountain was secure, it should be this hall. The sanctium-keeper had probably been dragged into Bataar's councilors' meeting. He'd been dead-set on interrogating the old man.

"I'll wait for you outside," Qaira said, but Nohra took her hand and threaded their fingers.

"No, come with me. Oktai, you stand guard."

He grimaced but nodded, holding his saber at port arms like a wooden toy soldier.

They walked through the open archway. The floor was littered with crunching gravel, dust, and plant litter. There were pieces of white sticks, desert caper bushes, and yellowing branches of other shrubs. The whole mountain city was full of debris. The air in the room was stale, musky and acrid. Ignoring the signs of neglect, Nohra's gaze flitted to the tall ceilings and over the sculptures. Words were carved into plinths at the bottom of blood-colored pillars.

"If you hear anything, we leave and call for more guards," Qaira warned absently, stepping closer to the columns. She pulled Nohra's hand, dragging the lantern close. The inscriptions weren't written in modern Dumakran. "Can you read that?"

Nohra squinted. "It's Old Rayenni. A dead desert language. The Book of Reconciliation in the Godsbreath was written in it, so most clerics can speak a little. Cali knows more of the characters than I do—?"

She held the flame closer to the plinth and scrubbed a hand over the letters. Her touch brushed off rust-like flakes of dirt. The fire dancing around the lantern's cotton wick lit the shadowed words.

"This is religious text," Nohra murmured. Qaira knelt and leaned in. Her warm breath was a distracting cloud against Nohra's cheek. "The words were conveyed directly to Nuna's daughters. After they penned those pages, the order swore a vow of silence."

Nohra rose on her tiptoes to reach the candles set in niches along the walls. Candlelight danced on the red stones, turning them into breathing flesh. Where its glow didn't reach, the large room faded into pitch-blackness. Anything could seep out of the gloom.

Qaira used her slippered foot to swipe some of the mess out of the way. As Nohra knelt, Qaira came down beside her, legs curled around her. Nohra screwed her eyes closed and tried to focus, conjuring up divine words.

The godswar played like a puppet show in the shadows, pulsing red and black behind her shut eyes. Her mother had believed everyone deserved gentleness and forgiveness, that no one would mourn the Goddess's daughters as Nuna would. Nohra imagined a funeral for godsblood, a litany for djinn. The Paga her mind conjured had auburn hair and hazel eyes. The incarnation of chaos was a mirror.

In the quiet, where the only sounds were their soft breaths, she couldn't focus. Coming here had been a mistake. Nohra opened her eyes and stared at the woman beside her.

"She looks different from the paintings and sculptures in the capital," Qaira mused.

Warmth prickled in Nohra's chest as she followed her gaze up the statues. Love for a mother, reverence for a goddess. "Maybe the old artisans weren't skilled enough to carve Nuna's wings. It must not have been taboo to depict Her faces back then." Her voice was too loud in the perfect quiet.

Qaira looked between the statue of Nuna and Nohra. "I

like her better this way. Wearing faces you'd see on the streets of Kalafar." She reached out, her voice sounding far away as her fingertips ghosted over Nohra's features. "The curve of her nose." Nohra's eyelids fluttered shut again. "Kind eyes. The bow of her lips..." Her feather touch disappeared. Nohra cracked open her eyes. "So lifelike I could trace the veins on her wrist."

She scooped up Nohra's hand. Nohra turned on instinct. Qaira's thumb kissed the pads of each fingertip, searing, a hot iron branding her skin. She cradled Nohra's hand closer, drawing it to her face. Her nose caressed Nohra's open palm, skimming her wingbeat pulse.

Nohra's thoughts turned into smoke and the hum of bees.

"You wanted to pray." Qaira dropped her wrist, letting her arm fall. "I'm distracting you."

Nohra's leg knocked over the lantern. Fire curled through the detritus, illuminating shapes like bleached branches, broken pieces of eggshell-thin pottery, gilded secret treasure. The flame flickered, dying and flaring back to life in spurts.

Blackness. Nohra leaned forward. She kissed Qaira the way she'd seen Bataar touch her, burying his nose tenderly in Qaira's soft cheeks and breathing her in. Their mouths touched at the corners, chaste grazes of parted lips, wet and warm. Sleep breath overlaid the gingery licorice flavor of brushed teeth. Qaira's breath caught. After everything he'd taken from her, Nohra wanted to steal this from Bataar—this intimacy he was unworthy of.

Light blazed back to fullness, and it was Qaira who drew back. But surprise wasn't reflected in her half-lidded eyes and loose smile. The gesture might have carried no greater meaning than any kiss from a close friend or family member; aunts and great-grandmothers had kissed Nohra's cheeks more roughly. She might not have meant to invite Nohra closer, to draw her in.

But Qaira's whisper was reverent. "You belong here."

Nohra pictured herself: feral in a sanctium of rubble, drunk off the dark. The Goddess was watching, stone cold and demanding, reminding her of her duty. Guilt flooded her, jellying her arms and legs. Opening her heart to Qaira would hurt them both. She couldn't let her feelings turn her cruel.

"Qaira, I shouldn't have—"

A strange sound interrupted the thought, a wormy mewling. Bats?

Nohra's mouth went dry as she recognized the sensation of being watched. The gaze boring into her wasn't just Qaira's, wobbling with earnestness. Cat's eyes flashed. Nohra grabbed the lantern and pulled them both to their feet.

"Is someone there?" Qaira laid a hand on Nohra's arm. "Should I call for guards?"

They shouldn't have trespassed on this grave.

The glowing eyes disappeared. Nohra took the smallest step back, bumping into Qaira. She clenched their lantern tighter. A strange shape stirred at the entrance to the sloping tunnel that fed into the sanctium's catacombs, but those eyes were so small. Nohra stepped closer, pulling away from Qaira. Something crunched under her slipper, a slender white stick. No—a dry, old bone. Dimly, she registered that this was bad. The sound of the mewling grew.

"Oktai!" Qaira called.

"They're just cubs." Nohra's whisper carried in the cavernous space.

There were four pink bodies the size of house cats, naked, with blurry eyes, wrinkled skin, and gaping beaks. Scraggy, naked tails swished. One wobbled upright, placing a small, taloned foot outside its nest. Was this really a gryphon, small enough to break with a single kick?

Something flashed, catching the lantern light. Threads of gold snaked through the nest of debris. A broken necklace, a jeweled flask, a few coins that must have been arranged by a delicate touch. Safely nestled, new, cracked eggs dripped red.

Beside what looked like a bone from a human hand, something gleamed. A silver seal, the Naji family crest: two seahorses twined around a tower. In the twitching shadows, she couldn't be sure. He could have dropped it as his retinue fled deeper into the mountain. Bataar's men hadn't searched the old catacombs. But without their supplies they'd be dead anyway.

"The Grand Vizier was here," she whisper-shouted, as loud as she dared. She knelt, reaching out a tentative hand. A voice in her head that sounded like a chorus of Darya, Safiya, and Bataar called her reckless and foolhardy and infernally stupid. But if she just grabbed it quickly—

The cub's paw lashed out, sharp claws nicking Nohra's finger. Blood welled, and her head swam.

21

The desecration of mountains and rivers is remembered
by their bodies as well as their spirits.

— Utasoo saying

The sanctium-keeper delivered his words like they were a prophecy from a god, but Bataar knew Preeminence didn't communicate in mortal tongues. "Something is stirring, a power older than mortal kings."

"Now what the fuck is he talking about?" Tarken muttered.

The war room was dark, and the air smelled like mold. Water dripped from the craggy ceiling, and the walls glistened with dampness. In the blackest corner of the room, Boroo hung back as Bataar, Shaza, and Tarken circled the old man. The cleric's worn robes hung in pools around stick-and-bone arms.

"*Just tell me*," Bataar growled, glaring down at the cleric. "Did you become insane before or after you started watching the sanctium? Living amid gryphons' nests in crumbling ruins? How in Preeminence are you even alive?"

There were no scary cannibals living in the dunes, just this maniac in his sanctium-appointed station.

The cleric balked. "Th-these halls have been peaceful for the three years I've been the caretaker."

Bataar shook him by the shoulder. "I'm not stupid. There were cubs. There are human bones in the sanctium. The whole room reeks of gryphons." Like sulfur and wet feathers.

He pushed the cleric against the table spanning the center of the room. The carved topographical map of Dumakra that came down the wall and spread across the face of the table was out of date and misshapen.

The old man winced as he braced himself on one of the sharp mountain peaks carved at the edge of the table. "I warned the vizier's party not to disturb the sanctium! When they arrived at the mountain, I said which rooms to keep out of. I would have told you, too! They must not have listened!"

Bataar ignored his twitching eye and tried to compose his expression. The cleric gawked at him, trembling. "When you were assigned to this post, were you not instructed to inform the clerics in Sinnobad in the event of any attack? If anyone invaded the sanctium, you were supposed to abandon your post until soldiers could clear the ruins."

"They were contained! They're Nuna's creatures, as holy as pegasuses," the old man sputtered. "I wouldn't dare cause the Goddess's Fell Incarnation offense."

Bataar snorted. "You've done worse. You caused me offense."

"She's pure chaos!"

Bataar shook him, hard. "I'll be worse."

Shaza shoved Bataar in the side. "Thrashing him to death will bring trouble with the High Sanctium. He's mad. Leave him for his order to pass judgment on."

Bataar let out another incredulous laugh. That wouldn't be enough. He readjusted his grip on the collar of the man's robes.

"Gryphons, ghouls, sea beasts, those are Nuna's creatures."

The sanctium-keeper's voice quivered. "Creatures of smoke and fire and the deep ocean—"

"Who said anything about *ghouls* and *sea beasts*?" Bataar blurted, tone sharp enough to cut.

The man shrunk back. "Word from Kalafar travels. There was a seahorse in the Scythe!"

Two, to be precise. Not that Bataar wanted to correct him.

"What are you saying, old man?" Tarken crossed his arms. He leaned his hip on the protruding carving of the port city of Marafal. "You think your chaos goddess is declaring war on our rhah?"

The sanctium-keeper shook his head, whitish-gray hair drooping. "Not a war on your king. It is an attack on mankind. She tests our strength. We can't win another godswar."

Bataar relaxed, taking a deep breath. This was an elder's ramblings. Godswars and demons were part of Dumakra's made-up monstrous history, along with djinn and harpies and a million other mythical monsters.

Boroo stepped away from her darkened corner of the room. Her frown was set.

"What is it?" Shaza asked. "Has the Preeminent Spirit communicated something?"

The shaman shook her head. Bone beads rattled. "Something unknown is at play here, a force hidden from Preeminence."

"And?" Bataar pressed.

Grimness pooled in her rheumy eyes. "The soul of this mountain screams."

Bataar clenched his jaw. "Nothing is hidden from Preeminence. If They haven't told you, it's because They don't care to speak right now. They see everything. They're *always* watching. Even here." He paused, before flippantly letting out what terrified him. "Perhaps I've just lost favor."

Boroo recoiled like he'd struck her. "You haven't."

"Then do your job and pray for me." His scar itched. "Is there a chance Naji's men are alive in the catacombs?"

Shaza gaped. "Who cares? Seal the catacombs and leave it alone, you dolt."

"Your Eminence," Tarken snapped.

"'*Your Eminence*'? Kiss his ass later, Tarken. Can you even comprehend what could be down there?" Concern made her brows twist up at the inner corners.

"The grand vizier might be down there." Bataar mulled his decision over. "Naji and his retinue might have taken cover in the catacombs. If anyone's alive, we'll need to find where they're holed up and get them out before we seal off the entrance."

Shaza blinked once, twice, shaking her head. "You're unbelievable. You don't give a cow's teat about Naji. You think there are gryphons down there, and you just can't leave a battle unfought. It's why we're marching on Rayenna instead of pushing for a truce."

"*Shaza*," Tarken warned.

Bataar put a hand on her arm. She threw it off. "I'll only take a scouting party. Tarken and some of his men. You don't have to come."

Her dark eyes gleamed. "Can't you please just listen to me for once?"

He turned away, wringing his hands. "I'm securing Anhabar before we move on."

"The topmost rooms are clear, and the skies are empty," Tarken reported.

"Good. Once the catacombs are clear, we'll seal them and leave for the Sister City."

"But—!" the cleric started.

In a dangerous tone, Bataar warned, "If that displeases you,

I'll seal off the whole sanctium. Demolish all your pretty pillars and statues."

The old man's lower lip wobbled. "You won't be able to navigate the tombs; the markers are written in Old Rayenni. My mentor instilled the dangers of wandering the catacombs. The dead still reek of the disease that ended Anhabar. I'd sooner bite off my tongue than be forced down there to guide you to your deaths."

First the assassin in Kalafar, now this fool. There was a lot of tongue biting these days.

"Anyone who knows the language could guide us?" Bataar asked.

"Only an inducted maven has the education required to understand such esoteric script."

Victory spread, warm in Bataar's chest. He smiled. "Send for Princess Calidah."

The cleric's face fell.

"And what about the gryphon cubs?" Shaza's gaze was icy. "They could have attacked my sister. Should we cull them?"

"No!" Tarken burst out.

Bataar and Shaza both turned in surprise.

"Keep gryphons alive?" Bataar asked. "*You* want that?"

"It would just be a waste, is all." A sinister smile tugged at his mouth. "We have the war dogs, but imagine war gryphons. They call you the gryphon king. We could finally give the rumors weight."

Bataar hesitated. "If you think you can tame and train them," he finally acquiesced.

When Tarken crossed his arms, a lock of brown hair flopped in front of his face. "I can break anything."

"Sure you can. How's the Princess Nohra?" Shaza's fingers skimmed the cliffs on the stone map table, traveling up to Marafal.

Bataar soured. "Feverish. Delirious. Calling out for her mother like a little girl. She's too weak to move." The fever had hit her harder and quicker than he remembered all those years ago.

"It was like that for all of us, when we were marked."

Bataar's scowl deepened. The three of them had been children when they were attacked. Young, with bodies still growing and taking shape. Nohra was an adult.

It could have been Qaira.

"She won't die," Tarken said. "Even if it feels like dying."

Shaza smirked. "Maybe she'll grow feathers. Make her a real Harpy Knight."

The corner of Bataar's mouth twitched. He addressed his shaman. "Boroo, you'll watch over her?" The old woman nodded. Bataar slung on his sable cloak. The chill seeping from the stone walls covered his arms in goosebumps.

"Should you check on her, before we go into the catacombs?" Tarken put down a hand, caging half of Marafal in his fingers. Shaza's trailing hand stalled, prepared to lay siege to the port city in Tarken's grip. Bataar wished they would end their decade-long farce, tangle their fingers, and get out of Bataar's face.

"Why in Preeminence would I visit her?"

With Nohra slipping in and out of consciousness and under guard, Qaira was safer than she'd ever been. Besides, Bataar wasn't going to sit by Nohra praying and fretting like an inconsolable lover. She was strong; she'd survive today to burden and betray him tomorrow.

❧

The cavernous entrance to the catacombs loomed like a beast's maw. Bataar readjusted his grip on the torch. Its flickering fire illuminated columns and statues with ancient inscriptions, but no amount of light could pierce the darkness capping the sanctium. The walls were too tall.

"Come on," he commanded, turning and nodding for Calidah and the soldiers to follow. Hands trembled on bows, and throats bobbed as young men swallowed the fear filling their mouths. Bataar tasted it, too.

"*Spirits*," Tarken swore.

He was so far ahead that his silhouette bled into the inkiness. Bone crunched under boots. Bataar stepped forward, tripping on something pale and hard. He squinted. A femur.

"What's that old man been doing out here?" Tarken demanded in an angry hiss. "How many merchant caravans have disappeared on their way to Rayenna? Or are these the scary religious dissenters?"

Calidah mumbled her own curses, eyes round and wide behind glass lenses. The mother-of-pearl inlay on her crossbow shone in the torchlight, glimmering a hundred iridescent colors.

Bataar watched her warily. "Whoever they are, the bones are old and brittle. These aren't Naji's men." Footprints led deeper into the tunnel, smeared from running, and blood stains made dark, hardened spots in the dirt. He nodded at some words inscribed on a plaque above the stone passageway. "What's that say?"

"It just looks like Paga's blessing for the dead," Calidah said. "It's common language near sanctium tombs."

A small body ran past, streaking over Oktai's feet. "What was that? What was that?!" he screamed, stumbling into Tarken's chest.

Tarken smacked him on the back of the head. "It was a rat, pisshead."

Up ahead, the passageway forked. Tarken stopped and turned, tapping his foot. "Which way? The idiot old man didn't know what he was talking about. These paths aren't labeled."

Bataar looked at the Harpy Knight. She'd wrapped her arms around her torso. She stared back at him, shivering. Sighing, he unclasped his cloak and swung it over her shoulders.

"Paga is associated with the left side of the body," she answered. "Nuna with the right. I'd expect we'd find the unlabeled crypts for the worst kinds of criminals that way. Wife murderers, child rapers."

Bataar drummed his fingers on his scabbard. "And to the left?"

Calidah shrugged. "Everyone else."

The two types of men.

"Which direction would the grand vizier and his men have gone?" The dust that poured into the tunnel at its mouth had cleared, and now the floor was unyielding stone, the faint trail lost except where bloodied handprints streaked the wall.

"Unmarked graves are taboo. Even if they were hiding from gryphons, Naji's men wouldn't shelter there."

"We go left," Bataar ordered. Up ahead, Tarken bobbed his head.

"Why do you care?" Calidah's tone leeched suspicion, and she wouldn't meet his gaze. "Is the grand vizier's life worth so much to you?"

Soldiers filed around them, leaving Bataar and Calidah alone in the silent red depths.

"I care enough to look." His tone was clipped. "I don't suffer losses well." Not to mention, if Naji died, Lofri's son would become grand vizier right away. The *idea* of Bataar elevating Jawaad was a more powerful motivator to Lofri than actually letting that oaf run the country.

Calidah squinted, watching him from the corner of her eye now. "You aren't superstitious?"

"Not at all." Bataar thought of the stone crypts in Choyanren, of the eyes that watched. He'd grown accustomed to the burn of gods' gazes. He bit his tongue, pressing down hard enough to taste iron. He knew what happened to the dead. Bataar could trust his own eyes. Souls didn't linger.

She kept watching him with that inquisitive expression.

"We need our little maven." Tarken's voice echoed down the passageway. Calidah bristled.

"After you," Bataar said. "Princess."

"I'm not a princess." Her thin mouth twisted into a grimace. "Only the zultam's ward. Just because my mother is the queen in Rayenna doesn't mean I'd succeed her."

Bataar had forgotten to ask about that. He kicked a stone. It skipped across the dirt, disappearing into darkness. "Who would? Who rules the Sister City when your mother abdicates?"

"If Rami had become the zultam, he would have appointed one of his sisters."

"Who would he have chosen?" Not that Bataar wanted a child making critical political decisions.

"Nohra's been a mother to him, but Saf's his best friend." She hummed. "I'm not sure. Neither one of them has those kinds of ambitions, really."

"Done chatting?" Tarken swiped at the thick layer of dust obscuring a placard. The grayish-red soot merely smeared over the recessed words. Swearing, he uncorked the stopper on his waterskin and poured it over the plaque.

Calidah leaned in, her lips pursed. "'Lords'? That wing could be for Anhabari viziers or zultams? I don't know for sure. If you'd allow me a closer look at the sanctium-keeper's map, perhaps I could—"

"The map stays with me." Tarken folded the vellum and held it up, out of reach. "I don't want you getting us lost on purpose." The impressions of footsteps were entirely gone, but a trail of dark stains wound down the hall to this barricaded room. "Anyone in there?" Tarken called out. No one answered.

Sighing, Calidah crowded Tarken, squinting to make out the words. "'Hall of Kings'."

"Aha." He flashed his teeth. "Thought it looked nice."

A slab of rock blocked the entrance, letting in a few finger-lengths of outside air. Soldiers heaved as they shoved the makeshift door in. Bataar stepped into the cavern first. Oktai's eyes followed his movement, brows furrowing in worry. Long lines of gold caskets stretched into the shadows. The air was shallow and dead.

Bataar drew in a breath like a lungful of stagnant water. "How many zultams died in Anhabar?" he asked. He couldn't tell if the markings in the dust on the floor were bloodstains or from moisture dripping.

Calidah's fingers twitched in the air as she counted. "Something like ten, but their families are probably entombed in this room too."

Tarken whistled. "Just one of these must cost a fortune. How has this place not been looted?" He stepped forward, prying at one of the coffins. "Maybe because these lids are damn heavy."

"Don't touch that!" Calidah scolded. "You shouldn't disturb the graves."

Bataar traced the carvings on top of one coffin. "Is the fear of vermilrot strong enough to keep away grave robbers?" The designs were cruder than the complex death mask and fine details on Zultam Ramzi's casket.

He swallowed around a knot in his throat. An eerie sweet-ness swirled through the air, like the scented smoke balls the priestesses had thrown in before closing the lid on Ramzi. It had been hundreds of years since these corpses were entombed, so how could those smells linger?

"Take the lid off of one of these," he ordered, tension coiling through his body.

"You shouldn't disturb the dead!" Calidah protested. "It's just wrong."

"I need to see. To be sure."

"To see *what*?"

He didn't know.

Soldiers grunted as they jammed weapons into the seam between the lid on one of the stone sarcophagi. They groaned and huffed as it slid off with a painful scrape. Bataar raised his torch over the casket, peering into its pitch-dark corners. The glow illuminated bits of exposed, yellowing bone and patches of dry, puckered skin. Strands of stringy hair still clung to the scalp on top of the skull. The eye holes, nose, and mouth were craters.

"Eehh." Tarken scrunched up his face in disgust.

"I'm going to be sick," Oktai groaned, wincing back.

Golden links of chainmail lay in puddles in the sunken chest. Insect-eaten scraps of fabric clung to the ribs. The scent of dust overlaid the decay, and the round incense holder lay empty and rusted red.

"What were you expecting?" Calidah grumbled.

"Next one," Bataar ordered, ignoring the princess's angry snarl.

"You're mad!"

"Anyone here?" Bataar called out, hoping to hear moans from a few emaciated survivors, desperate for food and water.

"Bataar, Your Eminence, uh, this one's already open," Oktai's voice carried to the border of the room.

Tightening his grip on the hilt of his saber, Bataar plunged into blackness. Flames whorled around his torch. The odor of burning oil clouded his senses, temporarily masking the smell of the mummified bodies. There was still that sweetness, and it wasn't incense. He recognized it from the doctor's tents outside Tashir's walls and from his father's deathbed.

Vermilrot.

"What—?" Calidah started. A horrified expression twisted at her lips as Bataar used his teeth to pull off his glove and swiped a finger through the film of grime on the bottom of the crypt box. He lifted it to his face, sniffed.

"Just dust," he said, wiping his hands on his pantleg.

"It's possible that the body meant for this casket wasn't entombed," Calidah suggested flatly, staring into the empty depths. She caught her glasses before they could slide off the bridge of her nose.

"Why would that have happened?"

"The person probably died just before the flight from Anhabar. If they caught the rot during the panic at the end of the epidemic, they would have been burned instead of entombed."

"I thought your religion doesn't allow cremation."

"It doesn't, but there were massive funeral pyres to try and stifle the spread of the rot. The records make it out to be a very virulent strain." She hugged herself tighter, nuzzling into the sable lining of Bataar's cloak. "The Nights of Flame was the inspiration for 'Ashes Over Anhabar'."

"That a song? A book?" Tarken asked Bataar.

He shook his head. "How would I know?"

"It's a ballad," Oktai supplied.

Tarken clapped his younger cousin on the shoulder. "I can always count on you to know something useless."

"The musicians played it at Lofri's party, actually, toward the end. You were probably too drunk to remember."

"Watch it, boy. I'm still telling your mother you've been a little shit, I haven't forgotten."

Bataar still carried tension in his back, like a string pulled taut. The cloying odor made his stomach churn.

"Someone bring me a torch, please," Calidah called out. She was a few paces away, prodding something with the toe of her boot.

"If you see something strange, step back." Bataar approached cautiously, drawing his saber.

"There's someone dead here. A cleric."

"How can you tell—" He broke off, staring down at the body. He sheathed his sword.

Tarken declared, "It must be one of Naji's retinue."

There were two corpses, one prone on the ground, the other face up, spread on a casket lid like a body to be dissected. This one was long-dead, wearing threadbare rags as thin as paper. The skin was gray. Squares of its desiccated, leathery flesh had been carved off by a precise hand. It wasn't the gryphons that had been chewing these bones. Though the face had been cleaned before this body was embalmed and carefully preserved, Bataar alone recognized the sunkenness of rot.

"More empty crypt boxes," someone muttered. Jagged stone chunks from broken casket lids cast mountainous shadows.

Bataar glanced down at the body Tarken had been staring at. This corpse's clothes weren't so time-worn. A flicker of hope died as Bataar nudged the dead body with his foot, rolling it face up. The grand vizier's group had mostly been made up of mavens from the Conservium: expert scholars of history, architecture, and religious symbology.

"He went with the vizier," Bataar confirmed, recognizing him from the audience hall in the palace. "Everyone step back."

Torchlight fell on the corpse's face, and red-crusted eyes flashed in the flames. Shouts broke out as grown men jumped away from the supine body.

"Nobody panic. Vermilrot is treatable with the right medicine and proper sanitation," Bataar explained. "It's a normal sickness, like bleeding pox. Just don't touch him."

The dead man's pupils spun in Bataar's direction. The corpse surged up and lunged.

"*Bataar!*" Tarken shouted, pulling him back. Tarken's saber met the dead man with a rotten thunk.

"Cover your faces!" Bataar ordered, as blackish red sprayed out of the slice across the maven's gut.

Someone stumbled out of deeper darkness. The figure was broad-shouldered and tall, even hunched over. Bataar almost didn't recognize him. The usually perfectly neat beard was disheveled. Thickened blood dripped down gaunt cheeks and trickled from the two open nose holes torn in his face. More spilled around cracked lips. His fingers ended in long, broken fingernails like dirty claws.

"Princess!" Oktai stepped in front of Calidah. Her hands shook as she raised her crossbow.

The ghoul stumbled forward, and Oktai smashed his lantern against Grand Vizier Naji's bleeding face. Glass cracked and shattered. The ghoul made a choked sound, spitting blood. Oktai shoved him, and Naji stumbled back. He crouched and lunged, hissing, congealed red spittle flying from his mouth.

"Back to the door!" Bataar shouted. His pulse was coldly calm. "Seal the entrance to the catacombs."

More death-pale arms reached out of the shadows. Bataar pulled his short bow off his back. Talon-like fingers ensnared Oktai. His eyes widened, trained pleadingly at Bataar as teeth sunk into his neck. He didn't even scream.

"No, no, no," Tarken mumbled, fumbling with his bow.

Bataar nocked and released his first arrow. Then another. And another.

22

To the Greater Demons, the cities of man are as insignificant as anthills to be destroyed on a whim, or by accident.

— Author anon

Nohra was dying. She shivered under the blankets as fever roiled through her. Her legs and arms were leaden. When she tried opening her mouth, her tongue was too heavy to move. She couldn't even groan.

"Something's happening near the sanctium," Safiya announced, grabbing her scabbard. *Queen of Beasts* sang out as she drew the wootz steel sword. "I'll be back."

"Wha—?" Nohra's voice was too weak and hoarse to carry.

"*Shhh.*" Qaira dabbed Nohra's brow with a damp rag. The salt water stung, ice hot. "Don't worry. Focus on beating this fever." Fingers gently combed against Nohra's scalp. Qaira's voice was a lullaby, cutting through dizzying pain.

Nohra tried lifting her head. Darya sat near the cot, wringing her fingers in her lap. Hana, one of Nohra's half-sisters, crouched on a sleeping roll, fastening her armor. Near her, Hana's twin, Syreen, sharpened her blade against a whetstone. Metal screamed.

"Come on, Hana, or it'll all happen without us," Syreen complained. "Saf, wait for us!"

Everything was obscured through a fog. In the corner, two serving girls whispered, their own hands hovering over their weapons. Bataar's shaman was in the room too, head lolling as if she were asleep, or in a trance. In an instant, her gray eyes shot open, and she said something in Utasoo.

"What was that?" Qaira blinked, brows knitting. "Block the doors?"

Darya tilted her head, her fingers stilling. "They're louder now."

"Hm?"

Shouts carrying from down the hall crescendoed. Screams came from just outside the doorway. Stronger than pain, a sharp slash of fear cut Nohra. Pushing past a wave of nausea, she dragged herself up.

"My scythe." Her words slurred painfully. Furs slid down her body, pooling around her hips as the sweat on her skin turned to frost.

Qaira's lips pursed. "Lie back." Her hands trembled slightly as she tried easing Nohra down.

But she'd finally found her voice and refused to lose it. The words scratched in her sore throat. "What's going on?"

One of the doorkeepers fell through the threshold. "*Aggg,*" he grunted, thrashing against a sallow-skinned man biting him. Biting him?

Utasoo soldiers poured in, forming a semi-circle. Behind them, men lunged into the room. Their heads whipped left and right. Red leaked from their eyes and mouths and the cavernous holes where cartilage should have covered noses and ears. A sickly sweetness seeped off them.

"*Spirits.*" Qaira's mouth formed a small, shocked circle.

Bataar's eagle streaked inside, diving through the doorway into one of the red faces. Her hooked claws sunk into blood-crusted eyes. A scream like steel hitting a boulder tore out of the attacker's body. Nohra fell forward, her heavy fingers reaching for the snath of *Bleeding Edge*. But her grip was as weak as butter.

"Vermilrot," Qaira whispered. "It has to be. But it can't—I've never seen a patient like this."

The eagle screeched, and one of the bleeding ghouls made a sound halfway between a groan and a growl. Ghouls, they had to be, like the stories from the Godsbreath, monsters who haunted tombs.

Nohra willed her hand to close. Her muscles strained as she tried to pull the sickle-staff into her lap. Her head swam. Wincing, she shut her eyes. White starbursts exploded behind her eyelids. Still so weak. If she could just stand and fight, she could protect them.

Her hand grasped something: fingers. Darya, smelling like a camp cookfire instead of fresh-baked bread and the palace's lavender soap. She could recite the names of all the constellations and would feed sugar water to dying butterflies. Nohra's little kitchen mouse. Darya's hand was even hotter than Nohra's feverish skin. She couldn't shield her now.

One soldier fell, then another. The doorkeeper howled in pain as teeth continued to tear into his neck. The crimson spray suffused his tunic, dribbling down his linen trousers. A man without a helmet fell back. His head cracked against the stone floor, and the spark of light in his eyes died. His expression glazed over in an instant, mouth hanging slack. Just like the assassin in the sanctium a lifetime ago, with her eyes like honey.

If that woman could see Nohra now, she'd laugh. The Goddess would laugh too.

Paga reborn with a bloody scythe. Ha. What a joke. If Nohra couldn't fight, what good was she?

Qaira's arm shot out, drawing a fallen soldier's bow out of loosened fingers. Nohra's heart raced. Qaira fitted an arrow and pulled the bowstring taut, cursing under her breath, elbow shaking from the strain. There was a flurry of brown feathers as Bataar's golden eagle raked an attacker's sunken cheeks. Qaira gave a sharp command, and Erdene was recalled, flitting to Qaira's side. Her beak was painted in blood.

"What a good bird," Qaira praised. "Did Bataar send you?" Clenching her teeth, she released the stretched bowstring. The string left an indent on her mouth, a perfect valley cutting down her lips.

The first shot missed. It *pwinked* off the stone wall, shaft snapping. Qaira breathed in a deep, steadying breath. The second arrow sank into the center of an attacker's chest. A snarl ripped from his mouth. Blood burbled out around the shaft, thick like tree sap. The third arrow struck true, right above the first. He lumbered closer, somehow moving faster.

Darya's hand tensed, fingers straining under Nohra's. Her skin was like a hot iron, searing down to the bone. "You need to let me go." Her voice pitched oddly. Dread was etched in harsh lines on a face turned foreign.

Nohra's blood curdled. "Dar?" She tried to fight the headache. A fog still lingered, but she could ball her other hand into a fist. The room spun, then stilled.

"Something is wrong with me," Darya whispered. Her voice was like rain hissing against a hot rock. "I can keep you safe, but I don't know if I can control it. When I start, you should run." Darya's fingers slipped through Nohra's and she stood, climbing in front of Qaira. She'd left her knife lying on Nohra's lap.

Nohra tried to shout, but her dry throat strangled her words. The man with arrows lodged in his abdomen snarled, stepping close to Darya. She dug her fingers into his muscled neck and pulled his body down. He fell to his knees as Darya snapped his chin up, twisting her knuckles into his jaw.

"Holy Preeminence," Qaira swore. Boroo started rocking back and forth, loudly chanting some ward against evil.

Something had been wrong, different, with Darya since the invasion. It seemed like Fahaad knew, but Nohra hadn't questioned it.

The flesh and the muscles underneath the man's skin molded to Darya's grip like clay. His fingers scrabbled against her arms, nails scratching, making ribbons of her sleeves but not drawing blood. White wisps seemed to ooze out of Darya. His head twisted, and scarlet-stained teeth latched onto her wrist. She didn't flinch as he gnashed down. The servants wore horrified expressions, mouths gaping as they retreated deeper into the cavern, away from Darya. The man stopped biting and looked up at her, eyes bulging, bright red from the pressure of her grip. Her fingers wrung and his neck cracked, head falling limp. His body collapsed, its dead weight smacking the stone.

Nohra couldn't breathe.

Darya looked over her shoulder, her eyes becoming black glass. Turning back, she dissolved into shadows. The smudgy shape of her blew around the room, seeping into the attackers' bodies. With a pop like a play ball breaking, each exploded, showering the far corner of the room in chunky ichor. Nohra couldn't blame Qaira for ducking behind her. One of the remaining serving girls threw up, and another burst into tears. Shock pricked like barbed thorns in Nohra's mouth.

Darya, what did you do?

When she rematerialized, Nohra didn't recognize the abyssal

pits of Darya's eyes. The edges of her body didn't make sense. They were hazy, glowing like electricity veining a storm cloud. The cavern reeked of flame. This was a fever dream, a nightmare.

"I need you to walk," Qaira hissed, yanking Nohra up. Nohra's legs shook but didn't buckle.

❧

In the hallway outside, blades sunk into rotten meat. The sound of boots pounding against stone carried down corridors as hunched shapes fell through the darkness. Nohra leaned heavily on Qaira's side. Boroo grunted with each step, the shaman's weight dragging on Qaira's other arm.

"Just a little farther," Qaira assured, pulling them both forward.

Erdene flitted ahead, screeching as she flew down the hall. Nohra's perspiration-dampened hair hung in front of her face, swaying with each step. She squinted through the muddy curtain of it, choking on the scent of her own sweat. "Rami," she croaked. "Where's Rami?"

Where was the Goddess? No prayers could reach Her here.

"With Fahaad—" Qaira was cut off with a stifled squeak as a body flew out of an open doorway.

It slammed into the right side of the hallway where it slumped, a steel-tipped javelin pinning it to the wall. Its eyes blinked open.

"A little faster," Qaira prompted, fingers pinching tighter. They were running from Darya as much as the ghouls. Nohra's mind swirled. This all had to be the fever.

"They're coming from the direction of the sanctium," Nohra rasped.

Qaira's body shook. "Bataar and Tarken went into the catacombs."

What had they awoken?

Shapes emerged around the bend up ahead. They stopped. Nohra pulled away from Qaira, shifting her weight onto *Bleeding Edge* to use as a crutch. The metal was cool against her hot skin. She planted her feet firmly, searching for stable footing. Her elbows quivered as she drew Darya's knife. Beside her, Qaira nocked another arrow.

"Oh, thank Preeminence," a man said. Nohra recognized the timber and cadence of Bataar's voice. She'd never been so relieved to inhale his balsam and musk.

"Bataar." Qaira's voice broke. She dropped the bow and quiver. They clattered against the rock floor as his arms wrapped around her body, spinning her off her feet. His gasping lips breathed in her skin, and she shook as she burrowed her nose against his cheek.

Calidah stood beside Bataar, wrapped in his sable cloak. The three soldiers accompanying them had dirt smeared on their faces. Tarken's face was spattered with ruby flecks of blood. He held something in his arms. No, not something. Someone.

"Physicians," he grunted. "Where are they?"

"Is it, Preeminence, Oktai…" Qaira trailed off, looking down at the wincing, blood-covered face cradled in Tarken's arms. "They should be in the same quarters as the soldiers, tending to the men with gryphon fever." She locked eyes with Nohra and then glanced at Boroo. The shaman was out of breath and shaking.

"Princess," Bataar prompted, holding out his arm for Nohra.

"I can walk on my own." She gritted her teeth against the whole-body soreness, not meeting his gaze.

"Then give me the boy, Tarken." Bataar's tone was insistent, imperious.

Oktai's body started to slip in Tarken's arms. He adjusted

his grip, movements jerky and hard-edged. "No. I have to carry him."

"Don't be prideful." Bataar's fingers clenched. "It's a bad time to play the hero. Drop him, and you'll kill him faster."

"He's my blood!" Tarken snarled. "My burden. Not yours."

Bataar pressed a bloody fist to his mouth and grit out. "Fine. Make this your hill to die on. We'll clear the way."

Biting down her pride, Nohra reached out. Her fingers shook slightly on Bataar's sleeve. "My brother. Rami," she whispered. Darya—

Sweat dripped from Bataar's black hair like ink. "I've already given the order to protect the boy by any means necessary. You"—he grabbed one of the grime-covered soldiers by his leather armor—"bring the princess her brother."

"Y-yes, Your Resplendentness."

"Something happened," Qaira interjected. "Her talmaid—"

Bataar cast a pitying look at Nohra. "Later."

Ahead, a Dumakran soldier crumpled backward, falling to his knees and howling in pain as a figure with a gory mouth snapped at his shield, hands like fishhooks digging into the man's thighs. Grunting, the soldier slammed the circle of steel down, again and again until he heaved and a lumpy wave of blood burst against him. Bataar fired. His shots weren't as perfect as Qaira's, forming neat lines of dove-colored fletching, but both splattered into the attacker's head.

The soldier fell back, collapsing, laughing deliriously. "Thank Paga, oh thank Paga."

"Get him up and to the infirmary," Bataar demanded. "The disease is bloodborne, spread by direct contact. We'll quarantine everyone after the catacombs have been sealed."

"Everyone?" A guard looked between Qaira and Nohra. She'd shielded Qaira from the gore Darya painted the room with.

Bataar's lip curled. "Everyone. Anyone."

There hadn't been a major vermilrot outbreak in Dumakra since the flight west. Conservium mavens still feared its spread, and the High Sanctium's bells rang whenever a rot patient died, but Nohra had never witnessed someone in the throes of the disease. This couldn't be that. These were more ghoul than man, demons haunting tombs in the Godsbreath.

Ghouls, like the races of djinn, were almost annihilated in the godswar. The survivors of Nuna's army were locked in the fell pits, chained to molten earth.

"Nohra!" Bataar called out. "Behind you." She stumbled back, swinging blindly with *Bleeding Edge*. Her legs nearly folded when her blade sliced under the head of an infected man. The curving sickle blade wedged into his neck with a meaty splat. Nohra stared at the exposed muscle and sinew dazedly.

"Come on," Bataar said, dragging her and her sickle-staff forward.

Guards were posted outside the makeshift infirmary in the soldiers' quarters. Their bodies coiled with tension and fear flashed behind visors. Women pushed through the doorway carrying bloodied bodies on thrown-together cots.

"Mmm," Oktai groaned. His eyes were unfocused as Tarken set him down in the center of the room.

"Make this boy your priority." Bataar's voice was punctuated with a new roughness. At his order, physicians abandoned their convulsing patients.

Fahaad. Rami.

Nohra gripped Calidah's wrist tightly, her gaze roving the room for a tall, dark-skinned man with short hair and a little boy with her father's eyes. She blinked. Not Rami, but another of her brothers had taken refuge in the infirmary. Nassar sneered and looked away. Embers of rage smoldering in her core, she refocused instead on the doctors hovering around Oktai.

"He's lost too much blood," the physician reported. "His eyes aren't tracking my finger. He's anemic, like the others. I fear he'll fade quickly."

Bataar dragged the man up by the front of his tunic. "Do something about it. There has to be something you can do."

"A-a new procedure," he stammered. "It's the talk of the Conservium, but it has risks."

"Try it. Anything."

The man's breath quivered. "The chance of failure is lower if there's a close blood relative. A brother or sister or—"

"A cousin?" Tarken's voice cracked. "Tell me what I have to do."

"Your arm." He pulled up Tarken's soiled sleeve.

Bataar stepped close, taking his friend's elbow and ripping the fabric. "There. Go on then."

"This is my fault too," Calidah whispered, sinking to the ground. She wrapped her arms around her knees, pressing *Covenant* against her legs. "That stupid boy put himself in front of me. That should be me on the floor."

"Thank the Goddess it isn't you," Nohra said quietly. She laid a hand on her cousin's shoulder. Calidah shrugged it off, and Nohra almost toppled over.

Cali's nose wrinkled. She shook her head, covering her ears. She was swimming in Bataar's cloak. "I don't deserve to be a Harpy Knight."

Nohra patted the back of her head. "That's not true." She winced as she dragged Calidah to her feet.

Her face was red, her eyes glistening with unshed tears. "I broke my vows, in the audience hall. I chose Aalya over the zultam. I couldn't let her bleed out, but... I don't even deserve to breathe on *Covenant*."

"You're here now." Nohra kept her voice steady. "Rejoin the fight. You can do more good outside with your bow than you'll do in this room." It was what Nohra wished she could do. Calidah's glistening eyes wobbled. "Give your life now, for your new zultam," Nohra told her. "You're a knight of Dumakra, a princess of Rayenna, and your heart burns for blood."

Calidah's knuckles tightened on the stock of her crossbow, and she drew herself up, fearsome in the gryphon king's cloak.

Nohra pulled her close and pressed kisses to both her cheeks. "Go." She hoped she wasn't sending her baby cousin to her death. "Give Saf hells for me."

Calidah was gone with a swish of hair.

Sparing few words, the physicians gathered supplies. One cracked a glass ampoule, protecting their fingers from shards with a cloth barrier.

Tarken accepted the vial of analgesic. "What's this?"

"Drink it. The boy can't swallow, so we'll get the medicine into him through your body."

A woman wearing the midnight-colored hood of a medicine maven stepped forward. "You'll need to keep a hold of something, to keep the blood moving through the limb."

Qaira reached out. "Take my hand, Tarken." Another maven candidate pulled a thick line from a leather bag, unwinding a coil that looked like an intestine. He produced a long needle and pricked the crook of Tarken's arm. The doctor ran the other end of the line into Oktai's inner elbow. A trail of blood slunk slowly down the membranous line into the boy.

"We need to try to stabilize the lacerations now," the woman in the maven's hood said.

Bataar crossed his arms, shoulders taut. "What else can we do?"

She bowed her head. "Pray to Paga that his body doesn't reject the blood."

Nohra's throat constricted, every breath the scrape of steel. Oktai had been her shadow for the last two months, more like a floppy-haired puppy than a guard. Seeing him on the floor like this was grim beyond her imagining.

"*Bataar*," Oktai said, a small, strangled murmur as the physicians undid the field dressings and stitched shut his bleeding wounds.

The silk catgut made black criss-crossings over Oktai's chest. When they were done, they wrapped gauze around the leaking bite marks below his ear. Bataar knelt and took the boy's hand.

"Y-you won't tell my mother about this part, will you?"

Bataar sighed. "Oh, *Oktai*." He rubbed back and forth over his fingers.

Oktai's face twisted in pain. "Promise you won't. She'd be so sad."

"You little pisshead," Tarken swore, clenching his hand tighter in Qaira's. Her lip quivered, and she choked on the sob that slipped out. Tarken twisted his head away, studying the bare stone wall.

"I promise." Bataar squeezed Oktai's shivering fingers once, twice. Blood had already suffused the clean bandages. "Only how brave you were. A perfect soldier, a prince of the world."

Nohra bit down hard on her tongue, blinking away moisture accumulating at the edges of her eyes. The mavens were on the forefront of medical advancement. Their blood transfer would work, she was sure of it. *Ward him from—*

More useless prayers, sour in her mouth.

"I wanted," Oktai gasped, "to tell her about the poppies—"

"Keep it down!" Nassar shouted. "Nuna's tits."

Bataar dropped Oktai's hand and spun around. "Forget about your tongue. I'll rip your soul out of your body."

Nassar sank back, eyes widening. "Watch the way you speak to me, rhah. I only asked if you all would"—Bataar swept across the room, stepping easily over the bandaged bodies lying prone on cots—"quiet down," the prince finished in a squeak as Bataar pulled him up by his neck. More words choked in his throat. His eyes rolled backward, feet kicking. He clawed at Bataar's face, but Bataar didn't flinch.

Lofri's guards wore haunted expressions, too slow to act.

He was going to choke Nassar to death.

"Bataar," Qaira called out, her voice so soft there was no way he would hear.

Wordlessly, he flung Nassar down. The prince scrambled back, knocking over a bucket full of reddened rags. "What in hells?" he heaved.

Bataar sneered. "Not another word, or I'll end you."

"F—" Nassar started. Bataar reached for Nassar's shirt, but his fingers slipped through air. Nassar's head fell back. Though no hands touched him, his face whitened with pressure. He coughed, clawing at an invisible adversary.

Bataar's long fingers twitched like they held something, fabric no one could see, pulling tighter and tighter, coiling invisible material around his fist. A muscle in his forehead pulsed as he drew some unseeable thing from the prince.

Nohra's chest twisted. This had to be the fever, too.

The old shaman growled words in a dialect Nohra didn't understand, but Bataar did. A flash of fear twisted his mouth.

Sweat-damp hair flew in front of Bataar's face as his fingers loosened. His expression shifted as Nassar fell forward, dropping like the force strangling him had eased. Guards rushed to his side, helping the prince stand on wobbly legs. Nassar wheezed, watching Bataar with wide, terrified eyes.

"Stay there," Bataar snarled. Nassar's guards were already hauling the prince toward the door. Bataar looked to his own men, opening his mouth as if to bark an order. He paused, then closed it and let them leave.

Nohra was going to throw up. Darya, Bataar, it was all some nightmarish hallucination. She should have killed the damned gryphon cubs.

Boroo shook her head, speaking some other admonishment. The beads in her spun-silver hair clattered. Her craggy voice blurted out Utasoo words Nohra knew: "The boy is dead."

Nohra turned back to Oktai, her vision blurring. She swallowed around the hard lump in her throat, tasting salt.

"Bataar, water from the Heartspring," Qaira whispered. "It helped the princess wake up. There was a cleric traveling with Naji. There might be a vial in their supplies."

Bataar's breath was jagged as a serrated blade. "It's just red water, and he's already dead."

Tarken started to pull away, untangling himself from the throng and dropping Qaira's hand like it had burned him.

"Wait," the physician said. "You gave too much blood. You'll need to sleep off the effects of the painkiller."

Tarken ripped the needle and line from his arm. Blood leaked from the hose. One of the young physicians tightly tied off the crook of his elbow. Tarken waved him away, his scowl deepening, creasing his face. "I'll get the catacombs sealed," he mumbled. "This ends now." His eyes glazed over as he turned, leaving the sickroom in the direction of the sanctium.

"Spirits," Bataar cursed, gesturing for soldiers to follow Tarken. "Stay here," he added numbly, pushing Qaira toward Nohra. "Watch them," he ordered his guards.

Nohra stumbled, still weak from the fever. She looked into Qaira's shimmering eyes, watching tears fall, running like rivers down her perfect face. When she couldn't keep looking, she turned to Bataar. "What are you doing?"

He unknotted his leather belt and knelt in front of Oktai's unmoving body. "Restraining him. The dead don't lie still in this mountain. Until we know how, we'll keep them down."

"Nohra!" someone called.

Shadows stood on the threshold. Blood dripped from the curved shortsword Fahaad held. Beside him, Rami shook, looking like a specter in his dirtied tunic and pants. Standing between them was Darya. The tension in Nohra's chest broke.

23

"Wise and handsome king of demonkind, please accept
my meager gift, though it pales in comparison to your
black-fire eyes and is unworthy of your magnificence."

— Nuna tricking the Demonking

In the crowd gathered outside the war room, high-ranking
Dumakran soldiers spoke shrilly, their voices cracking like
frightened boys. The guards posted at the cave-like threshold
stood rigid and pale. The clammy skin above their lips beaded
with perspiration. Everyone's eyes were wide, distant and
unseeing. Some officers whispered they should never have
trespassed on Anhabar. Others watched Bataar with unveiled
deference; he'd won their respect for clearing the mountain that
had terrified the country for centuries. He couldn't let any of
them know that through that door, a monster was unrestrained
in pitch-darkness.

Keeping his voice level, Bataar repeated his question to the
princess. "How dangerous is she?"

"Darya isn't a threat." Nohra's voice wavered, and sweat
sheened her forehead. It was a miracle she was even standing.

The fever couldn't have passed so quickly, but Nohra was stubborn enough to hurt herself. "She protected us. Like she protected Laila and the other girls the night of the invasion. She would never hurt her friends."

Frightened chatter from the soldiers was like the drone of insects.

Bataar scraped a hand over his face. "What is she?"

"I'm not sure." A flicker of apprehension passed over Nohra's features. A nerve beside her mouth spasmed.

"Can you control her?"

"I-I don't know."

Bataar thought of the constellation embedded in the hilt of Darya's knife—the chain Nuna used to control the Demonking. In the Dumakran legends, their goddess controlled the djinn with chains and trickery. But Bataar couldn't put his faith in myths.

"Is she a demon?"

There was silence as Nohra held his gaze. Desperation welled in her watery brown eyes. "What about *you*?" she blurted out. "What did you do to my brother in the infirmary?"

He shot her a warning glance. Bataar thought of Oktai, the blood spurting from his neck, his last desperate, stupid request about his mother. "Nassar choked on his spit. I had nothing to do with it."

Nohra's face softened. She seemed eager to believe the lie. She didn't want another beast in the mountain.

"Are you not concerned that he ran away?" Bataar pressed. In the confusion and chaos with the vermilrot, Nassar had fled with Lofri's son and all their family's soldiers. He could claim the city and spread the disease through her home.

"He's just slunk back to Kalafar," Nohra said firmly. She swallowed, and Bataar's eyes followed the line of her throat.

"He's still Lofri's dog. If Lofri doesn't bring him to heel, I'll remind him of his place."

Bataar wasn't so sure. He tilted his head and shouldered into her space, invasive. Grand Vizier Naji had warned Bataar that Nohra wanted *him* dead, but would she really kill her own blood? She seemed to value family loyalty more than common sense.

"I should have let your father smash his skull in." His utterance was barely a whisper, but Nohra flinched.

"*What?*" Her hair fell in her face, obscuring her expression. "My father was going to…? No. Don't lie to me."

Bataar didn't care if the truth hurt her. He wanted it to stab. "I've never told you a lie. Your brother moved on your father, and Ramzi tried to brain him with that lion-paw club, and I got in the way. Insurrection looks like blood killing blood."

"No. Nassar wouldn't—my father wouldn't—"

He twisted the knife, shattering the mirage she'd put her faith in. "If you'd been there, you could have chosen who died."

Maybe she was grateful to have been spared that decision. Her voice dropped even quieter. "No—"

The shadows inside Anhabar's war room shifted. *Darya.* They both stiffened, flinching at her quiet shuffling.

Yesterday, after they'd sealed the catacombs, Bataar had made it his mission to learn everything there was to know about Nohra's talmaid. Rumor had it, Darya's mother had skipped Kalafar with a caravan merchant more than twenty years ago, abandoning her daughter at the palace to be raised by her grandmother. The zultam had tried to arrange a match for Darya, to an old, rich widower, some minister, but someone had broken it off—probably Nohra.

The Daheer woman had been entirely unremarkable until the invasion.

He'd heard what Darya had done. It was elemental, her strange strength and cold, animalistic cruelty. It was magic pulled from old lore. If the rest of those stories were true and Darya could change shape or control storms, the power she wielded was older than empires, as strong as the cosmos.

But what good was it to be afraid of an entity with the force of a god? If Darya wanted him dead, Bataar would have stopped breathing months ago.

And if those old stories were true, her will could be bent. He had to put his faith in children's stories, in Nohra, in Darya.

"Forget your family right now. Darya is confused and needs direction," he whispered. "Can you give that to her? Can you control her?" If anyone could put shackles on her, Nohra could.

"You mean control her *for you*." Nohra's glare sharpened. She raised a hand to stab her finger against Bataar's chest. "You want to kill everything dangerous unless it's useful, and then you want to own it."

He almost laughed. *I thought we had that in common.* "I want to keep everyone safe. Don't you think Darya wants that too?"

The whispers quieted. In that thick silence, something shifted in Nohra's expression, a crack in marble. Bataar held out the hammered metal links, a crudely constructed necklace that connected to handcuffs as thick as leg irons.

"What is this?" Nohra spat.

"Our feeble attempt at exerting control."

She took the restraint in uncertain fingers, watching him with rage-filled eyes. Silence swelled. Then the concerned voices of military officers fought for Bataar's attention as Nohra stalked between the guards and disappeared into the darkness.

Bataar gripped the hilt of his saber, clenching it to count off the seconds.

General Fakier spoke up in hushed tones. He was the

only official who knew about Darya Daheer. "You'll have the fanatics *and* heretics shitting themselves and pointing fingers at you." The Dumakran general had a lined face like petrified wood. He was only ever snarling.

Bataar ground out, "Do you want me to kill her?"

"Can you? Will you?"

"Men win wars by building bigger weapons, by drafting more soldiers, better soldiers." Bataar motioned for his nervously shifting guards to follow him into the room. His black cape swished around his legs, fire twining around his torch.

Nohra positioned her body in front of Darya to face him down. The torchlight cast strange shadows on the topographical map in the center of the room and bright sparks turned the spires on the cave roof into red teeth. Water dripped off the stalactites, filling the tense lull with wet noise.

"Don't come any closer." Nohra reached over her shoulder for her sickle-staff. The chain still hung in her grip. Metal scraped against the scabbard as she drew *Bleeding Edge*.

Bataar's fingers tightened around the hilt of his sword. "Easy, princess. I just want to speak with her."

Darya's black eyes roved over his body. Bataar stiffened at her probing gaze. He was suddenly conscious that his face and dark clothes were still painted with crimson spatter from the previous day. Swiping roughly at his beard made flakes of crusted blood fall like dandruff.

The guards flanking Bataar hulked even taller than him, but they were still tensely coiled with fear. One nocked an arrow and leveled it straight ahead.

Darya didn't flinch. She wasn't blinking, and her chest didn't rise and fall. In the depths of her eyes, a black fire burned.

One of Bataar's guardsmen stumbled back.

"On your souls, keep your composure," Bataar snapped,

clenching his jaw. He stepped closer to Darya. "How long have you been like this?"

"Am I frightening you?" He didn't even recognize the voice Darya spoke with. It was rough, like a sheet of rain hitting hot coals, or tones the wind would scream. Bataar shrunk back, and her eyes zeroed in, perceiving his apprehension.

He took a sharp breath and stood taller. "How long have you known you're like this? Just since we took Kalafar?"

She didn't flinch, but her silence was damning. Fahaad, Safiya's talmaid Laila, and the other maidservants, everyone Bataar shook down after the fighting yesterday said that Darya had been acting strangely since the invasion. Laila had finally broken down in tears, explaining between hiccupping sobs what she'd seen in the courtyard when Darya saved her. *'I was so scared. She wasn't herself, but she had to become that for us. She became a monster, but she was our monster.'*

"You're not a monster." Bataar stepped closer, taking the iron necklace from Nohra's limp hands.

"Bataar." Nohra warningly looked between the two, swiping at her wet eyes. "Don't."

He softened his voice. "I want you to walk out of here, but I need you to put this on. You can do that, can't you?"

Darya looked away, shaking her head, slowly at first, then faster. She scratched against her palm, deeper and deeper, clawing desperately until steam broke through her skin.

Nohra wrapped her arms around Darya. "Everything'll be alright. I promise I'll keep you safe."

Darya's hands stilled. She looked over Nohra's shoulder, right at Bataar. "Will that work? Like in the stories? Fahaad had—"

"He supplied the words, from the old texts he's been looking into. It's the language from the Demonking's chain."

Bataar gave her the reassuring smile he usually reserved for scared children. It would work better if Nohra was the one holding the chain. His pulse pounded, a drum in his ears. Words pulled out of a religious fable and hastily engraved on shit-quality metal weren't going to keep her contained. He hoped she couldn't sense he was bluffing, or worse, hear his betraying heartbeat.

"That flimsy thing will keep me restrained?" she growled, her voice deadly low. "When I'm like that, you all look like bugs to me. I become something horrible."

Bataar licked his lips. He might want her to become something terrible. They might need her power, and if she thought they could compel her with magic chains, all the better.

"I've smashed enough ants already," Darya, or the thing occupying her body, suddenly hissed. "You want me to butcher bleating lambs, strangle birds with broken wings."

"Darya, please." Desperation made Nohra's voice break. She grabbed the iron chain and threw it over Darya's neck.

Black lightning flashed in Darya's eyes. "You can have your wars, but you can't use me to end them."

"Wait. No, no. Darya! You can't!" Dimly, distantly, Bataar watched as Nohra tried to keep hold of her friend while Darya's body transformed. Nohra reached for her arms, hands, shoulders, and grasped only smoky white tendrils of cloud and then air.

"Darya, don't do this. You're surrounded." Turning, Bataar shouted at his guards, "Hold your fire!" The men's grip shook on the taut strings of their bows. "Block the doors!" She'd become a soul, a sheet of mist, invisible, disembodied.

Nohra's eyes swam with pain. "Darya, please don't leave me." But it was too late. Pulling back, wisps slipped through Nohra's fingers, and Darya was gone.

The chains clattered to the ground. An argument outside escalated, and the crowded corridor broke out in shouts, but when Darya disappeared, she left no dead bodies in her wake.

❧

Bataar sank into a steaming bath. As the salt water lapped his wounds, blisters and old scars seared. He scowled down at the new scratch on his arm. Oktai hadn't been the only one the vermilrot-infected corpses made a mark on. Taking a gulping breath, he descended under the surface of the thermal pool. Fire burned on his skin where cracked fingernails had raked, scratching through the sleeve of his tunic. Under the surface of the stone bath, the water glowed yellow and orange like embers burning.

The shambling, slathering half-humans hadn't had souls. *Ghouls*, that was the name for the lesser djinn in the Dumakran holy book, but Bataar had recognized Naji and his retinue in the catacombs. They weren't born demons. It must have been vermilrot, but nothing like the cases he'd seen outside Tashir, or the outbreaks when he was young. Naji and his men must have awoken a dormant strain of disease in those crypts, and now Bataar wasn't sure how far it would spread.

He scrubbed his skin raw. It might be a blessing Darya had left. She was another dangerous uncertainty. Even if Nohra could have chained her, who held Nohra's leash?

Bataar touched the tiny braid in his hair. Ganni had plaited it before they'd left Kalafar, and he couldn't make his fingers unweave and brush it out.

"Bataar?"

He pulled himself out of the pool. Steam swirled off his skin and warm water ran down his torso and legs, puddling around his feet. The chill off the stone walls inside the mountain made hair all over his body stand on end. Qaira stood in front of him, slumping from exhaustion.

Bataar wanted to collapse against her, but he had to be strong for her. He wavered but didn't move, standing there dripping water, feeling lightheaded at what a nightmarish vision she made, glowing like the sun in this hellish cave.

"Your arm," Qaira murmured, reaching out.

Her words broke the spell. He pulled back, drying and dressing quickly. "Don't touch it. I already told Boroo."

She opened and shut her mouth, letting no words fall. Her hand trembled in the air between them.

Pinpricks of fear made Bataar's hands shake. "This new strain… you weren't bitten, were you? Or scratched? If anything touched you, you need to go to the infirmary."

"I've been closer to the rot before. Nothing touched me."

He let out a long breath. "Good. Then stay out of the sickroom. This is the one time I'll order that of you." They didn't know yet how this version of vermilrot spread.

He left his wife standing in the hollow room, her weighty gaze conveying all that they'd left unspoken. They'd talk later, when he could be sure he wasn't infected.

The constricting halls leading to the old sanctium were slick with red puddles. Bataar stepped over the corpses littering the slippery floors. Smoke from the pyres clouded the tunnels. The smell was acrid like death, but cloying too, a sickly-sweet perfume. Most of the dead were lined up in the room with the statues. Remains were still scattered: pieces of fingers, ears, and chunks of hair attached to bits of scalp were strewn over other debris littering the stone floor. Naji only had around forty men, but the ghoulish rot had made them difficult to kill.

"We searched the catacombs." Calidah delivered her report shakily. "The dates on the caskets with the missing lids were consistent with the flight west. That corpse that was cut up must have been infected before they'd resorted to burning the bodies. Naji's men must have been... exposed to the dormant disease."

They'd done more than just open those sarcophagi. They'd been desperate, hiding for weeks in the catacombs without food or weapons to fight the gryphons, and no way to leave if they reached the surface. The barricaded tomb had become their sanctuary and their grave. Bataar had seen the missing chunks of flesh. The Conservium didn't prepare a person to clench their gut through hunger pangs, not like the red steppe's winters. When they couldn't take the hunger any longer, they'd resorted to eating a well-preserved, mummified dead man instead of cannibalizing each other. They hadn't recognized the remnant signs of rot... but could consuming diseased flesh mutate vermilrot into *that*?

"Did you come in direct contact with any of the infected?" Bataar probed. "Scratched, bitten, their blood in your wounds?"

She shook her head, eyes shiny. There were tear tracks in the dirt stains on her cheeks. Guilt pulled at her frown.

"Then don't touch the corpses and get out of this room. Spread my order to isolate until we can determine how this strain spreads."

Near the barricaded entrance to the catacombs, Tarken grunted as he threw the corpse of an Utasoo boy over his shoulder.

"I've already been scratched," Tarken grunted. His eyes were red-rimmed, his face smattered with infected blood.

Careless idiot, recklessly endangering his life because they'd lost one boy. Wordlessly, Bataar picked up another body.

"I heard your order," Tarken said. "The princess's demon escaped and you're sending patrols to look for her?" Beyond the sanctium, the hall that led from the mountain fortress was full of slumped shapes in armor. Soldiers shielding their faces and wearing thick gloves tugged bodies through the corridors. "This Daheer girl, she's the princess's pet?"

Bataar covered his mouth and nose with the scarf he'd worn on the ride to Anhabar, unsure what good it would do. "Her *friend*," he corrected. He wished Tarken would lower his voice.

"Servant."

"Sure." Outside, night was falling, shooting streaks of purple through the sky. "If she won't listen to the princess, she wouldn't be much use to us anyway."

She was a cosmic power, chaos pretending to be human, a creature beyond their understanding. What was Darya Daheer? No fable about demons in the Conservium's libraries would shed any real light on her kind. No mavens truly understood the djinn. It was like that everywhere. The oracles at the School of Thought in Choyanren struggled to describe the granite gods. Bataar knew the face of Preeminence but couldn't guess what They wanted, from him or anyone.

Here in this hellish mountain, the face in the sky was distracted. Their gaze didn't sear as hot into Bataar's back, but that gaping mouth still devoured.

He adjusted his grip on the body he was carrying so he could grab the guard rope. Crimson trails leading to the infected corpses oozed down the steps to the courtyard. The stench of the bodies on the ground hit Bataar long before he descended the crumbling stairs. The reek of rot was layered. Fruity notes melded with decomposing flesh. Carrion flies buzzed thick on the dead, their black stick legs wading through gummy ponds of viscera.

They could burn these bodies, at least, before they transformed.

"Watch your step," Tarken warned.

"I know." The stabbing pain near his ear meant a headache was coming on. His eye twinged.

In the courtyard below, dead soldiers lay in mangled heaps. Tan bodies of lifeless camels were splayed across the sand, torn open and emptied. It had only been a few days since the gryphon attack, but the cracked, sunbaked white bones had been gnawed on and were pockmarked with scratches. Soon they'd be as scavenged as the pack animals that conveyed Naji and his men to their fates. Though the funeral pyres burned in the far distance, the air in the courtyard hung thick with foul-smelling ash. Bataar threw the stiffened body onto one of the sand sleds.

"We'll divide the ruins between anyone potentially infected and the rest," Bataar said. "If symptoms start, we'll restrain them. If it progresses to what we saw in the tombs, we'll sedate the infected and kill them."

Tarken's glance was impassive. "Fat lot of good that'll do. Your little prince has already run off back west. We can hope he dies in the desert; otherwise, this'll spread, to Sinnobad or Kalafar or Zeffa."

Bataar clenched his fists tight in his gloves. He remembered Nassar's eyes rolling back in his head, his choking gasps as Bataar almost ripped the soul out of his spasming body, over nothing but some words. That hadn't happened before. Would it happen again?

If Bataar's mind had started fracturing all the way back in Choyanren, now those cracks had fissured wide. Something was spilling out, a power he didn't understand, that he couldn't contain. If Bataar couldn't control his own body, and they'd hardly won the battle against ghouls in the ruins, they had little hope of taking Rayenna.

"I'll send a bird to the palace and the city guard in the capital," Bataar spoke firmly, trying to formulate a plan, grasping for a fleeting sense of control. "Tell them to keep the prince's retinue at one of the guardhouses until the quarantine period's passed."

"Ervan Lofri's city guard? I think you need to be a little more concerned that your princeling's finally snapped."

The pain behind Bataar's eyes flared. "If I wanted someone to treat me like I'm an idiot, I'd find Shaza."

Tarken put his hands up. "I'm only pointing out—"

"My mistakes. My shortcomings." His face burned. "If you think you could do better, *you* should have challenged the steppe lords when we were boys."

Tarken snorted humorlessly and placed a bloody hand on Bataar's shoulder. "My *brother*"—his smile made Bataar want to hit him—"unlike you, I don't have to start wars to prove I have a huge cock."

Bataar did hit him. Right in the side of the head. Tarken swayed dizzily then lunged, diving and grabbing Bataar's legs and slamming him to the ground. Bataar's scarf fell off, and a feeble wind carried it a few meters away into the sand.

A few guards that had been hanging back closed in. Bataar waved them off.

"Don't pretend like you're better than me," he ground out, gritting his teeth. "Like you haven't become a sadistic warmongering bastard."

Neither of them had slept all night. Grief and exhaustion made their movements weak as they rolled in the courtyard. Red sand stuck to a cut on Tarken's face.

"It's all been for you!" Tarken yelled. "I made myself a monster for you. I've fed people to dogs *for you*!"

"Poor Tarken, pissing his pants and getting none of the glory," Bataar spat.

He let his friend hit him over and over. The pain dulled as he grew numb to it. His teeth sliced the inside of his mouth. He tasted iron, maybe his blood, maybe Tarken's. They were bloodsworn brothers. What ran through Tarken's veins was his, too.

"Which one of us should tell his mother, Tarken? Do you want the honor? We should be used to little boys dying." Bataar spit a red glob onto Tarken's chest. "Wanna argue about whose fault it is?"

They hadn't fought like this since they were seventeen, when Bataar broke Tarken and Qaira's marriage contract. Tarken had ripped out a handful of Bataar's hair. Bataar remembered kneeing Tarken in the stomach so hard he coiled up, retching. That fight had been over hurt pride. It was an arranged match. Bataar had thought they'd both be happy if he dissolved it. They could both marry girls they really wanted. Tarken had just been infuriated that Bataar had overstepped.

Bataar blinked, and Tarken's features sharpened. A few fine lines appeared at the corners of his eyes, and strands of silvery white wove through his hair. They weren't children anymore. They weren't fighting over a marriage match. This was about another dead boy.

"*Did you see it?*" Tarken seethed, his voice half snarl, half whisper. He straddled Bataar's waist, pinning him down.

For a second Bataar couldn't remember where he was, or when. "See what?"

"Don't play stupid. I know. Someone dies, and everyone looks at the body, but you always gawk at the sky. You think no one notices, but I do. I know you see souls. Did you see Oktai's?"

Bataar couldn't tell if he'd lost his breath because Tarken had punched his collarbone or because of the sudden panic that grabbed his ribs. Tarken knew. He'd seen, and Bataar hadn't even noticed him watching.

Tarken pressed, pushing and pushing. "What did you do to that stupid prince, huh? I saw that too, idiot."

Bataar bucked Tarken off and threw him. Angry tears were running down Tarken's cheeks when Shaza's guards shoved through, stepping in and pulling him away from Bataar.

"Get up," Shaza said, holding out a hand. Bataar stared up at her gloved fingers. "If you wanted someone to beat your ass and tell you you're a failure, you should have sent someone to get me. I'm better at it than Tarken. I'm better at cleaning up your messes, too." She kept muttering, about recklessly spreading the infection and fools playing chicken with their lives.

He didn't take her hand, just kept staring up at the cloudless sky, daring himself to meet Their gaze. His jaw ached. He prodded it tentatively. It throbbed under his fingers. Bataar realized, dimly, that he'd wanted to be punched, a distraction from all the other pain.

"He didn't even break your nose," Shaza observed. "That's a good friend for you."

Shaza had scratches up her arm, gouges dug by one of the ghoul's cracked nails. Bataar finally took her hand and let her tug him up. His mouth was filling with blood. He traced his tongue against his incisors and molars.

She sighed. "It's just a split lip. You still have all your straight teeth, Your Eminence."

He recoiled. "It always sounds like an insult when you say it."

"Good." Her smile was false, and didn't reach her eyes. "If you want to wear such a heavy crown, your fat head better bow under the weight."

Tarken hung limply between two guards. The men tugged his wrists, pulling them in opposite directions, shoving him forward like an offering.

"Let him go," Bataar ordered. Tarken fell forward, wiping his cheeks and refusing to meet Bataar's eyes.

Shaza looked torn, her body angling toward Tarken as she resolutely faced Bataar. She wanted to go to Tarken, comfort him. She'd loved Oktai too. They'd all seen reflections of Chugai in him.

An unspoken accusation hung in the sour-smelling air. If Bataar had the ability to strangle Nassar's soul out of his body, could he have kept Oktai's spirit in his until the maven's blood transference worked?

Shaza squinted at Bataar. "Are you going to try to punch me? I'll have you gumming on soft food for the rest of your life. My sister better be happy with two kids, because you won't be making a third."

"I'm not going to punch you." Bataar spit out the last of the blood, but the taste lingered, metallic in his mouth. They might all be destined for the pyre now, as much vermilrot as they'd been exposed to. "We need to finish cleaning out the tunnels."

❧

During the fortnight that Anhabar was under quarantine, a film of red dust settled over everything at the mountain. It covered the charred heaps in the funeral pyres outside and blanketed the topographical map table like crimson snow. The Dumakran officers were pleading for Bataar to turn back to Kalafar, to retreat before facing Queen Clemiria. The disease had run through the soldiers, shattering already fragile morale.

This strain skipped the early symptoms of vermilrot and

killed quickly. Then, its victims became like the ghouls in the catacombs. This was a different, more powerful illness, a devilish one—a djinn sickness. Mavens and scholars would need to be consulted in greater depth about how a disease could transform the body after stopping the heart.

Bataar knew of four people who had come in direct contact with vermilrot and developed no symptoms: himself, Shaza, Tarken, and Nohra, all of them gryphon-marked. The losses they sustained had weakened his army, and the absence of Lofri's troops enfeebled them further.

Bataar broke the seal on a letter from Kalafar, Lofri's poppy sigil imprinted in the orange wax. The advisors assembled in the war room watched, the tension thick enough to cut. His eyes roved over the short correspondence as he worried a rough spot in his mouth with his teeth.

"Prince Nassar has taken Lofri's daughter to wife," he summarized in a dull monotone. "They were married in Thora's Sanctium in a ceremony officiated by the Minister of Faith."

Qaira pursed her lips, staring expectantly. She stood at the head of the table, where the stone map spilled down the wall and protruded. He tried to convey with a look that the children would be fine. Bataar had left a small army behind. The palace was well-defended, even if he couldn't trust the city guardsmen.

"That's all?" Nohra blurted. She was seated beside Qaira. "A wedding? I'm guessing that means they weren't able to quarantine his retinue at the gates. Did the infection spread? Does Lofri mention anything strange like... is Darya in the capital?"

Qaira squeezed Nohra's arm. The new levels of familiarity they'd reached made resentment claw inside Bataar. He scratched his face.

Tarken looked up, tilting his head. The bruises they'd given each other had yellowed and faded, but they still couldn't meet each other's eyes.

Shaza reached for the letter, though she couldn't read Dumakran script. Since Oktai's death, she and Tarken had stuck together like feathers in tar.

Everyone waited for Bataar's word. He had to deliver the rest. This was a war declaration, not a friendly missive.

"He doesn't mention the rot, but that doesn't mean it can't still spread. I've sent word to lock down Craullstreet and the Gold Road." The seedier districts and sections of town. Any infections would need to be contained and put down quickly. "Lofri also wrote that he's taken the Dowager Queen, Merv Attar, and Princess Aalya with him back to Zeffa. Nassar has fled for Aglea."

"What business could he possibly have in the north?" Nohra snapped.

"He's planning to take a second wife. Meric Ward's daughter."

"What?" Nohra slammed her fist down on the table, unsettling a cloud of sediment. She winced, hitting the sharp peak of a stone mountain.

"If I were a worse sister, I'd steal his wives," Safiya whispered, smirking. A few advisors snickered.

Bataar didn't laugh. "He declares himself zultam and plans to march on Kalafar in the spring."

The room erupted in cries and curses.

Bataar didn't suffer losses. He hadn't lost, yet. Just because Nassar had snuck into Thora's Sanctium in the middle of the night to have that pig read marriage rites in secret, didn't mean he or Lofri could lead a direct assault on the trained soldiers stationed in the city. Lofri controlled the city watch, but he didn't have experience commanding loyal, battle-hardened fighters. Even with this alliance, some northerner's vassals wouldn't stand a chance against the full force of Bataar's army, as long as they won in the east.

Nohra shrugged off Qaira's hand. "That treacherous dog will never deserve to be king!"

Safiya's gaze roved over the table, up the wall. "You need to turn back for the capital." She squinted at the carving of the strait and waved a hand flippantly. "March on Aglea, and rout his troops at the land bridge."

Now, not only would they be taking the Sister City without Lofri's troops and with weakened numbers after the outbreak. If this fight lasted two seasons, they could be returning to a city under siege.

But if he left Rayenna unclaimed now, Clemiria could work with Lofri's forces to pin him on two sides. And to stake his claim in Aglea, he needed the full strength and support of an unbroken Dumakra.

Still, Bataar shook his head. "Rayenna first. Then I'll come for your brother, if you're prepared to fight him."

24

To move the roc to steal, roll four times. An unlucky outcome such as one 2 and three 1s can be beaten by the single roll afforded the cat.

— *Games of Strategy and Chance*

The caravan trudged slowly forward, camels and horses lumbering through the ocean of red sand. They'd gone five days without water except the hot and quickly depleting contents of their waterskins. The inside of Nohra's throat fissured like dry earth. When her brother Nassar had fled, they'd lost Lofri's men, and the rot had taken even more. The rest of the army was on the move east toward Rayenna to challenge Clemiria. It was a battle Nohra didn't want to win, and now it seemed impossible that Bataar would be victorious in the Sister City.

Most importantly, it had been weeks since Darya disappeared, since Nohra tried to put that damned chain around her neck. Her constellation dagger was feather-steel, but it hung like a dead weight at Nohra's hip.

"I don't think you should—let me at least saddle him— listen to me—" Fahaad protested, helping Nohra climb onto

Mercy's bare back, boosting her up with interlocked fingers in lieu of a mounting block.

Nohra tensed, carrying tension in her shoulders tight enough to ache. "You should step away, Fahaad."

He stumbled back, but not quickly enough. The black gelding whickered and nipped, drawing blood. "Paga's holy ass. I'll roast you, you overgrown pigeon," he growled, cradling his hand. "I swear they've been more feral since we came to the desert. Hey, listen to me, would you?"

"I'll be fine." Nohra knotted the reins around her knuckles, hard enough the tips of her fingers turned white.

Fahaad pursed his lips, eyebrows drawn. "You do know you can die, don't you?"

"You're the first to say so." Not everyone had survived the gryphon fever like she had; fewer still who were attacked hadn't caught the rot.

"I know your skull is incredibly thick, but it can break like all your other bones. Just be careful. If Dar was here, she'd tell you the same thing."

"Well, she's not, and I'm the only one who seems to care that we lost her." Nohra wanted to twist the knife, make him hurt like she did.

She was losing her mind. Shapes trembled on the distant horizon: horses with birds' heads. They vanished like smoke, but the feeling of being watched still lingered. Mercy flattened his ears, keening in agitation.

Fahaad's gaze darkened. "I was the one at the palace during the invasion. I begged for her life after she massacred those soldiers." His voice wobbled, but he didn't stop when Nohra winced. "I watched her catatonic, covered in blood, pull herself back together so you could *cry on her shoulder*. I noticed she'd changed and I tried to help her. Did you?"

"Why didn't you tell me?" she whispered.

"What in hells would you have been able to do?" His eyes brimmed with accusation. "Besides, it was Darya's secret. If you didn't know, it was because she didn't want you to know. And because you closed your eyes to something so obvious."

"Oh, fuck you."

"Fuck you!" He let out a long-suffering sigh. "One of the patrols will find her." Crossing his arms, he applied pressure on his bleeding hand. "She's probably at the mountain right now. She'll return to Kalafar with us and then we'll help her escape to someplace safe."

Nohra jerked away. "When we get her back, she's never leaving my side."

Mercy's wings flexed, inky feathers ruffling. Every time someone mentioned Darya's name, the damned pegasus's ears pricked. Dar had never failed to deliver him a pitted date or a mouse she'd trapped in the palace kitchens.

Fahaad kept his gaze locked with Nohra's. The other soldiers in the caravan were too far away to overhear, even though the desert air carried. "If creatures like Darya can be controlled with chains and words, as long as you're one of Bataar's generals, it's not safe for her to be with you."

"I'm done talking now."

"I'm not saying it's even possible—"

Nohra pulled away and pushed against Mercy's sides. The flapping of the pegasus's wings made whirlwind clouds of crimson sand. Fahaad shielded his face, stepping back as she rose into the sky. Nohra's veil partially obscured her view, but it kept her eyes from stinging and her chest from rattling. A faint breeze ruffled her shroud, stirring her loose-fitting riding clothes and unkempt hair.

Mercy's pulse beat a drum that reverberated in Nohra's legs

as she tucked in close, pulling the pegasus into a dive. Then she straightened Mercy out, straining her thighs to keep her purchase on the sleek back.

They rode on the weak updraft until Mercy wobbled in the air, his wing muscles strained to exertion, sweat lathering his bluish-black fur. They drifted until the winding caravan below them became a trail of brown ants. Until they were alone in an unending sea of sky.

Nohra needed Darya if she wanted to challenge Bataar now and later beat Nassar. She had seen what Darya was capable of. She could wipe out a whole battalion. In the old legends, djinn could even turn into animals and manipulate the weather. Nohra couldn't waste power just because her friend was afraid of it.

Bataar, a monster himself, had looked at Darya in the war room with hunger in his eyes. He viewed her the way Nohra did, as a weapon. Her stomach lurched to know they were so similar.

Her knees shook and perspiration pooled on her skin. Mercy whinnied, shaking out his mane. Above, Prudence's expansive black wings flashed into view, silhouetted against the burning light of the white sun. The pegasus swooped down and leveled out beside Mercy.

"Trying to kill your horse?" Safiya shouted. "We're not supposed to be flying while water's scarce. Bataar sent me to retrieve you." Saf's eyes sparkled as she signaled below, her hair bouncing in the wind. "Look down."

Nohra leaned over. Under them, small clusters of blue and emerald shimmered. The tops of palm trees spread across the sand, and sunlight flashed on the surface of clear water. Mercy's wide wings twitched on his downstroke. His strained muscles and tendons spasmed as he came down to land.

367

Nohra pulled *Bleeding Edge* off her back and threw it down. Her feet landed next as she clumsily dismounted. Her legs shook and bowed as she crashed down into the sand.

Was this real? The image of the oasis in front of her trembled, feather-light in the air. Mercy's muzzle splashed into the water, guzzling greedily. He waded in, and Prudence followed, nipping at his brother's flank. Not a mirage. The pack camels loped close to the pond's edge. In the distance, Rami's laughter echoed as he ran toward the pools. Fahaad's scolding voice carried after him.

A grin split Saf's face as she tugged Nohra into the water. "My boots," Nohra protested weakly, letting herself be dragged.

"They'll dry. Five days without a bath! I thought my skin would turn to sand." The water wrapped around Safiya's thighs, then stretched as high as her waist. She leaned back, floating on the surface, her clothes soaked. "Rayenni merchant caravans maintain oases like these, to serve as waypoints on the route to Kalafar."

Nohra hadn't heard of that. She squinted. "Where's the water coming from?"

"An underground river. An aquifer, who knows."

The water was cool, unlike the steaming thermal springs in the mountain ruins, and it didn't smell of salt. Nohra cupped her hands and drank. "Holy Goddess that's good."

She tried to wriggle out of her leather boots, but they were plastered to her riding pants. She gave up, tugging off her sopping-wet shroud and flinging it onto the shore. She pulled out her jangling earrings and laid them down carefully. Around them, the rest of the war caravan approached the scattered ponds. Utasoo and Dumakran soldiers stripped off their clothes, shouting and jumping into the water.

Safiya straightened, standing up, and drew her sword. "I

don't think so. This pool's ours," she said, training her blade on two Dumakran boys. "Keep your clothes on or get out of my sight."

The tip of *Queen of Beasts* poked one in the sternum, pressing a white indent into tan skin. Safiya's curls hung heavy with water, drip, drip, dripping as the boys' faces paled.

Prudence and Mercy loomed behind her, monstrous in the crystalline water. They could pray it was as close as they'd ever be to seeing a seahorse.

"Your Highnesses," the boys squeaked, splashing back and climbing out in a tangle of slipping limbs.

"I should carve out your eyeballs for searing the image of your bare asses into my head," Safiya shouted after them. "If I see either of you again, I'll slice off your noses and feed them to our pegasuses." When Saf turned back, she winced.

"Sore?" Nohra prodded.

Her sister pulled up her sleeve, revealing a yellowing bruise. "It's like you were trying to break my elbow." Saf pulled her tunic up over her head and sank back into the water in her underclothes. Scars made a pinkish patchwork across Safiya's skin, and Nohra had matching marks on her own body.

During the two weeks at the ruins, Nohra and Safiya had exercised out in the yard. The severed head of the heretic sanctium-keeper had rotted outside, posted by Bataar's men, watching them train with bulging eyes and a bloated tongue. His fanatical worship of Chaos resulted in countless deaths, but Bataar couldn't pass the Goddess's judgment. Forced to look at the dead man, spite and revulsion became powerful motivators.

"My legs haven't stopped shaking since we trained," Nohra complained.

"Running up and down those stairs shouldn't have gotten you so out of breath."

They each had older silver-white lines too, from years of fighting, training to earn their titles. Harpy Knight. Strange, Nohra had almost lost that name just to become an Aglean lord's wife. Stranger still that relief swelled in her chest to have escaped that fate, to have lost so much and kept so little.

"I came in contact with infected flesh." Nohra peeled off her own shirt and shucked it onto the edge. "My blood might have been congealing."

"Paga's ass 'your blood was congealing'." Saf squeezed out her hair and propped herself up on Prudence's flank.

This strain of vermilrot killed swiftly. After the first few restrained corpses transformed, those still living who'd begun crying thick, bloody tears had been coaxed to swallow a euthanasic tincture derived from snake venom. Contracting the disease was worse than a death sentence. The fact that Nohra was alive was a sure sign of Paga's favor.

Nohra stiffened. The hair on her body stood on end, prickling like she was being watched again. The pegasuses were agitated too, cooing in warning and ruffling their feathers. Her unease growing, she scanned the caravan. Everyone was absorbed with the oasis.

She counted heads at the pools, inventorying their losses and determining how many troops they now moved with east. Between the gryphon attack, the ghouls, and Lofri's men, they were down almost a quarter of their original number.

In the distance Bataar leaned over a map, talking with his gray-bearded commanders and the Dumakran general, Fakier. Unless Nohra had been hallucinating during the ghoul attack, she couldn't shake the fear that Bataar was something like Darya. It was nothing she could explain to a maven, but the power he'd held over Nassar wasn't human. Already the people around Bataar saw him as a force like a god, but that scar meant he could bleed like a man. Calidah stood at his side, pointing at something.

"Bataar's been keeping Cali close," Nohra observed.

"She's made the passage through the Gash four times. More than almost anyone except trade caravans," Saf said.

"We're through already."

When they'd cut across the canyon in the mountain range days ago, the desert tides had been forgivingly high. The wind was gentle. There hadn't been sandstorms, rockslides, or mazes of rock spires to get lost in. The aeries on the red cliffs were quiet. Rocs, birds bigger than horses that nested high up in the mountains, hadn't given them any trouble. Every year their numbers dwindled and there were fewer sightings reported.

"He's watching Cali like he suspects something," Nohra noted. Like he was holding her hostage, but with a grip loose enough to ease suspicion. "You told Clemiria about Bataar's plan to blockade the ports with his Choyanreni fleet, right? At Rayenna, when we break from the caravan and declare for her—"

"Lower your voice," Safiya hissed, leaning around Prudence's wing. The gelding preened, ears twitching. "You still want to take Clemiria's side, after everything?"

"Why wouldn't we?"

"Think. Nassar made a serious misstep. If our brother and his conservator have finally lost Bataar's favor, that puts us in a better position with him." Safiya scrubbed her fingers against her scalp, detangling her curls in sections. "He could name Rami king in Kalafar now."

Nohra shook her head. Water droplets flew. "Not good enough. Father named him heir to Dumakra."

"Then pressure him for that. He might listen, if you're in his good graces. Besides, what deludes you into thinking our beloved aunt will make Rami the zultam?"

"She loved Father."

Safiya threw up her hands. "But she hated your mother. If Aunt Clemiria thought she could take it, she'd want his throne for herself."

"We wrote that we'd stand beside her. I won't go back on my word."

"Your word means dirt to her," Saf growled. "Less than dirt. Worms."

Everything she was saying, Nohra had already thought herself. "She's our aunt. We can't ask Cali to stand against her mother." It was exhausting the way Saf kept steering this tired conversation. "We don't have any other options."

"Of course we do." Safiya held up one finger. Her voice was so quiet, Nohra had to squint to read her lips. "First, we need to assess the situation in Kalafar. We need to pick a common enemy: the gryphon king or Nassar, and only one of them wants Rami dead. Forget Aunt Clemiria. She's too hard to manipulate. We need to think three steps ahead."

Nohra wished she would shut up about her three steps. Saf talked like this was all a game and she was the only one with an unobstructed view of the playing board. As if Nohra didn't even know the rules.

"You're stupid if you think Bataar stands a chance of winning in Rayenna now. The rot and Nassar have made sure of that."

"Bataar has been winning wars since he was sixteen. I don't think he picks fights he can't win."

Qaira and her sister were making their way over, Shaza glaring like a hawk. Nohra sloughed more grime and sand off her arms.

"We need Bataar to beat Nassar. Lofri has a sizable private army in Zeffa," Safiya continued. "And he's been buying the protection of Aglean free companies, sellswords hungry for money. They don't have a stake in who sits on the throne in Kalafar. They just want purses full of honors. Goddess knows, Lofri probably bribed Meric Ward too."

"Ervan Lofri is well enough off." Clean now, Nohra traced stars in Mercy's twitching hip. His tail swished, slapping her shoulder. "But he must be draining his coffers now."

Safiya gazed pityingly at Nohra. "When his purse is empty, he'll still have mining gold. Lofri, Attar, these are powerful families you'll have to stand against. Rich ones." She pulled herself onto the bank. "I don't know if your memory's lapsed, but our mothers were concubines. Bought like livestock and dressed up to look like royalty. Neither of us has a fortune to buy an army." Nohra sulked, but Saf wasn't done berating her. "Then there's the sickness we need to consider. If there's the slightest chance vermilrot is spreading in the city, that's another mess to clean up. Bataar has experience controlling the spread of vermilrot in Choyanren."

Zira, the concubine Safiya loved, was in Kalafar, where that ghoulish disease would ravage the streets. Nohra thought her sister would be rattled, but apparently she wasn't about to start showing weakness now.

"Even if the disease spreads, at least the palace is safe with Grandmother," Nohra reminded her. She still carried out her duties as queen mother. "And against Nassar and Lofri, we have her support." She wouldn't like that they were entertaining an alliance with the traitor Sartarids, though, and her wealth *was* spread thin.

"Wonderful. She can rule Kalafar and clean up an epidemic, and later, let's see how well an old woman manipulates courtiers from the front lines of a war." Saf was being unfair. Their grandmother was a master of poisons and could hold her own in a fight. "With Nassar's marriage match, you've lost Meric Ward and Aglea. Do you really want to waste the opportunity you have with Bataar now?"

"'*Opportunity*'?" Nohra was out of those, empty of luck. Darya was gone. Aalya was a prisoner of her uncle in Zeffa. Now they were going the wrong way, to deal with Clemiria instead of protecting the capital.

"Goddess, Nohra, be realistic for once. Bataar is the only person who can keep Kalafar out of Nassar's hands. You said he's receiving reinforcements from the west."

Nohra ground out her final answer. "When we get to the Ivory Gates, I'll break from the rest of the caravan and defect to the Sister City. Are you with me, or will you fight against me?"

Safiya took a heavy breath, pursed lips holding back a swell of words. Then, she softened. "I'm with you. Remember this: wherever I am, I'm always on your side. But whatever happens in Rayenna, as soon as it's done, I'm making for Kalafar. Zira is leaving with me, and we're going to get my mother, and we're never coming back."

Bitterness twisted in Nohra's gut. "You'll abandon us?"

"I have other people to protect. I'll do this much; the rest is your responsibility."

Nohra blurted out, in a low, deadly whisper, "Did you know? About Nassar?"

Confusion washed over Saf's face, but she wielded ignorance like a sword. "That he was born daft and ugly, shriveled like a date? Of course."

"That Father *tried to kill him*, and Bataar—" She choked on the rest. Qaira and her sister had come close enough to overhear their talk now.

"We all make mistakes and carry those burdens. Of course I heard. I'm surprised you're only just learning now, but I see it doesn't change things." Saf turned, ducking her head with practiced politeness. "Your Eminence." The hot desert air made water evaporate in wispy tendrils off her body.

Shaza was taller than her older sister, her darker image. Bataar's prickliest general cast a suspicious look between Nohra and Safiya.

Across the oasis, at another pool, Rami was riding on someone's shoulders—Tarken's judging from the auburn tones of his hair. Bataar was rolling up his maps and waving Cali away. Heat flared in Nohra's chest. She smothered its embers.

Qaira kicked the water, splashing Nohra. "Enjoying yourself?" She had stripped to underclothes and let down her hair. Nohra thought of palace baths, shared saddles, and the darkness of the abandoned sanctium, of growing feverish before she'd contracted the gryphon sickness. When she betrayed Bataar at Rayenna's gates, all those memories would wilt. "You should cool off, Shaza." A playful push sent the general flailing into the water.

On reflex, Nohra caught and steadied Shaza in the pool so the pegasuses, who were currently nipping at each other's withers, wouldn't decide to put their canines in her. They'd turned enough barn cats to pink stew in their watering troughs for Nohra to be afraid. *See, friend*, she tried to convey. At least, a friend for now.

Shaza squirmed free without a grunt of thanks. She grabbed Qaira's legs, pulling her squealing into the water. Qaira came up and coiled her arms around Nohra's neck. Her laughter was aimed with the same perfect precision as her arrows.

⌒⌁⌒

The stale bread was chewy. Bland, even smothered in cream ripe from the heat. Nohra could hardly choke it down. When a hand appeared, extending a drinking skin, she raised her lips to its mouth and drank.

Fermented mare's milk filled her mouth, sour and foamy. "How are you supposed to get drunk off this?" she muttered, swiping her lips.

"That's not really the point." Bataar slumped down beside her.

Nohra's ears and neck warmed. Shit, she'd thought he was Fahaad. "What're you doing?"

"Eating." He offered her a cookie, a date, and cheese.

She should reject it all. Her stomach growled. *Praise to the farmer, the Scythe, and the Vessel of Peace.* This desert had drained their stores. Most Dumakran soldiers could put aside their religious convictions and eat the dried gryphon meat, scarce as it had clung to those ravenous bones. Not Nohra. She was making herself even weaker leaving out half her rations each night, wrapped like a gift for the desert, for Darya, who was gone.

Bataar's eyes were faraway. He might be seeing impossible shapes out on the dunes too. "No matter how hungry I get, I'm never eating gryphon again."

"Is it the flavor?" It smelled disgusting.

"It tastes like bad memories." When their shoulders brushed, Nohra didn't jerk away. Against her better judgment, she blurted, "What memories?"

"I was fourteen. I didn't save a boy who was like a little brother to me. His funeral pyre burned near the cookfire, and the smells never separated in my head."

Nohra imagined a younger Oktai, a baby like Qaira's son Bato. If Bataar were anyone else, a woman or a servant, Nohra would have rested a hand on his leg or squeezed his shoulder. But she hated him, and he was all stone anyway. Comforting touches would slide off his marble edges.

"Do you want my sympathy?" she whispered, not hostile,

but still simmering. "Do you think I can ever forgive you for what you took from me?"

He sighed, moving his food around on the handkerchief. "I've made peace with the rot that killed my father, pardoned the people who stole my mother." He cast a sidelong look at her. His eyes swiveled like a pegasus's, all raptor. "Do you forgive your father and Nassar? They badly wanted to be each other's killers."

Nohra stiffened. "Don't."

"What?" He stood. "Vengeance and guilt are sins. Cast them off, and you'll be stronger."

⁓

On the distant horizon, support beams encased the limestone walls around the Sister City, jutting from the ground like a giant's ribcage. The full moon beamed down, an unblinking white eye surveying the war encampment. Soldiers huddled around blazing cookfires, laughing and drinking. Above the tents, purple silk banners and Bataar's red-and-black horse-hair ones flapped in the cold desert breeze.

No heads turned their way, but Nohra still felt the weight of eyes boring into her.

She unclenched her fists, shook out her fingers. Maybe Safiya was right about Bataar's chances. Tonight, the Dumakran and Utasoo fronts were united. Liquor and the attention of camp followers flooded the soldiers with courage. But who were they united against? The Sister City was Dumakran. Nohra recalled the boy she'd given her necklace to, worried about fighting outside the city his family lived in. Who knew if he was even still alive.

"We need to go now," she told Saf. "Fahaad's tacking the pegasuses. Where the hells are Rami and Calidah?"

"Rami had to take a leak. Cali said she'd keep watch."

"Well, did jackals eat them? How long have they been gone?" The camp was big, but surely even Calidah couldn't have gotten lost. "We need to be over the gates before daybreak." Bataar planned to move in the morning, and by daylight Nohra's little brother was always the gryphon king's hostage. They had to hurry. They were already going to have hells trying to convince Rami to get on a pegasus. They'd probably have to put a blinder on him and the horse.

Nohra herself thought it was wrong. Wings were for daughters, like the Goddess's. But Paga would forgive this one trespass.

A young Choyanreni boy, one of the clerk's pages, wove through the crowded bodies. He wriggled out and skidded to a stop in front of Nohra and Safiya. His head bobbed in a clumsy bow. "His Eminence requests you in his war tent," he said.

Nohra's blood curdled, turning lumpy in her veins. She shared a look with her sister. They were so close. She tried to school her expression into something calm and nodded at the page.

"Bataar doesn't know," Saf whispered as they strode through the encampment. "But if you're nervous, he'll read it on you. You have a stupidly honest face."

Drinks sloshed in cups as soldiers pressed close to the outdoor fires, whistling and cheering for a girl as she sang loudly and not too well. Lucky the pretty thing had avoided a fate dissolving in a gryphon's belly, and hadn't been maimed by ghouls.

Nohra pushed into the white tent. Her voice was a razor's edge. "Bataar."

He beamed, all perfectly straight white teeth. "Nohra." That easy tone made her skin crawl.

His seated advisors encircled a table spread with hide maps and tokens lifted from a game board. Bataar's generals looked up as Nohra and Saf entered, acknowledging them with curt nods.

"What are you doing?" Nohra's gaze fell on Calidah, standing wide-eyed to one side of him. Rami stood on the other, yawning and rubbing unfocused eyes. Qaira was there too, pulling a sweet orange apart and handing separated sections to Rami.

Bataar's lips quirked, brow furrowing in mock confusion. "Conducting a war meeting."

The gryphon nestlings screeched in their cage in the corner of the tent. They'd already grown bigger, with more downy fur. Bataar's eagle ruffled dark feathers at the shrill sound.

Nohra tensed. "Why does my little brother need to be here?" Bataar couldn't play the fool when he was grinning like the cat that had slunk into the palace aviary. He knew. *He knew.*

"Hey," Safiya said warningly, a breeze-light touch on her elbow. Nohra stepped away. Qaira's gaze flitted between them, mouth pinched.

Bataar patted Rami's hair, and he winced. "He'll be a man soon," Bataar answered. *Trying to get away?* Nohra read it plain on his smug face. He didn't even have to say it aloud and could still lord his victory over her. "Why shouldn't he sit in on the war council?" He turned to Calidah. "What are those support beams on the walls made of? Stone, feather-steel, something else?"

Cali's expression was cold, but not entirely closed off. "No one knows. The city predates Dumakra. Those walls are older than Kalafar, than pegasuses. If you didn't know, the Qadishals and Carisars tried to besiege Rayenna hundreds of years ago.

Their armies are buried in the sand outside those same gates. You can't pierce them."

"We have cannons on the Choyanreni junk ships." Bataar rubbed his short beard. "When those reinforcements finally arrive with the siege equipment, if we can't break through the walls, we'll come through the harbors."

Bataar knew they were planning to betray him, and he was patting Rami's head and asking Calidah inane questions. He'd taken her brother and cousin, made them hostages, and he had the nerve to smile at her.

Nohra's face burned. She *raged*.

"Ruo's damned ships. Always late," Tarken mumbled. "'Fickle winds favor no man'. Gryphonshit. A sea beast from the Thirst probably devoured her flagship."

"That was a gamble from the start," Shaza said, her fists clenched. "Even with the delay in the mountain."

"You don't have time to wait." Cali traced Rayenna's wall on the map. "The desert will drain you dry."

"That's why we'll have to rely on our contingency in a direct fight. Pegasus knights fly above the walls, launching an aerial assault." Bataar straightened. "It's why I brought you, why I took Dumakra. I wanted your sky power."

Nohra chewed her tongue. "Rayenna is a second home to my cousin. You can't ask her—"

"*Nohra*," Saf hissed.

"But your mother has pegasus fliers, too," Bataar interjected, looking at Calidah.

"They're not Harpy Knights," Saf answered. "They haven't trained like we have. They're young and untested, scared Rayenni girls. In the air, they'll be no match for us."

"It's archers and ballistae on the battlements that'll pose the problem." Cali swallowed thickly.

They were all ignoring Nohra. She grasped for something, anything, trying to force a semblance of composure. "Safiya, Calidah, and I can lead the aerial assault—"

"No," Bataar interrupted. "Your cousin will be more useful away from you all. I can't have her getting hurt." His gaze bore into Nohra's soul, cutting like a cleaver. He could break her apart like Qaira's sweet oranges, squish through her innards, pluck out her heart like a carrion bird, and devour it. "She's valuable collateral. I need her and your brother to keep"—he rolled his next words languidly in his mouth—"*your aunt in line.*"

Nohra barely resisted putting Darya's dagger through his face. Her neck burned with embarrassment, anger, shame. It was over. She'd lost. If she betrayed Bataar now, it was Rami's and Cali's heads on the line. The price was too steep, impossible to pay. He'd beaten her.

Her head pounded, her thoughts and heartbeat too loud for her to hear the rest of the councilors speaking. When the meeting ended, she tore out of the tent, ignoring Qaira calling her name.

25

The nomads host wrestling and archery competitions until
the sun sinks. Near the witching pyres in the darkness,
even I can hear the spirit that whispers to their shamans.

— A traveler's account of the Utasoo tribes

When the rest of the councilors filtered out of Bataar's war
pavilion, his friends and Boroo stayed. They stood around the
maps, wearing expressions both accusing and expectant. The
last to leave was Safiya. She shared a look of understanding
with Bataar, harshened by her drawn brows. Grand Vizier Naji
might have tipped him off, but it was the princess who'd found
him that morning and told him about Nohra's plan to take
Rami. Her confession was unexpected, and his first instinct
had been not to trust her, but she probably thought she was
protecting Nohra.

Now he had Calidah and Prince Rami to deal with. The boy
yawned, shuffling to stay awake. Bataar delegated guards to
escort his prisoners and keep them under tight watch.

"What was that about?" Shaza finally snapped. "You knew
the Harpies were going to betray you, and you made them

generals?" Her gaze shot to her sister. Qaira shrunk back. Then Shaza turned on Tarken. His expression stayed cool and guarded. "Was I the only one who didn't know? You don't trust me?"

"I didn't require your counsel." Bataar kept his tone impersonal. "I knew what you'd say."

Shaza opened her mouth, stopped short, then tried again. "To not do it? Shouldn't someone say that?"

Tarken clicked his tongue. "We already decided you'll command their troops on the ground tomorrow. Just drop it."

An outsider looking in might think Tarken was taking Bataar's side. In reality, they still hadn't made up. Tarken was impatient and aggressive with everyone else because he couldn't publicly disagree with Bataar again. He'd become single-minded in plotting to take Rayenna, more focused than any of them.

"If there are any other traitors you know about in our ranks, tell me before day breaks." Shaza slammed a fist down, rattling the tokens. "If I find a blade in my back tomorrow, I'll pull it out and put it through your eye, Bataar."

He rubbed his neck, working a hand through his hair.

"Wait, Shaza!" Qaira reached out.

Shaza brushed past, storming out before her older sister could pacify her. She didn't want to be made mellow.

Tarken exhaled heavily and took a swig of something from his drinking skin. "I'll go calm her down," he promised, looking only at Qaira.

"I need you two well rested tomorrow, not fucked out," Bataar warned, before Tarken could chase Shaza into the thick crowd outside the pavilion.

Qaira smacked Bataar's arm, without any real force behind it. *"Don't."*

Tarken sputtered, angry splotches of red coloring his face. He stomped out of the pavilion, tent flaps rustling.

Bataar grunted. "Sorry, was I supposed to keep pretending we're fourteen and they still hate each other?" He thought they were done ignoring the obvious things. That's what Tarken had claimed, anyway.

"They both deserve to find some peace in their lives," Qaira murmured.

"Tarken's been complaining to you."

"No, but I heard about what you both said when you fought. The soldiers talk."

He swallowed. His secrets danced in the cool air between them, their clouding breath like the spirits he saw.

"I know you both blame yourselves for Oktai."

Bataar exhaled a strangled breath. He almost laughed. "We both blame me."

She shook her head, the ornaments in her hair rattling. Her hazel eyes shone with intensity. "That's not true, but even if it was, I'd let you shift some of that burden to me. I'll tell Oktai's mother."

Her touch was too much on his wrist. His head pounded. "What would you know about losing a child?" Bataar regretted the question as soon as it spilled out, intended to hurt because he was annoyed at her and her gentle words. Qaira didn't cringe back, but her gaze hardened. That stung worse.

There had been babies between Ganni and Bato. Ones that scarcely quickened in her womb, and one born unbreathing, the same way Bataar had been, skin tinged blue, choked before he could take his first breath. They hadn't had souls yet, just empty vessels—

"We both know what it's like to lose a child," Qaira said. Her tone was ice cold and just as delicate. "Just because you think you're the most important person in the world, that doesn't mean you're the only one. I was there when Chugai died, too."

"Is anyone ever really lost?" he mocked. Bitterness welled, spilling out even as he fought to keep it contained between his teeth. "Since we all peacefully rejoin with Preeminence?"

Her soft, smoky voice shattered. "How could you, of all people, say those words like you don't believe them?"

She didn't know the truth of it. No one did but him.

Qaira stalked out of the tent, and her guards who'd been posted outside flanked her. Bataar almost ran after her. Not loud enough, he muttered, "Wait. Qaira, that was wrong—"

Boroo watched with her clouded eyes. He and the old shaman were the last lingering in the war pavilion, just them and the muffled sound of cheering for grapplers competing outside. And the screeches of the gryphon cubs.

Boroo stepped close. She set her gnarled hands on his arm, peeling back his sleeve. The scratch marks from the vermilrot ghoul were scabbed over, a healthy dark red. For the sad sods who'd been infected, the wounds stayed wet and gummy. Bataar snatched his arm away.

"You didn't get sick," the shaman hummed.

"You're a good medicine woman."

The beads in her snow-colored hair chimed when she shook her head. "The gryphons already claimed you children, or something else did."

All manner of dark and violent things wanted a part of Bataar, if he'd give it to them. "We're not children anymore."

Her smile was missing a handful of teeth. "To me you're still the squalling baby I helped deliver."

Bataar sighed. "Then I should be concerned that your memory of the last twenty-eight years has failed you." He should go. He needed to apologize to Qaira, try to get some sleep before they moved on the gates at daybreak. "Shouldn't you talk to Them for me? What does the Preeminent Spirit say?"

"Silence, since the mountain, and even before. Something has stirred that makes even Preeminence deliberate."

Through the threshold of the tent, red embers danced in the black sky. The smell of smoke drifted on the cold air. The war encampment would need to be more conservative with their fires tomorrow and in the days after that. Bataar wasn't sure how long this siege would last before Ruo's delayed reinforcements arrived. In the meantime, the barren sands had little to burn.

"I don't fear Preeminence," he lied. "Provoke the spirits to speak."

Boroo watched him expectantly. "Observe for yourself the way They're silent. Come."

"If you wanted to train me, you should have started ages ago," he grumbled. Would the steppe tribes have followed a shaman king? Once, he'd been too afraid to learn the answer. Too afraid of everything. Now he was the hand of Preeminence, or the hand that fed Them.

He begrudgingly followed Boroo as she hobbled out into the raucous crowd of soldiers. His guards outside the pavilion moved to follow, but Bataar waved them away, craning his head to keep sight of the old woman's hunkered shape in the darkness.

It was strange to think that decades ago, Bataar had been in a camp that carefully rationed food scraps every winter. Now, even with their depleted stores, his army was probably the best fed in the world. All around there were faces that didn't remember hunger and scarred bodies that had encountered every beast except for it. He tried not to sneer or let bitterness poison his mind.

Thank Preeminence Tarken had his men tightly controlling the flow of alcohol in the war encampment: stronger Dumakran pomace brandy and milder fermented mare's milk. As long as no one was hungover or exhausted tomorrow, eating, drinking, and a little sex were all good for morale. And this noise and ash would likely keep jackals, snakes, and anything worse away from camp.

Boroo led him out of the fray, toward her tent on the outskirts, where the din faded to a dream-like hum. She ducked inside and emerged from behind the flap gripping the arm of a young girl with hair as black as a raven's wing. The acolyte Boroo was training to replace her had been born fully deaf. Bataar had no idea if in this girl's silent world, the Preeminent Spirit spoke to her, if she read rune signs, or if all of this was guessing and speculation anyway.

She was a sweet girl, nicer than Boroo. Give her eighty years and she'd turn out just as crotchety.

Bataar signed and spoke hello, so she could read his lips. She ducked her head, her cheeks reddening. Boroo asked her to fetch something from inside the tent. He was surprised that the knotted, rheumatic joints in her hands still let Boroo's fingers move so nimbly.

The sound of metal ringing, stone knocking in a mortar, and a sheep bleating all seeped from inside, along with the smell of iron and ammonia and pungent herbs. She was killing one of the sacrificial animals. A soul was the price They demanded to answer Boroo's questions.

Bataar folded his arms and watched the distant city wall. It wound like the sun-bleached skeleton of a serpent through the night. All was still under a canopy of stars and the penetrating eye of the moon. Tomorrow those clean walls would see blood.

Something slithered out of the tent, floating through the air like smoke carried on the wind, snaking up into the blackness to be devoured by a hazy face.

Boroo emerged again, now holding a wooden bowl filled with something watery red that gently steamed in the cool air. She poured in a powder, and the liquid thickened into a spreadable paste. Her shamanic acolyte knelt by a neat cone of interlocking sticks, coaxing a tiny flame into a blaze. The girl upturned the contents of the stone mortar into the lapping fire. Glowing red turned blue-green, the color of ocean glass. Bataar grimaced at the lamb's blood.

Boroo tapped her foot. "You must disguise your face. You fear attracting the notice of the weaver and unmaker. We all do."

It was easier not to look. "How would you know what I fear?" Still, he bent, accommodating her short reach.

She dipped her fingers into the mixture and traced patterns on Bataar's face, interlocking swirls and sharp lines. Bataar couldn't help but think this was similar to the Dumakran ritual with the water from the Heartspring. But that iron-rich water didn't have the heat of real blood. He wrinkled his nose at the chalky metallic smell.

Bataar remembered the words Boroo had spoken in the mountain before Oktai died. She'd told him to remember himself, recognizing he was pulling the soul out of Nassar.

"You've been playing a dangerous game, boy." Her hand shot forward, surprising him. She pulled his saber from its sheath, so fast he didn't have time to stop her. Looking into his eyes with a serious expression, she held it out for him, blade-first. "Take it."

He glared, reaching for the hilt. She pulled it farther from his reach. "You want me to slice my hand open?"

"There's a reason children shouldn't meddle unguided in

the matters of souls. This world is full of dangerous things."
She shoved the saber into the red sand with shocking strength.
"Without teachers, little boys cut themselves open playing
with swords."

He felt the heat of an embarrassed flush. A nerve twinged
in his face. "I'm not a little boy. You're just a very old woman."
Bataar drew the saber out and sheathed it.

Her rheumy eyes sharpened. "To me? To the universe?
You've lived as long as a windflower." She hooked her claw-like
fingers into his forearm and dragged him toward the flickering
blue fire. A trail of white smoke wound up into the sky. "Look,
and listen. Speak, when you're ready."

Near the entrance to the tent, the girl watched eagerly. It
was annoying to be a learning experience for the diminutive
shaman.

"What do I say?"

Boroo tutted. "The words will come. But know the voice of
the universe does not speak in mortal tongues."

What did that even mean? He thought of the language of
wind, the sound of water bubbling over rocks in the Lugei
river, waves whooshing and crashing in the Thirst, the hiss of
mist.

A sheet of rain hitting hot coals. *Darya's voice.*

Bataar swallowed a thick glob of spit that threatened to
choke him. Boroo pushed him, and he grimaced into the
flames. He could pretend to make out a face in the light and
shadow. He could imagine a scene played out in the smoke, but
he just breathed in a choking cloud. Logs cracked and popped,
suffusing the clearing with the scent of sweet burnt wood.
He could almost taste ocean salt, carried from the sea beyond
Rayenna's gates, all the way from port.

The face of Preeminence was almost as wide as the sky,

waiting amidst the stars, hungry for tomorrow, to devour what Bataar would return to Them. He didn't need to ask what Preeminence wanted, what price he would need to pay to keep Their favor. How he would have to supplicate like a winter hare.

He already knew the language of death.

Bataar thanked Boroo, promising to come back and learn more from her, to seek her wisdom later. She frowned, confused or disappointed. Her fingers still clung to his sleeve as he pulled away to look for Qaira. He'd find the words to apologize, and she'd forgive him, because she was good, and for her, he'd pretend to be decent. And he would ride into battle tomorrow with nothing heavy hanging between them, the taste of her on his lips.

26

A well-fortified city has more than just strong walls. It is built in such a way that the nature of the landscape around it defends against its besiegers.

— Obeyd's *Wartime Strategies*

Fingers of orange and pink shot across the sky as Nohra hauled herself onto her pegasus. Her armor clattered as she hastily adjusted the straps on Mercy's saddle. Tumbling thoughts distracted her. If she died today, what would she be dying for? Bataar?

Bathed in morning light, the encampment was full of ringing steel and shouts as soldiers donned armor and sharpened weapons, hurriedly forming ranks with sweat already dripping down their faces. Weak wisps of smoke curled off dead campfires, and evidence of revelry littered the red sand: licked-clean bones, torn clothes, dry drinking skins. The only fire still burning was Bataar's shaman's pyre.

A sea of limp and feebly flapping silk bore the Zultama pegasus, and the tangled hair girdled by gryphon insignias were Bataar's banners. In the war pavilion, soldiers held Cali and Rami prisoner.

"If you must, lay down your lives for a united country," Safiya told the dozen riders holding the reins of stamping pegasuses. "Their wings are yours. Your heart is theirs, and it beats for Dumakra."

These were all their half-sisters who could fight. They were old enough that if they'd been born boys, they could have been conscripted into Dumakra's army. They still looked like little girls.

A united country.

It was almost like Saf genuinely believed what she was saying. She'd always been a convincing liar. "We have the skies," she continued, her voice carrying with forced strength and sincerity. "Clemiria couldn't take them from us, even if she had a hundred girls and a hundred pegasuses."

Curious soldiers halted and stared, looking to them because they were Dumakra's Harpy Knights, their imperial princesses.

The heat of so many eyes, seen and unseen, burned pinpricks in Nohra's back as she led Mercy away, toward a clearing distant from the tents and fringed banners, with space for the pegasus to take off. She couldn't listen to Safiya's stupid speech to rally their sisters, trying to convince them that this was their fight, their war to win.

"Slow down," someone said. Hands covered Nohra's, refastening the metal buckles carefully. She blinked incredulously down at Fahaad. Qaira hovered back behind him, her hair unbrushed, disheveled like a bird's nest.

"I was looking for you," Qaira said. "You weren't in the sanctium tent. You skipped breakfast."

"Don't be reckless, alright? We'll make sure Rami's safe," Fahaad promised.

Nohra's voice spilled out, hollow. "Can't promise anything."

"I don't have a favor, so—" Qaira hurried over, took up Nohra's fingers, and pressed her lips against her chainmail-veiled hand. It wasn't a kiss, didn't even connect skin to skin, but it pierced her to the bone.

Nohra couldn't stay and look too long into their pleading eyes. She pulled free, and Mercy kicked off.

The force of his black wings battered the sand. Fahaad shielded his face against the stinging cloud, an arm around Qaira. Their concerned frowns shrunk smaller and smaller.

The last time she'd flown outside this city, Nohra had been a gangly girl still wearing bandages from the assassination attempt in the sanctium. As the caravan had cut across the Gash, she'd gazed admiringly at her aunts' gleaming armor, longing for the day when she'd be a Harpy Knight. Her mother hadn't wanted her to go, but Nohra had promised she would be back in Kalafar months before the baby came.

The Sister City had been a shimmering mirage in the desert, walled with giants' bones. Saf had said Nohra was just doped out on pain medicine. The stone fortifications enclosing Rayenna were sun-scoured, capped in glittering spikes and white reinforcing bands, all bright enough to burn eyes. It was more splendorous than any illustration of the other Marvels of Man.

As Mercy gained altitude, Nohra's stomach swooped even though it was empty. The Ivory Gates rose as she did, stretching endlessly into the sunrise. Buried under the dunes sprawled a graveyard of sand-weathered skeletons, remnants of ancient armies. Mercy circled. On the ground far below, Bataar's men formed long rows aimed at Rayenna's impenetrable walls. Shouted orders carried on the still air as Clemiria's troops moved on top of the battlements. If players were beating war drums, the sound became too far away to hear.

Without pegasus fliers, the Sister City could have held out in a siege until Bataar's junkrig ships arrived to seal the port. Those reinforcements from the west could take weeks or more. He'd wanted to lure Clemiria's troops out today, but it turned out Clemiria didn't need to be baited.

Rayenna had a Harpy queen. Clemiria wouldn't wait, for reinforcements or to be trapped. That morning Bataar's emergency patrol had raised the alarm, sending soldiers jumping from their tents: the Rayenni military was forming ranks outside the gates.

It took more than a few months to teach someone, an adult especially, to fly a pegasus without vomiting, to train them to adjust to the dizziness and vertigo. Even Shaza was still unsteady in a pegasus saddle. Only Nohra's sisters would be in the sky today. She and Safiya had transferred command of their ground battalions to Shaza.

This day, Nohra was Bataar's dog. And... it was almost *good* to follow orders, to cast off accountability.

Nohra pulled Mercy in wide arcs like a hawk, scanning the ocean of red and the white wall for a target. An archer took aim in one of the embrasures atop the crenelation. This Rayenni soldier was far from the ballistae, separated from the press of the other soldiers.

Without hesitating, Nohra drew *Bleeding Edge* and dug her heels into Mercy's flanks. Her body strained against the fastenings on the saddle as they dropped. The rest of the battlefield far below smeared. The extent of Nohra's world was as far as she could reach with her weapon. With a jolt that rattled her teeth, the sickle blade slid down the Rayenni soldier's shoulder, across his chest, hooking into his other arm.

Red welled. His screams were distant noise as Nohra pulled Mercy back into the sky. First blood was hers.

"Nohra!" Safiya shouted. Her condescending tone cut through Nohra's smug victory. "We don't have any cover. Think, please."

Raising *Covenant*, Safiya readied a barbed bolt. Calidah didn't need her crossbow to be Bataar's prisoner, so she'd surrendered it to them. Squinting, Saf pulled the trigger, releasing the bowstring. One of the tiny shapes manning a ballista on the wall dropped, then another.

"I'll cover you." Safiya still sounded annoyed.

Nohra didn't thank her.

The heavy blade in her hands made her arms shake as she nudged Mercy into another dive. A ballista operator feebly drew a sword to try deflecting *Bleeding Edge*. She sliced him on her pegasus's upstroke, tasting his blood as it sprayed up the length of the sickle-staff. Mercy's steel-shod hooves scraped the surface of the wall walk, sending up sparks.

Nohra's heart was a dove beating its wings against her ribs.

On the battlefield, the Rayenni spearmen advanced in stiff, blockish formations. Bataar's Utasoo horsemen dispersed, breaking into smaller groups that jabbed at the sides of the units. His cavalrymen struck like daggers, cutting in and peeling off, then regrouping together in powerful clusters, hitting harder, and pulling back again.

Bataar's army had experience, but Clemiria's soldiers knew the terrain.

They wouldn't stumble in the sand or sag under the shooting heat. Some of her men were used to combat in the hot coliseums. And the city had an endless supply of fresh water and food pouring in each day at the port. In a siege, unless the Choyanreni ships arrived, as the days wore on, they'd stay well supplied, while Bataar's army would be forced to ration. What Rayenna lacked in numbers, the desert made up for.

Dumakran infantrymen littered the dunes below, and Utasoo horses lay on the sand. Clemiria stood a very real chance of beating Bataar on the ground.

But not in the sky.

The only problem was how long the pegasuses could stay aloft, warbling on the weak desert wind, suffering the heat of the sun. Already, Mercy's flanks were lathered with sweat. They both perspired, sweating out their body's water. Nohra's skin boiled where her chainmail coif touched her neck and the sides of her face. Her tongue was parched. If she had any spit left, she'd be choking on it.

Black, gray, and white bodies unfurled huge wings and flew off the walls, wavering toward Nohra, Saf, and the other riders. The sky filled with the sounds of pegasuses shrieking as Clemiria's fliers clashed with Nohra's sisters. She adjusted her grip on *Bleeding Edge*, finding a balance that didn't pull out her shoulder, and pushed forward.

Saf shouted, "Try to just hold them off. They're only girls."

Nohra snorted humorlessly.

This was a battle with lives being lost in the hundreds. Aunt Clemiria's soldiers were turning Dumakra's into a feast for carrion birds and jackals. Nohra wheeled Mercy in a wide arc. She couldn't just hold the girls off when she was full of so much white-hot fury. She dove in, cutting between one of Clemiria's riders and one of her sisters.

Wide, wild eyes blinked at Nohra through the visor of a feather-steel helmet. A lance shook in uncertain hands. The girl looked fifteen, maybe sixteen. She was probably some street urchin Aunt Clemiria had thrown on a saddle, bribed with empty promises of a more noble life.

Was she fighting for a family? Her city? Her country? Probably, she was just trying to survive.

It didn't really matter anyway.

Nohra spurred Mercy forward and took off the girl's head. Wrongness suffocated Nohra as the rider's brown braid whipped around her helmeted head and plummeted down, becoming small and then vanishing completely from sight.

Nohra's palms dripped, her grip faltering. Panic made the world spin. Killing had never stung like this before. It ached like an arrow through the arm, the leg, the heart.

She fought to control herself, to regulate her breathing. Every breath was ragged. She couldn't make her lungs take in enough air. Something was gone, missing. Like a shirt ripped off her. She couldn't feel the Goddess.

"Look out!" Safiya yelled.

Nohra saw the ballista leveling on her, the bolt hurtling toward her. She was numb, drenched in cold sweat when the huge broadhead tore through the junction of Mercy's wing and shoulder. The pegasus's whinny grew ear-splittingly high-pitched. Blood streamed across the sky as Mercy spun out of control, losing altitude. The broken wing buffeted Nohra's face, obscuring the world through obsidian feathers. It hit her over and over again until it tore off, wheeling away from Mercy's body.

When *Bleeding Edge* flew out of Nohra's grip, the long, hard snath cracked against her head. Pressure built behind her eyes. Her stomach flipped over, and her lungs filled with the smell of brimstone. The world faded to white as she waited to hit the ground.

27

The horizon was bone, and she was a galaxy.
The desert tasted like dread and the blood of my Sister.

— "Rayenna", a poem

Bataar rode behind the front lines as his soldiers pierced the flanks of the Rayenni spearmen. From head on, the phalanx formation was impenetrable, but Shaza's archers rained down a volley, and Clemiria's infantrymen in the middle of the formation stumbled, collapsing and weakening the tight shape. High above, pegasus fliers picked off bowmen on the wall. The air was full of death; the sky was full of souls. Like a vision in the firmament: black eyes, teeth, and horns sharp enough to pierce stars.

War in the desert reeked of sweat, bile, and hot sand, and the battle was just the beginning. The queen could send units out for days, weeks, maybe, until Ruo's ships reached port to deposit siege equipment to take the wall.

If those ships ever came.

Red-and-black flags pressed forward, and Bataar pulled ahead. With two firm shrieks, Erdene jumped off his arm and flapped up.

Tarken rode close behind, drawing his saber. Bataar turned, sharing a look with him. Understanding passed between them. Excuses and forgiveness were words they didn't need to say, and couldn't now.

Tarken grunted, "Where are your hostages?"

A pike jabbed toward Bataar's horse. He hit her flank with his heel and the mare shuffled back, narrowly avoiding the sharp blade at the end of the shaft. The Rayenni man coughed at the sand kicked up by the horse's hooves. Tarken cut him off from the rest of his formation and struck him down.

"With Qaira at the war pavilion, under guard."

Tarken stabbed for an opening in an infantryman's plate armor. His sword sank between hauberk and chain. A wave of steel pressed toward them. Bataar gave the order to fall back. Princess Calidah was cooperating for now, more than the other Harpies. She knew how many garrisons were stationed in Rayenna, and she'd borrowed a counting frame to estimate how many soldiers her mother could have recruited from the populace in the months since Bataar took Kalafar.

"She can't have more than twenty pegasuses, and her riders won't have seen battle," Bataar repeated. "Calidah said her mother favors tight formations, and most of her garrisons are infantrymen led by arena fighters. The walls are a strong defense, but she'll act offensively."

In exchange for Calidah's information, Bataar promised to spare her mother's life when she surrendered. He'd sworn in blood and put his seal to the terms.

The battlefield spread as far as the eye could see, stark against the ivory wall and crimson sands. Men fell around Bataar's horse. Souls seeped from corpses. Other bodies soaked the sand with blood. Their fingers spasmed, eyes straining to keep seeing light. These fighters died when Bataar was already too far away to witness their final wheezing moments.

The skirmish had a tide, an ebb and flow that lulled when ranks re-formed and pulled back, stopping to catch its breath when the grating on the gates rose to let out another flood of soldiers. At his order, Bataar's units charged forward to try to break through and funnel into the city. The sticky sheen cooling on his skin and wetness of his horse's fur choked him, and the iron tang of other people's blood against his lips made him gag. He let the fog of battle and fear of death spur him forward.

A flash of silver sparkled in a pile of corpses. Bataar swayed in his saddle, shielding his eyes from the glare.

His mare reared, and Bataar's gut lurched. He flew off, landing hard on his back. The current of sand lapped like waves, and his ears rang.

"Qaira?" Their tents were far from the battle, but he recognized a necklace glinting amid the dead. Bataar crawled forward, his cape an anchoring weight on his shoulders.

He gulped in a breath of the sick-smelling air, gaping at the splayed limbs of a cut-open Dumakran boy. Bataar reached for the chain of a necklace. His fingers brushed the words inscribed on the pendant. *Chaos begets order.* It was impossible.

The boy's skin was waxy, warm from being cooked in the hot sun. Black blowflies had already colonized his unmoving body. They swarmed on his glassy, wide-open eyes and crawled down into the collar of his tunic, where blood spread over his hairless chest. High above, dark shapes reeled through the cloudless sky, vultures waiting for an intermission in the fighting.

In the greater distance, there could be gryphons.

"Your Eminence!" a guard shouted. Bataar ripped the silver chain off the dead boy's neck and whistled for Erdene. He was still holding the necklace in his fist when Rayenni soldiers closed in.

"You shouldn't be in the vanguard," Tarken called out, voice straining as his soldiers organized into a defensive half-circle.

"Neither should you," Bataar shot back, climbing to his feet. Erdene swooped and landed on his shoulder.

"Guess we were both hungry for blood."

One of Tarken's personal guards fell, a spearpoint protruding from the middle of his back. Tarken's horse went down with a pained sound, taking a pike through its neck. Tarken cursed, fighting to disentangle himself and dismount before it crushed one of his legs. They were both on foot now, fighting for a square of sand the width of a bed.

High above, Clemiria's pegasus riders dropped off the wall and careened toward Bataar's fliers.

"Pay attention!" Tarken yelled.

Bataar jerked his gaze away from the winged horses clashing in the sky. Blood gushed around his saber, droplets spraying in a hard sheet across his face. A soldier's soul dripped out, dissolving into the air a little at a time until his body fell back and folded. Something firm pushed against Bataar's aching back. He recognized the press of Tarken's body from their nights camping together when they were boys, the smell of the cinnamon bark Tarken chewed and the scent of his milk soap under sweat. Tarken's shoulders against his filled him with boyish courage he hadn't been high on since their first war.

They didn't move with the same synchronicity Bataar and Shaza did. He and Tarken didn't think the same or move with equal precision. They protected each other's weak sides, completing each other, two halves of a whole. Bataar pulled his bow off his shoulder and nocked an arrow. He spun, picking off one of the men lunging toward Tarken, and Tarken twisted around him, parrying a blow and kicking an armored Rayenni infantryman down with a grunt.

Bataar's guards fell, desperate, blood-slick fingers clutching the shafts speared through their abdomens. More of Tarken's soldiers died, bodies purging their souls.

Erdene dove toward one man, talons extended at his eyes. He screamed and swiped at her thrashing wings, but Bataar had already recalled her, leaving the man clawing his own gouged face.

They were outnumbered, the odds stacked high against them. Hopelessness made their movements stiff. This was worse than his and Nohra's chances at the docks. These were Rayenna's soldiers, trained for years and desperate to live, to go home to their families or their honors in the colosseums. His muscles burned, the bow an anchor dragging down his hands. If it were just his life, Bataar would have fallen to his knees, but right now he was fighting for Tarken. He'd sworn when they were little he'd keep him safe. And Bataar had a family too, one he'd burn the whole world for.

They'd lost the upper hand on the sand, but they still had the skies.

He held out the silver chain for Erdene to take. She'd been his bird since he was a boy. She was an extension of Bataar's will—tumultuous and dissident when he was young and unruly, cruelly cold and cunning now that he ruled half the continent. Like ashes on the wind, when he died, Erdene would be free of him, too.

"Go to Qaira," he ordered her. Erdene tilted her head. Then she shrieked, flitting away from the arrows and crashing swords.

If this was his last chance, Bataar had to tell Tarken what he couldn't say at the mountain.

"I didn't see it," he shouted to be heard over the clang of steel. "I wasn't looking. I didn't see Oktai's spirit leave his body."

"But you saw Chugai's." Tarken's breathless voice broke as he parried a blow. "You saw Chugai's soul rejoin Preeminence, after the gryphon"—he heaved up the word—"*ate* him."

"Yes." He couldn't say it was like watching Tarken's little brother be devoured twice. "I saw him. *I saw him.*"

Panting, Bataar reached for the feeling he'd had in the infirmary with Oktai, the anger at Nassar that had radiated off him.

He thought of Mukhalii Rhah's smug face when he'd sworn fealty. He remembered the rainy day when the first girls were stolen from camp. It had stormed again when they got them back. He remembered Chugai's body sliding down the gryphon's throat, Tarken's mother dropping a tiny dismembered foot, a strangled sob tearing from her throat. The Dumakran merchant spitting on him at a market in Zeffa when he was just a boy, the zultam's emissary refusing his people aid in the years after the Sunless Months. Bataar thought of all that and everything worse, reaching for memories as dark as he dared.

He burned with anger.

I did it for you, he wanted to scream. *Everything was for you.*

For the briefest second, he was fourteen again, pressed down by a gryphon, stabbing it over and over. He turned the Rayenni soldiers into monsters in his head.

The man pushing his spear hard against Tarken's saber sagged, his soul spewing out through his eyes. Like toppling tiles, a dozen men fell in quick succession, their spirits spurting out of their heads as if their skulls had burst.

Bataar's head lolled back. He stared up at the sky, locking eyes for the first time with that searing gaze. What he felt went beyond primal fear. He'd been Preeminence's meek servant. Now he would be Their king.

"Bataar?" Tarken's voice hit him. "What did you just do?"

Panic unfurled slowly, spreading under his skin. Exhaustion hardened his muscles, turning his limbs sluggish and clumsy.

It wasn't enough. A dozen men were nothing in the face of the wave that trapped them. Stiffness turned to a fatigue that hadn't hit him since the gryphon attack, fever ravaging his body. His knees went weak, and stone settled in his stomach.

Whistling arrows fizzed past Bataar's face. The air bent around them, stroking his cheek. *Shaza.*

"A decade later and I'm still saving you oafs' asses," Shaza grumbled, pulling in front of them with her soldiers. Fear and fervor swirled in her eyes, but she commanded her bowmen capably, with quick, shouted orders. They swept up the last of the Rayenni unit and dispatched them, their volleys aimed with exacting accuracy.

"Shaza!" Tarken cried, collapsing against Bataar. "You won't believe how glad I am to see you!"

"It's damned hard to win a battle when you're searching through the dead bodies for your idiot friends!" she shouted.

Tarken grinned deliriously, wavering and punch-drunk. His arms shook and his saber fell into the sand. "I missed your beautiful face!"

The tips of her ears colored. "It's been less than an hour. Shut up or I swear I'll kill you myself."

Bataar's pulse was so loud, separating him from the world through a sound-dulling film. Above, the pegasuses screeched. One made a distressed noise that cut through the din of the fighting like a peal of thunder. Bataar looked up. A black speck wobbled erratically in the sky then fell, becoming a larger shadowy shape, a meteor.

"Was that one of ours?"

A black pegasus, speared through by a ballista bolt. Cold

dread prickled Bataar. His eyes landed on one of Shaza's men. He pulled the soldier off his horse. The man hit the sand with an aborted grunt. Bataar climbed up, grabbing the reins, kicking the horse to a messy gallop over the writhing bodies and hot sand.

"A fire!" someone shouted, their voice distorted by the speed of the horse.

Bataar turned, glancing at the wall, prepared to pull the army back if the Rayenni soldiers were pouring vats of burning oil from the embrasures. Under the sun, the stone was blazingly bright. He raised a hand, shielding his eyes, and cast his gaze out at the battlefield, over the heaps of prone figures and tattered flags.

The falling pegasus was close enough for him to see its wing separate from its body, breaking off. It was still too far away to see the rider or make out any distinguishing detail in her hair or armor. He spurred the horse faster, ignoring the fatigue untangling his nerves. His scar itched, and pain stabbed behind his eyes.

There *was* a fire.

The column of smoke was twenty yards wide and growing steadily. No, not smoke—a storm cloud, a distortion. In seconds the formation was tall enough to graze the sky. The hazy pillar began to take shape, the curve of a hip, a plume like an arm, a face almost as immense as Preeminence. Human features lingered, too clear to be imagined. The entity was alive, and the falling pegasus was swallowed up by its cloudy hand. One, two, five fingers unspooled from the column and curled around the pieces of the pegasus and rider.

Bataar yanked the reins. His horse reared to a stop. All around the battlefield, soldiers stopped fighting to watch in fear as the figure eclipsed the sun. The giant's eyes were two black fires like hot coals. Stars burst in their depths. He knew them.

Darya Daheer.

"Demon!" Dumakran soldiers shouted. And they were right.

The rest of her shape pulled out of the column. Reconciling the short, mousy woman with the monster now billowing over the battlefield was nearly impossible. It wasn't Darya. It was nothing like her. But it was her. It had the same luminous gaze and soft edges. It had the same round lips and wisps of shadow hair brushing its shoulders, the same short arms and wide hips. This was the woman from the kitchens. But also a demon unraveling from its human shape, furling out wider and wider.

The Darya at the palace shrunk into herself. This one would tear the world apart.

Steam flooding off her shrouded the sky, covering the terrible face of Preeminence, dimming blue to an angry ash gray. It wouldn't matter if he had one god's favor, when another was burning with rage. Light splintered in the depths of her, like veins of lightning fissuring steely clouds. Bataar's horse nickered, rearing again. Its shivering terror bled into his own. His heartbeat was a rabbit, kicking off the walls in his skull.

Darya's head moved, left, right. She cast a dismissive glance toward the other face in the sky before her gaze fell to her hand. She stepped forward. The sound echoed, a vibration that made sand on top of the dunes skitter. She displaced the red desert. Crimson blankets swept over corpses. The battle stopped. Infantrymen fell back from the impact as horses were thrown. Soldiers were crushed, their shouts and high-pitched noises of fear cut short as they vanished into the typhoon of Darya and fell silent. Bataar made himself shut his gaping mouth. She wasn't turning the tide of the battle in their favor; she was blotting away entire units on both sides indiscriminately.

He braced for the gust of wind as she moved through the thick, electric air. A storm of sand blasted him back, stinging his eyes. He wheeled the horse around, pushing tight at its flanks to urge it toward the wall. Screams poured from the parapets. Dust-mote flecks of people jumped from the Ivory Gates and vanished into the red below. A volley of arrows was fired, and one of the huge ballista bolts shot through her face. Darya swept up the ballistae, wiping clean a length of the wall-walk thirty yards long. Screams died with a whoosh.

"Shaza!" Bataar shouted.

"What were you thinking?" she yelled back. "Were you going to catch a whole damned pegasus?"

"Send the order to fall back! Get everyone as far from the wall as possible before—"

First the limestone cleft open, torn apart with a sound like a mountain breaking in half. Chunks of the wall fell in huge, rough slabs larger than siege towers, crashing down and splashing into the sand. Bataar didn't see the bodies lost in the hissing wave of rock and dust, but the air filled with the fibrous, wispy flesh of souls. Reinforcing beams on the wall still stood, looking more than ever like the jutting ribs of a giant.

Perhaps they really were.

Darya pried one experimentally with her empty hand. She strained harder. It protested with a bone-scraping screech, then gave a crunch like the biggest tree to ever grow snapping in half.

Tarken's mouth hung open. "We aren't going to need the ships."

The impenetrable Ivory Gates were wide open, and Clemiria's reinforcements behind the wall were buried under the waterfall of rubble.

The air had been kicked out of Bataar's lungs. He'd never seen anything so magnificent or so terrible. Rayenna's fortifications crumbled. If Darya didn't stop, the entire city would be flattened. Clay-tiled roofs and public baths and fountains, the bustling port connecting the continent to the scarcely explored countries to the east, it would all be wiped clean. Who could say if Darya would even stop here, or if the whole world would soon be a heap of ruins and ash?

The pillar of star-cloud shrunk, fizzling into a thin column like smoke swelling above a campfire. Bataar took a strangled breath. When the sky cleared, for a moment, the face of the Preeminent Spirit was gone too.

28

Above the fires on the sand,
  white ash flew in the air
The pyre burned bright as a star
And the children exclaimed there was
  snow on the mountain

— "Ashes Over Anhabar"

The scent of fire enveloped Nohra, but she wasn't suffocating on smoke. She'd lost consciousness falling into a cloud of warm vapor. When she opened her eyes, the world spun, pitching forward as she tried to drag herself up. A body, large and black, slumped close to her, making ragged noises.

Nohra swore, touching her scalp. Her head throbbed like she'd been cudgeled. For a terrifying moment, she thought she'd be able to press through her broken skull and feel squishy bits leaking out. Instead, her fingers met skin and hair and only a little blood. Chalky air coated her mouth. She swallowed, squinting through the slowly dispersing cloud of dust.

The straps from the pegasus saddle were still tight around her hips. One of her legs was pinned under Mercy. Instead of crushing weight, she only felt a slightly searing numbness. Around her, red spilled over white bricks. Nohra wasn't sure if it was her blood or Mercy's or someone else's. Her fingers kept slipping as she tried to unstrap herself. Mercy's jagged breaths grew desperate as the gelding rolled, stumbling to his feet and limping forward.

There was a gash in Mercy's shoulder where his left wing should be. Nohra curled over and dry-heaved into the debris. The crushing realization was back: Paga wasn't with her. Nohra had abandoned peace long ago, when she was still a girl in the sanctium, cracking a woman's head open on marble steps. She had a new benefactor, one whose sulfurous voice seemed to hiss in her ear, compelling her to climb to her feet. Ignoring a sharp stab of pain, she obeyed.

Nuna must have cursed her to keep living, to keep killing.

She ripped off Mercy's saddle blanket, wadded it up, and pressed it against his wing stump to stop the bleeding. Clumsily, she fumbled one-handed with the pegasus's feather-steel barding, pulling loose the bindings fastening plate and chain.

The incarnation of chaos had sent Nohra a demon. Now she demanded a river of blood. The pain lancing through her was a reminder she was alive, urgent enough to prickle at her eyes and make tears roll.

She limped through the rubble, and for a moment the years fell away. She was a child again, arm in a sling and mind foggy from analgesic, walking through the Ivory Gates into Rayenna. But the buildings in the outer ring closest to the wall were in ruins now. Roofs sagged and caved under large chunks of stone. Water gushed from a broken fountain, making a milky pink river on the split-open cobbled street. Dirt spilled from shattered pots. Branches and trunks of olive trees lay in splintered pieces across a courtyard that had been churned up, like in the aftermath of an earthquake. Paper torn from books and downy feathers from ripped-open pillows wheeled in the air.

Walls had been cleft open, exposing tiled kitchens and broken clay ovens. In bedrooms, straw filling leaked from mattresses and small, unmoving bodies were pinned under hunks of rock. As the dust cleared, the twisted, contorting corpses of smashed soldiers came into view, scattered around Nohra. Her ears stopped ringing. Men moaned the Goddess's names, reaching out with broken fingers.

Demon.

Nothing else could have brought the wall down like this. No siege equipment was capable of entirely obliterating the impenetrable gates of Rayenna.

Her eyes fell on a familiar form slumped nearby, and her thoughts stilled.

"Darya," Nohra gasped, tripping over the rubble. Darya was so small, naked and curled up, wearing a blanket of ash. Wisps rolled off her body.

Nohra swayed. More soldiers poured over the broken wall, infantrymen scrambling up and flooding into the city. Their battle screams didn't stir her to action. She needed to find something to cover Darya.

Sweet, gentle Darya. The most dangerous thing she'd ever done was bake cookies so delicious, Nohra ate too many and had to have a rotten tooth pulled. Darya wouldn't go on a slaughtering rampage, killing families, smashing armies.

Darya had only done this because of Nohra. Suddenly, the feeling of being watched she'd felt since they'd left the mountain city made more sense. Dar would never truly stray from her side.

Nohra took a shaky breath, knees wobbling. She felt for the

feather-steel dagger and found its sheath empty. If she picked up a jagged shard of limestone or fragment of the wall embrasures and sunk it into Darya's neck, would she die? She slept now. But when she woke up…? She wouldn't have meant to—

Nohra had made her a monster.

Darya had tried to tell her, but Nohra couldn't see her as anything other than a loyal friend, an agreeable servant. Her little kitchen mouse. The girl who knew the names of all the stars and predicted futures from the lumpy shapes left behind in coffee cups.

Nohra should never have become something weak Darya needed to protect.

No. It was all because of Bataar. His war set this fate in motion.

Soldiers shouted. Women and children screamed, the blood-curdling kind ripped out of mouths. Nohra blinked through the clearing cloud of white. Entire units swarmed around, pushing into the city. They needed cover. Leg quivering, she slowly lowered herself and scooped an arm under Darya. Every muscle in her body protested, but she couldn't leave her here, couldn't kill her, couldn't just stay hunched over her as soldiers ran around them and horses vaulted over the shifting mountain of debris.

Mercy swished his tail and stamped, keening painfully and then screaming louder when his eyes landed on Darya. As if he were terrified of her. Nohra couldn't put weight on his back, not with all that blood, and he fought to keep distance from her. She seized his reins and trudged forward, a slow, hobbling limp. Darya was as still as death but too warm slumped against her, feverish. A fire burned under her skin. Her flesh boiled, blistering Nohra's hands, but she couldn't drop her or stumble. Any weight on Nohra's broken leg made pain flare like nails hammering into the bone. In pulsing intervals, the world went numbingly quiet.

Her scythe. She needed *Bleeding Edge* to protect them. But if she swung the sickle-staff now, the momentum might make her fold and snap in half.

She had to find Bataar. He was the one whose head she should be bashing open with a chunk of the wall. It didn't matter that Nassar and her father had forced his hand in the audience hall. It didn't matter that he could protect Kalafar, that Qaira—

"Nohra!" someone yelled hoarsely.

She stiffened, turning, and nearly tripped.

"You idiot!" Saf shouted, rushing forward and enveloping her and Darya both. "Nuna's tits, she's burning up."

"Did she black out?" *Bataar.* Nohra recognized his scratching voice, bearing none of its usual wry amusement. "Is she unconscious?"

"Your leg! You look like death." Safiya ignored Bataar's questioning completely. "Your eyes are bloodshot. Shit, your arms—"

Her skin was irritated, torn up from fresh burns where she'd held Darya. Nohra mumbled, "What happened?" She needed someone to say it, make it real.

Safiya gave her a knowing look. Bataar unclasped his cloak and swung it over Darya. Her skin singed holes in the fur. Nohra offered no resistance as Bataar winced, lifting Darya into his arms. Her heart was in her throat. She was supposed to keep Dar safe from Bataar, not hand her over to him.

But she couldn't carry Darya herself.

Tarken's eyes lingered on Dar's unmoving body, glassy, like he'd seen a ghost.

Leaving Nohra's side, Safiya moved to placate Mercy,

attempting to soothe him while she tied his bridle off to one of the horses. He thrashed, flapping his remaining wing, and their eyes rolled to the whites as they reared away from Darya. Safiya grimaced.

"Take her back, put her under guard." Bataar passed off Darya's limp body to a soldier. He recoiled from the heat, exposed skin reddening. "Restrain her and keep her unconscious."

"No!" Nohra's voice broke in desperation. "Don't tie her up, please."

Bataar's face twinged. "If you really didn't see what she did, look around. The rubble paints a detailed picture. There are a few thousand men you could try asking for further clarification, but I'm afraid the dead aren't chatty."

"How could Darya have done this?" She'd seen the pictures in the chronicles and fables of demons as tall as the sky. "Why?"

He shook his head. "You know why. None of us know *how*. She's more than dangerous. Darya didn't just turn the tide, she made a new ocean."

"Let me look at your leg." Safiya knelt, and Nohra winced. "How are you even standing? You've got to be in shock."

"Get them both back to Qaira." Bataar gave the order to soldiers whose faces Nohra didn't recognize. Hands grabbed her arms, lifting her. She couldn't contain the strangled sound she made.

"It could hurt her more to move her like this. Find me two dowels or straight branches," Saf ordered the soldiers. She held up her hands. "About this length. Bataar, I need your belt." She took off her small leather bag and unrolled it, exposing rows of vials stuffed with gauze and tinctures. "Drink this." She pushed an amber-colored bottle into Nohra's shaking fingers.

Nohra choked on the bitter, reddish-brown liquid inside. "It's just a sprain."

"It isn't, and setting it will hurt like a bitch. Try not to bite through your tongue."

"Here." Bataar drew his blade and unbuckled his saber's sheath, thrusting it out at her. Nohra took the tooled leather in her hands and bit down. Underneath the taste of tanning chemicals, sweat, and iron, it was earthy.

Tears burned in Nohra's eyes as Safiya bound the splint with Bataar's red silk belt. Bones scraped against each other, wriggling in the muscles of her leg. Nohra wrapped the length of leather hard around her clenched fists. She hissed at the pain of it touching her burnt palms. Her stomach begged to be emptied, but she fought to keep from throwing up. Waves of pain battered her until every sense dulled.

Once Safiya was done, Nohra tried taking a step forward.

"You still shouldn't put weight on it," Saf told her.

"Get them both back to the triage tents," Bataar said. "Then bring *her* to me."

Bring who?

Ignoring the pain, she grabbed Safiya's breastplate. "You're not coming back with us?"

Bataar answered for her. "We need to pressure the queen for a surrender now."

"I can walk." She turned on her sister. "Don't do this without me. I know what Aunt Clemiria's thinking better than anyone. I'll make sure she understands."

Saf sighed. "Fine. You can come, but only if you take this."

"What is it?"

"Something stronger for the pain. Riding with a bone like *that* will stir the meat in your leg at every step."

Nohra didn't have time to argue. She knocked back the

contents of the vial and swallowed. The flavor called to mind the surgery from when she was a girl. It was potent valerian root extract, which was a dark, rich color and tasted like a mouthful of moss and dirt. There were notes of poppy too, nutty and bitter. Her vision fogged over, a crushing wave of exhaustion hitting her like a kick in the gut. She didn't even have time to feel betrayed.

☙❧

Nohra blinked awake on a cot. She tried bucking off the dizziness, attempted to sit up, but something tugged her arm. Her pulse quickened. Bataar must have ordered she be restrained, too. Her fingers groped an intestine tube like the one the mavens had put in Oktai. Red-brown dripped down it into her arm. She yanked it out and covered the small trickle of blood, applying pressure to stanch it.

The long, curved weapon propped against her cot couldn't be *Bleeding Edge*. It had been buried, when, when—

"Nohra." Qaira's concern was a gentle caress. "You can't get up yet." A patronizing caress.

"Where's Darya?" Nohra's voice was groggy.

The sick tent was full of bodies. Most breathed shallowly, their skin powdered with dust from the collapsed wall. Countless tourniquets encircled bloody, sawn-off limbs. Dreading the worst, Nohra glanced down—her leg was bound tightly now, stiff with layers of gauze and a thick plaster. She let out a sigh of relief. Someone must have properly set it while she was unconscious.

"Fahaad, could you help her lay back down?"

Nohra breathed in apples and musk. Her eyes landed on the sliver of Fahaad's chest where his tunic was always undone. Qaira leaned over her too. Nohra jolted at a prick in her arm as the line was reinserted.

"Darya's fine," Qaira said. "It's your turn to get well now."

"Saf drugged me." Nohra couldn't help that her tone was bitter, childlike.

"She was just worried about you. She didn't want you to hurt yourself," Fahaad attempted to reason with her. His fingers pressed her shoulder and then brushed her face, pushing back a damp lock of hair.

"Let me go or I'll bite your hand." Nohra pushed herself up. Fahaad wrestled her back down. The other physicians wore horrified expressions, like someone had thrown a lion onto the sickbed.

Qaira crossed her arms. "If you promise to keep the line in, we can take you to Darya."

"Fine!"

Fahaad grumbled as she leaned on his shoulder and limped around the cots and bedrolls full of moaning, convalescing patients. Qaira walked on her other side, letting Nohra brace herself on her arm. Nohra managed to knock over a stone mortar full of yellow paste and spill a carafe of water. A Choyanreni doctor went red-faced trying not to yell.

"You're a pain in the ass," Fahaad grumbled. "You can't do anything anyone tells you to do, can you? *Bite me?* You wouldn't try to bite me."

Nohra focused on dragging her foot forward. They led her to the Utasoo shaman's tent on the outskirts of camp.

Qaira passed between the guards posted outside to pull back the flap. "Bataar thought it was the safest place."

"Before you see her, just know—" Fahaad started.

Nohra had already stumbled past him. Inside, Darya was awake. She sat up, watching the light spill in from the entrance of the tent, wearing a bemused expression. Nohra had expected restraints binding Darya's wrists and ankles. Of course Fahaad and Qaira wouldn't be as cruel as Bataar, or stupid enough to think iron shackles could constrain her.

Boroo and her shamanic apprentice knelt at the tent's fringes, ritual markings still painting their faces in bloody streaks.

"Dar," Nohra said, collapsing against her. Darya's clean shirt pressed against her face, cotton soft and uncharred, smelling like an orchard. A necklace pooled around her collarbones, the metal molten warm against her skin. Nohra recognized the shape of the pendant the cleric had given her years ago. But that wasn't possible. That boy from the palace courtyard had it.

"I was worried about you." Darya's speech was slurred. "Fa'aad told me you were riding and had a bad fall."

Nohra drew back. "You caught me."

She giggled. "*Pfft*, how'd I do that?" Darya's black eyes were as warm and gentle as she'd ever remembered, puddles of a summer night. A smile pulled at the corners of Dar's mouth.

Nohra grabbed a candle and held it up to her face. Her pupils, almost indistinguishable from the irises, were dilated. "She's high."

"Bataar wanted us to take precautions," Fahaad explained in perfect monotone. "She's out of it, but at least she's not transforming into a giant rage monster and destroying any previously unbreakable city walls."

Beads rattled as the shaman took a sharp breath. Qaira cast an apologetic look at Boroo's pursed expression.

"Huh?" Darya tilted her head.

Nohra pulled her tighter, willing her prickling eyes not to cry. Fahaad prodded her shoulder, urging her to ease her grip.

"Where's Rami?" Nohra asked, not letting up.

"He's shaken. Scared." Qaira measured her words carefully. "We all saw the wall crumble. It was unsettling."

Fahaad's fingers twitched, then tightened.

"Is he in the war tent? I'll go to him and Cali."

Finally, Fahaad's hand fell off her. "Your cousin was called to accompany some of Bataar's soldiers. Queen Clemiria's holed up in the Municipal Hall, and Bataar wants to use Calidah to force a surrender."

Nohra's blood ran cold. "That won't work." She dropped a dazed-looking Darya. "I should go. Fahaad, you have to help me get to them." He started shaking his head. "I'll never ask you for anything ever again," she pleaded, looking at Qaira now too. "I swear."

"Don't make promises we both know you won't keep." But his sigh was him agreeing.

Qaira swore that few in the camp knew where Darya was being kept. Bataar had promised the high-ranking commanders answers, and action, when the dust settled in Rayenna. Confusion was etched onto the faces Nohra passed. As far as they knew, the demon that attacked Rayenna's walls had vanished into dust like the bodies buried under the sand.

Nohra dressed hurriedly, too unnerved to feel awkward as Qaira helped her into her chainmail and buckled her plate. So low it would be a miracle if Qaira overheard, Nohra whispered, "I'm not sorry." For plotting to betray Bataar, even as her and Qaira's heartlines knotted tighter. She would do it all again, no matter what came unraveled.

Qaira's fingers skimmed Nohra's neck, pulling out her hair trapped under her armor. "I'm not either." For manipulating Nohra, attempting to make her malleable for her husband. Any tenderness was collateral damage.

Nohra kissed her hand, but it wasn't forgiveness. Qaira's skin smelled like antiseptic, medicinal herbs, and metal; blood and feather-steel. She cradled Nohra's cheek. Emotions swam in her eyes, ones Nohra didn't have time to wade through.

Outside, Nohra couldn't flex her foot in the stirrup, but at least she'd recovered enough from the painkillers and tranquilizers to keep her balance.

The pegasus Fahaad had fitted for her to ride, Honor, bunched his wings and shook his rump like a finch in a bird bath. As her fingers brushed his white mane, a question Nohra had been dreading spilled out. "Where's Mercy?"

"Grounded." Fahaad crossed his arms, scowling down at the sand. "I made the decision. Cut off his other wing to save his life. He was going to break a leg trying to fly."

"But he's alive?"

"If the wound doesn't get infected." Fahaad sighed. "He lost a lot of blood, and the mavens could hardly figure out how to sedate a horse, let alone attempt to transfuse blood."

He's alive. Right now, Nohra couldn't think about if it would have been better to put him down.

Qaira tapped Nohra's good leg. "You really shouldn't exert yourself. It's not worth the risk of hurting yourself worse."

"Bataar doesn't take prisoners, and my aunt doesn't surrender. I thought he was using my cousin to control *me.* I didn't think he was really going to try something so obviously—". *Stupid. Reckless.* She bit her tongue. Qaira's brows knitted.

Nohra looked searchingly at Fahaad, who nodded. "As much as I hate to say it, Nohra's right. It's dangerous, but not as risky as cornering Clemiria. Nohra might be able to talk her down, make her see reason. I'll say it was my idea to let her go." He met Nohra's gaze. "Try not to die, would you?" And he swatted the dappled gelding on the flank.

❧

The destruction branched deep into Rayenna, cratering the streets. Homes, shops, and sanctiums sagged, their roofs concave and walls riddled with holes from fragments of the wall. Nohra heaved from the pain as she landed the pegasus outside the city's Municipal Hall. Her clammy fingers slipped on the metal buckles of the straps. The thought that she might be too late was a knife stabbing in her head. Soldiers positioned around the courtyard yelled, poking their sabers toward her pegasus. The world spun, the sky the same color as the gray paving stones in the plaza.

"I'm a Harpy Knight!" she shouted, dropping ungracefully from the saddle and limping forward through the soldiers. "Let me pass."

Each of the five steps up to the doors hurt like smashing a different toe. At the landing, guards stationed outside the entrance to the capitol building crossed long Choyanreni glaives, barring her way. She drew *Bleeding Edge* to use as a walking stick and hobbled forward. Her blade threw up sparks when it clanged against one of the steel poles the guards held.

A woman's voice inside delivered an order, and the guards parted. Shaza emerged from the middle of the men. She cocked her head, a hand on her hip. "You cause people a lot of problems, princess. But you brought down the wall."

Nohra's voice was gravelly. "I didn't—"

"You have good timing. The lion queen just agreed to talk to your sister."

Before Safiya, Clemiria had wielded *Queen of Beasts*, the lion-hilted sword. Nohra winced and dragged herself forward into the dimly lit hall.

There were so many stairs down into the queen's audience room. Sweat sheened her forehead as she stared into shadows.

"Take my arm." Shaza's flat tone conveyed her displeasure. "I won't offer twice."

With her roping braids and passing resemblance to Qaira, Shaza was the kind of irritating person who, like Saf, looked good even with blood and dirt and perspiration covering her. She didn't look like she'd been thrown from the sky and squished under a horse.

Nohra bit her lip to keep from crying out at every step. Shaza's glare wasn't sympathetic.

At the end of the hallway, a large group of soldiers clustered outside the tall door leading into the audience hall. Calidah was dressed in plain training clothes, with light leather armor. She hovered near Bataar. He shot Nohra a vexed look. She searched for Safiya's armor gleaming in the light of the torches. Her chest clenched.

"You're harder to shake than a case of vermilrot," Bataar grumbled. "You're not needed. Your aunt's already treating with Princess Safiya." Lioness eyes shined in the pommel at his hip. Clemiria must have wanted Safiya unarmed.

"And not my cousin, I see," Nohra bit back. Cali winced. "Or did you decide she was more valuable out here with you? Let me in too."

Bataar's gaze lingered on Nohra's leg. He exhaled deeply and turned away. "Don't mention who brought down the wall."

He made it sound like Nohra had given Darya an order. "Who's in there with her?"

Calidah wriggled, shifting her weight like she had a rock in her boot. "Her palace guards and some highly trained soldiers. It doesn't matter though. Mother's backed into a corner she can't fight her way out of."

"What about her servants? Darya's grandmother?"

She aimed a sympathetic look at her. "Iba Daheer is dead.

I'm sorry. Some of Mother's staff were sheltering in one of the buildings that collapsed, near the palace."

Nohra's heart plummeted. She flinched, grip tightening on the snath of *Bleeding Edge*. Chunks of wreckage had been flung at storm-like speeds into the heart of the city. Darya couldn't find out. That guilt would crush her. And along with Iba Daheer died their chance at uncovering the truth of Darya's parentage, the origin of her djinn blood.

"She's opening the doors again. Go, before she changes her mind," Bataar ordered, waving like Nohra was a fat fly buzzing around his head. The soldiers at the door had weapons raised. "Back up."

The braced doors had parted infinitesimally, a bright white sliver just wide enough for Nohra to squeeze through. Before the doors soundly shut and were rebarred, guardsmen jerked her forward.

"I need it to walk," she snapped, when one tried confiscating *Bleeding Edge*.

The walls in the audience hall were made up of large sandstone blocks. Chipped mosaics encircling the top of the room depicted fiery red and blue phoenixes. Rayenna, the impenetrable city, had never had to rise from ashes.

Safiya already knelt at the foot of the dais and turned to fix Nohra with an incredulous, eye-bulging glare. A soldier's steel boot against Nohra's legs sent her sprawling and gasping into the room. Her fingers opened reflexively and *Bleeding Edge* clattered onto the stone floor.

"What in hells happened to you?" Clemiria opened with, in a tone that almost sounded like sympathy.

"My pegasus fell on me," Nohra ground out, scrambling to find a way to keep her broken leg straight.

Clemiria's lip curled in disgust. "Stand up. Both of you."

The Zultama banner behind the throne spanned half the wall, rippling purple silk and golden embroidery. Years had turned strips of Aunt Clemiria's black hair silver. Nohra wasn't used to the sight of her in plain clothes, a tunic and pants. Her fingers rested on a reloading crossbow in her lap. The Harpy Knight version of the queen in Nohra's head still wore armor and carried a sword dripping blood. Nohra gripped Saf's hand tightly and let her pull her up.

Maybe Qaira and Fahaad were right; she shouldn't have come.

"As I tried to convey," Safiya started. "Bataar swore to our cousin that he won't hurt you. There will be a peaceful turnover of power and—"

"Turning power over to whom?" the queen interjected. "*Bataar?* He seized the city. If he wants my throne, tell him to come in and take it from me."

Nohra braced herself against the handle of *Bleeding Edge*. Her vision throbbed. "Do you really want to keep fighting right now? Rejoin the battle another day." She stared up at Clemiria, meeting her steely gaze, unblinking. Nohra wasn't sure whose ears were pressed to the door. "Turn over the city and abdicate. There's more blood to be had later, other wars. You wouldn't have reigned in Rayenna forever. You belong in Kalafar with the rest of our family, not dead in the desert."

Nohra registered a flicker of understanding in her aunt's eyes. Surely Clemiria's mind worked the same as hers. They were Harpy Knights. They'd sworn the same vows. All Nohra knew was her duty, and revenge. She would win their retribution. She'd kill Bataar, for both of them.

Aunt Clemiria straightened, composed, as she gave the order to open the doors. Bataar was close to the front of the group that entered. His personal guards fanned out around him.

Behind them, the rest of his soldiers funneled through the doors, weapons drawn. The tension in the audience room was cutting. Cali squeaked as Bataar dragged her forward, keeping her in front of his body like a shield. The blade he held at her throat was a short, squared-off knife, similar to the one he'd given Rami.

Nohra held her breath. The corners of her vision darkened. The room spun.

"Step forward, Clemiria," Bataar called out. He pressed the blade down and Calidah squirmed. A tiny trickle of blood made a thin line down her neck.

Clemiria didn't move.

"Surrender," Nohra hissed after a few tense moments passed. "Surrender the city. Step down." She stepped closer to the dais, bracing herself for the pain as she took the first stair, the second, and finally stood at Aunt Clemiria's side. The queen of Rayenna looked small and pathetically bitter, nothing like the golden beast of Nohra's childhood nightmares.

Clemiria's gaze was level and cold as her finger pressed the trigger on the crossbow, firing bolts in quick succession.

Nohra didn't understand. Couldn't.

Across the room, Cali's face twisted in surprise. She reached for the shafts projecting out of her chest, for the one lodged in her stomach. Bataar's eyes were wide, his scarred mouth open in shock. Calidah's blood pattered on the floor. She coughed, and red phlegm splattered her lips. Her body slumped, exposing Bataar's armor, and Clemiria fired another bolt, clipping his arm.

Cali's body blocked more shots. Bataar's soldiers were already closing ranks, forming a barricade of steel and plate. Nohra watched her cousin's fluttering eyes, her blood-tinged lips parted, her legs folding as her hands pawed at the shafts of the arrows.

For a terrible, too-long moment, Nohra was frozen. Soldiers grunted as they clashed. Blinking away the numbness, Nohra raised her arms to swing.

Pain made her weapon arc slowly. The blade rammed into her aunt's neck and wedged deep, but not deep enough to sever.

A mother looked like gentle hands on Nohra's broken arm, fingers brushing away tears, lips forming nighttime smiles in the noisy concubines' quarters. A parent looked like Father beckoning Nohra to his side, lifting her up with his own hands and setting her on the deck of a boat with purple sails.

"Nohra," Aunt Clemiria gasped as she choked on *Bleeding Edge*, dredging Nohra from her cloying memories. The sickle blade ate those burbled final words. Fury soured in her mouth. Her aunt was going to hells. Nohra would probably be joining her.

Saf tried to grab her, but Nohra had already dropped *Bleeding Edge*. She wallowed forward into the press of fighters and swinging swords, tripping onto the ground beside Cali's unmoving body. Nohra cradled Cali's head, pulling her onto her lap. Guards closed in around Bataar. In an opening through soldiers' legs, Nohra could see the medics working on him. He flinched as they dabbed at the gash cutting across his arm, cleaning and disinfecting the wound, stabilizing the shaft of another bolt. He was alive, and Calidah was fading in Nohra's arms. Her eyes were already glassed over, her parted lips cold.

Breathing raggedly, Nohra pressed for a pulse. She thought Calidah's chest rose, but it was her own hands shaking her body that she'd mistaken for movement. When she touched Cali's cheek, her fingers left a smear of her aunt's blood.

"Get up," Safiya shouted, coming up behind her and jerking

her to her feet. Nohra immediately sunk back down, limp as a doll in Saf's arms.

The skirmish was at a climax, peaking and surging down into a slow, end-of-battle dance, tepid and passionless. Swords sunk into squirming figures on the ground and medics collected people not choking on their own blood, dragging them out to be treated.

Nohra still cradled Calidah's wilted body when Bataar approached, saying something. Apologizing? Planning what came next. She wasn't listening. They'd lost the only ally who could have helped them defeat Bataar. Nohra didn't care who would rule the Sister City now that Aunt Clemiria was dead. Nassar and his army didn't matter. She didn't care how Bataar would use Darya to take the land of the lords in the north. For one peaceful second, she didn't care if Rami was king in Kalafar or the zultam or just a little boy like Safiya wanted him to be.

Bataar was responsible for all the pain and death that war brought to Dumakra, for breaking up her family. But Nohra's missteps had played a role in creating the corpses surrounding her. Nohra was the reason the gates fell and all those innocent people died. She'd let them turn Cali into a shield. She should have known her aunt's pride was worth more to her than her daughter.

If Nohra wanted justice, she'd have to put her own neck on the executioner's block and let the blade fall.

Calidah's body dropped from her shaking hands.

29

Fickle winds favor no man and weather all stone.

— The Supreme School of Thought in Xincho

The docks bustled with activity as the *Iron Orchid* moored, and salt air stung Bataar's eyes. Ruo's ship had green batten sails that glowed under the white sun. Its towering masts dwarfed the fleet anchored in the distance at the lip of the harbor. The curious crowd shrunk back, murmuring, as the prow twisted and a snarling horned dragon leered down at them. The wooden figurehead was carved with detail so fine its whiskers floated on the bare breeze.

Since the battle, Rayenna had been a city of whispers and fear. They'd found out that demons were real and no walls were unbreakable. The day of the attack, most of those inside the Ivory Gates had probably only seen a pillar of cloud and heard the earth-rattling sound of stone splitting. They'd likely been more concerned with taking cover from the army rushing in and stone falling like hail, but rumors of monsters spread. Apprehension was as far-reaching as the kilometers of sprayed wreckage.

"Watch out," Bataar warned Rami, motioning for the guards.

"That rigging looks like a fish's fins," Rami murmured. He stepped forward. "One, two, three masts. What's that flag mean?" A crewman dozens of yards up on the top deck threw the mooring line. The rope smacked the creaking boards, coiled up like a thick snake.

"It's the council's insignia. A dragon devouring its own tail."

Nervous exclamations erupted as the bores of cannons appeared to point at the clustered throng. Bataar approached the foot of the gangplank as a woman with short brown hair and stained lips disembarked. Her fingers glided over the ornate railing.

"You're late."

She crossed her arms. "You don't look like someone who won a fight."

He tried not to wince as he took her hand, his bandages straining. Her hair had been longer when they were in Choyanren, and she'd only worn dresses. Now it was cut straight across her shoulders and she was dressed like a pirate, in men's clothes. She was always a fan of theatrics and disguises.

"I thought you'd send a representative," Bataar told her, as he stepped back, making room for her personal guards to flank her.

Ruo smirked. "I thought you knew me better than that."

He fell back into speaking her native language inelegantly, already out of practice. "Did you meet unfavorable winds?"

The Choyanreni empress shook her head. "Inhospitable waters. You didn't say there'd be so many monsters. We lost two ships in the Thirst."

"I warned you it'd be dangerous."

Turtles the size of islands, seahorses with a taste for human flesh, gryphons terrorizing the half-sunken ruins of Noor, and probably more horrifying monsters, ones no man had lived to describe to the authors of bestiaries.

Rami hopped for a better look, straining so close to the edge of the dock he might splash into the harbor.

"You shouldn't have abandoned court with your council on alert," Bataar warned Ruo. "There's still the issue of the dragonlords' allegiances. What if they make a move while you're a world away?"

Their youngest daughters were wards of her council back at the palace, but she would be too far from the islands if the dragonlords tried taking the capital. Plus, Ervan Lofri controlled the distribution of opium and many other trade goods. That was going to pose a problem.

She smiled, baring sparkling teeth. "Those men wouldn't dare. I took their daughters with me."

A row of girls stepped down, walking shakily onto the bobbing dock. A couple of them looked younger than Ganni. All five wore cloud jade combs carved into serpentine shapes.

"Hostages will probably keep them in line," Bataar begrudgingly admitted. "Dragging children into war, though?"

Ruo arched a thin eyebrow and inclined her head at Rami. "Is that the zultam's boy? He looks very young."

Excited chatter dulled. Merchants and fishermen got back to unloading nets and crab pots. Ruo's traveling chests and her caged hunting birds were unloaded expeditiously and stacked onto carts to convey to her rooms in the palace. Rami's hungry eyes never left the lacquered hull of the huge junk rig, except to glance briefly at the strangely colored hawks.

"I'll take you on a tour of the fleet tomorrow," Ruo offered. "If you're curious."

Bataar sighed. "You never miss an opportunity to show off."

"I pride myself on my country's innovations. Which reminds me, bring me that case!"

One of her guardsmen bobbed his head and rushed off to retrieve a long silver box decorated in filigree. Bataar handed her into one of the waiting carriages. Ruo's overprotective guards eyed him warily as he moved to follow.

"I'm her husband." By law, at least.

They wrinkled their noses but finally stepped out of his way.

He and Rami settled into the seats on the bench across from her. As the carriage jerked forward, she grinned and unlatched the box spread across her legs. Its edges hardly fit within the confines of the cabin, so she angled it up toward one of the lattice windows. Inside, on velvet lining, was an apparatus like a miniature cannon. It had the trigger of a crossbow, but no string to hold a bolt.

"What is it?" Bataar asked.

Ruo beamed. "A firearm! It's comparable to a handcannon, but more precise. It uses gunpowder stuffed down its throat. It does quite a bit of damage with a single silver bullet." She sunk into the cushions with a sigh.

Bataar lifted the weapon out of its case. "It's heavy."

"Because I had my silversmiths make this one." She gave a dismissive wave. "Others can be made of iron and wood. They can be constructed smaller, too, to keep under a skirt, but the long ones are more accurate. Careful!"

Rami reached forward.

"I don't think so." Bataar shut the idea down quickly. He'd already given the boy a knife. He preferred him with his head not blown off.

Outside, a pillar-shaped chunk of the city wall protruded from a sanctium. Bataar drew the curtains, hiding the glare of the sun off the bleached, debris-pocked cobbled streets.

Ruo ripped the curtains back open. "Where's the famous fighting arena?"

"You wouldn't like it. There's no strategy to winning those matches, just desperation. Most of the combatants are basically slaves. We won't be in Rayenna long—don't get comfortable." They needed to repair Rayenna, secure Kalafar, and move on the land bridge before Nassar and his Aglean army came south.

She tilted her head. "War calls?"

"War calls."

After a while, Rami fell asleep with his face propped against a velvet bolster pillow. Ruo turned to Bataar with a concerned look. "You killed the boy's father. Tell me, are we both keeping our enemies close?"

Bataar watched her from the corner of his eyes with apprehension. His siege had killed her father. Ruo's family's rise to power had only been made possible by stomping on the dragonlords in Choyanren; now their young daughters rode in a carriage behind theirs, thousands of miles from home. A little boy wasn't his enemy. In light of everything that had happened since Nassar fled, Rami might have a more useful purpose than as Bataar's prisoner-ward.

"There are rumors you're pregnant. Are they true?" Bataar asked.

That cut the tension. She balked, looking down at her belly. "How would that have happened?"

"Do the granite gods believe in divine conception?" He snorted. "They're rocks. I assume they copulate strangely."

"You misunderstand my gods. We believe in absolutes and immutable truths. The granite is a metaphor."

He smiled teasingly. "You're right, I don't understand any of it."

Outside, the city blurred to white. With a tired yawn, Rami

wriggled, feet tucked against Bataar's side.

When the carriage halted, Bataar gently shook the prince awake. He directed the footmen unloading Ruo's luggage toward her quarters. Everything in Rayenna looked carved from ivory, sun-bleached and weathered by wind and sand. The harsh Municipal Hall was no different. Apparently, the outer courtyard had once contained date palms, but Queen Clemiria thought keeping them watered was a wasteful extravagance. Now the courtyard was barren, bone-dry.

Ruo stepped around her trunks and picked up one of the cages. The bird inside screeched. "One of Erdene's fledglings," she explained. "This one's for you, as promised. I have the other at my mews. This one's got muddier colors."

Bataar squinted at the overgrown hawk. "That thing's a monstrosity." He'd let her breed Erdene with her ferruginous hawk and was just now regretting it.

"It's progress. In a few generations, I could have a pure white eagle."

"Which would accomplish what?"

The Choyanreni empress smiled demurely. "It'd be pretty."

He shook his head, fighting his own smile. "You sure you don't want to attend the war meeting?"

"You know how I feel about crowded rooms. A side effect of growing up with only my father's company." Ruo sounded sheepish. She'd been hidden behind silk screens and tall shrub walls her entire life. "I'll meet you in the library when the meeting's out. You can tell me what plans they contrived, and I'll come up with something better."

❦

Bataar dragged Rami onto the packed councilors' terrace where a heated discussion was already underway. Shaza leaned on the table, rearranging the war tokens. Tarken stood over her shoulder, looking ready to draw his saber if needed. Squares of shade stretched under the canopy of bright tarps, but the air winding through the balusters was still stiflingly hot and stale.

"—leave people to repair the city, but no amount of feather-steel could build stronger walls," Dumakran General Fakier mumbled.

All Bataar's high-ranking officers were present, engaged in multiple arguments. The space would only grow more chaotic with Ruo's fleet commanders on their way. No one looked relaxed except Safiya, which was standard. Her feet were kicked up on the table. Fahaad stood rigidly with his arms crossed, and Nohra looked as dead and defeated as she had for days, her expression glazed over, saying nothing.

"It'll be quicker to go north through the mountains, then strike Aglea here," Shaza insisted, drawing a line across the hide map with her finger. "A smaller force can secure Kalafar."

Across the table, Safiya scoffed. "Quicker, sure. If we don't all die getting there." Her easy smile made Shaza bristle. "I'd remind you that just because it's drawn on a map doesn't mean the mountains are this neat. They're full of man-eating birds and carnivorous flying horses. We can't trust cartographers to have made faithful measurements."

"We'll go back the way we came. Through the Gash." Before Safiya could interject, Bataar added, "We'll hire merchant caravan guides. They should know how to navigate the sand tides better than… anyone."

Their cousin's death was a fresh scab Bataar didn't want to reopen. But judging from Nohra's blank face as she slumped in a tall-backed chair, that injury festered.

A yowling screech made the hair on Bataar's neck stand on end. The gryphon cubs were getting too large for their cage.

434

He rubbed the old scar on his face as he studied their feathered purple heads. Firearms, pegasus knights, gryphons, the seahorse at the Conservium, a djinn—they had strange new weapons, but they needed a solid strategy to use them well.

Bataar stepped close to the map and repositioned a few of their markers, dragging a carved ship into port and picking up the piece shaped like a hawk, moving it from Choyanren to their current position.

"Ruo's here?" Shaza asked. Tarken and Qaira both perked up.

Bataar nodded. "If I send her back to Choyanren, she can sail south, through the Thirst, dropping off the boy in Marafal."

"Or she can go north. We go back through the Gash, but she circumvents the mountains to the Aglean land bridge."

"She was late before," Tarken huffed. "She'll probably be late again."

"Granite gods don't control the winds." Shaza recited the words they'd all heard a hundred times. "I'll ask her if she thinks the journey would be favorable."

"Between her soldiers and Clemiria's, plus the reinforcements from the steppe, Nassar would be smart to surrender. We'll rest in Kalafar, put down any cases of the rot, replenish supplies…"

There was more business to discuss than just how they'd box in Nassar's growing army in Aglea. Bataar swiped the sweat on his neck.

"There's still the matter of Rayenna. There's more to rebuild in the outer ring than the walls, and this city needs a queen—"

"Does it?" Tarken interrupted.

"It's too far from Kalafar to run on the zultam's word alone," Safiya sing-songed. "And there isn't even a 'king in Kalafar' anymore."

"And I'm assuming you want to rule here?" Shaza asked.

Safiya threw back her head and laughed. "I don't think any of you could ever guess what I want."

The Sister City always had a queen, but Bataar couldn't afford to spare any of the Harpy Knights, and he had only crumbs of trust for the princesses. "Ruo could help set up a council of the wealthy families. We'll appoint a head from some suitable candidates," Bataar decided.

It wasn't a permanent solution, but after the war ended, he could instate a queen of his choosing.

"We should start on alliances in the south." Bataar cast a glance at Fahaad. "I told you I'd make you an ambassador to the Moshitu tribe leaders. Could you negotiate for their support? You'd be saving them from war later."

Fahaad's expression was shrouded. "I'd need a ship, and some translators."

"And some good liquor," Tarken added. "No one likes a dry deal."

Bataar watched Nohra for any reaction, but her face was an emotionless mask. Nohra Zultama was finally broken. It might be impossible to build her back into the kind of soldier Bataar needed. He was already counting her as a lost cause.

Where the map didn't reach, the table was crowded with picked-over trays of dried apricots and nuts. A plate full of husked-out oyster shells was starting to stink. Overhead, gulls squawked.

General Fakier stood stiffly toward the back of the terrace near some of the Utasoo generals, hidden behind the furiously scribbling scribes. Clearing his throat, he stepped forward. "What will you do about the demon?"

Eyes turned, and everyone quieted. Bataar looked toward Fahaad. He'd been scouring books in the city's famous library until long after midnight for four days, leafing through weathered tomes with barely legible brown pages, searching for any usable information.

Fahaad shook his head. He'd already spoken to Bataar last night. "One manuscript mentions steel as light as feathers and links of unblinking sapphire eyes," he'd said. "Most reference a chain of words, but I can't puzzle out the meaning." Shadows pooled under his eyes. Books and fragile fragments of illuminated manuscripts were piled in his quarters, a mountain of esoterica with a summit neither man could reach.

"She's under guard, and she's cooperating," Bataar told those on the terrace. And she was so high she couldn't perceive a person when they were standing in front of her. "We have methods in mind to control the djinn. Of science, and of faith."

Around the room, tense shoulders settled. The Dumakrans would be even more reassured if Nohra spoke. Darya was her loyal servant. If Nohra stepped up and controlled her, the soldiers would think they were seeing a story from their Godsbreath playing out on the battlefield. Nuna and Her demon queen.

"You'll face greater resistance now," the general continued in his gravelly voice. "From the families in Dumakra and all the viziers."

Bataar grimaced. "Because of Darya Daheer, or because I lost Lofri?"

"Because you lost the Attar girl."

Aalya *was* gone, stolen back by her family. With her, Bataar had lost alliances with most of Dumakra's wealthiest families.

The general pressed on. "You should prove your commitment to the country, pick a new wife and swear vows. The zultam had many daughters, Goddess be blessed."

The audience fell quiet. Bataar thought of all the women in

the harem; who would make the most impressive match and be the least unpredictable.

Safiya had a respectable reputation with the soldiers in the Dumakran army and some favor among the people, but even with her confession, the amused glint in her eyes made him wary. Besides, she was a more useful source of information through the concubine she confided in than she'd be as his unhappy wife.

There were several princesses who were pretty enough, with luminous brown eyes and agreeable figures, girls who would make a good picture on his arm and didn't seem likely to put a knife in his back. Though no one would make as strong a political match as Merv Attar's daughter would have made with Oktai. Aalya's inheritance would have promised control of the Merchants Guild, and Bataar could have made further powerful marriage matches for the people closest to him, to broaden the distribution of power in his army.

At this point, any girl would do. He'd rather betroth Tarken to one of the princesses. He'd had enough of weddings.

"Make me a list—" Bataar started to say.

Nohra stood, the clouded-over look in her eyes clearing. "Marry me." Her voice came out strong and unshaking. Her expression had sharpened into steely regard.

Bataar's pulse kicked, a surge of adrenaline spiking. Her proposition was dangerous, the exact opposite of what he needed. Danger was the thrilling price of power. Nohra was a double-edged blade with no hilt. He'd be shredding his own hands to cut down their enemies.

"I'll control the demon." The corner of Nohra's mouth twitched. She was almost smiling. "And you'll control me."

Bataar almost scoffed at that. "Marrying you isn't any guarantee—"

"The Harpy Knights are unpledged." Her firm voice was filled with determination. Beside her, Safiya's eyes widened. "Pledge your daughter's hand to my brother and name them heirs to Dumakra, zultam and queen. If you let my sisters give their vows to Rami, I'll swear *my* Harpy vows to you."

It didn't matter how sincere she seemed. He couldn't trust her. But in this world, there were few people Bataar placed faith in without question. A weak breeze ruffled the canopy above the terrace. Higher than the rustling tarps, Erdene screeched, her shadow flitting across the roof. Above that, the face of Preeminence was a scar on the sky. He'd bargained with a deity, starting a dangerous game. What was one more deadly gamble?

Loudly, Tarken grumbled, "Oh, you can't be serious."

The rooftop erupted into a quarrel, but Bataar didn't focus on any of it. He looked at Qaira, searching her stone expression for cracks. She nodded her approval.

That was all he ever needed.

EPILOGUE

[1] Two girls served the battle-proven princesses at Mineva.
The talmaids were not only dutiful servants but also the
Harpies' dedicated friends.

— Footnote from *A Dark Era*

Her grandmother had never taken a class at the Conservium, but Darya thought she was as wise as a maven. Grandmother didn't bring Darya to the sanctium to learn about the Goddess or read her adventure chronicles about demons and monsters. She sat on Grandmother's lap in a creaking chair in the servants' quarters and listened to the histories of the heroic and cunning deeds of real people who'd existed before anyone alive was born, the kings and their architects who built Kalafar, and the warriors who conquered Noor, hundreds of years ago.

Darya realized when she was still very young that her name would never be written in a history book.

The only other children at the palace were the zultam's brood, and the princesses treated Darya like she was invisible. She only had one friend, a boy she spoke to through his shut door. The apothecarist had Darya bring the prince his sleeping drafts, which was a considerable responsibility for a little girl. But when the prince was let out of his quarters, he stopped talking to Darya. He only sneered and called her names.

She was seven when she made friends with one of the imperial princesses. The physicians told Darya that Princess Nohra fell off a pony pegasus. She had a broken arm, a fractured collarbone, and a sprained ankle. They needed someone to sit with her in the infirmary, to keep her entertained so she didn't run around with her wild sisters and hurt herself worse. Everyone agreed mousy little Darya, if she'd step out of her grandmother's shadow, would be perfectly suited for the task.

Of course she'd known about Nohra. They were almost the same age, and soon they'd be having lessons together, but Darya had only ever spotted her across the yard, sword-fighting with sticks or hopping at her mother's skirts. Darya took her fraying ragdolls to Nohra's sickbed and she used them to act out stories of a brave knight fighting a king, keeping her sisters safe from his evil clutches. She figured it was the sort of story the princess had a taste for.

When Nohra got better, and the physicians let her leave the infirmary, she called on Darya to come swimming with her at the wading pools. She took Darya by the wrist and dragged her to a pegasus foaling. Darya threw up watching the baby pegasus slide out of its mother, sticky in its amniotic sac, with slimy, slippered feet. Nohra laughed so hard she cried.

She made Darya help her and her older sister Safiya torment Queen Merv's son, Nassar, but somehow only Saf and Darya got swatted with the birch switch when he'd run crying to his mother. Nohra was the youngest of the three of them, an expert at batting her eyes and weaseling out of punishments.

"Look, it's Nohra's little dog," Nassar would say. When Darya swept and scrubbed the floors, he'd bark at her and kick over her bucket. A brown wave of soap bubbles would flood over the tile. But he only did all that when Nohra wasn't around to hold his face down in the mess he made or make him cry until he wet his pants.

Nohra dragged Darya to flying lessons, even though she was terrified of heights. The princess laughed loudly in Darya's ear, telling her to open her eyes, but the wind blew so ferociously, she could hardly see. It pushed her screams back down her throat. Days after lessons Darya's hands would still feel wrapped in the reins.

Nohra wanted to be a Harpy Knight, and she'd become one, if she didn't die before she could be sworn in. She wasn't the best of her sisters, but no one would fight for it harder. Darya started to think she *would* be in the history books after all, as a footnote by Nohra's name.

It was nice, being more than just her grandmother's hazy little shadow. Ever since she became Nohra's favorite toy, Darya was invited to play building blocks with the princesses in their quarters. No one even got cross with her when she'd trip and knock over the wooden castle.

The memory blurred. Panic clawed at Darya's throat. *A wall breaking—*

She took a few shaky breaths, searching for stories that made her heart flutter in a different kind of panic, gold-tinged times when her world was small and so was she.

When the zultam's soldiers dragged a scrawny boy into the audience hall one day and threw him down at the foot of the dais, Darya had been refilling cups. The boy looked at her, and she read the desperation in his dark eyes. Then he turned, hacking spit at Grand Vizier Naji's feet. He spewed a stream of Dumakran vulgarities and words in other languages, each spat so venomously that the translators wrinkled their noses.

"Ferocious little thing," Naji said flatly, not sounding impressed.

Ramman Mytri, the Head Eunuch, waved a hand at the guards. "Send him to the stables. Orik can break the boy." Everyone knew the stablemaster had the firmest hand of any of the servants.

Later that day, the head physician asked Darya to bring a blue vial from the infirmary to the eunuch's quarters. Darya watched, horrified, as Ramman Mytri squeezed the boy's cheeks and poured the infertility tonic down his throat. "So he becomes accustomed to the taste early."

When Darya told Nohra about the boy, they sprung him from his room, but only after nine-year-old Nohra—who thought she was already in charge of palace security—could be certain that he wasn't a threat to her father's life. Neither of them knew what his name had been before he came to the capital. He wouldn't tell them, but Orik called him Fahaad.

The surly, Dumakran-born stablemaster had a soft spot for Fahaad. He never got a lashing with Orik's infamous whip. Even when Fahaad mouthed off, he was only sent to bed with a little less on his already full plate.

Darya recognized the way Nohra looked at their new friend. Nohra saw him as someone below her, a servant, and she looked at Darya the same way. She loved them both, but what if Nassar had been right, and it was the same way she loved the hunting dogs or Mercy, her spindly-legged pegasus colt?

But Darya knew Fahaad was different. The best she could hope for was to become a homely wife for a vizier's unlucky third son. Fahaad's father was a king, somewhere. He was royalty like Nohra, even if Dumakrans thought the zultam was more important than the southern tribe leaders. Darya could see it in the way Fahaad walked, in how his head hadn't bowed even when the soldier forced him to his knees in the audience hall.

When Darya turned eleven, the servants in the kitchens realized she was useful because she was short and could squeeze behind the stoves and other hard-to-reach places to clean.

Nohra had a dangerous sweet tooth, and Darya could make her amenable with the right food. Under careful direction as an apprentice in the kitchens, Darya learned to make syrupy sweet cheese and flaky cookies stuffed with crushed walnuts. She perfected a gooey honey cake that could give even the pickiest eater a rotten tooth. She made marzipan, butter cookies, ice cream, and rice pudding.

But the cooks said making the same food as everyone else didn't win you favor in court. Chefs in Kalafar had to devise new recipes, meals beautiful enough to enrapture the eyes and delicious enough to captivate royal palates. So Darya made sugared tansies, caramelly honey-custard in phyllo nests, cardamom cakes topped with candied blood oranges, and everyone loved them.

The kitchen maids said she had raw talent, since Darya never burned her skin on red-hot iron cook pans and never cut her fingers, no matter how close a knife sliced. Strange. She'd never even been bruised.

"You're a goddess in the kitchen," Nohra praised her. "What would I do without you?"

"It's good, Daheer. Really good." Fahaad's smile was bright enough to burn a hole in her field of vision.

Her face warmed when he beamed at her like that, but he didn't seem to notice. Or probably he did, but was too kind to tease her. The kitchen mouse loved a prince. She was a joke too pathetic to poke fun at.

Darya knew they were both better than her. What she

didn't know was how long she'd have until Fahaad took his Conservium learning back to Moshitu, or until Nohra went to rule the Sister City. Even if her friends pretended like they didn't know what tomorrow would bring, Darya knew the paths they'd walk as if they were spelled out in the stars.

Her grandmother left for Rayenna when Darya turned fifteen. She'd lose her friends next. They had important roles to play, and to most people, she was just an afterthought.

Of course, being invisible wasn't always bad. Darya didn't get the same unwanted attention some girls attracted at the palace from old viziers. She didn't have the same weighty responsibilities as kings and queens. No one died if she ruined the laundry. If Darya measured wrong, dinner was spoiled, but no city would be blotted off the map.

"You should write your recipes down," Nohra told her. Some maven had been at the palace, sifting through the library, collecting research for a book about the era after the Sunless Months. "It's not as exciting as you'd think to be the subject of a historical book. I can already tell that woman's going to make me seem bloodthirsty. If you write a cookbook, at least you'll be remembered for your lemon cake."

Darya hadn't read the fantastical adventure stories where men had to bargain with demons to become rich and important. Even though Nohra often dragged her to the sanctium, Darya hadn't memorized the words in religious texts, where two halves of a goddess fought wars and blood burbled from a red spring for thousands of years. Everyone knew the stories anyway. Only queens and kings were remembered.

❧

Darya blinked blearily. The room in the palace in Rayenna wasn't a prison cell, but it was as bare as one. The window was boarded up, the door locked from the outside. There was nothing sharp, or anything long enough for her to strangle herself with. Guards stood sentry—the sound of their breaths was deafening through the door. As she sat on the bare bed, slowly coming to consciousness, her thoughts drifted between past and present.

She was a girl again, lying in the straw with Nohra and Fahaad, looking up at the stars. Darya used to fall asleep with the shape of the constellations imprinted behind her eyelids. Once, Fahaad had made a joke of telling her the wrong names, so she'd learned all the correct ones out of spite. *Nuna's Whip*, *Abayae the Trickster*, *Saffa's Crown*. They were magnificent, casting light on Kalafar from so far away. Darya wanted to pluck them from the sky and savor them on her tongue.

The shirt she now wore was long enough to be a chemise on her. It smelled familiar, musky and apple-sweet. When night fell, and a chill crept into the room, someone came in and stoked hot coals in the brazier.

Someone refilled the cup of tea near the bed. Someone else whispered it was *dangerous, giving her that*, but there was a weapon in the room stronger than the shards of a broken cup. The wisps of steam had dissipated, and the water was tepid.

"They don't own you, Dar," a familiar voice said, deceptively soft and calm, caught between a boy she'd once known and a man already out of her reach. His back turned, Fahaad inspected the barred window casing. "That's not what's containing you, is it? You and me, we have different chains."

He faced her, leaned in, and the scent of his closeness enveloped her. Long fingers adjusted the blue shawl around her shoulders. It was gorgeous, beaded with pink flowers.

"That's a good color on you."

His hands moved to the chain around her neck, lifting the

metal pendant that had nearly softened against her hot skin. Finally, lips brushed her fluttered-shut eyes, or maybe that was his fingers wiping away star-silt tears.

I'll be back for you, Daheer.

And then he was gone. Had he said that, or had she imagined it?

The fog in Darya's head made it difficult to grasp anything unhappy, but every minute it cleared more and more. She remembered a boy with long eyelashes pushing her into a fountain. It was in the middle of Kalafar, and he pointed and laughed as her face reddened and her wet dress dragged her down. Her shoes slipped on the piles of wishing coins. The memory collapsed in on itself. Huge slabs of white stone plummeted hundreds of feet before smashing into a public fountain. The Rayenna city wall crumbled, stone turning powdery as flour when her hand smashed the ballistae.

She hugged herself, wrapping her arms around her stomach to keep from exploding into smoke and scattering, squeezing out through all the cracks in her prison cell. Fahaad was right. She could escape, but where would she go? Darya's breaths came in ragged gasps. *She'd killed people*, nearly destroyed an entire city.

It hadn't been the first time she'd lost herself. The night of the invasion, rain mixing with blood redder than strawberries, ripping out men's entrails and feeling nothing...

She wheezed in a gasp that didn't fill her lungs. Darya didn't need to keep pulling air inside her. Breathing, blinking, those were things she *used* to do. Through the walls, spying from somewhere else, *their* gazes bore into her back, the ones who watched her. She squeezed her head, covering her ears to try and block out the voices, but they already screamed in her mind.

They hissed that her name wasn't Darya—that was just one she'd been given, like Fahaad, by her captors.

Shame on you for letting them make a slave of a storm.

Come find us, or not.

It took you so long to wake up, you poor creature, and here, isn't this yours?

The knife Nohra gave her kept coming back whenever she lost it, brought to Darya by shadowed hands. Darya buried the dagger under her pillows.

It wasn't just the faceless voices whispering. Darya knew how the stars breathed. When she closed her eyes, she saw the shapes of constellations. Fire called to fire, and she was an inferno. So hot. Her blood boiled, skin constricting too tight, stretching and bursting at the seams. All her life she'd been dying embers, but this war had stoked her into a beacon flame. She needed out of this body, but if she unwound now, she'd never be whole again.

She didn't need to breathe, to blink, to walk among ants. Darya could let her inhibitions go and become nothing, become everything, go somewhere else, with creatures like her, with the other celestial bodies made of divine fire. In their cities, light never died, and time was a game. Darya could claim dominion over the ocean, the desert, a river, the sky. She could let go of this body and this life, step out of her skin and unravel her mind.

Instead, she reached a desperate, trembling hand for the cup Qaira had left. She took a shaky sip. The mint tea was numbing on her cracked lips. The drug slunk through her body, fat as toads down her throat. It spread roots through her wound nerves. Then the cup slipped from her loosened fingers, and Darya fell back into haunted dreams, yoked by chains stronger than steel.

ACKNOWLEDGMENTS

I would like to first thank my critique group for giving me the motivation to write this book and the feedback to improve it. Thank you to my agent, Lane, for believing in this story first. All the gratitude in the world to my editor, Katie, for making this book a million times better and for answering all of my questions, and for loving my characters who have all the charm of wet cats. I'm so grateful to Bahar and Katharine, who regularly deal with my emails, as well as Kate, Charlotte, Amy, Isabelle, and every other amazing person at Titan. And I want to offer my endless appreciation to Nat MacKenzie for making this cover fit for royalty (Bataar would approve).

To everyone who read some version of this book early, I'm so thankful for you. I'm especially grateful to Katie, Shannan, Tori, and Kelsey for all their help with romance, ballad writing, holy text naming, pegasus birth, and a million other things. Thank you to my agent siblings, debut group, and all my writer friends for the support and community.

I would be remiss for not mentioning my dad, for believing I could be a published author, for making the priestesses look cooler and for making Nassar better (worse?). My mom, who read no fewer than a million versions of this book, including one memorable occasion on a one-day turnaround (it paid off!) and said she really liked this one. And my brother, who shares my love for fantasy fighting and was a true tactician suggesting war strategies. I wouldn't have written this story without my big baba telling us stories about historic battles, my nana who had me visit her in Istanbul, leading to my slight obsession with the Ottoman Empire, and my grandma who made me fall in love with books by reading to me every night as a child. I must also mention the creatures: Stitch, who didn't make it to publication day but will live forever in the palace of my heart, Ayla, and Percy, for being there for pets. Anti-acknowledgment to Reuben, for turning my computer off no less than twenty times when I was editing. He did everything he could to stop this.

Lastly, I would like to thank all the teachers who gave me space to write strange stories and nurtured my ambition to become a published author.

ABOUT THE AUTHOR

Sara Omer is a Pushcart Prize-nominated short story writer. She's been a technical editor for medical and engineering publications and is now pursuing teaching. You can find her (sometimes unsettling) poetry and prose in places like *The Dark, PodCastle, Small Wonders,* and *Strange Horizons. The Gryphon King* is loosely inspired by history and culture shared by her Turkic and Kurdish family.

For more fantastic fiction, author events,
exclusive excerpts, competitions, limited editions and more

VISIT OUR WEBSITE
titanbooks.com

LIKE US ON FACEBOOK
facebook.com/titanbooks

FOLLOW US ON TWITTER AND INSTAGRAM
@TitanBooks

EMAIL US
readerfeedback@titanemail.com